THE PLACE OF THE SWAN

As Australia's gold-rush opens in the 1850s, Raunie, heroine of AND THE WILD BIRDS SING, follows her lover Brick O'Shea to the Bendigo diggings. Their marriage is destined to be passionate and stormy and Raunie's son Jamie drives a wedge between them as he gambles his way to adulthood. The open secret of O'Shea's mixed blood has barred him from political office so he concentrates on his business and lavish entertainment.

With the arrival of the Moynans from Belfast to start a new life in Sydney, O'Shea sees an opportunity to expand his empire. Owen Moynan is soon absorbed in the O'Shea wool mills. Young Conall falls prey to the temptations of Jamie's tearaway life while Alannah is torn between homesickness and the challenge of a new land.

Raunie, resentful that she cannot give O'Shea the child he craves, becomes ever more capricious, and he, finding in Alannah some of the qualities of his lost love, Barbara Merrill, cannot resist the demands of her infatuation. Raunie hits back with all the fury of her gypsy blood, but revenge only drives her husband further from her . . .

THE PLACE OF THE SWAN, the second in a planned Colonial Trilogy, evokes the Australia of a century ago, when the taint of the convict settlements was being glossed over in the rush to make fortunes.

Also by the same author,
and available from NEL:

AND THE WILD BIRDS SING

About the Author

Lola Irish was born in Sydney, New South
Wales. She cannot remember a time when
she was not writing, all through marriage,
family, diverse jobs and varied experiences,
graduating from the excellent training
ground of magazine articles, short stories
and radio plays. She has also written for the
stage. AND THE WILD BIRDS SING, the first
novel in the Colonial Trilogy, was published
by New English Library, and she had
previously written THE TOUCH OF JADE,
SHADOW MOUNTAIN and TIME OF THE
DOLPHINS. She is a keen pianist, loves to
paint — portraits for preference — and has
travelled widely. She has been awarded
Fellowships from the Literature Board of the
Australia Council and AND THE WILD BIRDS
SING won her an award from The Society of
Women Writers (Australia).

The Place Of The Swan

Lola Irish

NEW ENGLISH LIBRARY
Hodder and Stoughton

Copyright © 1986 by Lola Irish

First published in Great Britain in 1986 by
New English Library

New English Library Paperback edition 1987

British Library C.I.P.

Irish, Lola
   The place of the swan.
   I. Title
   823 [F]   PR9619.3.I/

ISBN 0 450 41349 7

_____

*This novel is a work of fiction. With the exception
of historical personalities, names, characters,
places, and incidents are either the product of the
author's imagination or are used fictitiously.
Any resemblance to actual persons, living or
dead, is entirely coincidental.*

Printed and bound in Great Britain for
Hodder and Stoughton Paperbacks, a
division of Hodder and Stoughton Ltd.,
Mill Road, Dunton Green, Sevenoaks,
Kent (Editorial Office: 47 Bedford
Square, London, WC1B 3DP) by
Cox & Wyman Ltd., Reading.

For
Matthew Francis Coble

Author's Note

In this, the second book of The Colonial Trilogy, I have utilised a wide background in keeping with an expanding Australia. The novel is complete in itself, yet the reader will resume acquaintance with many of the characters first met with in *And the Wild Birds Sing*, together with meeting new ones.

My thanks to the librarians and staffs of city and country libraries, in particular to those of the New South Wales Public Library, and the Mitchell Library, Sydney, as well as the staffs of city and country newspapers, during my years of research involving biographies, histories, newspapers, journals, diaries, letters, pamphlets and so on, amounting to hundreds of publications, to compile the period background to my story.

Some less familiar words and expressions can be found in the Glossary at the end of the book.

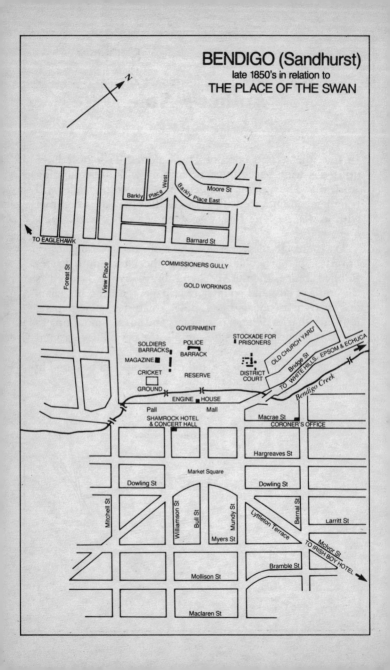

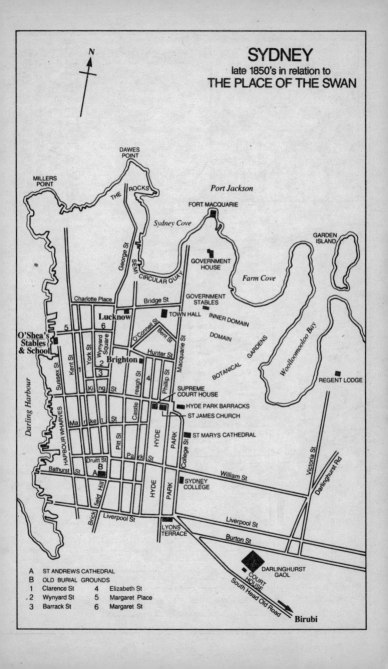

SYDNEY
late 1850's in relation to
THE PLACE OF THE SWAN

N

DAWES POINT

MILLERS POINT

THE ROCKS

Port Jackson

FORT MACQUARIE

Sydney Cove

GARDEN ISLAND

George St

SEMI CIRCULAR QUAY

GOVERNMENT HOUSE

Farm Cove

Charlotte Place

Bridge St

GOVERNMENT STABLES

Lucknow

TOWN HALL

INNER DOMAIN

O'Connell St

DOMAIN

O'Shea's Stables & School

Wynyard Square

Kent St

York St

Bent St

Hunter St

Macquarie St

GARDENS

Brighton

BOTANICAL

Woolloomooloo Bay

Sussex St

reagh St

King St

Phillip St

Castle

SUPREME COURT HOUSE

REGENT LODGE

Darling Harbour

Market St

HARBOUR WHARVES

Pitt St

HYDE

Castle St

HYDE PARK BARRACKS

ST JAMES CHURCH

ST MARYS CATHEDRAL

College St

Park St

PARK

Druitt St

B

A

Bathurst St

Brickfield Hill

WILLIAM St

SYDNEY COLLEGE

Victoria St

Darlinghurst Rd

HYDE

PARK

Liverpool St

Liverpool St

LYONS TERRACE

Burton St

DARLINGHURST GAOL

COURT HOUSE

South Head Old Road

Birubi

A   ST ANDREWS CATHEDRAL
B   OLD BURIAL GROUNDS

1   Clarence St
2   Wynyard St
3   Barrack St
4   Elizabeth St
5   Margaret Place
6   Margaret St

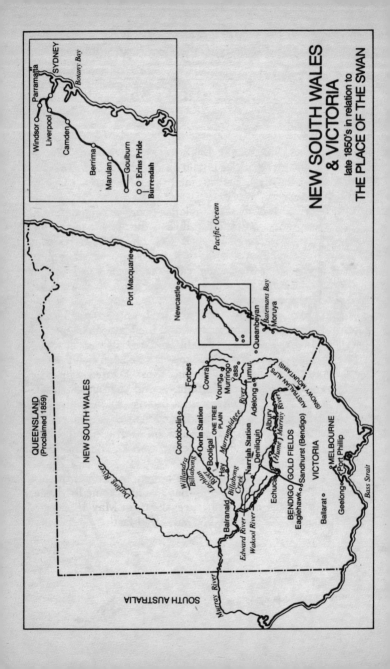

Australia, 1852

THE GOLD-RUSHES of the 1850s jolted eastern Australia to new life and growth. The inland opened up for other reasons than the pasturing of stock; men wandered it in search of quick fortunes.

Commerce thrived and speculation boomed. Money poured into communication: roads, railways, the electric telegraph, and the coach-lines of Cobb & Co. The great rivers that flowed to the Murray and so to the sea were utilised to distribute wool, wheat, and meat on the hoof. A new kind of immigrant landed at the ports, seeking gold. As many more craved, as always, land.

Slab and bark gave way to brick and stone. Sydney acquired pretentious suburbs – and the loathsome slums of failed dreams. Fustians and cabbage-tree hats were elbowed aside by the frock-coats and top-hats of men of business. Melbourne, capital of Victoria, grew bloated from the proceeds of the rich fields of Ballarat and Bendigo. Adelaide was becoming respectable and a little smug. Tasmania, a fertile island of sheep farms and orchards, was growing out of its convict era, but Western Australia's farmers and squatters, isolated from the east by desert, were still dependent on convict labour.

In a north that was wild and largely unknown, the old convict settlement of Moreton Bay would become Brisbane, capital of the new state of Queensland, in May 1859.

Australia was growing up, out – and fast!

Prologue

HEADING THE long straggle of pilgrims, the hardy and the dogged paused to look out over the flat of the Bendigo Valley. They grew silent and still, affecting the children scrambling down from the drays or their fathers' backs to join the group and stare as mutely as their elders at the promised land. Women sank on the hillock to cry when they had not cried before, from exhaustion but more from the balm of this climax of months on a road that in its hundreds of miles had become rougher and drier, dwindling to a barely defined track as it verged south-west into the new state of Victoria. Through the droughty dusty summer, under a sun that burnt through their clothes and seared bare skin and hair to the brittleness of old paper, they had dragged themselves along, often in sickness, passing death on the road side by side with birth when an overworked Doc Peter pressed help from those who would not hinder, with always the prick of thirst at their throats, for what water there was must go to the children – always the children first with O'Shea. 'Be glad of the dry,' he had thundered at grumblers. 'Bogged down you'd be digging yourselves out for weeks to come. And be glad you're in the first rush to these fields for it can mean good claims with time to settle in for the winter.' Goaded by his passion, his confidence, his knowledge, and his supply wagons even if the bulk of his load was to stock his store at Bendigo, they had kept on.

But at Yass, until recently the end of the terrible Great South Road, they had found settlement creeping out and on; and some with small children, fearful of the emptiness ahead, had dropped out to work as timber-cutters or, possessing skills, anywhere O'Shea could find them a place. Some regretted not having trekked west to the Turon diggings where it was said there was still payable gold to be scratched. Others yearned, crazily, to cut across wild country to the Braidwood rush. Still others feared they could not last the distance and quailed at the warnings of diggers met with on the road:

'The traps'll hound you day and night. They clap a hand on your shoulder, "Your licence, mate", and if you've left it in your tent or another pocket it's five pounds for your bail or the logs to await the magistrate's pleasure – then half your fine going to the informer so don't tell your secrets. And thirty shillings more for your bit of paper. And don't let 'em catch you calling the warning "Joe Joe", or it's another fine. It's all they do, hunt licences and sly-groggers, and they'll drag your tent about your ears, aye about your wife and bairns too in seeking the grog. There's trouble brewing over the police and 'twill be worse when they bring in the troops as they're sure to do before long.'

'O'Shea will fight the traps. O'Shea will give 'em whaffor,' they boasted, but uneasy all the same. Would O'Shea really fight their battles? They hung back.

'Hell, man!' O'Shea urged on the timid, 'you can't give up now. It's as hard to go back as to go on. You can rest a day at my camp on the Edward where there's water, again at the Murray. From then on it's only a matter of days, a week at the most with the worst over.'

But was it over? The women wondered, waiting for the laggers, putting their babes to breasts that gave scant sustenance, staring through the haze of heat and dust at the tents with only an occasional hut to proclaim the fortunate or the industrious. It was said men were making fortunes out in those gullies . . . Well, fortune or not, rich or poor the women vowed, this was the end of the road. Here they would settle and make a home.

The rest came straggling and struggling up, weary and dishevelled, three hundred or so of the four hundred who'd left Sydney months before. The hesitant waited as always for decisions and directions, for men had ridden ahead to form a dispersal camp. Besides, O'Shea was bringing up his well-watered horses brought from the Edward River to sell to the highest bidders where horses were worth more than gold, so there were mounts for those in great need. The impatient argued with wives, partners or sons: they had heard much gold was coming from the White Hills back there, who was for the White Hills? Others were turning west to the Eaglehawk. But the Irish almost to a man voted for Irishtown where the Back Creek met the main stream with swards as green as any in Ireland, and bird-life swarmed in the wattle, and where there would be water, surely, at least in winter. Then they stopped arguing, intent on dodging Mrs Malamud's goat on the rampage again, a source of milk for the small children (at a price, trust Mrs Malamud) but a sore trial the way it devoured all and everything, even Mrs Malamud's own bonnet. Strangers on the road joined in the chase, then lingered to jeer at the Sydneysiders mad enough to trek overland when it was hard enough tramping up from Melbourne – more new-chum bastards to fight over the water and, of course, the gold. 'Victoria's a state now,' they boasted. 'Victoria should keep its gold.' 'When we've paid for our licences and staked our claims, what comes out of the ground is ours,' the New South Welshmen shouted their fighting decisive threats.

Bored by the droning argument, Raunie Merrill moved to a patch of shade to tie up the remains of her dress. Here she would wait for Jamie to take her up and ride in beside O'Shea, a triumphant cocky young Jamie now that her presence was known and she could ride with him openly. It was a miracle in its way that she was here at all. Without Jamie bringing her food and drink while keeping her hidden, if reluctantly, from the Duchess and Abigail Luff and O'Shea's men when they made their rounds, more importantly (if more reluctantly) from O'Shea himself when he rode the lines, she could not have survived the first week. She had huddled in the Cummings' small cart, venturing out only at night to stretch her limbs, for she had been close enough to Sydney for Brick O'Shea to send her back by coach if he were angry enough. But at Goulburn, when the Cummings had dropped off to relatives and she was without shelter, she had known panic – where to hide?

Where to run? Not to the Duchess taking round the hat after her troupe's bawdy campfire performances; the Duchess would flaunt and use her again. She had been forced to settle for the grudging remains of Abigail Luff's friendship that had granted her a corner of the crowded Wickler cart.

Abby was no longer her loyal companion-housekeeper, nor was her daughter maid-servant or her son-in-law groom to the young fashionable Mrs Merrill of Macquarie Street's imposing Winthrop. No longer were they mistress and servants but weather-worn travellers on the road to Bendigo. Abigail had become a querulous harpy, thin where she had been plump in Raunie's service, obsessed with the survival of her sickly grandchild, forever bickering with the shiftless Herbert, and scolding her erstwhile mistress for her foolishness as to refuse William Dover's offer of marriage and instead follow Brick O'Shea across Australia. ''Tis nought to us if you want to follow the man secretly but where's your pride, woman? At least you always had that.' But when the anonymous sheltering crowd had thinned out further Raunie knew that even with Abby's help she could no longer hide. Besides, Jamie was sulky, threatening to expose her. Gathering her rags about her she had mounted behind the boy who whooped in triumph as he galloped to where his father led the way.

'*Papa!*'

Brick O'Shea had turned in his saddle and her heart had given a great thump as she met his stare, Jamie laughing from one to the other. It had been a game to Jamie O'Shea, an exciting game hiding this woman he knew and liked. There was something between her and his father, he sensed it. They were aware of each other yet never came together, divided in some special way, and the mystery of it had made the journey intriguing. Now he had brought them face to face and he, Jamie, was part of the mystery!

'Ride on to the Gamble station for water,' Brick had ordered him. 'Enough at least for the children. Beg if you can, buy if you must. I'll see to Mrs Merrill.' As Jamie galloped off with his young cronies, Brick had dismounted to lead his horse. 'I don't suppose I should be too surprised you're here. What does surprise me is that you've managed to hide yourself so well.'

'I have friends.'

'Jamie for one by the look of it. I object to his taking bribes.'

'I didn't even have to offer one.'

'I can still leave you with the Gambles.'

'But you won't,' she bluffed. 'Jamie wouldn't like it.'

'You had no right to make him your partner in deceit.'

'Why not? After all he *is* my son – no,' she added as he glanced at her, 'he doesn't know. At least, I've never told him. You insisted you must be the one to do it, remember? When the time comes, as you put it. Well, I believe the time has come for he's ten years old and curious. How long do you think you can keep him hoodwinked?'

'He shows no curiosity as to his parentage. All he knows is that I adopted him.'

'Well, he doesn't seem to like the idea overmuch. He speaks of you as his foster-father.'

'He likes to tease – and irritate, just as you do. You'll earn your vittles on the road and at Bendigo. We have sick children along, and pregnant women, too many of both for easy travelling.' He gave a wry little laugh. 'But I can't stop couples finding comfort in each other's arms, they have precious little else.' He paused. 'Saving Jamie, who hides you?'

'Abigail Luff.'

'I might have known.'

'She suffers me, no more. I want to ride with you.'

'You'll stay where you are.'

'We're too crowded.'

'Everyone's crowded.'

'Then I'll travel with the Duchess.' Scared but defiant. 'I danced for her at the Thames Hulk, I can do it again.'

'The Duchess and her women will finish up in the brothel tents. I assume you draw the line there?'

'I always have,' she flared, 'and you know it.'

He shrugged in his maddening way. 'To my way of

thinking there's a thin line between that and the role of the colonial *demi-mondaine*.'

'Nor was I ever that.' She fumed. 'I married men who loved me – and did not let them touch me till we were wed. And I could be Mrs William Dover this minute if I'd wished it, with a fine house in Sydney and a carriage of my own.'

'Dover the grocer?'

'Merchant. And a rich one.'

'He should be. He managed to cheat even me.' He made a gesture of impatience. 'Leave your dead husbands – and lovers – be, as it seems you've left all else. If you were foolhardy enough to dispense with soft cushions and couches – and your William Dovers – for this cursed road and a hazardous life on the diggings, you'll take your chances with the rest.'

'I did that when I followed you.'

He ignored the remark. 'You'll finish the journey with the McKees. Hannah makes a Scotch broth so close to ambrosia it will be wasted on the boarding-house she means to run, so I'm encouraging her interest in my hotel-to-be. Meanwhile, she needs help on the road, most certainly on the fields.'

'I'll do as I please at Bendigo.'

'Then starve for all I care.'

He turned from her to stare out over the brittle and forbidding bush, striding out so strongly she could scarcely keep up. He was as brusque as ever, harsh, often brutal, yet, as she had seen along the road, with those strange brief flashes of compassion that surprised all who knew him. He had passed forty she supposed, but was as agile and certainly as youthful-looking as ever. What had happened to him in those years when he had disappeared from Sydney? Years of defeat yet of financial success during which he had become something of a legend, almost a myth; years when she had existed only to hear that he was alive until, abruptly, he was back announcing he would lead a trek to the newly-discovered goldfields of Bendigo. Abby and the Wicklers were throwing in their lot and there was nothing to hold her in Sydney. With her only weapons her determination – and her son with whom to bargain, for reportedly O'Shea took

8

the child everywhere – her only possessions a dress, flimsy shoes and a flimsier shawl, she had burnt her bridges behind her and set out to follow Brick O'Shea wherever he might go.

She stopped dead beside him, her feet raw and aching in what was left of her shoes. She could not keep up. He could leave her where she stood to starve or die of exposure or the less-than-tender mercies of anyone who might take her up, but she must get her breath. She stood, dejected and miserable while the carts and wagons creaked and jangled around her, conscious of her straggling hair, rough skin and torn clothes – and still only halfway to the Bendigo fields. He turned to stare, then slam his saddle with impatience.

'Up with you then. We've no time to dawdle.'

He was giving her scant welcome, but it was a start.

The sun was dying a vivid livid death as they crawled along the line of the Bendigo Creek, now no more than a straggle of muddy pools, to the thud of axes: by the look of it the trees were fast being destroyed leaving uneven forests of jagged stumps. Great mounds of earth overhung holes from which men emerged to stare, then burrow deep again like so many moles; an army of men, heads down, panning for their very lives. As newcomers the New South Welshmen appeared less than welcome. Pleas for water were met with derision; there was no water but scum and what they could beg or buy so they must learn to live with thirst. A thick frost of tents clung to the creek banks with few women to be seen, only men of all nations and colour, dragging, beating, gouging the land as if the end of the world was at hand and they must buy their way through the Pearly Gates.

They crossed the rough bridge to straggle past the wooded rise on their right that was the tent- and hut-studded Government Camp comprising Police Barracks and Lockup and all the other impedimenta of determined law and order, seeming in the glare of late afternoon to look out and down on the world with an ominous superiority. Picking their way through the squalid disorder of yellow mud, scavenging native dogs snuffling about groups of aborigines, and the begging brigade of drifters that always followed the strikes, they settled about the tents and store-wagons of O'Shea's camp. It did not matter that the tents were few, the earth bone-hard and they were hungry and thirsty: for the moment this was journey's end. It was enough to lie out under the Bendigo stars and sleep the sleep of exhaustion.

Through the hot dry autumn the mutilation of the land went on: from first light on into the night by lamp or candle-light the shush-shush of cradles and the thud of axes penetrated the valleys, as if the vandals of old had descended to pillage and chop and slash, then move on to desecrate again. Everywhere was the shock of firearms; a revolver or even a musket was a prized possession. Next came a woman. But most valued of all was a horse, even though there was no pasture within a ten-mile radius and oats cost three pounds a bushel. Stealing was rife so O'Shea sold his horses promptly and profitably, and proceeded to set his personal wheels-within-wheels in motion. To the east of Pall Mall, away from the disorder of the valley but still convenient for trade, he had bought a former shepherd's hut as quarters for himself and Jamie. Beside it, flag flying over its entrance, went a great square of canvas as his general store, well stocked, with supplies expected regularly from the south, even water it was rumoured but at a price to those who could afford to pay – and O'Shea decided who did the paying. Another tent for a crèche and another for a hospital where Doc Peter dispensed what remained of his stock of medicines. Along with such amenities O'Shea was negotiating for a grog shanty along the McIvor Road owned by one Kurt Herlicht, a suave (and slippery, many insisted) Austrian adventurer, as the basis of his hotel. With so many irons in the fire O'Shea seemed everywhere at once, barking out his orders, settling brawls and directing those in tithe to him, for he was equipping men in fours with horses, dray, rations and tools in return for a fifth share of gold obtained and the proviso they return to work on his stations at shearing-time. He seemed always up on Government Hill paying someone's fine, though the disgruntled insisted he was there to cultivate the law for the day when liquor licences would be handed out. The Duchess's women were blatant in their bargaining and Raunie kept away from them, as she kept clear of the Duchess – but she had been unable to escape her, finally, at a roadside camp when, washing her hair in a bit of a stream, she had looked up to meet the woman's mocking eyes.

''Pon me Sammy, 'tis the widder Lorne!' As brash and vulgar and certainly as confident as she had ever been as Madam of the Thames Hulk.

'The widow Merrill.' Raunie had stood her ground.

'Widder agin? By the look o' fings, husbands ain't done y'much good.' A doleful shake of her fiercely scarlet streaky hair. 'Fancy-men neither. Never larned did y', milady, to make the most o' the Hulk pickings, and by the look o' y' now ye've larned nought since. Take m' tip, gal, if ye're still too uppity to come in wiv me filch gold dust from some varmint – if we ever get to the bloody fields that is – and set y'self up in a tent of your own, nice and cosy. From what I hear there's room for us all, and more.' Her fierce booming laughter had sent birds flying.

Making up Hannah McKee's tightly packed rows of stringy-bark cots, preparing the five-shilling meals of mutton, damper and tea, and tripping over near-blind Grandpa McKee fumbling his way to the woodstack or hunting out scarce chamber-pots, Raunie fretted for Brick. But all she saw of him was his back as he rode off in search of carpenters for his hut, nurses for his hospital and crèche, and milk for ailing children – Mrs Malamud was importing a billy to found a goat farm, more profitable she insisted than grubbing for gold. Or he would be galloping off to Irishtown to enjoy the scrape of fiddles and the stew simmering in steaming pots. Or to search for a child lost in the Whipstick, the thick earthbound jungle of strange growth where the Italians congregated amid evil little grog shops. She was forever watching someone go by: the Duchess in a new bonnet with outsized plumes, off to keep house for a Yankee in California Gully, shouting her ribald invitations from her perch atop her commode . . . Abby, Herbert, Kitty and the baby on their way to try their luck at Eaglehawk . . . and would give her damper extra savage thumps. She had not followed Brick O'Shea half across Australia to endure the life of a slavey, and grasped her chance when Hannah ordered them to start packing. They were moving out to Eaglehawk for better pickings.

'If ye'll no' come wi' us then fend for yeself,' she snapped at Raunie's blunt refusal. 'But take heed, Raunie or whatever ye call yeself, run to O'Shea wi' excuses or tales o' woe an' ye'll get scant sympathy. He sent ye here, remember? 'Tis an awfu' hard mon there!'

He was also an angry man as he paced the dirt floor under the herring clusters melting in the heat and dripping into the sugar. 'You'll go with the McKees for the sake of your bed and board. There's too much talk of you around here.'

'There's always talk of me. There's been talk of me since I was born.'

'It might die down a bit if you kept away from womanising Austrians.'

'Kurt Herlicht has fine manners.'

'Herlicht's a dandified sham of a card-sharp.'

'I'm not staying because of Kurt. I like the town.'

'Then you'll work in the hospital.'

'I'll not go near the hospital.' Screaming her horror and defiance. 'If I must work I'll work here.'

'In the store?' He stopped dead. She pressed home her advantage.

'Why not? I can count – enough – and give change and measure cloth and talk to the women the way they like. And do it all better and quicker than that dragon who scuttles about at your bidding.'

'Bridget McElhone can keep accounts.'

'Then I'll learn to do that too. Send Bridget McElhone to the hospital.' Had she gone too far too soon? To her relief he began to laugh.

'I'll be damned. I believe you could learn to run the place if you set your mind to it. The same old Raunie.' He frowned. 'But you can't serve in those rags. Respectable matrons – and we have a few – expect respectable garb.'

12

'Then I'll choose from stock.' And she flew to tear open the bundles of women's clothing.

'Suitable clothes, mind,' he called. She laughed. As if she had ever worn 'suitable' anything; besides, when had he ever given a 'suitable' woman a second chance – except Barbara? She dragged out a yellow silk kept for the public women – why not? Everyone would notice her. Besides, she would wear what she pleased, and the town – and Brick O'Shea – could lump it. Bendigo was out there, a new town, a new world to be conquered. Before long, she was determined, both town and Brick O'Shea would be hers.

She made up her bed in a corner of the store shielded by spades and shovels and great piles of miners' boots, all redolent with the odour of oats and liniment and pungent goods she could not identify. There she could keep a quiet eye on everything while cultivating Jamie as her ally; he was in and out with news of the town or to play cards in secluded corners with his cronies, young but often too old, risking the stock going up in flames by passing round Brick's finest cigars. She turned a blind eye to his pilfering of the store's few luxuries of currants and potted anchovies, well aware he peddled them about town at a handsome profit. He delighted in sitting by her to polish his saddle and munch stolen candy. He had knowledge and guile beyond his years, was forever in trouble and would come to her for sanctuary and condolence but mainly for what loose change she was able to scrounge for him. They were together so often the townsfolk grew accustomed to 'O'Shea's lot' as they were dubbed. There was not a digger on the fields who did not know the dark, beautiful, if somewhat mysterious widow Merrill, and she could have married a dozen times over but turned up her nose at them all. She would have no other, it was rumoured, but Brick O'Shea.

'You like her, don't you?' Jamie teased his father, his black all-seeing eyes gleaming. 'You watch her all the time.'

'Don't I always note a beautiful woman?'

'Are you going to marry her?'

13

'I have no plans to marry.'

'You'll die without a wife, then?'

'Probably.'

'Well, I won't. When I'm old enough I'll marry Raunie.'

'Mrs Merrill from you. It's polite.' He grew serious. 'In the meantime, you will go to school.'

'*School?*' The child was horrified.

'You don't imagine I'll let you spend your days lolling about grog shops and mullock heaps, do you? Certainly not around the store eating up the profits. I mean to open a school.'

'You've no teacher.' In triumph.

'I'll bring one up from Melbourne. But until I do you'll go to the Catholics.'

'It's the windiest tent on the fields,' the boy wailed.

'You'll weather it. You'll start tomorrow.'

The drought persisted. What water there was was brackish and bad and there was much disease, the most persistent a dysentery that affected almost everyone. Even worse was the sandy blight, as bad a plague as the flies, so severe men walked about with red and running eyes, sometimes struck blind.

'The dust doesn't help, and only rain can settle it.' Doc Peter, overworked and forever watching the road for medical supplies, was impatient because wellnigh helpless. 'I can do nothing but send the worst affected to Melbourne.'

Jamie came down with fever. They hovered helplessly about his bed as he whimpered and tossed in his struggle for life, lost in hours of delirium. But at last his burning skin felt a little cooler and when Doc Peter gave him some of his precious laudanum the boy slept. Hunched beside the slab stretcher, Raunie smoothed the dark curls from his forehead. What was he doing in this parched wasteland, prey to disease and death? What, for that matter, were any of them doing here, forever weary and thirsty, lonely even in mateship? She studied the handsome young face, a child's face; her child, until now a stranger, conceived to a husband dead before the boy was born, left as a baby with his Aunt Betsy Witherstone then, on Betsy's death, adopted by O'Shea. She, Jamie's mother, had had no choice then but to agree to the secret bargain, but now the years came back to torment . . . A child she scarcely knew except for brief path-crossings as Brick O'Shea's fosterling, then adopted son; a boy who though ignorant of his kinship had always been drawn to her, but a child she had seldom thought of in those years in which she had married again, been widowed a second time, had contrived and survived with but one thought, one love – Brick O'Shea. She had left her Sydney house, bare and impoverished yet a roof over her head, for what? For a man who had always blamed her for being no more than herself? Yet he did want her son, perhaps because he had none of his own, perhaps because of undefined, only half-understood reasons. Whatever the reasons, Jamie had been and could always be a link between herself and Brick O'Shea, part of the strange tangled criss-crossing of their lives, so much part of their existence that she and Brick could never be entirely separated while this boy lived. Here, fighting for his life, was her ultimate weapon.

She pushed her hair from her face with a tepid rag – ah, to float in clear and sparkling water cooling the very roots of her body. Would it ever rain again? It was well into April and in the south frosts were endangering tender crops, though here they suffered an Indian summer with fierce and angry winds to torment. But tonight was still, with a heaviness in the atmosphere that caused limbs to move languidly. She straightened at Brick's muted tread. He stood beside her looking down on the boy. He had tossed water over his head and shoulders and it gleamed, dripping down his bare arms and chest. He snuffed out the light. 'Leave him be and come out into what air there is. He'll sleep a long time.'

She followed him to the bit of trellised garden that someone, perhaps the shepherd's wife, had planted with care, and hope no doubt, long ago. He was a darker shape in darkness that burned the skin no less than did the sun of day; even the stars seemed to glow sharp and hot as torches.

'Out there,' she said slowly, 'is what I think the moon must be like; bare and dry with gaping holes of dust. Nothing but dust. How can anyone love this place? I thought I could. I came ready to love it but it's no use—'

'It won't always be so. Soon there'll be nothing left to tear apart and the – despoilers I suppose one could call them – will move on. But others will stay and build a town. And the rains will come, they always do – May at the latest.' He moved about, rubbing his body dry, pausing to pluck at leaves or break a small branch with quick sharp gestures, and his restlessness transmitted itself to her where she was already tense and waiting. He said slowly:

'Jamie can't be fobbed off any longer with fairy tales. I've known it for some time. I shall tell him of you, his mother. It's what you want, isn't it?'

'And what will you tell him of his father?'

'The little I know.' She caught the sudden gleam of his smile. 'He wants to grow up, in a great hurry at that, and marry you.'

So he had finally faced the fact that he could no longer possess the boy or use him against his mother, and in a sense it was capitulation, unprofessed, disguised and as much as he was capable of. For the first time it made him vulnerable before her and she would use her power: she had waited long for this. He was quiet, but abstracted she could tell, rubbing his chest with vigorous rhythmic movements. Sounds drifted on air so still she could hear her own breathing. She sensed his eyes on her. Her throat felt dry and she ran her fingers over it, seeking relief from the very flavour of dust. As if suddenly aware of her discomfort he fetched a bowl, dipped in a pannikin and held it out.

'It's not much but it's safe. Never mind the taste.' She drank thirstily but left a little and watched him drain the mug. Somewhere a fiddle played a high and wistful air, eerie and far away. 'He's telling of County Wicklow where the stone walls are high and the trees higher in lush gardens,' he mused 'The high walls of Wicklow hide green places.'

'He'll get well, won't he?'

'He's as hardy as yourself.'

16

'I don't feel hardy. I feel . . . drab. And old. Yes, *old*.' She who had always been afraid to use the word flung it at him in her desolation.

'I cannot imagine you old, Raunie.'

'I feel ugly too. Yes, *ugly*.'

'You? Why, even now . . .' He reached out and pushed her hair that had not been washed in many weeks, from her face. His hand lingered on her and she held her breath but he turned aside and moved to the big tree. It was green there as she remembered. And soft. He placed both hands against the trunk as if to support himself. 'Ah . . . Egypt.'

His old pet name for her came so softly she could not be certain he had said it, for he was not looking at her. He was looking past shadows and shapes to the distant camp fires. Slowly, very quietly, she moved to him through darkness that was like thick and oily water.

'I'm here.'

Her voice was as soft as she knew how to make it when she wanted something, and she wanted him. She had always wanted him. She leant against him and he did not move from her. She slid her hand slowly down his arm in a long soft caress, then folded her hand over his. Still he did not respond – yet did not move away. She had never seen him so vulnerable, if such could ever be said of him, with the fight, the antagonism against her, dormant or dissolving. She stirred against him. She didn't care about a poet's song of Ireland conjured out of an alien country by longing and despair. She didn't care about this Bendigo torn and scarred by greedy men; it could wither or tear itself apart or burn itself out, she did not care. She didn't care where she was as long as he was beside her. And he was beside her now in the lee of a long-ago shepherd's hut with her son asleep inside it and nothing but the brittle powdery bush to surround them and the soft green at their feet to make a couch. She held her palm to his cheek, pressing to him, and felt him tremble. He did not speak, just turned his head and put his mouth to her palm, not quickly or roughly as he usually acted, but hard and surely. She dared not move or speak, nothing to halt him or stop him; he must be the one to act, to move, to decide, for

17

once long ago she had locked a door to keep him beside her and he had turned from her all the same. He drew her round to face him, gripped her elbows and drew her down with him, kissing her hands then her neck, caress by caress as if he had done it all before in his mind and she knew he would not draw back, not now, not ever. The years had gone and there was only the present. If it were simply because he needed a woman and there were none but the harlots in the tents he would not touch, it did not matter. If he were undressing her as he might any passing slut, that did not matter either. If this was the result of a mood, or anger, or loneliness for unknown or unexpressed things, she did not care. If he were starved she would feed him. She had waited a lifetime to do so. It would never be an easy love between them, there would be unease and, quite often, hate, as there had always been, and they would tear at each other as they had always done. But whatever it was that held them it would stay as it had always stayed, a bond as necessary to their lives as the connecting tissue of Siamese twins that could not be severed if they would have life. There was no sound but the soft slur of their bodies meeting and folding into each other. As he came down on her, hard, their combined gasp was a jar, a shock in the heavy silence. Strange, she felt more than thought, looking up into the face she could not see clearly as he moved above and within her – in all the years, ten since she had first known him, years filled with her longing and his resistance, she could not have guessed they would mate in the night heat of a parched goldfield under stars gleaming on a burning world. There was no sound outside themselves until his ultimate gasp of 'Egypt!' that seemed to shiver the grasses and leaves around them and assured her he knew it was she and no other who lay beneath him, loving him in the hot dark quiet night.

Chapter One

SYDNEY HAD been *en fête* from the first bells greeting the New Year to picnics at the Cremorne Gardens (furnishing enough brawls and scandals to titillate the town for a week), the crowds at the Races and the Regatta, and the packed houses applauding the San Francisco Minstrels. Now the élite were entertaining more intimately in their elegant white-painted colonial homes lining the Harbour and the River inland as far as Hunter's Hill, and even in those mansions which pierced the grey-green density of the North Shore and depended on ferries to bring guests southside again. In the most brightly lighted, most lavish and most widely known of the villas hugging the Harbour's southern shore, the talk and laughter and clink of ice against glass dwindled when the host, Black Brick O'Shea – as more than his friends had come to call him without fear of broken jaw or bloody nose – called for glasses to be refilled and a final toast downed to this New Year's Day of eighteen hundred and fifty-eight.

Owen Moynan, watching the whisky slide into the finely-cut crystal, knew he should decline for he'd had more than his share, but how to refuse the purest Scotch, malt Scotch at that? 'Try this Lowland malt, sir. An excellent pre-dinner drink.' And the local wines had been remarkably good; a surprise that, but Australia was full of surprises. All through the superb dinner of new and exotic flavours – he'd found the haunch of kangaroo venison particularly fine – then the masculine talk over port and coffee, the dancing and singing and the elaborate supper, he had moved in a comfortable lethargy induced not only by the hot summer's night but by an unaccustomed swimming-with-the-tide. It had taken hold of him from the moment of leading his son and daughter through the opulence of the house and into this room with its windows framing the flush of sunset above the glow that was the city, the darkening sweep of the North Shore and Harbour broken only by lights from anchored ships, and the long vista of water and woody shores to Sydney Heads. In all this, Birubi glowed as an oasis resplendent with glittering mirrors and chandeliers, its dining-room aglow with its *pièce de résistance* on its eastern wall, a mural of sunlit plains and grey-green gums and a sky that was the sky of Australia, clear and sharp and fiercely blue.

'Erins Pride, Mr Moynan.' His host had lifted his glass in salute. 'My station in Argyle County. Perhaps you will let me show it to you? If you dislike the idea of riding up, there is a coach service to Goulburn; I regret no railway as yet but men would rather grub for gold than cut railway sleepers.'

'Moynans are born to the saddle, Mr O'Shea,' he had interrupted, too sharply but piqued by what he regarded as the man's patronising air. 'When one rides in Ireland one rides everywhere.'

'Even so, you do not know the Australian roads.'

'And you, Mr O'Shea, do not know my family. Particularly my daughter.'

Annoyed with himself for having dragged Alannah into it, he had responded to O'Shea's invitation, offhand as it had been, without committing himself; he would be happy to view Erins Pride but at present he was settling his family into a house after too long in hotels. But his eyes had returned again and again to the dramatic magnificence of the man's painted acres; was everything in this house and about these O'Sheas designed to impress, from the lavishness of cognac and French champagne to the trained obsequiousness of waiters, and flowers and fruits out of season? It certainly appeared so where the man was concerned, with his fashionable, almost foppish, evening clothes that yet he wore so casually he gave the impression he was at some masquerade. But his signet ring and diamond pin were as extravagant and dramatic as the thick incredibly black hair, with not a streak of grey that Owen could see, for all the man must be well into his forties. And how did one meet the amusing niceties that flowed so effortlessly from his lips – God damn the lot of you, he seemed to be saying to the world. And in particular, to Owen Moynan and his kin.

'The New Year!'

Owen put his glass to his lips sincerely and with hope for it was the reason he was here – the New Year. And a new life, the old one left behind in the Old World, his familiar world of work and comfort and fulfilment – yes, Belfast had been kind to Owen Moynan. But Belfast was not prepared to be kind to his son. Belfast had no place for a lad of nineteen who had wounded and almost killed his young friend in a tipsy brawl over a girl, no girl from a back street either but one of their own social standing, and this at a ball of the season. Young Moynan had been judged and condemned by his own society for his victim had been of a wealthy and influential family. Indeed, whenever he, Owen Moynan, longed for Ireland he could block homesickness with gratitude that he had managed to save his son from the gallows or, at best, a prison term, while accepting Belfast as it was – moderate, self-reliant, proud. Hard, too, of course, an eye-for-an-eye sort of city, but he understood for he was Belfast too. But Conall? His son knew pride, too much perhaps, yet he, his father, had not been able to pass on to his children the virtues of sobriety and self-sufficiency by birth or by training, and he was often uneasy over the fact. He had known the same unease with their mother, for he had spent his youth struggling to understand Mary and her Catholic piety as well as the fierce county from whence she had come, bringing him a dowry generous enough to set him up in the linen trade. Compromise, after all, was all he had been able to manage – his son must follow Moynan ways. And a boyish foolishness must not be allowed to condemn Conall for life.

But where was there a country that would not judge as harshly as the old? America? Emigrants came streaming back from New York with tales of hardship and disappointment. Well then, England had colonies – though Australia, it was said, was growing resentful of the term. With a sick heart he had ridden to Cave Hill to look on his city, flat and unbeautiful, enclosed within its hills. There . . . Belfast Lough. There . . . south to County Down. Leave all this for Australia? To his world that strange and distant island had always been a penal settlement with a garrison and black savages and the strangest of flora and fauna. But the transports no longer sailed for Botany Bay and he had heard the place was changing; sheep country, of course, with long droughts and great heat and floods such as few had seen the like of, but towns were becoming cities with at least some of the amenities of living . . .

He savoured his drink, making a pretence of heeding his erstwhile dinner companion, a garrulous *modiste* dealing in French bonnets even if she did fashion them herself; women, it seemed, could make their mark here in commerce on their own terms. But he had not come to Australia to idle in a city; cities seemed to touch Conall too sharply, sweeping him along with their fleshpots. No, the Moynans would not loiter in urban grandeur, they would return whence they had come – the land. Con must have his chance in this new country and never mind the man who had left his life's work behind him. So Owen had locked away his letters of introduction to Governor Denison, to a distinguished barrister, to a master at a city academy, locking away confrontation and so, possible danger, for though they had come quietly and unannounced to New South Wales who knew what gossip had preceded them? He would not chance exposing his daughter to further insult or his son to ostracism, not unless all else failed. He would move with caution, feeling his way, sensing the pulse of the place, absorbing where it pleased him to do so this deep new timbre of colonial life. He had turned the key in his desk and turned to confront the New Year. And a new life.

The laughter of women broke in on his thoughts. Taffetas shimmered; jewels, both precious and paste, sparkled. The curve of fans made brittle arcs before the lips of these noisy colourful foils for their argumentative masters who drank as stolidly as they talked. 'Another shipload o' blasted Chinks to foul up the trails and the water. They're pouring into New South Wales since Victoria put a tax on 'em and we'll soon

have all the troubles o' Californy in this state' . . . 'Most big
nuggets have been found on the Ballarat diggings and there's
more to be dug there, you'll see' . . . 'They'll pay anything
you ask around Bendigo for hosses. Not even a hack to be
seen these days . . .' Male talk, trade talk, and his pulses leapt
to hear it. Even so he avoided eyes, unwilling to be drawn
into conversation let alone controversy, preferring to listen,
watch and wait. That heavily-jowled fellow with the outsized cigar – Mason, was it not? – had landed with only a few
shillings and was now a miller, with grain stores enough to
deck his bold-eyed brassy-voiced wife in expensive furs. And
why not when the fields paid three pounds the bushel for
oats? And that square-set man with the burr had made a pile
from the collection of 'dead men' and sunk five hundred
pounds into a public-house, cheap at the price with the
whole city seemingly guzzling itself into extinction. No
government officials or politicians present, not a hint of the
judiciary or professional classes, for these were Counts of
Commerce, Princes of Trade with the same unblinking
inscrutable look he had known in the business dealings of
Ulster – but with a difference. The men and women of Ulster
did not pretend to be otherwise, they did not appear to be
honest and hearty and rather boyishly naive as they shook
your hand and poured you their choicest liquor. Here, who
could tell what men were really like, what they were going to
do or whence they had actually come? Jam-packed ships
rolled the sea-lanes to Australia – steamships, too, in recent
years – with polyglot loads of riff-raff in search of easy
fortunes torn from the earth in gold, or in liquor deals, or
prostitution, or more subtle and secret dealings, snatching
up the spoils in their greedy peasant hands to be shovelled
out again on personal comforts and pursuits. Now he and his
had been tumbled out to deal with them. Well, he could deal
with such sharps, there was even a sense of excitement in the
prospect of beating them at their own games. But his
convent-bred daughter? His impulsive headstrong son?

His eyes lingered on Conall's handsome moody face as the
youth hovered about their hostess who had glittered and
gleamed within a circle of admiring males all night. Con had

23

the male Moynan build, broad of shoulder and squarish of body, but his look of strength belied him for he was often tongue-tied and awkward. Yet with a sudden change of mood he could be bombastic from the need, his father supposed, to convey the confidence he could never seem to acquire. The body of a Roman soldier with the face of a pre-Raphaelite saint, someone had once said of Conall Moynan, extravagant in phraseology though not unreal: an uncertain reticent young man but one who had loaded his father's pistol and shot at his friend, the motive so obscure he had never been able to explain it clearly. Yet he had gone out to murder, so much was clear, and Owen went chill when he considered it. Was it for this hasty and unreliable youth that he had torn out his own roots, even more despairingly, Alannah's, for she had come from a country where she had been happy, with determination yet open suspicion of their unseen refuge. Indeed, with something deeper – fear. And fear was something new to Alannah Moynan.

Owen studied her closely as she gave her attention, or appeared to do so, to the curious nasal patois pitted with French phrases of the overdressed girl at her side. In contrast to the peacock brilliance of the other women her dress was a simple one of ivory moiré and even to his somewhat provincial eyes, old-fashioned, for it came high about her breasts and shoulders, its only colour a lilac sash. Her pale springy hair was drawn back on the nape of her childlike neck and twined in her most frivolous adornment, a satin ribbon bow. No flowers, her only jewel Grandmama Moynan's cameo brooch. She looked an anachronism, he decided with mingled pride and unease, certainly she looked different. She was not shy – Alannah was too proud to be shy – but she was unworldly, unversed in the sophisticated world of Society, nourished by the curious overlay of cultures that was Ireland. First, an isolated and, he had realised too late, unhappy childhood with her dead mother's people in Derry. Then an adolescence moulded by the fierce piety of the Dominican nuns warring with the Protestant puritanism of her Aunt Delia. All this with the added touch of the pagan mysticism of the Mournes – how could she be anything but a

24

trifle fey! Overlay upon overlay, so much it was sometimes hard to know what the girl was really like. But if she were still outwardly untouched and untried she was not demure about it, for there was something of the peasant in all Moynans. In Alannah it was there in her honesty, her uncomplicated needs and impulsive enthusiasms that caused her aunt confusion and not a little shock, and himself unease over her future, particularly in this country.

'Thank you, but I would rather not.' Her precise disciplined young voice that could never quite hide her emotions brought him sharply to the present to see their hostess touch her playfully on the arm with her fan.

'But you *must*, Miss Moynan. Your first New Year in the colony is a special occasion.'

A long pause. 'Oh . . . very well.' The girl drew herself up even straighter, folded her hands together and moved one palm against the other, a childhood habit when disturbed. 'If I *must* then I shall take two glasses of wine, and together.'

'Alannah!'

She turned to her father, her eyes glittering. 'You heard Mrs O'Shea, Papa – I *must*. It seems I cannot refuse to drink something I have no taste for so I shall drink a double toast in the hope it will atone for my ungraciousness in refusing the seventh – I counted, Papa – *seventh* invitation to take wine. And it will be Mrs O'Shea's fault if I am sick all over her beautiful and, I'm sure, expensive carpet.'

A long silence while their host inspected the sparkling perfection of wine glasses. 'Miss Moynan shows discrimination in refusing what she doesn't enjoy. But when a lady dislikes wine it usually means she has not tasted one sufficiently mild yet matured and interesting.' He turned to Owen. 'If she will try this sherry, as good as any Spanish. Or this Cawarra of the true colour and flavour of Moselle, very light—'

Miss Moynan did not wait for further explanations. She snatched both glasses and drained one then the other with scarcely a gulp between. O'Shea's eyebrows shot up. 'Along with discrimination a lady must learn moderation—'

'*Must* again, Mr O'Shea?'

'Should, then.' He laughed it off. 'One *should* savour—'

'Then I'll never learn discrimination or moderation,' she throbbed through the struck-dumb room, 'for I am hardly likely to be taught civilised habits by a – a—' Whatever she was struggling to say was strangled in a distinct hiccup.

'Roughneck colonial?' Laughing at her stricken but stubborn face. 'There are those of us who deem such a description complimentary. And given twelve months you won't hesitate over insults, for Australia will afford you a colourful vocabulary. May I?' He took the goblets from her indignant and trembling hands. 'Venetian glass. Importations are costly.'

As a hasty ripple of conversation broke over them Owen moved to his daughter's side, knotted by a tight core of anger. This was the girl who had sat quietly all evening touching little of her food though there was everything to tempt, speaking only when spoken to, looking the epitome of the convent-bred maid, only her eyes moving from one guest to another, evaluating, separating and judging in that special way she had. He should have heeded his sister and sent apologies, but the invitation in expensive-looking gold engraved on ivory had been as intriguing as it had been concise: Owen Moynan, Esquire. Conall Moynan, Esquire. Mrs Carney. Miss Moynan. The O'Shea carriage to call at seven and await their pleasure. So they were known individually and as a family. Why, when they had slipped so quietly into the colony, had they been singled out? His sister had refused point-blank to 'have truck with the vulgarities', for all she had heard of the O'Sheas set them far outside the orbit of a Carney of Stonemore, County Down. But he had accepted, intrigued by the name of O'Shea heard frequently as he moved from shipping-office to bank to eating-house.

'I knows a Belfast voice when I hear it!' The host of their first hotel had beamed on him, leaving Owen reflecting that it was one thing to land discreetly in a country but another to disguise a particular inflection of voice. 'Well now, a gentleman like yourself will want to talk of home and there's none knows Ireland like Brick O'Shea for he's travelled the north and south of it many times. Your paths will cross sooner or later, all paths do in Sydney, so ask for him in any coffee room.'

'An odd name.'

'It's all we know him by.'

Then the carpenter mending his travel-damaged desk had been only too eager to answer questions concerning the villas across the Harbour. 'Aye, they're spreading out there now, sir, for there's money about even if a lot of it is ill-gotten; there's some in those fine-looking mansions over there, this side too, wouldn't lie easy in their beds if I was to spread what I knows about 'em. But Mr O'Shea now, the one they calls Black Brick among other names – that's his, there on the Harbour front, but empty many years – is one I'd trust for I've done many a chore at his house out at Rose Bay and he's paid me fair and square. More, he gave my boy a chance at his school then put him to a shipping place where he writes figures so clever you'd scarce believe.'

Even more revealing was the digger flashing gold nuggets who'd flopped at Owen's luncheon table without a by-your-leave to slam a fist on the damask and slop the mulligatawny. 'New chum,' he'd shouted to his cronies. 'Moynan by name. From Ireland's Black North and come out to take up land – am I not right, sir?' Grinning with triumph at Owen's surprise – where on earth had the fellow heard all that? Delia gossiping before cab-drivers and parlour-maids? Con bragging or grumbling in some bar? But the bearded giant was so friendly Owen could not take offence. 'A warning from an old hand: the town's full of tricksters so if you ain't too sterling about a man's forebears seek one by the name of O'Shea to show y'the country. He knows it as few others which ain't surprising seeing there's native blood in 'im; only a touch, mind, but enough to keep him below the salt with the nobs and snobs. And no cause to look as if all the fiends of Hell are after ye for 'tis common knowledge the man's a darky, the truth of it came out years back with him just elected to Council and set to marry into the military when, *wham*, his dark secret is out!' A guffaw at his own little joke. ' 'Tis said he knew nought of his touch of the tarbrush which is as may be but his feud with Major Merrill is a tale you'll hear soon enough.' A stream of tobacco juice on its way to the spittoon barely missed Owen's boot. 'But O'Shea picked himself up from the debacle to make a fortune from pubs and stores and one of the richest quartz mines on Bendigo's quartzopolis, and another fortune from his Riverina cattle. Some swear it's his black blood that makes him so canny but I reckon he was born shrewd, knows the way the wind will blow so to speak for he's back with wool, swearing it's the future now that cotton's like to get scarce in Americky. He could be right but I'll stick to m' curse of God.' Stuffing his gold back in his pouch he had thundered at the waiters. 'Measures of rum for the comp'ny if ye're not too grand for such grog. And whatever his lordship here fancies.'

But Sabbatarian Temperance broker Purdue had given a different, quite venomous slant on the man, his spite heightened perhaps by the pallid effect of his mineral water against the glow of Owen's sherry. 'Sydney is becoming a city of substance, Mr Moynan, with railroads out and better roads in and the electric telegraph through this month to Liverpool, only twenty miles inland but a start. But we need more than the measure of law and order we've gained, for the scum of the earth infest our diggings with an equal number of rogues in our cities engaged in commercial skulduggery, not to mention politics. As for the Demon Drink, sir, it rules rampant!'

Owen set down his drink in haste and picked up his knife and fork. 'A prime roast, Mr Purdue.' But the man refused to be distracted.

'At last count eight hundred taverns in this city alone and by now, I'll warrant, over the thousand. Taverns and race-courses, whore-houses too, patronised and often owned by those who should be upholding the dictates of the Good Book. And the most blatant and avaricious upstart of all is one O'Shea, of coloured blood, residing in a house of Baal he calls Birubi, a heathen native name to match its heathen goings-on—'

'Am I to assume, then, that you do not conduct business with this reprobate?'

'Business?' The man's face assumed a curious expression,

one that could only be described as a conflict of reverence and revulsion. 'Well now, Mr Moynan, business is business as a man like yourself will know.' A moment more in obeisance to the world of money and he returned with vigour to his obsession. 'A house of sin, sir, where decent God-fearing citizens are affronted and their wives insulted by the painted woman he did not make his wife till the scandal got so bad he was forced to it. Picnics on the Lord's Day, sir, with loosely-clad women cavorting on the beach in view of passing craft.' He jabbed the air savagely with his fork. '"Ye shall keep my sabbaths and reverence my sanctuary; I AM the LORD." Leviticus 26 Verse 2. As for the boy, for all he's only sixteen and for all it appears he's hers by a former husband born a gentleman, respectable parents seclude their daughters when Jamie Lorne's in town.' He mopped his forehead, brooding, Owen surmised, on young Lorne's one extenuating feature – honourable, even aristocratic, birth. Then gripping the table as if the demon O'Shea might leap from under it he became conspiratorial. 'Fathers are doubly vigilant when the boy's buck nigger of a stepfather is on the prowl.' True Sabbatarian Temperance outrage conquered discretion along with all laws pertaining to slander, and his fist pounded the table before shaking in the general direction of Rose Bay. 'As a God-fearing Christian and Elder of Chapel I consider it my duty to warn you and yours of that tangled household – a Temple of Baal, Mr Moynan, a Temple of Baal!'

So what was he, Owen Moynan, to make of such diverse talk, together with the innuendos and gossip drifting about restaurants and counting-houses, of O'Shea's ruthless business dealings, the lash of his tongue and sometimes fists, his prowess with stock-whip and gun? Here he was in the aforesaid Temple of Baal by no more sinister route than the most formal of dinner invitations, his suspicions dissolving like the morning mists through the agency of fine food and liquor if not of conversation, and entertained with skill and charm by the painted woman herself. He ran his whisky-mellowed and, by now, indulgent eyes over their hostess. Painted she certainly was and doubtless as bold as she

29

looked but he could not find it in his heart to censure his son or anyone else for their admiration, for she was more than beautiful with strange magnetic eyes, slits one moment, flashes of greeny-gold the next. And ah, the caramel gleam of her shoulders, or would one call them honey-coloured – and don't make a fool of yourself, Owen Moynan, for she'd be too much of a handful for such as yourself whose life has been made up of industry, love for a beautiful but stifling wife, the demands of a spoilt son and daughter, and a well-meaning martinet of a sister who promised to become a problem in meeting Australia even half-way. But gazing on the woman O'Shea he felt twenty again – and why not? It always came as a surprise to realise he was still in his forties and at this precise moment rather deliciously aware of his vigorous pulse beat . . . The room was becoming distinctly fuzzy-edged and he pushed his drink aside, shaking his head to clear it. There! The O'Sheas came sharply into focus. A handsome pair but he found the man an enigma. Why, after slipping discreetly into the colony and depositing his assets even more discreetly – assets more modest than expected for mills and town houses were valuable until one needed to realise in a hurry – had the Moynan family been invited tonight? Was it the man's habit and pleasure to spy out newcomers? If so, what could O'Shea want of an Ulsterman who had severed all business and professional ties and sailed across the world to seek a haven for himself, a second chance for his son and, hopefully, suitable social contacts for his daughter?

For Alannah, of course, must marry. Advantageously and as happily as possible to compensate for the humiliation and defeat they, as a family, had suffered over Con's unfortunate affair as much as for her own social inadequacies. In her brief Belfast 'season' she had been reluctant, even gauche, with her few – very few – social flutters eclipsed suddenly and dramatically by Con's disgrace and ostracism. It was a wonder she had not come to hate her brother. Clearly, a suitable marriage at home had become impossible though she had made light of the situation. 'But I do not wish to marry, Papa. Not for years and years, perhaps never. There

30

are so many wonderful things to do besides become a wife.'
What things? he asked, puzzled. She had laughed at his
expression. 'Don't worry, never the cloisters. You know I
have never been a true believer like Mama. I wonder over it
all too much. I mean, it's so . . . well . . . *improbable*, don't you
think?' But a woman could take up her own land and
manage her own estates . . . A woman could breed fine horses
on fine acres . . . A woman could travel the world . . . He had
brushed such excuses aside as foolish schoolgirl fancies. Of
course she would marry, all women married, all women
wanted to marry – well, did they not? She had shrugged it off
and he was left with the rather unpleasant feeling that he
might be more than a little old-fashioned. But even if she
were eager to wed who here was a potential husband? The
place was full of tradesmen, pub-keepers, counter-hoppers,
scrub farmers . . . The prospect was enough to tempt him to
flaunt his letters of introduction and cultivate what passed
for the colonial élite. He even found himself considering their
fellow-passenger from the *Elizabeth Anne*, a polite if overly-
proper young man with a somewhat tiresome formality, an
apologetic little cough and an awesome volubility of facts:
the population of Paraguay . . . the habits of migratory
seabirds . . . the mechanical wonders of the Great Exhibition
. . . setting all about him yawning. Even so, calculating
Northern Ireland expediency had prompted Owen to keep
the young man's card: Simon Aldercott Esq., Tuition
in Calligraphy. Grammar of the English tongue. Latin.
Greek . . .

  Greek, eh? Despite his old-fashioned, slightly frayed
clothes – Owen had actually seen him wearing an elaborately
folded stock – Aldercott possessed a classical education
which denoted application and thrift ,if not an affluent
background. The latter was in no way evident. Unfortunately,
scholarly young men without private means were too often
destined to become poorly-paid clerks or overworked tutors
with no provision for a wife and family. But he recalled that
by the time the ship had anchored in Sydney Cove Alannah
was hiding her yawns and had even smiled upon the
obviously smitten Mr Aldercott.

O'Shea was at his elbow. The man moved like some jungle animal, or perhaps it was a deliberately cultivated tread to daunt newcomers. 'New Year toasts can lead along too many conversational paths, Mr Moynan, keeping a host from his guests.'

'My apologies for my daughter's lapse of good manners. Ireland has produced many saints but Alannah has never aspired to their ranks.'

O'Shea laughed. 'And *my* apologies for my wife's New Year enthusiasm. And for my own, I'm assured, often macabre brand of humour.' His fine teeth gleamed and Owen's eyes travelled over his face: a little broader than most perhaps, the eyes more deeply set, but these were traits among whites too – no, nothing of the savage that he could see. All the same, it must be there. He felt distaste for his own emotional reaction. Besides, he had the conviction that if this man could not actually read his thoughts he could surmise them. Finely cut crystal was pressed into his hand.

'Try this Islay malt, sir, full-bodied and peaty. I'd like your opinion.' O'Shea grew more expansive, almost genial. 'You must allow me to prove that we are really hospitable folk. My wife will be delighted to assist your daughter in any way she can. And Jamie will do the same for your son.' He paused, frowning. 'My son is late – very late.' His nails made sharp rhythmic clicks against his glass. 'For my part, there are concerns here apart from our surface pursuits that I believe will interest you. I plan to breakfast at the Crimean Arms tomorrow at ten – you know the Arms? Good. Will you join me there?' Owen's first impulse was to refuse but before he could do so a mocking young voice came from the doorway.

'Any hospitality left for the son of the house? I've been at thirsty work.' And heads turned to the youth supporting his slim body by a grimy hand braced against the door jamb while he flourished a greasy topper. His mother flung her arms wide in a dramatic welcoming gesture.

'Jamie! I thought you'd never come.'

'I was ordered home, remember?' He crossed the room to kiss her heartily and without embarrassment.

'For dinner,' O'Shea snapped.

The boy's grin took in the assembled guests. 'Considering the real rowdyisms are just getting into swing I think I've shown conscientious . . . *ness* . . . in getting here at all.' The slurred sibilance made O'Shea stop the waiter weaving a path towards the boy. 'Besides . . .' Jamie's grin was transferred to his mother, 'orders are orders, aren't they, Mama? But I took time to win the greasy-pole, see?'

'By the state of your clothes I'd say you earned it,' O'Shea broke in.

'It's a fine topper, worth a few smears of oil.' He rubbed his hands up and down his beautifully tailored breeches, making himself even more raffish-looking, then set his prize at a jaunty angle, strutting, greeting the men with a flourish of handshakes and the women with exaggerated bows, sweeping his hat to the floor in dramatic arcs. Even playing the clown he moved with a beautiful fawnlike grace, and in the sheen of his black hair, the smoothness of golden skin and his charming insolence there was a startling resemblance to his mother. The men cheered, the women laughed, and all seemed to find him amusing and engaging. All except O'Shea.

'We're accustomed to your dramatics but newcomers can't be expected to be so tolerant.' The boy ignored him. '*Jamie!*' O'Shea stood tapping an impatient foot until the boy turned to face the Moynans. 'Mr Moynan. Miss Moynan. Mr Conall Moynan. My son.'

'Stepson,' Jamie drawled. 'Jamie Lorne, stepson. Formerly foster-son. He swears he adopted me at a tender age but I choose to disbelieve it.'

'Enough of that nonsense—'

'In any case, I choose my own name.'

'Foster-son, adopted son, stepson, it matters not,' Brick fumed, 'for you bide under my roof and eat at my table – when you do condescend to grace it – and that gives me the right to decide what curfew to impose upon a boy of your age who arrives smelling of the gutter.'

'You're surely not going to fuss over a few pesky cabbage leaves?' Brushing himself down with long delicate fingers he straightened and grinned at Alannah. But she felt that behind his smile his eyes were calculating and shrewd.

'You're unfit for drawing-rooms,' his stepfather snapped. 'Upstairs and to bed.'

Jamie turned his back on him, clasped his mother and kissed her again with enthusiasm. 'My one consolation in being sent to bed like a brat is a kiss from Mama-Raunie – with an extra one for New Year.' She nuzzled his ear, laughing at him. It was clear she adored him and he her. 'Don't know what we'd do, do you, Mama, without new chums to spark things along? New chums, that is, who've not had time to learn our colonial tricks.' His attention was transferred to Con. 'Mama is not the only one to melt at my bussing, the girls love it. Most currency lads trip over their upcountry boots when they try to bend from the waist.'

'Upstairs, Jamie. *Now*.'

Even Owen jumped at O'Shea's command but still the boy took his time in sauntering out, pausing in the doorway to throw his mother a final kiss. But in the silence all heard with painful clarity the female giggles and scuffles from the hall. The glass cracked in O'Shea's hand. There was an awkward hasty rustle of skirts and bustle of servants to summon carriages and collect wraps. Owen bowed his farewells, returned compliments and sparred with invitations, his mind on Jamie for the lad had left a disturbing impression. No doubt most here were aware of the cross-currents beneath the surface affability of this disparate worldly family, but why should he and his suffer the youth's rudeness fostered by the wealth of a notorious stepfather and an over-indulgent mother? Con would do well to avoid the boy.

He was suddenly, and briefly he supposed, alone in the room with the lingering perfume of women and flowers, the massed candles glinting on the china, the Venetian glass, and the lavish brilliance of fat black grapes and rosy peaches and golden slices of melon. The broken glass glowed redly amid the spilt wine. He moved to the French doors. The scent of honeysuckle mingled with magnolia, and the distant lap of water on the beach tantalised. The exotic semi-tropical opulence by which these O'Sheas had fashioned

34

their lush Australian existence was new to him; it disturbed, and he felt himself resisting his surroundings as a monk might resist some pagan house. Pagan? He laughed softly to himself. These people were simply unlike others, folk through whom ran some vague but exciting thread of decadence. And, after all, they could afford to be so: wealthy, self-indulgent colonials engaged in pursuits with which he was unfamiliar in a country he did not yet know so had no right to criticise. The room was coming to life, men drifting back for furtive last drinks while wives exchanged plans and portents. Owen thanked his host and was gallant without being effusive to his hostess, but as he made his way into the open to the waiting O'Shea carriage O'Shea called: 'The Crimean Arms, Moynan. At ten.' And to his surprise, and consternation, he found himself nodding assent.

Dora's pail thumped to the ground, tipped over and they slithered in its ooze as Jamie pushed her hard against the scullery wall and dragged her blouse below her waist to pin her arms and bare her breasts. Her skin gleamed, outlined in what light penetrated from the house to their dark angle of the yard.

'I only came out to empty m' slops,' she gasped. 'If Cook catches us it's me what'll get the whipping, not you.'

'They're all busy with coats and carriages,' he murmured, fondling her, maudlin in his caresses.

'You didn't oughta do it.' She squirmed under his hands. 'You didn't oughta—'

He slapped a hand over her mouth, pressing her back so tightly she could not move. And there was nothing fumbling about his thumb and forefinger plucking at her nipple, gently at first then harder, pinching and plucking with a hard persistent rhythm that made her moan behind the gag of his hand, then whimper.

'You'll be crying for it soon,' he mumbled, biting her lips and throat with quick teasing little movements. But he ceased his handling of her to stare into the scullery. He released her abruptly. 'Come out, you miserable cripple.'

35

And dived into the dark to drag forth a blinking protesting Gondola. 'Stop that gibberish. You've been spying.'

'He sleeps behind the tubs.' Dora scooped her rubbish back in her bucket. 'He sleeps all over the house, anywhere. Fair gives me the creeps, he does.'

'Run with tales and I'll boil you down for tallow, you cretinous pimp,' Jamie hissed, shaking the dwarf till his misshapen legs flapped like those of some grotesque rag doll.

'He doesn't know what you say,' Dora scorned. 'Only a word here and there. He talks all the time in his foreign lingo. The mistress is the only one to make him understand anything.'

'He understands the boot.' Jamie sent the creature sprawling. Gondola's eyes gleamed, infuriating Jamie further, and the youth hauled him upright, wrenched him about and sent him off with another kick.

'You don't have to hurt him.' Dora collected her torn blouse, her dignity and her bucket. 'You like hurting people. You like hurting me—'

'Cover yourself up,' Jamie hissed, 'and keep a tight mouth. You'd like the whole house to know we're out here, wouldn't you. I know you.'

'You think you're a real swell but you're no better'n anyone else with your breeches down,' she dared, and darted into the black silent regions of the house.

'Slut!' He swayed, but regained his balance and felt his way up the back stairs, only distant voices and carriage wheels breaking the silence. He stood blinking in the untidy comfort of his room with its guns and pipe-racks, jackets of kangaroo fur and finely made boots, trophies and stuffed fauna for he was a skilful and avaricious hunter. Nausea twisted him and he crouched ready to dash to the basin, but the urgency passed. He hated the feeling of nausea, the only reason he eased up on wine but, after all, this *was* New Year. Actually, he hated sickness of any kind, as Mama did. But more than anything he hated deformity – as Mama did – and he could never understand, quite, how she suffered that wretched midget. She found him amusing, she insisted. She needed to laugh. But it was his guess the creature's twisted limbs and eccentric ways enhanced her own perfection – he knew his mother! He prowled, fondling artefacts. Those Boylands, no, *Moynans* . . . The girl attracted him in a way, but then all women attracted him, at least initially, simply because they were women. But this one was too tall and thin for his taste; he liked women plump and nicely rounded, like Dora. Dora really wasn't so bad; warm and strong and responsive; at least he knew how to make her respond. He moved about the room, restless. The Moynan girl's eyes had been cold in sizing him up. He didn't like to be so appraised. But her brother might, just might, make a fitting riding companion, for the Irish rode like centaurs; besides, he was rather tired of the same old crowd – Tom Pearson for ever boasting of the family money, ironmongers that's all they were, and Myron spoiling stableboys rotten so he could bully them – something more than a little odd about Myron. Con Moynan might, just might be worth cultivating if for no more substantial reason than a temporary diversion.

Moaning, he threw himself on his bed to toss in vague discomfort. He didn't have to rush to the bowl, that was something. A long sleep and he would be fine, he always was. He wanted sleep badly. Actually, he wanted many things badly – as Mama did – but O'Shea was acting meaner than ever, a man as rich as Croesus too . . . Who the devil was Croesus? Perhaps he should have stuck with his book-learning. But he knew the things that mattered, like choosing a gun and a well-drawing pipe and clothes of the best cut and cloth, and how to judge a horse – and a woman; what a world to explore there! Exploration of women would be much easier, though, if he lived close in to theatres and restaurants and dives, for all Birubi really provided was good stabling – and of course Mama. Mama would love Lyons Terrace . . . Trouble was, she wouldn't leave O'Shea, at least not for long. Only one place might tempt her to turn her back on O'Shea even for a time – the house in Bendigo. She'd always loved that house. Actually, he rather liked the place himself, right by the Irish Boy with something always doing in the town. If the pub was his own he'd settle with her. Plenty to do around the fields, too. Besides, he could run down to

Melbourne when he felt like it, cut a figure – Jamie Lorne, hotelier! Jamie Lorne, entrepreneur! How could he fail with Herlicht to advise on running the place: Kurt knew everyone, and if not exactly everything, would know how to make the place pay. Between them they could make the Irish Boy a household word, a place as fine as anything in Melbourne.

Sometimes he had a dream of Mama-Raunie walking out on O'Shea. Just walking out. How *that* would set the man back on his heels. He hated O'Shea when he acted paternal. He didn't want O'Shea as his father. His real father was dead. Mama understood how he felt. She understood so many things about him.

He turned over on his back and lay limp. The world was slipping away . . . He slid quickly and easily into the deep uncluttered sleep of youth.

Chapter Two

'WILL PURDUE is peddling coach-building. You taking it on?'

O'Shea made no answer though Mason knew he had heard; O'Shea heard everything but answered only when and what suited him. Hard to catch O'Shea off-guard at anything but worth a try for the man didn't take on a thing, at least openly, that didn't pay. The others had dribbled out to impatient women waiting in impatient carriages but Nance could wait, he'd waited around enough for her in his time. His stomach tormented and he belched loudly, for the maids hovering at the door impatient to clear up didn't count. Finally O'Shea turned, full glasses in hand.

'Odd,' he grinned, 'considering Purdue as some genial-sounding "Will".'

'Takes him down a peg.' Mason smacked his lips over the brandy and water. 'A sanctimonious pander but knows how to make brass make brass. Trouble is, he talks too much. He'll gossip himself into a real fix one of these days.'

'And talk himself out of it just as easily.'

'You investing, then?' Mason persisted.

O'Shea shrugged. 'In "Will's" eyes I'm a black pagan profligate with dirty money, but money he'd still like to get his hands on. I'll let him stew a while.'

'Noan so bad, the coach-building trade,' Mason brooded. 'Trouble is, railways are set to take over.'

'Not entirely. The coach-lines will work with them. A coach can go where rails can't.'

'Oh, aye.' No doubt of it, the man had instincts for success as well as survival, and worth a bit of crawling to be in on something profitable. Always some scheme up O'Shea's sleeve: he, Mason, wasn't the only one to regret not having been around in the early fifties when, Victoria eating itself out of meat, O'Shea had run up slaughter-yards on the fields and started the great cattle trek south from the Riverina, charging beef-hungry gold-gorged diggers through the nose for steak. Rumour had it he'd made twenty thousand pounds in one year. No one doubted it.

'Rumour going around you're standing for Assembly,' he prodded.

'I doubt you heard that, Mason.' The man's cold stare was, as always, disconcerting and Silas could escape it only by inspecting his glass. 'For one thing, we all know it's too late for this year's election. The most you might have heard is that I'm considering getting my own man in – no secret that, it's my constant consideration. But it takes time to groom a candidate, even a suitable one.'

'You've found the right one, eh?' Blurting it out.

O'Shea ignored the question. Mason fretted. He rather fancied himself in politics, even the step-up of one of the newly formed municipal councils. Something to write home about there: Silas Mason, fifth son of a Liverpudlian cooper, kicked around Merseyside as a lad, emigrating penniless or close to it to the colonies, clawing his way up to the Legislative Assembly! Even a suburban council would take brass of course, but he was making brass. As for Nance, she'd grab at the life, might just handle it too with a bit of dolling-up here and toning-down there – might. There were times he rather regretted Nance: no canny ambitious Lancastrian should saddle himself with a pub-keeper's daughter from a Southampton back street, plenty of her sort here already. His stomach gurgled uncomfortably. Could O'Shea possibly be promoting 'Will' Purdue? Incredible, but stranger things had happened. After all, the man wielded power among his Temperance Sabbatarian cronies. And if not Purdue . . . the newcomer, Moynan? He looked the sort who'd cultivate the right people and say the right things at the right time, presenting a respectable dependable public image no matter what he was like off platform. He, Silas Mason, had disliked Owen Moynan on sight.

He brooded on O'Shea's broad uncommunicative back. An upstart after all, an off-colour descendant of convicts, yet he ran the place – almost – while Silas Mason, grain-merchant, was left to make his mark the best way he could. He took an angry frustrated gulp of brandy. It burned. Bile rose in his throat. He'd up prices, that's what he'd do, and he'd start with the man before him. The odd awful thing was that whenever he tried to deal with O'Shea, the man's cognac, malt whisky, imported champagne, all and everything, turned bitter to his taste.

'Go to bed.' Raunie jerked her hair from Abby's hands.

'But your hair—'

'I can't bear brushing tonight.'

'I'll unhook you, then.'

'I've a husband to do it.'

Abigail threw the brush aside in one of her tight-lipped tempers. 'I sometimes wonder what I'm doing here when I could be off with my Kitty.'

'You're here to save me trouble.'

'A mistress should manage her own household.'

'I pay you to do it instead.'

'A careless mistress makes poor servants. They're not only insolent, they pilfer.'

'Then take the strap to them. As for your precious daughter, she doesn't want you because Herbert won't have you; he sets the tune in that tent. And tent it will always be no matter how you beggar yourself sending them money. They'll never acquire even a lean-to, let alone a house.'

'Kitty wants me—'

'You fool yourself. You always have. Go to *bed*.'

But still the woman lingered, folding and sorting clothes, tucking things away or moving them from one place to another unnecessarily, until Raunie grew angry, then abusive. Even so Abby went reluctantly, puffing a little, not solely from indignation for she was growing plump again with the good pickings of the O'Shea household. Raunie tore impatiently at her hooks. These days she needed to do little for herself; if Abby was out of her range there were servant girls a-plenty to keep running. She was at her mirror when the door

41

crashed open and Brick stumbled over her clothes left where she had stepped out of them. He swore, kicked them from his path and banged the door.

'You keep this place like a gipsy camp. If it weren't for Luff—' He broke off, glancing at the closed doors.

'I sent her to bed. I knew you'd stay drinking with Silas and finish up in a temper and I don't choose to have her hear your ravings.'

'Mason drinks, I bargain. He's manoeuvring grain prices. I stopped him in his tracks.' He looked about, frowning. 'Knowing Luff she's at some keyhole right now – doesn't she ever sleep? You should have left that predatory harpy at Bendigo instead of dragging her back here to play your spy.' He snapped the hall-door bolt and key flap in one movement. 'Foiled! And she'll not hear anything she's not heard before.' He dragged off his coat and loosened his shirt. 'Damn this heat. And damn that son of yours, spreadeagled on his bed fully clothed and snoring. He's been drinking and you know it.'

'He never takes more than a couple. And only wine. And it *is* New Year.'

'You believe everything he tells you.'

'You're in no position to act the prude over liquor.'

'If you're set on ruining him with your indulgences, I'm not. You've no more knowledge of human beings than a rabbit has. Oh, I'll grant you've a highly developed animal intuition that leads you to triumph in most of your dealings with the human race, particularly with the male of the species, but more than intuition is needed with Jamie. What does he ever do but spend the money you feed him, lording it over a gang of young bucks roistering from cock-fight to race-track to saloon – and, from rumour going about, the town's whore-houses.'

'If he does he'd have the good taste to choose the best, just as he does with restaurants. Did you know,' she preened, 'that he's an expert at chess at the Café Français? And quite the connoisseur of its stewed kidney?'

He laughed. 'He goes to ogle the hostess and wager on billiards. He'll wager on anything.'

'And why not? You did. You cut your teeth in the best places and the worst – and that goes for whore-houses too.'

'More sensible than becoming involved with predatory housemaids. Put that girl – Dora, isn't it? – to work in the scullery where Jamie's less likely to prowl. Blast this weather.' He blundered through to his dressing-room to throw boots about, swearing as he searched, apparently for a dressing-gown, cursing Jonathan – give the fellow free time and he was off with some strumpet forgetting to come back. He'd send him packing when he did turn up. Raunie smoothed her hair thoughtfully. He'd had a good deal to drink and was in a vile mood, but when was he not over Jamie? He appeared wiping his neck and the thick black hairs on his chest with the elusive gown. 'The curse of supporting a stable of lackeys is that you become helpless without them.' He tied the gown about him with a savage knot, his eyes as cold as his voice. 'You excelled yourself tonight, didn't you, Egypt.'

'You did ask me to take trouble over the dinner.'

'Dinner be damned. A houseful of servants can take credit for that. You know exactly what I mean; your more than usually expert performance of a trollop.'

She swung about angrily. 'I weary of being polite to your procession of protégés and tonight they were worse than usual, particularly that freckle-faced Irish milkmaid with her ribbon bows and folded hands and stupidly superior airs.'

'You're overlooking your quite exceptional talent for manipulating men and stupefying women. I would say the girl is straight from convent life and terrified of your, what is usually referred to as worldly glitter. You could have helped rid her of her awkwardness if you'd wanted to please me.'

'Then you should ask more interesting people to my dinners than bog-reared peasants.'

'These particular peasants, as you call them, might turn out to be useful to me, which in language you can understand means the father is not to be despised, the daughter ridiculed or the son bewitched.' A tiny smile lifted her mouth. 'Do you understand me?' he snapped. 'I don't pay my spies of ships' captains, bank-managers and cab-drivers to keep me informed as to who enters the country or leaves it, to have my expensive information wasted.'

'What do I care about an ogling boy and a frumpish girl? Or their prig of a father looking down his nose at all and sundry? I'm bored with living out here without even gaslight.'

'You know my views on living close in – it would be bad for Jamie. He gets himself into enough trouble as it is.'

'Jamie . . . always Jamie. You're obsessed with my son.'

'My son too, all legal and binding. He only raises doubts over the matter to annoy me. As to living out in the bush as you call it, you've carriages, a stable of horses and enough bodyguards and servants to man a mediaeval castle; I even suffer your court jester creeping about my halls and sleeping under tables. If you were to rid yourself of even a few of your stubborn dislikes and suspicions you'd find more to do than flaunt new clothes and sit over cards.'

'There's nothing else to do but flaunt new clothes and sit over cards.' She flung herself on the bed to pound her fists into the cushions in temper. 'Nothing else, now or ever.'

'I suppose, being you, there is nothing else. If you were any other woman you'd come with me to the Pride to take your rightful place as its hostess and set it at its best before the county and my guests.'

'I hate Erins Pride. I've always hated it and you know it. Isn't it enough that I'm forced to look at it on my own wall knowing you had it painted there to spite me?'

'That's a crazy notion.'

'It's true. And each time you gloat over it I wait for you to announce that *there* is where your wife made her start in the colony, as a slavey in its kitchen for three shillings a week. If you ever do that I'll deny it.'

'You'd be wasting your breath for there are those who know it to be true. It's an odd thing, Egypt, but you never seem to mind people knowing you're a gipsy yet you go through life terrified they'll discover you soiled your hands in my kitchen. I'm often tempted to let fling your fearful secret, which is not a secret, if only to witness your lying performance of shocked denial. You might not be as successful at it as you imagine. No one watching your performance tonight as an over-dressed courtesan – a more flattering title than Cypriot – need be told it comes of long and detailed experience.'

'Who are you to talk of beginnings?' She spat the words at him. 'A *nigger's* beginning. *Nigger!*'

'Stop it!' He moved to fold her hands in his. 'No one knows better than I that spite is only one side of you. When it suits you you can charm the venom from a spider to leave it sitting meekly on your palm. And that's the way I want you now. I want you at the Pride. I need you there.'

She lay back watching him through half-closed lids. 'You have your precious Moll to play lady housekeeper.'

'Moll's too old to play at anything much longer.'

'She should be dead.' She flung it at him, at the room, at the world. 'I wish she were dead. But even if she were I wouldn't go to your Erins Pride. I ran away from it once. I'd always run from it. They hate me there. Particularly Joey.'

'You could remedy that. Or try.'

'I'll have nothing to do with Joey Bowes. I don't want him at Birubi. And if you ever bring Moll down, for any reason—'

'I'll bring whom I wish into this house.' He turned away but she grasped his wrist.

'To spite me.' Petulant but beguilingly so and he sank on the bed again.

'When will you understand that my reasons for doing specific things are not necessarily connected with you? This time you would be at the Pride as my wife and its mistress.' So patiently and reasonably that she looked at him with suspicion; he was almost begging, he needed her badly, she knew, and it made him vulnerable before her. 'Take trunks of dresses and jewellery. Give your splendid dinners. Give a dance and ask the county; I'll make all come if I have to call in their petty debts and my stud rams to do it. I'll even take you there in a pantomime chariot drawn by white horses

45

with bells to their harness and footmen in white perukes. Think of all that magnificence bumping over the pot-holes of the Great South Road.'

Laughing, she burrowed deliciously into her cushions. 'You can be so amusing when you like.'

'The Pride is a different place these days and I can't understand why simple curiosity hasn't enticed you back if only to fault the carpets and furnishings.'

'I couldn't bear to see what Moll and that smug Hetty have done with it.' She stretched her body languorously, her eyes distant and dreaming. 'But I'd ride in your fancy chariot to Melbourne when the wool sales are on. The city's gay then. Why don't you take me?'

He got to his feet impatiently. 'I've more to do than dawdle in the Café de Paris and flaunt you in a box at the Royal.'

'But I helped you sell your wool. I talked about it all the time.'

'God in heaven, brokers don't consider women when they're calculating wool clips. What attractions could you possibly add to the finest fleece in the Riverina?'

'I love cities,' she dreamed, 'full of rich and clever people where I can wear wonderful clothes and give dinners and balls. I like—'

'Flirtations and admiration and notoriety – I know, Egypt. You must let the world know you're alive.' He grinned. 'Which to a certain extent I condone. It's good for business.'

Leaning on her elbow she put out an urgent hand. 'Don't go away. Don't leave me.'

'I must go. Jamie must settle at the Pride and earn his keep. He'll learn to run the place if it kills us all in the doing of it. And when he's mastered all there he'll do a stint at Narriah. He was too young when we last went through.'

'I don't want him wandering the back-country picking up fevers from rotten meat and water. You've hands galore to do your work.'

'He'll learn to run my properties as he'll learn to manage my Bendigo interests. I want to phase out Herlicht.'

'You're too hard on my son. He's only sixteen. You hate him having fun. If you were his real father—'

'His real father would have left him to drink himself into the gutter or gamble himself into a debtor's prison – and Jamie's likely to do both if he's not watched.'

'His father was a gentleman.'

'The only gentlemanly thing James Lorne did was to die on an immigrant barque and be buried at sea before he made a gentlemanly nuisance of himself in this colony.'

'Why are you so hard on Jamie? You coddled him when he was a child, you promised him the world. Just because at his age you were working – no, not at work, but planning ways to do somebody out of their money or trick them into parting with something you wanted – while I was scrabbling for food enough to keep myself alive. I'll never let my son live as I did. Why shouldn't he have everything he wants and needs?'

'He goes to Erins Pride.'

'You can't make him stay there.'

'Rob will have his orders – a free hand with him. And I don't give a damn how he keeps the boy in line.'

'He'll run off. He's done it before.'

'And I'll find him. As I have before.'

'And while you're bullying my son around your stations, what of me?'

'If you won't come we must go without you.'

'Then *go*,' she raged. 'Traipse your pudding-faced Irish bores around in the dirt and hob-nob with your precious Blacks. *And* your precious Moll . . .' Her words trailed. Had she gone too far too soon? He was slipping away from her . . . Time for other methods. She turned the lamp low until it was only a glimmer, shrugged out of her thin négligé and lay back, the faint glow outlining her naked limbs. Reaching for him she drew him close. 'Don't go.' Her voice was soft, no more than a purr, that sweet throbbing voice that could twist about his heart and squeeze it till he had no more resistance than a willow frond in running water. 'Stay with me.' As she knew he would, he turned to her. 'Leave the Pride to Rob. I hate Erins Pride – why not? I hate your mill and your school and stores and the mine as I hate all things that take

47

you away from me. I even hate my little shop when we argue over it.'

'It's becoming a liability; you make too many inroads on the stock. There are better investments to be made at Moreton Bay.'

'I'm always lonely without you.' Clasping her fingers behind his neck she drew his face down to hers, whispering. 'Stay with me. Stay.'

He sank against her, kissing her. After a time he raised himself on his elbow, placed one hand behind her neck, his fingers splayed, and pinned her to his gaze. 'You'd come with me to Bendigo soon enough, wouldn't you.'

With a soft little laugh she ran her fingers down his cheek in a long slow caress. 'The golden town we called it, remember? The gold coming in with lights blazing . . . The crowds on Saturday nights – ah, those Saturday nights. And always the excitement of a new strike: "He'll dine at the Shamrock tonight,"' she mimicked. 'And someone always did.' Her voice throbbed as he settled himself alongside her, stretching out, kissing her neck.

'The town's growing decorous these days,' he murmured, intent on her, beginning to absorb her. 'Women everywhere. You'd have competition, Egypt.'

'You should go through more often – if only to keep track of Kurt.'

He paused in his fondling of her. 'Well now! If you insist upon talking of the old days, and of Kurt in particular—'

'*No.*' She quivered in his arms. 'I don't know why I said that. And you promised you'd never bring *that* up again.' She snuggled against him, sure of him. 'It was your fault. You left me alone too often.'

'I have but one thing to say concerning Herlicht: I make a point of knowing everything that ex card-sharp does and says as I know what each of my employees is about. Kurt knows better than to grow lazy over my interests – and my money. Even if Bendigo is over four hundred miles away, if it were a thousand I'd still know every move he makes.'

She stirred against him provocatively. 'I helped make your fortune there. It was I who insisted the men were ravenous for meat. It was I who endured the noise and the bull-dust and the awful lowing of cattle and the filth of your slaughter-yards every time I opened my door—'

'And spent the profits as if they had never been.'

'Kurt will never forgive you for winning his grog-shop from him at cards, building it up to an hotel and giving him the job of running it.'

'He's a smart manager, he saves me money. If he ceases to do so I would have grounds for suspicion. Giving him a free hand with my properties there doesn't mean I trust him, it means I trust others less. Herlicht won't put a foot wrong because I've made Bendigo his responsibility; besides, I believe that in some twisted way he's grateful to me, I taught him not to play poker when he's drunk – after being duly warned.'

'I miss the house,' she mused. 'It was the beginning of things there.' She felt him stir, then tremble and she knew she had him. 'You loved me so much in that house. I made you forget everything, yes, even Barbara – and I *will* say her name. *Barbara*.' Feeling him withdraw from her a little she drew him back, deliberately, soothing him, holding his head between her warm silky breasts till he put his lips to them. 'She's dead and nothing to do with us any more. And you were never really in love with her, it was always me you wanted all those years – wasn't it? *Wasn't* it?'

'It was,' he whispered, his lips moving over her shoulders, his eyes closed, drawing in the scent and sense of her. 'You made me forget everything I was running from. You did it then and you do it now.' His arms tightened. 'Sometimes the things you are and the things you do drive me near insane, and being bound to you – and I am – is like being bonded to a Circe, hearing some far-off siren call and helpless to escape it . . .'

She didn't know what a Circe was but she knew what a man meant when he called a woman a siren; a female something that rose from the sea and coiled about him and drew him down, just as she was doing now to fill the room and the bed with his male heat and faint scent of tobacco and strong flavour of whisky that meant he was here and loving

49

her. His kisses grew longer and deeper as his hands moved over her. 'You're talking about your wife,' she gasped, 'not your whore.'

He lifted his head and she could just define the shape of his face and the gleaming slits of his eyes. 'Wife, mistress, whore, it's all the same. I have no illusions about you, Raunie. And if I ever had illusions about Jamie they're dissolving fast. He hates my touch of the nigger but loves the life I afford him, just as you love your life, and I sometimes think that what you feel for me, and even for your son, is possession, a matter of degree beyond what you feel for your jewels and dresses and silver and crystal, and I know you can't help any of it.'

'It took me a long time to collect my jewels and dresses and silver and crystal,' she laughed softly. But she knew he did not hear her for his voice was slurring, becoming remote and indistinct as he grew intent on her body, obsessed by it, as she wanted him to be. Her barometer in life was Brick's voice, angry, bitter, passionate as now, and she set out to manipulate that voice as she set out to control him when he was stubborn or resistant or moody or furious, stamping about and shouting in his sometimes terrible rages. Yet no matter how he raged he always came back to her for she had long ago learned to dispel his moods by making love until all else dissolved and there was nothing but the friction they engendered together. She murmured endearments, drawing him in to her, breathing him in until he was part of her and she of him and they throbbed together in their, always complete, unison. And it wasn't until they were spent and still, breathing quietly, that she turned with a desperate little movement to bury her face against his neck.

'Don't go away. Don't leave me.'

'I must go.'

She clung savagely. 'If I had children you wouldn't leave me. Why don't we have children?'

'I don't know,' he said dully. But he lightened his voice deliberately. 'Don't fret so over it. Be thankful they don't stone women any longer.'

'Don't call me barren,' she raged in her despair. 'I'm not barren. I bore Jamie.'

'That was long ago. Perhaps—'

'I'm only thirty-four. That's not old.'

'No, it's not old,' he soothed in the tone he used to placate children.

Her hands moved over him, groping, pleading. 'I don't care what the doctors say – "In God's good time". What kind of an answer is that? What has God to do with it?'

His laugh was a little tired. 'Very little, I should think.'

'It could be your fault.'

'That's possible,' he agreed ruefully. 'I have never had proof of my fertility though there have been accusations. Perhaps I should have investigated them more thoroughly.'

'How can you joke—'

'Because I must make light of it,' he said sharply. 'Leave it, Raunie, leave it.'

She was making her sterility an obsession simply because her body foiled her in this thing and no other, for when she craved something its lack absorbed and possessed her. She had Jamie – as he did – for good or ill but it wasn't enough, she wanted more. She was crying and he stroked her hair and moved his lips across her damp lashes as she clung to him, and he tried to understand her despair and dispel it for there was something terrible about these anguished tears. Here was perhaps the only true sorrow she came to tears about and when he saw her like this he could almost wish her to bear a child, his child. But there were other times when he actually sweated at the idea of his own child, for even if colour did die out, the idea, the knowledge, the *fact* would always be there. No degree of business acumen or amount of money or power could wipe out the fact that he, Brick O'Shea, was born of convict-aboriginal parentage, and that, combined with Raunie's touch of the gipsy, would damn their child as a mongrel breed, to be regarded in white society as a pariah. The child's then the man's only weapon of defence would be a stubborn self-willed strength such as he, O'Shea, had cultivated to devise and scheme and fight a white society that had but a grudging place for the ex-convict and nothing for the aborigine – except, on occasions, the romantic European concept of the aborigine as the Noble

Savage! The world would have no secure place for his sons, even less for daughters for what could there be for a part-aboriginal woman? Before his colour had been made known to himself and the world he had held ambitions to found a dynasty with the woman he had chosen as wife, the keeper of his future and his name, but that was become a dead dream . . .

He moved uneasily beside his wife. The memory of Barbara came and went in his life, a woman long dead, unenjoyed and unloved before he had learnt to love her. A woman destroyed wilfully, if indirectly, as a casualty to his own ambitions and those of this woman in his arms with whom he had not only mated but whom he had finally married. His hand stilled on her hair and slid away for he was back with the sense of being divisible from her, an odd terrible sensation that came sometimes in the most intimate moments of their lovemaking to leave him desperate with a sense of being solitary even in the sexual act. He was well aware of what he enjoyed with Raunie, the intensity of his absorption in her body as he probed and trembled within her, bent upon the physical release he had never found so completely or exquisitely with another woman; so exquisite he no longer sought solace elsewhere which often amused and amazed him as his eyes passed over a lovely face or devoured breasts flaunted by some would-be temptress or breathed in the scent of a young girl at his elbow. The end result scarcely seemed worth the effort of pursuit – Raunie was always persistently *there*. Usually when he made love to her everything was resolved, even her selfishness and extravagance and lack of civilised anything, her grasping needs and the uncanny flair she had for getting exactly what she wanted, for in their enjoyment of each other they became outside all else. And yet . . . too many times of late, climax over and physically divided, he knew this vague dissatisfaction. There were even times when he felt an actual . . . distaste, and the injustice of it horrified him; incredible, impossible, but it was so.

He trembled, he could not help it, and half asleep as she was she murmured his name and clutched at him. He held

52

her close. Did she feel his turning away – no, she would not for it was enough for Raunie to possess him physically; to her all answers lay in the body and she would never understand the need for more, his hunger for a little of what he had tasted with Barbara Merrill, the unspoken promise of things to come.

He would not take Raunie to Bendigo. He must not, for once in their house with its aura of the excitement of their old life together, a house that would always be the symbol of their success and adulation and raw living, at times almost to debauchery and loving it all, he would lose himself in her again and, helpless, become as he had once been: less than fiesh and muscle, unable to resist her demands. And she would demand, she never ceased demanding, and would get all she wanted, even her absolute way with her son. He could not let that happen for in her attitude to Jamie there was a disturbing indulgence, a laxity, as if the boy were a favourite expensive toy acquired to amuse and stimulate her. A plaything. Jamie must not remain a toy, Jamie must grow up to the world he, O'Shea, had made. Jamie – Lorne if he wanted it so, what matter after all – had always been his future, the child then the man to take over his world-within-the-world that he had built so assiduously.

Raunie sighed and stirred and came to life, her hands moving over him, beginning to explore, to stimulate in her own unique way. She leant over him, pressing on him with her warm and yielding body, and her weight though slight was urgent.

'Love me,' she whispered. 'Love me.'

Her kisses and caresses were greedy. Her female scent enveloped him again and he closed his eyes and ceased to think, and desire for her grew till it became unbearable yet still he held back savouring the painful but exquisite drag of her but she drew on him until he could no longer resist and they joined lips, thighs and hands in the strong familiar ritual of their loving.

Irritated with himself as much as with his son and daughter, Owen sat silent but impatient as the carriage clopped the eight miles or so into Castlereagh Street, the dark spread of bush and the indifferent road defined only by the glow of distant cottages and their own carriage lights. It was late when they reached the city and there were only stragglers about. No, sir, the coachman yawned, he would not be taking the carriage back till morning, the master mostly rode in; in any case there were other equipages. He would stay over with his sister. He whipped the horses past a volley of stones from a brawling 'push'. A woman ran from an alley, sailors in pursuit, but no one answered her shrieks. A youth retched in a gutter, another propped himself against a fence and Owen felt his stomach turn; what was this rascal about, embarking on a tour of seamen's haunts? He pulled down the blinds. In God's name, what was he, a citizen and house-holder of Belfast, County Antrim, Ulster, a connoisseur of civilised living, doing in this market town, this port of charlatans and coloured men and ex-convicts, this haven for scavengers and runaways, confidence tricksters and squab-bling aborigines? A place of the wildest extravagance, great wealth and luxurious homes. Of disorder and torpid heat and dust and burnt-out scrub, of dingy alleys and sour streams and the marvellous heart-stopping beauty of sea and sky. A place where he was expected to break bread with a dandied-up buck nigger even if he did pass for white, and a woman of doubtful origins and career, and a boy who talked as if he would stop at nothing, had experienced too much and who obviously spent his life, his mother's mad-money and what he could scrounge, or even thieve, roistering in the town's pot-houses. He winced. When it came to roistering, Owen Moynan, who better at it than your own son? Indeed, Conall Moynan goes one better, he shoots his friends. Owen did not even glance at his daughter. Her manners had been as atrocious as any bare-foot wench from his Belfast mills – or any bold-eyed ex-mistress. Late as it was he had much to say to his children, but not in this box, prey to alien ears. He sat fretting for the privacy of his house.

But Con tumbled out and, clutching the banister, stumbled upstairs, Owen offering up a prayer that Delia was sleeping soundly, exhausted by praying for them in 'that den of

54

'iniquity'. Without even a lift of a hand Con Moynan closed his door on his father and sister and Owen knew it would be useless to try to talk to him that night. But he was determined Alannah would not escape. As she turned along the hall he followed her into her tiny sitting-room and closed the door softly but firmly behind them.

'Your behaviour tonight was unforgiveable. The prioress surely had no hand in the teaching of such gaucheries.'

'Mrs O'Shea was rude to me, Papa.'

'Even so, it was no reason to be insolent. Your aunt must attend more closely to your manners.'

She slipped off her cloak with a tired gesture. 'If I've upset you, I'm sorry.' Then, with a flash of temper, 'But I wasn't sorry at the time.'

'Are you so intent then on acquiring the habits of these people you criticise? No matter how angry you were, such an attitude to your hosts was unpardonable. Only that Mr O'Shea made light of the matter I would have made you apologise then and there.'

Her eyes blazed. 'It is fortunate you did not try.'

'Alannah!' Uncaring if his voice did pierce the walls. 'It is not loss of face to admit you were at fault. Nor the loss of your pride; indeed you can spare some.'

'Oh . . . *Papa*!' With a movement that seemed to have something of despair in it she turned from him and, troubled, his anger receded slightly.

'I fear I made a mistake in bringing you to a country you had made up your mind to dislike.'

'We could not have stayed at home.'

'Con could not have stayed in Ireland, no.'

'Then we could not.'

'No,' he agreed reluctantly. 'Therefore, we must try to be happy here and not criticise so readily.'

'Is it true,' she murmured, 'that Mr O'Shea is an aborigine?'

He hesitated. His sister was an efficient housekeeper, the reason he had brought her out, but was proving an inveterate gossip as well as too outspoken a critic of Australian *mores*. 'Part-native as I understand it,' he answered abruptly.

She turned slowly to face him. 'Then why were we told that the Blacks were ignorant savages?'

'I imagine the man cannot altogether escape his blood,' he said uncomfortably. He did not want discussion on such an explosive subject, most certainly not here and now, but since they were stumbling about in Delia's hotchpotch of fact and fiction, better to bring all into the open. 'In any case we must not cultivate prejudice. You were not taught to practise distinction.'

'There was no need for it at home.'

'Not of colour, no.'

'A strange man, don't you think?'

He cleared his throat. 'This is a strange country. The people are . . . well . . . different. They have grown away from England, indeed from the Old World. But to be different is not a crime or even something to arouse suspicion. We must accept much here whether it be to our liking or not.' Talking to her so meant that, in a way, he was talking to himself, soothing and placating his unease by reason. 'It could even perhaps be stimulating.'

'I have never heard you speak so before.'

'I have never been in Australia before.'

As always she met his eyes frankly. 'And I've never met anyone like Mr O'Shea before. I didn't know what to say or do. And so I became angry.'

'I know.'

'His wife is wonderful to look at, don't you think? Like a gipsy. A shining decorated gipsy. Did you notice her eyes?'

'I did.'

'And her rings? So many rings. Were they actually diamonds? The eardrops too?'

'They are wealthy people, I understand.'

'She invited me to visit her jewellery shop.'

'You are too young for ornate gems.'

'Her hair was sprinkled with gold dust. Real gold. I've heard of the custom—'

'You looked very charming yourself,' he said quickly, finding something a little unhealthy in her admiration. But she shrugged off his compliments, as always reluctant, seemingly a little afraid, to believe them.

'I'm sure she was laughing at me. They must all have been laughing at the way I do my hair, and this childish dress.'

'Then you shall choose a new wardrobe.'

'Oh . . . I don't know why I said that.' Laughing off her mood. 'You know I never care what I wear. Besides, I could never manage these new fashions, I'd be certain to trip over so many skirts.'

'You must learn to manage them.' It was suddenly important that she stand on a level with, preferably superior to, these colonial women even in the trivialities of fashion. 'I insist you shop for new things, and by your own choice, without advice from your aunt. But not *quite* so deep a decolletage, eh? You are not Mrs O'Shea in years. Certainly not in temperament.' He grew enthusiastic. '*Carte blanche* at the stores, for I have decided to do some entertaining.'

'But we've made few friends.'

'We owe a dinner to our shipboard acquaintances. For a start, that polite young man . . .' He snapped his fingers, making a great pretence at recall. 'What was his name . . ?'

'Aldercott. Simon Aldercott.' So, she had remembered. He couldn't decide if the fact pleased him or not. 'Aunt Delia took note of his boarding-house in Macquarie Street.'

So he would be close by. And in choosing to reside in a respectable street of residences side by side with academies he might, after all, be a young man of discernment and ambition. 'Aunt Delia,' Alannah went on, flippantly, 'is prepared to tolerate Mr Aldercott, not only because of the proverbs and prejudices they share but because she despairs of me matrimonially as well as socially. "At least he is a *respectable* young man," she assures me, and herself.' She turned clear grey eyes on her father. 'I hope, Papa, you are not conspiring with her in some match-making scheme, for when and if I decide to marry I will make my own choice.' In her words and tone he sensed a veiled threat and he hastened to change the subject.

'Take Con with you when you shop.'

'He'll be dreadfully bored.'

'I don't believe so. He likes to air his quite excellent taste.' He yawned, watching her untie her pale fine hair. He hated to see a woman's hair confined but then he was an old-fashioned man and, as he had sometimes been told, something of a prude. Had he perhaps been alone too long?

'Do you remember your mother, Alannah?' he asked, abruptly and impulsively, surprising himself for he seldom spoke of Mary now. Alannah was so still at first he thought she had not heard, but finally she answered.

'A little. At her prayers, mostly.'

'I insist you take Con with you,' he hurried on. 'He's growing lazy. A lazy country I fear.'

'It's nothing like home,' she mused. 'As you say – different.'

'Perhaps not so different. After all, we've never viewed home from a distance before.'

He remembered stirring in the night to the sound of bells and only half awake had believed them Irish bells – ah, the sweet ever-present bells of Ireland; a land of bells, beckoning, summoning, reassuring, saying all was well. But this was not Ireland and he had turned over seeking oblivion from the bells that were not Ireland's bells. Now he looked long and anxiously at his daughter but she was not crying, she was simply standing still and very straight, her long hair spread about her, staring from the window at nothing that he could see. Alannah would not even cry as others and for all he could tell she was crying for home, silently and inwardly, tearing away at herself, holding her unhappiness close, in a way nurturing it because that was the only way she could bear and conquer it. He wanted to comfort her, to assure her all would be well, but he did not know how, and even if he could, being Alannah, she would shrink from such an intrusion upon her mind and heart. He could staunch a cut, pour oil on a scald, but he could do nothing for her inner wounds, he could only fumble before her silent distress. It had always been so. Turning to leave he placed his hand over her slim one and pressed, feeling the fine light bones; would they, would she, be durable enough for this stark country? He closed her door softly behind him. Whatever she was, whatever they were, the Moynans were here to stay and must drive roots deep into Australian soil. Hard as it promised to be it must be done. And soon.

Chapter Three

ALANNAH STIRRED to the shock of raised blinds and blinked at the sun dancing on the wall. Stifling a yawn she struggled up and pushed aside the mosquito netting to meet her aunt's disapproving eyes. Aunt Delia Carney was pink and white and short and plump and moved with the precision of a prettily functioning doll. Her success lay in her ability to surprise; on first meeting no one could quite believe Aunt Delia capable of anything more forceful than the pouring of tea from her Irish silver teapot and the proffering of cucumber sandwiches, but she had never believed in tiptoeing to the day or to anything else for that matter, and had managed the ancient Carney farm to a thriving property, her husband into his grave and her progeny to the most affluent quarters of the globe. Her china-blue eyes missed nothing and disapproved of most while her plump but capable fingers could manipulate a hem, a suet pudding or an angry bulldog with equal zest and skill. By some unique fusion of delicacy and damnation life's most irksome hindrances vanished and lesser ones were kicked neatly under the carpet when Delia Carney took a decisive hand in things.

'Your father has left for town refusing breakfast. I'm here to make certain you eat yours.' With a precise finger flick she bade Effie place the tray before her niece, waited for the maid's thump downstairs, then folded her hands across her ample bosom, her usual preliminary to a lecture. Phipps the cook, Effie, young Ned the odd-jobs boy, and Jebediah Wimple who came in to garden, scurried (in Jeb's case, shuffled) from her path while Alannah followed from long habit, soothing injured feelings. But this morning it seemed she must defend herself. She laced her tea liberally with sugar and prepared to do battle.

'Your brother is still asleep. I hope neither of you is adopting this deplorable Sydney habit of lying abed. "Time and tide"—'

' "Wait for no man".' Alannah shuddered at the poached eggs shimmering in the glare and caught her breath at the heat. Mosquitoes still buzzed about the net and hovered at the wall. The house faced north, a bad aspect in a colonial summer, but even without that trial she hated Brighton with a fervour she usually reserved for horse-beaters and rag curls. An unreasonable attitude, her aunt kept reminding her, for the house was of brick and to be prized in a city of wood and stone, and occupied a prime position in the fashionable northern end of Castlereagh Street with its back windows looking over a small but well-kept orchard to Pitt Street and the city. Moreover, it boasted a pine in its neat garden and a bush of white-starred jessamine under the window. But Alannah hated its cramped stairways and hideous wall-papered drawing-room where her aunt sat under her large-framed 'Sermon on the Mount', in pride of place above the fireplace as it had occupied pride of place in their cabin coming out, happily criticising passers-by. This morning the cumbersome varnished furniture seemed about to topple over and crush her and she wished her head didn't feel as heavy as the chest of drawers looked. Surely she didn't feel so, simply because of two glasses of wine that terrifying man had dared her to drink with all those terrifying people looking on? Laughing at her no doubt. She pushed the eggs aside.

'Tea, that's all.'

'Some toast at least. You surely don't imagine I'll allow you to exist on the rubbish served up at dinner parties, do you?'

'It was lavish rubbish. Con positively devoured the wallabi tail soup and the breast of Wonga Wonga pigeon.'

'Both have a pagan ring!' Aunt Delia pushed toast fingers under her niece's nose. 'I cannot understand your father—'

'I know.'

'Then you must know that I still disapprove of your attendance at that dinner, or whatever it was called.'

'Rout would best describe it. And worse than even you could imagine with over-painted women and lewd men lolling about a salon decked with crimson curtains weighted with gold tassels,' she elaborated. 'Exactly like some vulgar expensive bordello.'

'And what, might I ask, would you know of such places?'

'I listen and learn, Aunt Delia.' Solemnly. 'I have learnt a great deal since leaving Ireland.' She paused significantly before striking further terror into her aunt's breast. 'Con flirted disgracefully with Mrs O'Shea. And I drank – or quaffed, rather – two glasses of wine straight off, right there in front of everybody.'

'Your brother and *that* woman?' Aunt Delia skipped the horrors of her niece's wine-bibbing to consider the greater horror of her nephew's possible seduction. 'There are things Conall must be told about these people. For one thing, *if* the woman is married to this O'Shea it would make her thrice wed – *thrice*, Alannah! But if they only . . . well . . .' She looked hunted by her moral dilemma.

'Co-habit is the word, I believe. If they *are* living in sin their wages are certainly not death for they positively thrive. As for Con's enlightenment, it's common knowledge Mr O'Shea is a Black – not that he looks it for he *is* three parts white and that Irish so there is no need to be afraid of him.'

'I am not afraid of any colonial, native or otherwise.' Completely out of her depth Aunt Delia passed a limp hand across her forehead in her favourite gesture of martyrdom. 'If the man is accepted in what passes here for Society I can only bear with the situation for all your sakes and struggle with my conscience as best I may. I have made my bed and must lie in it, uneasily I'll admit, but to the best of my ability. Nevertheless!' She straightened her already firm little back. 'Tolerance must end somewhere. I am convinced there is foundation to the rumour that the woman is of gipsy blood. Mrs Purdue has no doubts.' Alannah shuddered at Eveline Purdue's ceaseless tongue, her pug dogs that chased guests through halls, and her near-moustache. 'I understand,' her aunt continued,' Mrs O'Shea never actually denies she's a gipsy but neither does she admit it, just laughs off questions or changes the subject and everyone seems too daunted by her to pursue the matter.'

'But of *course*. A gipsy . . . It's in her eyes. And in that wonderful black hair.'

'She dances, I'm told.'

'Quite beautifully.'

'Not *our* kind of dancing, Alannah. Gipsy dancing. Pagan dancing. She was even hostess, or whatever such women are called, at a saloon in Bendigo – wherever that place may be. A *saloon*! I repeat such unsavoury details so you will understand why I object so strongly to you, a young unmarried girl, scarcely out of a – a—'

'Convent – a Roman Catholic seminary. You must say the dreaded word before the world sooner or later, you know.' And managed to slip slivers of toast between the sheets.

'I have never denied or argued with your father's promise to provide you with a Catholic education, as I supported him over his decision to provide Con with a Protestant one, consoling myself, if with difficulty, that yours was the Dublin and not the Galway house of the Dominican Order. But you are your father's daughter too. *And* my niece.'

'You know, I have always considered a bordello to be rather like a convent, in its seclusion and secrecy and all that drama behind the scenes. Much went on in my girlish retreat you would not have approved of. Nor would have the prioress.'

'Do not be impertinent. In any case I do not believe you.'

'To be quite honest,' Alannah pursued, 'I did think there was something . . . well, exaggerated, strange, even pagan about Mr O'Shea's wall-painting.'

'Wall-painting?' Her aunt's voice squeaked. 'Not—'

'Oh no.' Smooth as silk. 'I imagine even Mr O'Shea would have the good taste to keep his paintings of naked women from sight.'

'Naked women?'

'The mural is of his station – sheep and cattle properties are called stations here, you know – near Goulburn. I should like to visit it.'

'Wall-paintings are ostentatious gestures. But what else

can be expected in a country where vulgarities are accorded such prominence? The place is primitive, and the servant girls quite imbecilic, with what appear to be permanent head colds and nary a pocket-handkerchief in sight.'

'It's the dust. One can't escape it. We might begin sniffling ourselves soon. Papa did warn us of difficulties.'

'Difficulties are one thing, vulgarities another. It's bad enough to be forced to beat off scavenging goats without being terrorised by packs of vicious dogs.'

'Make Ned carry a big stick. And use your parasol, as I do.'

'Nor can one put one's nose outside one's front door without being assaulted by theatres and music-halls.'

'The one thing that makes Brighton bearable to me.' Alannah stretched lazily. 'Do cheer up, Aunt. Papa's planning a dinner party, so civilised I expect it to be boring. But perhaps the O'Sheas will accept and enliven the proceedings.'

'I shall refuse to entertain such people. "He that sups with the Devil—"'

'"—needs a long spoon". Papa will insist, you'll see. We are obliged to return hospitality.'

'There must be *some* respectable folk to cultivate. For instance, that young governess who asked so many questions about Moreton Bay – wherever *that* may be.'

'The one Con likened to Harlech Castle – mud-coloured, square and absolutely solid?'

'A most respectable person, Alannah.'

'Perhaps she's off prospecting. I've heard of a strike to the north.'

'Miss Trencham was taking up a position as governess, braving Blacks as thick as bees, and country with the roughest of settlers, predominantly male. She asked me to pray for her.'

'From all I hear she'll find a husband without your prayers for they won't have seen a woman, even one as spectrally mud-coloured, square and solid as Miss Trencham, for years.'

'Finish your toast.'

Alannah indicated her empty plate. 'Mr Aldercott is to be invited.'

'Aldercott?'

'The young man from the *Elizabeth Anne*. You know you've been wanting to invite him here for want of better fish on my matrimonial hook.'

'Matrimony indeed! I shall need more detailed knowledge of that young man before considering him even as an acquaintance. Lichfield, I've been informed by Mrs Purdue, is no more than a provincial market town. Besides . . .' her chin tilted a little higher, 'I rather suspect that he is Methodist.'

'You really are a most dreadful snob, Aunt Delia,' Alannah reminded her cheerfully. She didn't want to be reminded of Simon Aldercott for she had found him ponderous, obsequious and garrulous to the point of absurdity. Such solemn eyes – though rather handsome eyes as she remembered, behind spectacles that had a habit of sliding slowly down his nose until on the point of dropping into his soup he pushed them back with a pat, as if administering reproof to trusted but wayward friends. She tried to imagine those eyes coming alive if they should see her in the kind of gown she meant to buy – a rich sharp blue. Or as green as the Harbour waters close to shore. No more virginal white, on that she was determined! 'We might, you know, foster a match between respectable Miss Trencham and worthy Mr Aldercott and help them finish up absolutely solid together.' She sprang from the bed, dragging on her négligé. 'I am to shop for new clothes today. Another of Papa's decrees.' Her aunt's pursy-pink mouth made a perfect O of dismay.

'But Mrs Purdue is calling.'

'Con is ordered off with me,' Alannah added with silent thanks that she would be free of her aunt for the day. 'The idea, I believe, is that in sprucing up we meet and mingle with the native-born. We shall go up to Wynyard Square and admire the gold nuggets in the shop windows.'

'You're far too flippant about serious matters. I intend a serious talk with your father.'

'I believe he intends the same with you.'

65

She straightened her nightcap that never would stay straight and Delia Carney felt a stab of the alarm she so often felt in attempting to deal with her niece. Too wilful, too rebellious and, she feared, quite unsuited to this country. Harsh pioneering lands needed determined practical Presbyterians like herself and she wished, as she so often wished, that she understood the girl's evasive, sometimes malicious, young mind. Yet, quixotically, a girl of quick sympathies and responses. A sudden quicksilver girl, too intense, with far too much *feeling* about everything she did and said. Yet she could scarcely be blamed for the taint of popery implanted by that rather odd Cassidy side; all the Cassidys saw things in corners where practising Protestants knew that the real evils of life were right out there in the market-place. Mary Moynan, *née* Cassidy, should have taken the veil instead of Owen and left him to more durable flesh, but who could have foretold that her pious devotions would turn to fanaticism? Mercifully – and she, Delia Carney, made no bones about it – Mary Moynan had died young freeing Owen for more worldly pursuits, even though religious divisions would always war within his children, certainly within Alannah no matter how the girl rationalised. All she, Owen's sister, could do was remain vigilant and protective of his motherless children with their unpredictable ways grown out of a bizarre childhood lived on a see-saw of social and religious over-protection, over-indulgence. She reached across to fasten the button straining across the girl's breasts; full and lovely breasts she had to admit with a pang of unease for behind every tavern door and on every bullock-wagon in this vulgar and fearsomely virile country, danger lurked, yes, even for poor foolish Conall, a boy still sadly undisciplined and, as all boys, headstrong. Owen had done his best but his offspring seemed quite beyond his control. Still, young men *could* grow out of wild ways and who should know that better than herself having brought up sons and acted matron one busy term at Con's Academy for Young Gentlemen – except that most of them had proved otherwise. She resumed her look of disapproval: posing before her mirror Alannah had become unbuttoned again, her restless fingers straying about her throat and shoulders and moving up to twist her hair about her ears and atop her head in snake-like experimental coils.

'If you gave as much attention to your Bible as you do to your coiffure I would have little need to hunt you up for church,' her aunt reminded her tartly.

'My hair never keeps to its pins,' the girl laughed ruefully, twisting and patting. 'If I don't experiment how am I to compete with exotic women who give exotic dinner parties?'

'You are not expected to be exotic, whatever that means. Young girls of your age and station are required only to be modest and soft-voiced and—'

'Obedient, because potential husbands like them so. But, do you know. I'm not absolutely certain you're right. In any case, I'm not interested in the latest bargains on the marriage mart and won't be for aeons and aeons, if ever.' She swung about the room, excited. 'There must be many wonderful things to do here besides marry. It's such an interesting country – and there's so much of it.'

Crash! Aunt Delia swished to the door in a way that boded ill for kitchen carelessness. 'I shall try Effie in the scullery where there is less to break. Remember now,' she warned with her most pious expression, 'I expect you and your brother to attend church on Sunday, Papist or Protestant, even if your father reneges. I'm sure I don't know what I've done to be forced to endure such constant bickering over Divine Service.'

For the first time Alannah showed impatience. 'Con and I have grown past sermons, particularly thundering ones. Anyway, Con's a rank unbeliever, while I get in the most awful muddle when I ponder the Holy Ghost.'

'You are not supposed to ponder anything. And I will not listen to blasphemy, not even when directed at the Pope. I'm sure I've done my best to save all Moynans from Hellfire, even suffering the Mass when you were a child solely for your sake. In Latin at that.'

'You don't have to suffer the papacy now, in Latin or otherwise – all's left behind in Ireland.' But Delia Carney turned abruptly to the stairs and the unfortunate Effie without more argument. Alannah hastened to pour Con's tea, strong and sweet the way he liked it, and hurried along the little hall. She was opening the window of his tiny sitting-room, even pokier than her own, when he emerged sleepily resplendent in a gown of gold satin and she gazed her delight, glorying as always in his Beau Brummel taste while openly sympathising with her father over his tailoring bills. She gloried in Con altogether, not only because he was her only sibling but because he had been her companion throughout a lonely, sometimes ominous childhood.

'Tea!' Then, as he turned from it with distaste, 'I know, you hate everything this morning but it will waken you. You are to help me choose new clothes. Papa insists.'

'Play the wardrobe-mistress? No thanks.'

'Because of your excellent taste,' she hastened to placate. 'I think Papa imagines that if I deck myself out as a fashionable I might manage to outshine such colonial lights as Mrs O'Shea.'

'A sparrow to look like a bird-of-paradise?'

She laughed off his remark as she always laughed off his observations that hurt, the only way she could bear them. 'I could never hope to look like her, of course, for she's quite wonderful. I can well believe she's a gipsy.'

He stretched, yawning. 'Whatever she is she's the most glittering thing aside from gold nuggets I've seen in this country.'

'You'll feel different about everything once we're settled.'

'No one's settled here. They sing all night under your windows and talk all day of the outback and gold. And when they're not fighting or doing you and each other down they're arguing, but happily, loving their enemies, patting them on the back. Or wandering off to some new field, or back to Europe to spend their gains – and how they spend! They throw gold dust to the winds for the fun of it, and why not? They swear there are places where you can pick the stuff off the ground with knives and dig up lumps of it with potato forks. Maybe enough will settle on me to send me back first-class to swank it down High Street. Think what a dash I could cut around City Hall.'

'You can't go back, you know that.'

'With enough payable gold in my pockets I'd give Belfast another try.'

'Con . . . please listen.' She placed her palms carefully along the chair arms. 'Papa has plans for us.'

He yawned again. 'When has he not?'

'I'm sure they're good plans, even though he sets about everything so quietly, and often seems secretive.'

'Isn't he now!' She had never heard him speak so bitterly of their father. 'He decided on our emigration as if he was arranging an afternoon's picnic to the Bluff.'

'That's not true. We made the decision together.'

'What else could we do when he holds the money-bags? But then you don't care a fig for money, you're as happy as a lark if there's a horse left in the stable. But I'm tired of being without spending-money.'

'You'll soon have your legacy.'

'Not "soon". Twenty-one is centuries away. If our venerable papa is afraid I'll spend his coin if I get my hands on it, he's right. Another thing, I'm fed to the teeth of being tied to our venerable aunt's apron strings. That old biddy's born to the purple of spying.'

'Don't speak so of her. She left her good life for our sake.'

'She left nothing that won't be standing till the Day of Judgement, and if I know her she'll be waiting at Stonemore's gates on Doomsday to ward off intruders. She has her well-tended and sharp little claws so deep into Harvey he doesn't dare manage the place as less than a petty principality. A miracle Anne escaped to South Africa, and Vincent to Jamaica—'

'Just give her time here. She'll adapt, I know she will.'

'No time to waste. I'm shaking her off here and now. And if you want any life of your own, you'd best do the same.'

'She worries over us, as Papa does in trying to build a new life.'

'I don't want a new life. I want the old one and he threw it aside because a few snobs cut us in the street and left us out of

69

their soirées. All because of a bit of a fracas that would have died down if we'd sat tight. She wasn't worth this exile, not that tart.'

'Don't, Con. *Don't.*'

'She promised to marry me. I didn't tell you that, did I? I don't think I told anyone.'

'Minna Belgrave was twenty-eight and you only eighteen.'

'Well, everyone was after her,' he sulked. 'She had coffers of money in her own right. But whether I would have married her in the end or not doesn't matter. She tricked me. She was carrying on with Alex too. I wish I'd shot her instead of old Alex, that would have been better all round.' He gave a wicked little grin, the kind that could make a girl's heart turn over. 'Certainly better for old Alex. But I didn't think of it at the time.'

'You thought of too much. And acted on it. You can't go about shooting people.'

'They think nothing of it in this country. Guns are cheap, even if powder and shot are sky-high – ah, the tales I hear of life on those diggings.'

'Don't talk of guns. It's time you forgot that whole sorry episode. I know I want to forget it—'

'Go on, say it.' He stamped about, directionless in his anger, as he'd stamped about Stonemore startling the horses, and across the open fields scaring the cows. Con hated to be confined just as she did, but he was always plaintive and noisier about it. 'Tell me I've spoilt everything for you, dragging you out to a forsaken hole to hobnob with ex-cons and darkies.'

'There's more than that here, there must be, and we'll soon have a chance to find out. I believe Papa's planning to settle inland.'

'Upcountry? The devil he is.'

'A sheep station perhaps. It could be right for us.'

'For you, perhaps. I want comfortable living on a civilised estate close to town with lackeys to do my bidding.'

'Couldn't you give the country a chance? Oh Con, *try*. I hate this cramped little house. We've always had room to move, to breathe, to ride . . . I want my own horses.'

'Don't talk of home.' He slammed the table in his fury. *'Don't.'*

'I must talk of it.' She was equally furious, and stubborn. 'We need to talk things out, bring everything into the open and not . . . brood. I want home as you do but we can't have it; it's thirteen thousand miles away and behind us and we must accept that.' She brightened. 'We can still ride, and when we ride need never feel hemmed in.' Ah, to ride again with Con, her – arrogant, yes – but fun-loving, fun-finding brother who had devised and led while she followed, spurred by the excitement of his seemingly endless schemes. Memories crowded. 'Remember the summer days we rode south from Downpatrick along the coast and everywhere was the "lint in the bell". And we climbed Slieve Donard . . .'

'There are no Mourne Mountains here,' he said heavily.

It was true. There were no Mourne Mountains and she felt a small stab of hate for all else around her, yes, even for her brother for reminding her of the fact. Con would, Con so often did put a careless brutal finger on her heart. 'There are other mountains,' she rallied. 'There must be.'

'So I hear. And it looks as if I'm going to be driven over them to a sheep run to stomp around it with a bunch of ex-lags filling in their time till the next gold strike when they'll be off leaving us with the work to do – oh yes, I've been asking questions too. If you and Papa imagine I'll waste my time slushing about shearing-sheds and pig-pens you're wrong. I'm for the gentleman's life with all its trimmings.'

'You had the gentleman's life and it did you little good. You're here to forget all that.'

'I don't know what I'm here for,' he fumed.

'Couldn't you try to find out?'

'I know one thing. I won't be stuck on some blasted rural property watching the grass grow. If I must stay in this country – at least for now – I'll comb it for excitement, and I hear there's plenty if you scratch around. I'll go my own way how and when I choose and you can have our old biddy aunt *and* our old man Moynan.'

'Papa's not *old*.'

'I'll get something out of this damned exile, you'll see.' He was savage in his desperation yet curiously defenceless – after all, he was only nineteen. He wanted the old ways and places as she did, but with a difference; she was out to make the best of things. She made an effort to shake off her aching care that seemed to annoy him and got confidently to her feet.

'Let's see the town together. If I can't be beautiful I can be fashionable, with one of the new bonnets – but no silly flowers or ribbons, something truly elegant.'

'I'll bet that boy knows all there is to know.'

'What boy?'

'That Jamie. How to get the most out of the place, I mean. Knows his way around by the look of it even though he's only a youngster.'

'Oh, forget Jamie. Forget the O'Sheas.' She shook him playfully. 'Hurry before it's too hot to move.' To force him from his mood she flung her arms wide, breaking into a wild little dance. 'Plumes!' she laughed. 'Tall waving plumes, that's what I'll have.' And whirled him about in a mad jagged dance, urging him on until he laughed back at her with something of the Con of their growing-up years. But they stopped dead before the youth blocking the doorway, Phipps fretting and fussing behind him.

'As the sole sprig climbing my ancestral walls,' Jamie grinned, 'I enjoy watching siblings at play. I take it you *are* at play and not about to tear each other to pieces?'

'He ran up, Miss.' Phipps peered through the crook of Jamie's arm. 'He just ran up. He's not been announced, see, so goodness knows what the mistress will say when she comes in from the garden. I had to leave m'pastry and I'll give that Effie whaffor when I find her—'

'Don't worry,' Alannah soothed, 'I'll explain.' Even so the woman stomped down in her ill-fitting shoes; it was not her place to answer the knocker, all floured up at that! Jamie threw his whip on the table, careless of its polish, and flopped in Con's armchair to fix his gaze on Alannah so intently her hand moved instinctively to her top button that seemed for ever gaping. She hated to be stared at, particularly by boys.

'Surprised to see me at this ungodly hour, I suppose? I decided to ride in with O'Shea.'

'Why don't you call him father?' she retorted for he seemed to enjoy putting people at a disadvantage.

'Because he's not my father.'

'He seems to care for you as one.'

He shrugged. 'In his way, I suppose. I just don't like his way – it's sparse. Mama's better at caring; at least she doesn't argue over piffling accounts. I call her "Raunie" when we're alone, in public sometimes too just for the hell of it.' He gave one of his attractive laughs. 'Stops strangers in their tracks.' Swinging his boot idly against the table he turned to Con. 'It's a fine morning and I've slept off my head and a gallop over the sand-hills might clear yours. We can turn off to the Foresters' stables – the track as far as Coogee isn't bad, after that it's the very devil but I hear Irish roads aren't much better. Or, if you'd rather, ride straight out to the Sir Joseph Banks.'

'What are the Sir Joseph Banks?' Alannah put in uneasily for Con was already rummaging through cupboards.

'A hostelry five miles out on the edge of Botany Bay, with pleasure gardens and a zoo and so on; a great place to idle time away. I know the crowd, some of them too well.' He grinned at Con. 'But you might as well know the best and the worst of the place. I brought an extra horse. I knew you'd come.'

'Con is shopping with me,' Alannah sparked.

'For women's stuff?' He roared with laughter. 'He'd better put paid to habits like that. Dancing attendance on sisters and cousins and aunts doesn't go down too well with the local swells – unless it's some maiden aunt likely to leave a favourite nephew her fortune.'

She stood her ground. 'Papa insists.'

'Paternal edicts exist to be evaded.'

'Take Phipps with you. Or Effie.' Her brother brushed her aside none too gently as he slammed things about. 'And there's Ned to carry your things. Oh come,' with his patronising little laugh, 'you didn't really expect me to go on such a silly caper, did you? You'll choose what you want, anyway.'

'Papa won't like you going off so.'

'Papa! Papa!' he mimicked. 'Our venerable Papa can lump it.' He swung her about to face the door. 'Out with you. I want to dress.'

She didn't like his tone before this boy of sixteen, yes, *boy* despite his assurance which seemed to bring out the worst in people, stimulating them into competing with him. He was certainly having that effect upon her brother. A hateful youth, she decided, aware of his mocking eyes on her as she moved to the door. Feeling abandoned and rather lonely she went down to placate Phipps and soothe her aunt if the latter needed soothing, then make her own half-hearted arrangements for a day that had been spoilt before it had even begun.

It was good before the heat of the day, and before the roads came alive with carts and omnibuses and riding parties, to give the horses their heads past the gaol wall and along the flat of the South Head Road then ease them up the long hill by the Barracks before breaking into a canter again. The thickly wooded slopes leading down to the Harbour were pitted by little streams with, here and there, a waterfall coiling and dipping through glades and coppices. But on their right, to the south, spread the great flats of gentlemen's estates, market gardens and small farms petering out in the scrubby sand-hills fringing the Pacific. To the south-west, around Cook's River, smoke spirals proclaimed breweries and brickworks and family factories clustering decently together. It was growing hot as they turned south from the heights of Paddington and towards open country, cantering past neat cottages in their neat gardens all connected by little villages. Con felt a sense of well-being, a growing excitement; once he got the hang of this city, this whole country, he could do what he liked with it, he knew it – the world would be his again! This boy was the one to show him the ropes for he seemed to know a great deal about many matters, too much perhaps, but with a stepfather like O'Shea was reputed to be how could he be otherwise?

'Your father is taking breakfast with O'Shea at the Crimean Arms – did you know?'

'I was told nothing.'

'I'll wager they're cooking something up between 'em. Arranging your life would be my bet.'

'What makes you so sure?'

'Because I know my stepfather, even if I don't know your papa – yet. Besides, I hear things.' With one of his bubbling laughs. 'Through keyholes if I must.'

'I can well believe it.' Con made an offhand gesture intended to convey confidence. 'Well, no one's going to arrange my life or manoeuvre me to places that don't interest me, even if they do manipulate my sister. She'll have to wake up,' he went on fretfully. 'She's lived too long behind high walls kowtowing to nuns and priests, peering at the world through iron grilles. Now she kowtows to papas and aunts who aim to keep her in the nursery.' He broke off, embarrassed, for Jamie had actually yawned. But Alannah irritated him to near-madness by her romantic insistence on 'a fresh start' as she called it in a country where they had, presumably, only to cling together to finish up happily-ever-after. She needed a whacking great shove into life, that one! Heaven alone knew what frumpish Old World stuff she'd come home with today.

'She'll do well enough without you.' Jamie yawned again, for he hadn't quite slept off his head. 'She doesn't seem the kind to kowtow for long. Anyway, she'll make mistakes and wriggle out of 'em, as you will. But there's excitement in making mistakes – if you make the right ones. Can you use a stockwhip?'

'No. Must I?'

'If you want to join an emu hunt around the Lachlan, yes. It takes skill to swing the lash about an emu's neck when it's in full flight; you have to know just when it's tiring, then a sharp jerk at the right moment and you have it down on its back. Stupid birds, easy to catch really. Make good pets but peck at the horses' eyes. We'll start you off hunting 'roos around the Pride.' He paused, watching Con shade his eyes for the sun was growing fierce. 'Get yourself a cabbage-tree – a *hat*, man.' Laughing at Con's frown. 'New chums all wear 'em. They can't bear the sun, get drunk with it. With the light and colour too. *And* the women.'

'Haven't seen a woman yet to turn my head – except your mama.' Con grinned. 'A pity she's spoken for.'

'Mama's had long practice at turning heads,' Jamie said so solemnly Con glanced at him uneasily. 'There are women here, certain women that is, but you need to know where they're tucked away, places even O'Shea doesn't know these days.'

Con stared. 'What do you know about women?'

'I know they're different in this country, at least I'm told they are by those who should know. They *become* different, that is, not so precious or distant if you know what I mean? The place changes them. Perhaps it's the climate . . . Of course, currency lasses have always been that way, free-talking and doing.'

'So we heard last night. You were making the devil of a commotion out there in the hall.'

'Oh . . . Dora.' Infinitely airy and offhand. 'The Doras are always around, huffy when you don't notice 'em, sniffling all over your jacket wanting you to marry 'em. Safer with women like those at Julie's. O'Shea cut his teeth in the Julie's-that-was, like every buck of his time, but now the place is run by Annette who pretends she's French from a Boulogne *maison de pavé*, but everyone knows she was plain Annie around Piccadilly. She's just good with an accent so we let her act up, for the food's not bad and the champagne's better – if you can pay for it.'

'How old are you?' Con gasped.

'Seventeen.'

'Not quite, according to your father.'

'In June – what's a few months? And my father's dead.'

'Then he's no use to you. O'Shea could be more.'

'He could, if he didn't hang on to his money. Doles it out.'

'Scarcely that for you've a fine mount there. In fact you seem to live well all round.'

'He gives with one hand and takes back with the other,' Jamie grumbled. 'Too many rules, but never for himself.

Like his promise of the Irish Boy. He's promised me that pub in Bendigo since I was a nipper, used to bribe me with it when he got desperate and he was often desperate.' He chuckled. 'I grew up in Bendigo and I'd go back if I could run the Irish Boy my way: grand gaming-rooms, a theatre like the best in Melbourne, to entice famous actors and singers, you know? I know how I want the place; trouble is it would take money.' He was savage in his ambition and acquisitiveness. 'What can one do without money?'

'Very little.' Con gloomed along with him. 'I can't wait to get my hands on –' He broke off, embarrassed. Bad taste and worse policy to talk of personal finances, particularly to boys of sixteen. 'But shouldn't you have your head down over your school primers?'

Jamie's laugh was distinctly unpleasant. 'Got rid of the tutors early, made everything too hot for 'em. Got m'self out of the academies too. But sometimes I go back to my first school. It's down on the Rocks – actually Darling Harbour. Specially when I want to hide out a while, I work with the horses and such. I like that. I know how to handle Hugh Whaley so he turns a blind eye. No one thinks to look for me there, at least they haven't yet. Maybe they're just used to me taking off then turning up again when I like, for I always do turn up – for Mama you know.' He looked grim. 'Don't know why I told you. If you ever let on I stay there I'll kill you.'

'I believe you'd try,' Con challenged. He didn't like to be threatened even in fun. He certainly hoped it was in fun.

'O'Shea expects me to take over his lands, investments, everything, but I'm no clerk or even a sheep farmer. Can't stick in one place for long, not even when Mama is there. She knows that. I want to be a showman. An entrepreneur – and will be one day. I'm only going to Erins Pride without too much fuss because it's close to the Tumut and Adelong fields and everything's booming down that way. Plenty going on.'

'My father drives hard bargains too,' Con gloomed. 'The house would have brought a pretty penny, the business another. Yet he likes to cry poor-mouth.'

They were well out now in a world of small farms, self-sufficient little places with a few sheep and cows, a horse cropping the sweetest grass and sometimes an orchard beside the vegetable patch. As they walked their horses Con's eyes were held by a girl coming from a barn carrying a pail, a full pail by the way she walked, slowly and with heavy undulating movements from her bare feet up through her hips to breasts and shoulders. She provoked – yes, women even moved differently here, naturally and boldly, unconscious of the effect they made – or perhaps they knew only too well. Her skirt was looped up to show fine legs, dirty but beautiful, as her body was beautiful, he could tell, firm yet moving loosely within its clothing. He felt excited – and a long way from Ireland! She dumped the pail and passed her hands over her hips, to dry them perhaps, moving her skirt up and down with long sensuous movements. She noticed the youths and loped across, squelching her toes through the dung and rubbish to lean over the fence and balance on her elbows, half smiling, her blouse drooping open to show full and rounded breasts. Her hair was bleached pale by the sun. As she leaned, staring them out, she swayed from side to side as if she were singing to herself. It stirred him. He found something sluttish and infinitely wanton about her. Inviting. Jamie was right, there *were* women here. Easy-looking women. Exciting women. Jamie followed his glance and smiled.

'Milkmaids come cheap too.'

Con narrowed his eyes to look out to the flat wide horizon broken here and there by low and gentle hills. What was beyond that green and blue and milky cloud that a man like himself could use and enjoy? His mind returned to the girl leaning on her fence – all she needed was a good wash! He laughed softly. Excellent hunting all round it seemed, in a new country with all the time in the world in which to do it. His exile might not be so awful after all. A breeze played about his hair, stimulating him. He glanced slyly at Jamie and plunged in.

'Have you tried the native women?'

And instantly regretted it for the lad did not even look his way, just mounted his horse and sat waiting for him to do the same. Con knew he had made a mistake. He must learn, and quickly, the subtle interplay of local *mores*, what was openly discussed and pursued and what avoided. But, as he mounted, Jamie answered.

'No. I haven't tried the native women. I don't have to. Plenty of my own kind.' A mischievous smile began to play about his sensuous young lips. 'I was told, by sailors, that in the Philippine Islands native bucks have the penis pierced by a tiny spear with little bells attached that tinkle as they walk. Drives the women mad. Not that the women need urging; virginity is not prized among them.' Con stared then spluttered into a laugh that grew to a delighted roar. Jamie joined in and they laughed till they could scarcely sit their mounts. 'There's the Joseph Banks,' Jamie gasped, 'there where the flags fly.' He pointed with his crop to a large building hugging the Bay, surrounded by smaller buildings amid trees and gardens. 'Time to race.'

With spurs and yells of encouragement and rivalry, their laughter gusting off to lose itself on the summer wind, they galloped, evenly matched and side by side, towards the wide blue plate of Botany Bay.

Chapter Four

BRICK STROKED Glenora – the eagle – until the black and shining flanks quivered gently, then tossed the reins to the stable-boy with a coin substantial enough to dispel his alarm. It was as well, he reflected, that he could afford his penchant for stallions as most stables baulked at blood horses; they upset the hands. He ordered Glenora resaddled for three o'clock and was out of the gates and making his way with his light but confident tread towards the Crimean Arms but taking his time as he had more to spare than he'd planned for. Drat Jamie for overtaking him on the road in, bright as a button when he could be expected to be sleeping off his revels, daring him to race so arrogantly he had put in his spurs and beaten the brat. Jamie hadn't liked it, he never did, and had turned off in a sulk towards Castlereagh Street, and the Moynan house Brick felt certain, for Jamie valued riding partners at least his equal so that in beating them he could score a triumph. He had lived in the saddle since childhood and trained on the best mounts the country could provide, finishing up with the skill and stamina of an Overlander, but by all accounts Con Moynan would not only match him in the saddle but display traits Jamie would delight in exploiting. He glanced at his watch – almost ten o'clock. To hell with Jamie, at least for now. He had other fish to fry.

Pedlars and hawkers with their cries of 'Watercreesesses' and 'Pies all hot' and 'Muffins' were making an unholy babel as they wound their hopeful way towards the suburbs. A drunken old lag was enjoying a fight with an equally drunken bullocky. A gent on a fine palfrey put on a spurt and every dog on the Quay was off after horse and rider, lickety-split. China Men, bland and unsmiling, pattered by in twos on their way to God alone knew where. A horse omnibus crawled along George Street with a barefoot boy twanging his 'Na Wullumulu', and everywhere the town screeched and jeered and shouted, scattering the populace before the stamp of hoofs and the wheels of wagons. There was even the formality of black beaver stovepipes, if a little askew. The world was about again though rather bleary-eyed, blinking off its New Year head.

Ten o'clock. Still he dawdled. The Crimean was an old hostelry retitled and refurbished, which not so much stood as sprawled around a corner, with its apologies for pavements thronged with women gossiping on their way to the Markets, boys holding horses or running errands or squabbling over the pennies thrown them. A row of slim dark-haired greasy-collared youths leant against a wall on the lookout for mischief, if possible with profit, their cabbage-tree hats dangling black ribbons, hands in pockets, smoking cigars or just chewing them round and about their mouths. The public-house seethed with morning idlers. Jos Wiggins nodded to Brick then jerked his head towards a side parlour – so Moynan was here. Brick had rather expected to have to wait for him while certain he would come, if not with eagerness and even with a certain suspicion, but he would come out of curiosity. He was staking much on the Moynan curiosity.

'Breakfast, for two,' he ordered, then picking up a lime and soda made his way slowly and with ease towards the partly open door through which he could glimpse Moynan open his watch, study it, sip his drink, open his watch again then sit staring from the window into the street. The man was rattled – but not *too* much; it would take a much longer wait than this to shatter such a hard-headed man of business. But rattled he was. So Brick idled, slapping drinkers on the back, cracking jokes, moving women from his path with a kiss or a jest, hoisting children shoulder-high before setting them on their feet to fight over his fistful of coins. The women scolded, loving the attention, the young girls feigned outrage, flaunting themselves, while the children fawned on him – while the money lasted, O'Shea always insisted. It was after ten o'clock. Even so, he would make the man wait a little longer.

Owen knew he had made a mistake in arriving even minutes early and such miscalculation by a man of his experience had made a distinct dent in his armour. As ten o'clock came and went he began to wonder if O'Shea would appear at all but at ten-five he saw the man's bulk filling the doorway. Dazzled by the light through the street door he blinked, but it was not the light alone that confused him; in this casually dressed man in riding-breeches and boots, open-necked shirt and loose coat, his wide-brimmed country hat in hand, there was nothing of the dilettante of the previous night. In any case, O'Shea in a business topper would be something of a cartoonist's dream and Owen doubted he would ever see him sporting that insignia of respectability. O'Shea closed the door firmly behind him.

'My apologies. It's possible I'm losing my ability to hold my liquor –' his clear direct gaze belied his words, 'but I prefer my excuse of living out of town.' He spread himself comfortably at the table. 'I have no doubt you've heard I live out in order to perpetrate a libertine existence, principal among my more loathsome practices being the bullying of my servants and the beating of my wife.'

'Do you beat your wife?'

Brick laughed heartily. 'If I so much as made the attempt she would twist the whip back upon my flanks thoroughly and expertly. Furthermore, she's an excellent shot, I'd even say a deadly one, so I'm obliged to keep myself in training as something of a sharp-shooter. Your son and daughter this morning?'

'My son, I don't doubt, is still asleep. My daughter will be enduring with her usual fortitude her aunt's lectures on the evils of alcohol, particularly two glasses of wine at once, before escaping on a shopping expedition.'

'A fair enough tavern the Crimean now it has changed hands, for Jos keeps a generous table. Australians are greedy, one could say gluttonous eaters, but not connoisseurs of fine victuals, perhaps because in early days maggoty meat and weevily biscuits were manna from heaven.'

'I don't imagine it's your habit to apologise for anything

Australian, Mr O'Shea, for the country seems to have many compensations to replace gourmet cooking.'

Brick smiled. 'One being that a man with convict and aboriginal forebears can attain a position of, if not social esteem, notoriety? A freak success, Moynan. I make a point of "laying my cards on the table" on the subject of my mixed blood; I accept my touch of the tarbrush as so and let it go at that.' He paused to drink slowly, thoughtfully. 'At one stage I did more than accept it, I wallowed in it; but self-flagellation seems to have worn itself out. Now I accept the most miserable of my mother's people by managing not to see them if to date I haven't been able to close my nose to them. If others cannot accept me that is their problem. I've even come to believe it's their misfortune.' He threw the remaining juice down his throat. 'You'll hear many things of me and you will scoff at most of them – don't. I know just about every blade of grass that grows in this land and the worst and best of many men. I know an indecent amount about the women too. I have bargained and baulked and plotted, everything but begged, in the making of a consider-able fortune but I haven't lied too often or too seriously. I have schemed and bargained my way to the top of public life to be thrown back and down with a gesture some would call malevolent, and I began a long way back, at the primeval you might say. But I had the audacity to refuse to retreat. I have a keen and constant eye for the main chance and when I want something I'll do almost anything to get it, the "almost" applying to my particular code of ethics. I'll play foul if I must but fair for preference, never underestimating my opponent's ability to do the same, with the probable exception of my opponent playing fair at all—'

'Which seems to be a long and devious way of stating you want something from me. Furthermore, that you intend to get it.' Owen twirled his empty glass and waited.

'With fair exchange. A bargain with as much self-interest as you'd get over a snack in a Belfast entry, among the advantages to yourself being my knowledge of this country which means the cheapest and simplest way of doing everything and acquiring anything. Advice on investments, contacts in business, with smooth entry to enterprises such as communication – telegraph is haphazard but railways are about to boom—'

'I have no business, Mr O'Shea. I left it behind in Ireland. But it's true, I did come to Australia to invest, ideally to take up land, a sheep property perhaps, for my son, and for my daughter of course until she marries. Both are accustomed to country life; a greatly different country certainly but here or in Ireland it is all land, and land to the Irish . . .' He shrugged, knowing there was no need to elaborate.

'Your son's opinion of this country?'

'I doubt that he's formed one as yet.'

'And Miss Moynan?'

'My daughter's emotions, from love through to hate, have always been absorbed by Ireland, and I see no change as yet. What remains of her devotion belongs to her brother.' He smiled without envy. 'I come a begging third.'

'A divided heart is a deucedly uncomfortable one, it gives so much and no more to each objective. Your own opinion?'

'What could there be in Australia for me?'

'Not Moynan's Mills certainly.' As his companion's head shot up O'Shea leant back with a satisfied air. 'I have friends in Belfast. We correspond.'

'I see.'

'But there could be a substitute.'

'If you knew of my mills then you must know the rest of my story.'

'Some. From the version I received, your son's failure to kill his rival means he is either a woeful shot or he lacks the desire to wilfully kill. Let's hope it is the latter.'

Was there anything this man did not know of himself and his family, Owen wondered. His voice was cold. 'Perhaps you could arrange for your excellent spy system to be put at my disposal, for I have received but vague information to date concerning investments.'

'And you won't get more, not yet. Sydney's civic fathers and business tycoons are sizing you up. They'd know how to handle you if you'd gone straight to Government House and the sterling clubs but you didn't and they're puzzled.' He smiled slightly. 'And you'll learn nothing from me that I don't choose to tell you, but I do choose to tell you this: our first great influx of population ceased with the demise of the convict transports. The second was more-or-less organised immigration dwindled now to a steady trickle. Our third and biggest came seeking gold – and is still coming. Australia has close on a million people, most with nothing in their pockets but what they take from their cradles at day's end. If rowdies don't steal their loot it's frittered away in saloons, and the women grab what's left – not necessarily a bad thing since women plan . . . Contrary to what you hear few are making fortunes on established fields, for the alluvial's almost disappeared and one must go farther afield for it. It takes capital and skill to go down for the quartz; I know, I've done it, but I got in early. Yet fail or win men will stay on in Australia for their women are eager to settle. So! How to make use of this huge itinerant labour-consumer force?'

'Why, I have not thought . . .'

'Wool will be our produce now but to produce wool on the hoof and in the fleece is an expensive business. Likewise, turning wool into cloth. Through necessity we send our fleece out of the country to be made up. Why not make it up on home ground?'

'Textile manufacture?'

'It has always been here from the first rough convict blankets. It's still crude with what machinery there is obsolete and the labour and knowledge raw, the reasons I search constantly for mechanics, but somehow through the slump years I've kept my mill going. There are only three others in this state – at Bowenfels near Lithgow, at Parramatta, and Emu Plains – but between us we produced a lot of Colonial Tweed; in '52 alone two hundred and thirty-five thousand yards before the gold-rushes began to have effect. Well, now the country's coming out of its chaos, my weavers are even drifting back. I want to extend my mill, sir. A complete reorganisation.'

'But this is a pastoral country, thousands of miles from industrial centres.'

'You're right – in the main. But we have raw materials –

we're growing cotton in the North – and can find skilled labour, or at least try; there must be some tucked away. If not I'll stake my money on bringing out mechanics or have them trained here. Machinery can be imported and what cannot be obtained overseas can be locally cast provided we have the plans. It can be done, Mr Moynan, but only if I have the necessary link – expert knowledge.'

'And where will you find such knowledge?'

'Why, sir, in you. In *you*!' He leant back looking smug.

'I see,' Owen said smoothly, 'having ascertained that I am an engineer, and knowing that linen manufacture is akin to woollen.'

'Further, that you are fully acquainted with the Lister Nip-combing Machine.'

'A Nip-comb for worsted, here?'

'*Here*, sir! I imported it from Leeds. I turned England upside down to get it but I succeeded. A step forward, eh? And before long, I hope, carding machines for worsted.'

Owen raised eyebrows. 'You're not entirely unversed then?'

'I know too damned little.' He drummed his fingers on the table. 'My mechanic, Cameron, went home to find himself a wife but seems to have lost himself in some Highland glen. Wife or no wife, Moynan, no Scot leaves Scotland if he can find a way of existing there, so I don't expect to see him again. I need expert men.'

'Perhaps you are not aware, Mr O'Shea, that the Noble-comb is a more generally useful machine.'

'I was told that.'

'The Lister Nip-comb is a "tuft" comb, specially suited for combing long wools and hairs—'

'—giving more lustre and smoothness and is more "humane", so it is said, in its treatment of fibres, giving them a better arrangement for spinning; I was informed of that too. It's what I want, Moynan, a straight clear worsted yarn. And I mean to get it for we have the Merino wools, the finest of all for worsted.'

'But you seem concerned over employment. The Nip-comb will lessen it.'

'Only temporarily if we regard this machine as a means to

an end, that end the greatly increased production of woollen cloth.'

'Importation of machine – debit. Expansion – debit. Wages – debit. New machinery – debit.'

'But very much on the credit side a great untapped colonial market, a market I intend to be mine for as long as possible. I've already surpassed the old "Parramatta cloth", and I consider my tweeds the colonies' best – I've exhibited in London and Paris – but the necessity to produce cheaply enough to combat future low-priced imports means I must aim politically for Protection – a most unpopular cause. Nevertheless, Victoria will have it shortly. I lobby for it in New South Wales.'

'In that case I'm surprised you haven't stood for Parliament.' And realised he had touched a nerve for the man had actually winced.

'A man of my blood? You forget.'

'But surely in these changing times . . .'

'This country will change slowly if at all in its attitude to race and colour; it's British, white and privileged. Even so, it struggles with itself and will continue to do so. You cannot help but have heard of the Chinese Question? A bill is proposed to control and limit them but it will have a long and stormy passage. Kanakas and Indians are always being proposed, sometimes imported, yet resented. Labour, sir, or to be specific, the lack of it, is Australia's great problem for everyone wants to be a capitalist. So! I prefer to weave around stumbling blocks and nominate my own man. But he must be the right man.'

'And the Nip-comb?' Owen interrupted for the conversation had diverged too suddenly, and dangerously he felt, into the area of local politics of which he knew nothing.

'Assembled from blueprints by the only man I have with any knowledge.' He gave a helpless little shrug. 'And apparently little of that for the thing won't work, it just stands there. If it has been damaged in transit my man doesn't know enough to say.' He leant back and placed his palms on the table with a decisive gesture. 'So name your price, Moynan. Name your price.'

Seldom had Owen known such satisfaction for he had the man in the palm of his hand; furthermore O'Shea knew it and accepted it. But his reply was nicely offhand. 'My price will put you further on the debit side.'

'Perhaps not so far, for what I have to suggest might balance a mutual commitment. Adjoining Erins Pride is a fine property, its owner in England and fretting to stay there. Charles Huntly settled on the Swan River in the west but came round to Argyle for family reasons and built a fine house. Even so his son returned to England, his wife pined so all followed. Burrendah should bring an excellent price at auction even now when properties are difficult to run, but I am empowered to sell privately and outright if the right interests come along. The right interests, to the Huntlys, would be people who value the place and I believe you would do that. I have no axe to grind in this except that I like to see any property touching mine well settled and run, for Erins Pride and Burrendah work together in many ways. I could recommend properties farther afield but Argyleshire is almost civilised these days even from your view-point and standards. You had perhaps planned on leasing but the day is gone when a man could hold over five million acres on a ten-pound licence fee; now a man must buy his land to hold it, dig in and deep. And now is the time to buy for prices are down; hands would rather take pot-luck on the fields than grow crops. Burrendah has kept its hands, one reason being that manager Dan Charlton and his family have an affection for the place. It is a substantial station, almost as large as my own Erins Pride, and I can promise you as much grazing land as you might want to lease, all of it fine sheep country. The property has been much improved and can scarcely decrease in value even with poor seasons.'

'I'm afraid such a place would be beyond my pocket.'

'At present perhaps. But if mechanics are valuable how much more so an engineer? I am prepared to pay well for a works manager.' And Owen knew precisely why he had come for somewhere back along the conversational limb a phrase here, one there, had stood out in the rhetoric. Works manager. To work with machines again . . . 'Damn this New

Year tardiness.' O'Shea flung the door wide. 'Breakfast or I'll take over the kitchen,' he shouted, slammed the door again and slumped back in his seat. 'So my juggernaut of an engine refuses to budge and all continue to fret – and wait, no doubt, for you will insist upon time to decide. But not too long for in March I take my son through to Erins Pride. Jamie strains at the faintest suggestion of a leash as you have seen.' He grinned. 'Like his mother in many ways. But he'll learn to run my stations if it sets everyone's teeth on edge.' He paused. 'I have no son of my own, you see.' He moved his glass slightly to the right then returned it to its place. 'My wife does not care for the country so Erins Pride is in the hands of my foster-mother who has spent most of her life there. I would like you and your family to come as my guests, to stay some weeks, get to know the country and its people; more importantly, watch Burrendah at work. If the place is to your liking settle in then and there – why not? It is kept in prime condition.' He smiled. 'But my hope is that whatever your family should decide you will return to Sydney and take over my works.' He paused to light his pipe with its absurd ornamental bowl of a mermaid. 'However, if you don't care for the place you can be on your way with no harm done. But I feel certain your daughter will approve.' He frowned. 'The journey up will be slow for I'm taking young families through to Wiena and Calua stations. You and your son will want to travel with us but Miss Moynan and her aunt will find the coach comfortable enough.'

'We are all expert riders, I've assured you of that.'

'Nevertheless, it's rough living on our roads. Travel in this country is not a jaunt along Irish lanes to exercise the horses, with a gentle canter home – and there are no cottage teas served under rose arbours in our bush inns. Even if Miss Moynan thrives on dust and potholes I doubt that Mrs Carney would. They will go by coach.'

Owen had an unpleasant vision of Alannah chafing under such orders yet did not argue for he understood the reasons: Delia's expectation of Old World niceties and Alannah's arrogance – yes, arrogance – would only hamper the men. Sparks would fly, no doubt of it. The door opened and the pungent odours of hot food made him stir and O'Shea busy himself directing the waitresses. 'Leave the pros and cons till you've tasted our Harbour bream. It deserves full consideration.'

The scrubbed table was almost obscured by heaped and steaming plates. There was coffee, hot rolls, creamy butter – how Delia would gloat over the lavish gobs of butter. Owen peppered his careful selection of food with small talk but behind the trivia his mind raced. He had dispensed with his old life but for the first time since landing he was finding not only his way but a familiar foothold. Something of what had been his work and his world, left behind with regret, was represented here by this man who needed his specialist knowledge and was prepared to pay for it. He, Owen Moynan, had value again, and roots if he wished them. But could he, at this stage of his life, become involved in O'Shea's world of behind-the-scenes manoeuvring, a world built around the man's personality and drive and reputation as a colonial identity? Could he, in short, become an O'Shea employee? Indeed, if all he had heard was true, an O'Shea menial?

'The best table in Sydney if one insists upon it – I insist. So tuck in, man. Then, if you will, a glance through my mill.'

Owen concentrated on the breaking of a roll. 'Aren't we anticipating somewhat? After all, I haven't accepted your invitation to Erins Pride.'

'But I feel that you will for I don't intend to give up. Meanwhile, shall we look upon the situation as a challenge? I've never known an Ulsterman to refuse a challenge, have you?'

Owen smiled but said nothing. Let the man stew; two could play at the waiting game. The food was irresistible and he was hungry. He spread his napkin, took up his knife and fork and proceeded to tuck in.

O'Shea's Mill, as it was known, was a large barracks-like building distinguishable from afar by its tall smoke-wreathed chimney. It stood on a Sussex Street corner alongside the

O'Shea stables and school, its outbuildings sprawling over the land that sloped down to his wharf on Darling Harbour. He waved an exasperated hand over the mercantile squalor.

'Been silting up there for years. You'll find many problems, Moynan, I warn you, not the least of them my inadequate water supply.'

He led the way up narrow stairs – too narrow, Owen noted – to a big light airy room tormented by a furious and ceaseless din. Owen registered with growing excitement the familiar processes of the manufacture of woollen yarn, primitive but with attempts to turn the place into a modern woollen mill. Three scribblers prepared the wool for the carders, the latter in good order even from the cursory glance he was permitted before being urged on by O'Shea's vast enthusiasm, his mind boggling at the prospect of branching off to the manufacture of worsted. The place certainly needed reorganisation, complete at that, before the addition of machinery, all of which could, even with money, time and a free hand, take years. Close on seventy employed, O'Shea boomed at him, half women and children. But the children were not *too* young and looked well enough, for there were amenities – an eating-room, fireplaces, and all lit by gas.

'The weaving is in the annexe. At present twenty-one of my twenty-three looms are working, the machines kept going till nine at night. But my weavers usually work only from daylight to dark so don't heed complaints or swallow high-minded explanations as to why they work for me – I pay better than most with better conditions, that's all. Well, sir! Your opinion so far?'

'A hodge-podge, as I'm sure you'll agree, more suited to cotton than wool in its preparing stages – still, not as primitive as I expected.' He would not commit himself further, he felt he had already shown too much interest and was deliberately casual in his inspection of two pairs of large spinning mules, each pair working between nine hundred and a thousand spindles. O'Shea drew him to a window.

'The dye-house has been lately added, as you can see.

Wool-scouring for the finer cloth and the white yarn is carried out at my wool-washing establishment at Newtown, but some is done here in a section of the dye-house – much work is needed there too but I won't subject us to scouring so soon after our meal! I plan extensions to my engineer's shop, there's land enough, so bring in as many mechanics as you can find. And anything else you might need to add me a modern mill for worsted. Incidentally, a house goes with the job of manager – you can see its roof there – so all you need do is say the word.' But as Owen remained silent he added briskly. 'Now, the comb.' Leading the way down a side passage he flung open a door with a grand dramatic gesture. 'The first of its kind in the colony. And the best my money could buy.'

Huge, complex and inanimate, there was nothing in a glance to explain its fallibility but Owen knew he would find its weakness. He placed his hands flat on the great comb circle to absorb the coolness of metal, drawn back by its touch to the whirring slurring manufactories of Ulster and the flax drying in the green fields, the looms and shuttles of cottage weaving and the spinning-jennies of primitive machinery. Belfast had paused in its path fifty years before to cast wool aside and choose cotton, then cast cotton away for linen – he had come full circle to wool. His mind leaped. Ballantyne could ship out all he needed; it would take at least a year but if he wrote off immediately . . . And if he couldn't find good men here Ballantyne could ship men out too, O'Shea would pay. Meanwhile, he could search country settlements, towns and goldfields for what skills might be idling in miners' tents. It would take time and knowledge and organisation and technical skill – and force if there were any left in him. And it seemed there was for he was stirring to an old familiar excitement . . .

'Autumn is the best time to travel this country,' O'Shea was saying. 'Always some Indian summer hanging on. But no matter how satisfactory you find Burrendah, my hope is that you will return to this.'

Undemanding, deliberately so Owen knew, but dangling carrots just as deliberately, and he stiffened against the man's subtlety. He would not be coaxed into business again, or even into buying a property before he was ready. The golden acres of O'Shea's wall-painting were not difficult to banish from his mind but it was not so easy to ignore his life's work. His hands moved slowly over the thing he knew best, the cool smooth complexities of a machine awaiting his skill and command. As much as any inanimate object could compel his affection this was a beloved thing, a symbol of his life, and the touch of its metal, and thump-scream-and-jangle of its power was a stimulant, a nourishment, a kind of music to his soul. He straightened slowly. He had not agreed to O'Shea's offer – but neither had he refused.

'You could be surprised at how well the boy would run the pub,' Hugh Whaley observed before resuming the intent picking of his teeth.

'Have you gone mad? He's only sixteen.'

'But a precocious sixteen, as he was a precocious six. He has ideas, extravagant I'll grant but running that kind of hostelry needs flamboyance.' He moved his feet from his desk and straightened his dangerously tilted chair. The only difference in Hugh's appearance over the years were his puckish curls, grey-white where they had been black. He never bought new clothes and still flaunted his incredibly old, incredibly Irish, hat – all Sydney, or rather all waterfront Sydney, knew and delighted in the Whaley insignia. 'You've always taken chances so why not on Jamie and the Irish Boy? He's fed on your promise of that pub for years.'

Brick frowned through the grimy window pane. To the west the clutter of Pyrmont Bay was straggling out and it came as a shock to realise how long it was since he had last viewed Sydney from exactly this angle. He seldom came to the stables these days and had not intended to do so today, but after seeing Moynan on his way a restlessness had sent him in. Usually he left Whaley well alone in the running of what remained of his school, his philanthropy towards

Sydney's waifs and strays dwindled to the occasional ambitious or talented youth. Hugh ran his classes with a good-natured humanist discipline, still spry as a man, still able to grip a boy's ear with an agonising pinch, and still able to administer a thrashing with the same steel-like insistence. He still chased women but in an aged desperate way. Brick's only serious clashes with him over the years had been over Jamie, for the boy had always got his way with Hugh: Brick knew well that the boy ran off to the stables but, provided he did not stay too long, let him be. There were worse places in Sydney a lad could hide out.

The O'Shea stables had taken a giant leap during the Crimean War, another in the years of the Indian Mutiny, in the charge of Taffy Jones who had married a barmaid from the Inkerman pub and still carried the little scar on his hand where Jamie as a child had ground his heel into it. The stables made up a healthy part of the O'Shea income for he could not meet the demand for his horses, business likely to be even brisker if the rumour of the Artillery off to India were true. The clinic was no more for Doc Peter had retired to a Melbourne villa, his liver damaged beyond repair. Emmaline Banner had sailed back to her sister in Liverpool, and Margret Magouran, tired of widowhood, had married a retired whaler and managed her cottage in the Glebe and her husband's infidelities with the same dexterity with which she had managed O'Shea's street urchins.

'It all comes down to the particular in the end, doesn't it, O'Shea?' Hugh leant forward with an unaccustomed seriousness. 'To a Jamie Lorne or a Joey Bowes, or a carpenter's son with a head for figures. When one acquires personal ties one loses the required detachment of the Philosophical Radical – that "Greatest good for the greatest number".'

O'Shea made an impatient gesture. 'I don't pay you for philosophy.'

Hugh laughed. 'You don't pay me at all.'

'Is that a fact?' O'Shea frowned.

'You haven't yet come down to the particular of a skilful experienced clerk. Look for another like Ashby.' He shrugged. 'No matter. All I require is a warm and comfortable squalor. I have it.' His eyes followed O'Shea as he prowled the little room, a man who, these days, seemed to be going precisely nowhere, and pushing the boy before him, a lad who would not, could not, be pushed – the irresistible force meeting the immovable object. A Narcissus figure, Jamie Lorne, a faun of a youth who would love, hate, fight and pleasure his life with great charm and guile, as his mother had and would always do; mercurial drifters both, but superb survivors. O'Shea was strong but they were stronger because united. Jamie Lorne was the gipsy's son and not O'Shea's and there was the tragedy. Or perhaps, in the end, O'Shea's saving grace.

'Deed him the Irish Boy, man.' Rocking dangerously on his chair legs. 'Before someone else makes a play for it.'

'What do you mean by that?'

'Herlicht wants it back and you know it.'

'Herlicht will never get it.' Brick paused at the door. 'There could be a time for the Irish Boy and Jamie, but it's not yet. Not just yet.'

On his way out he paused at the partly open door of the room, now a storeroom, where Barbara Merrill had once sat writing her letters or making lists or frowning over the books he was for ever bringing her, many of them still piled, dusty and yellowed, on the shelves. Some had toppled to the floor and lay open, their pages torn or stained and it bothered him for there was something unbearably neglected and abandoned-looking about them and the room. He closed the door on it all firmly. But he would have the books sorted and stored. Ghosts haunted the place and he left it with relief, for it belonged more than ever to Hugh and his peculiar comforts. He hastened to retrieve Glenora. But, oddly, crossing the Circular Quay, he paused at the ferry across to the North Shore where his house mouldered in its overgrown gardens at the mercy of prowlers, despite the ex-lag chipping rock oysters and sleeping off his binges in the boat shed, kept on as caretaker. Sober, Benny Brack was a dead shot with his old musket but, drunk, became a wild one, and riff-raff kept away. Brick turned Glenora's head resolutely towards the South Head Road. Ghosts wandered about the house at Neutral Bay, too. But the time to exorcise ghosts was not yet. Not just yet.

'The girl's a slut,' Raunie throbbed. 'They're all sluts. I should have packed her back to her harridan of a grand-mother long ago but . . . well . . . she's strong, and willing most of the time, and can turn her hand to most things. But the father could be any yardboy round here and you know it.'

'And he could be Jamie as she insists. He hasn't denied sleeping with her, has he?'

'Don't shout.'

'Why not? There are no secrets in this house – how can there be? Everything we do and are seems common knowledge, including every detail of this messy episode – and get your feet off that chair,' he boomed at the lounging Jamie flicking paper caps at the walls. The boy obeyed though slowly and insolently. 'Did you sleep with the girl, Dora? And by that I mean, fornicate?'

Jamie grinned. 'Now *there's* a fancy name for it!'

'I want a straight answer. Did you?'

'Once or twice. Why not? Everyone else seems to.'

'Once or twice is all it needs – once can be enough. It seems we can look forward to a procession of your bastards conceived in squalid couplings behind wool bales or in outhouses.'

'Actually, it was on the beach and quite pleasant. Can't you remember what you did at sixteen? Or is it too long ago.'

'No, I haven't forgotten. But there were rules, crude and unwritten, but rules all the same. For a start, the girls had to be willing.'

'This one was willing. Eager, more like it.'

'That's not what she told her grandmother.'

'How can you believe that old stewpot of a washer-woman?' Raunie fumed.

'That old stewpot, as you call her, came down from

her Parramatta pub to face me with precise details of your son's . . . well, seduction is a more pleasant-sounding word than rape.'

'If Dora swears that she's lying,' Jamie shouted.

'You'd take the word of that strumpet against that of your son?' Raunie defended.

'So *now* he's my son.' Brick laughed shortly. 'The grandmother is a drunken old parasite but willing to see the girl through this which you haven't offered to do. Dora will go to Parramatta till the child is born and Jamie will contribute to her support till she's fit for service. Certainly he will support his child.'

'It's not my kid.' Jamie was near screaming point. 'It's not mine, I tell you.'

'You can't be certain of that any more than she can – you slept with her, that's enough. I'll take care of the matter and you'll do as I say. Meanwhile, if you think you can use the circumstance in any way to avoid your stint at the Pride, forget it. You'll stay there till I say you can move on – or be cut off with the proverbial penny.'

'When have I ever had more than the proverbial penny?'

'You get a generous allowance. Now it can pay for the brats you sire.'

'You've no right to take that trollop's word against his,' Raunie raged.

'If Jamie's not ready and waiting here the first week in March I'll comb the town for him and drag him along the Great South Road by a rope collar like the lowliest Black in the land.'

'You'll not touch him.'

'I'll touch him. And you'll watch.'

'He gets angry because you keep him poor and so he goes out and does wild things. He has nothing of his own, everything's yours.'

'He'll own property when he can manage it, with care and sense.' Brick stamped to the door. 'The first week in March, Jamie. And pack old fustians for you'll be working hard.' He banged the door on them and Raunie swung angrily on her son.

97

'Why do you do these things? *Why?* It's I who must suffer your father's furies.'

'Don't call him my father.'

'He will insist the child is kept.'

'It can go to a foundling home,' he sulked.

'She means nothing to you, this Dora?'

'She's always clinging.' He shrugged his slim shoulders as if shrugging her off. 'I can't bear girls who cry all over me.'

'He'll make you stay at the Pride, I know him. He's in a stubborn mood.'

'I hate him sometimes.' He almost spat it out.

She sighed. 'There are times, like now, when I hate him too – but they don't last. Sometimes I can't live with him, yet can't live without him.'

'What was my father like? Really like?'

She stirred uneasily. She hated him asking questions about his father and he had been asking too many of late. 'Handsome, as you are. Quick-tempered. A lush. He didn't live long enough for me to know more. But he was Lord Farleigh's stepson and that was something.'

'Let's run away, Mama.'

'Oh – *don't.*'

'We'll run off to Bendigo. To our house. We had good times there.'

'Don't talk so.' With a desolate gesture she rested her head against his shoulder and they were still, looking out over the Harbour. 'You know I can't bear to be away from him even for a night. I need him. We both need him – oh yes, you do,' she insisted as he made a sharp movement. 'What could either of us do, where could we go, without him?' She straightened and they stood holding hands, comforting each other as they did often and effortlessly, just being close. 'I love him,' she murmured, miserable, yet at the same time soothed and comforted simply because Jamie was home.

'I know, Mama.' He squeezed her hand. 'I know.'

Chapter Five

WITH THE 'plantation' of Ulster by English and Scottish 'undertakers' early in the seventeenth century the native Irish, though officially banished, remained and held what they might of their lands. The wildest proudest fighting men among them took to the woods and hills and 'stood upon their keeping', to become known as wood-kernes. And the strongest and most valiant and violent of these was called Dark Hugh Moynan. But when Dark Hugh crept – if one so strong could creep – one bright morning to stand, rock-body straight in its tatters, hands torn and face bearded and matted, to stare long at the slim tawny-haired daughter of a Scottish divine milking a cow with the grace and delicacy of any temptress witcheen, it became not so much in what church they would wed but which of them would thereafter have their stubborn will and way.

Owen Moynan had heard this old tale of the mating of his ancestors more times than he could count, but from its romantically garbled content of fact and fancy he could never decide, quite, whether paternal or maternal forebear had won out. Nor, it seemed, could anyone else. It remained, simply, a familiar story to argue about over winter fires while Ireland howled outside. So, when it became necessary to claim kinship with organisation, calling or church, the Moynans resorted to expediency as they had learned to do often and bitterly in all that touched their welfare. To an Ulsterman, expediency was not only profitable, it was necessary; and so deeply ingrained in all Moynans was the combination of Catholic mystical piety and self-reliant Protestantism that it became almost a simple matter to be baptized a Protestant yet absorb the learning and humanity of the cloisters. But no Moynan had ever doubted the persuasive powers of that remote ancestress; any woman who could do what the armies of England had failed to do and bring Dark Hugh down from his hills to work a tenant farm near a village called Belfast, teach him the English tongue and garb him in English clothes was no ordinary woman. Her descendants spoke in awe of that long-ago Jeannie Moynan.

Hence, Moynan roots were deep in the soil; expediency, necessity and inheritance had driven them to the factories and counting houses of modern Ulster. But Owen Moynan, reining up beside his daughter and O'Shea on that fine autumn morning to gaze over the sweep of Argyleshire towards the distant Maneroo and the largely unexplored vastness beyond, knew satisfaction at the misty hills before him. He would never work this land with his own hands – the dedication of the craftsman to the world of the machine was too strong in him – but here, he hoped, was a world for his son and daughter.

Ahead, Con and Jamie galloped the red dust road down to Burrendah homestead sheltered on its slight opposite rise within gardens and thick English trees, a row of willows behind it marking what O'Shea called simply the Creek. Owen felt a deep pride that his son kept pace so easily in the saddle with these colonials who were seemingly born in one, and could not stifle or always hide his dislike of Jamie. Lorne, as he called himself to spite his stepfather, spent his apparently aimless existence charming or vexing all who crossed his path and met O'Shea's commands with defiance and his bequests with such insolence Owen marvelled O'Shea kept his temper at all. It was clearly an effort, for their storming at each other on the road up had risen loud and clear as it did now above the good-natured banter of station life – but no one seemed to turn a hair. Actually, when the boy did apply himself to work he was quick, cheerful, knowledgeable and popular with the hands. He had, so to speak, taken Con under his wing and the two lived in the saddle, riding in to Goulburn to return with lurid versions of the district's scandals and crimes, and what bushrangers were hiding out in the hills – lounging about the police barracks with other no-goods, Moll Noakes accused to Jamie's amusement; he was always laughing at her, keeping her in a more or less permanent pet. Owen smouldered at hearing his son referred to as a 'no-good', but silently, for this rough-talking fearless relict of O'Shea's past was permitted freedom in all she said and did and seemed to have great influence over the man. Alternatively, the youths would be thundering the road towards Yass and the Creeveys, or to Wiena at weekends to fish upstream with Hal and Roy Elston. When they did deign to hang about home paddocks they played the gentlemen squatters in calf-skin vests with sleeves, Bedford cord tights, Napoleon boots and wide cabbage-tree hats in an attempt to outdo the Elstons in bravura. They interfered with the ploughing or rode hell-for-leather with supplies to the few shepherds left out in the hills, and planned possum hunts to relieve what they saw as their nightly tedium. Meanwhile, Alannah wove her own path between Erins Pride and Burrendah, sometimes with Ned along, but mostly alone as she wanted it. Now as they looked out over Burrendah to the immensity of the land beyond, O'Shea drew his riding crop along the line of distant hills.

'You see? Our mountains are truly blue.'

'No bluer than Ireland's, Mr O'Shea.'

'Well now . . .' He flicked a patch of dirt from his boots with his crop. 'I've travelled your country, Miss Moynan – my country too in a way – but I found it more of a blue-grey land and pale on distant mountains. However! I'll grant Irish woods are deeper.'

'Ireland is as blue as the sea near Belfast.'

'Belfahhst,' he mocked.

'Ireland is blue. *Blue.*'

If she had been standing her father knew she would have stamped a foot. She was growing up, yes, though in a haphazard lop-sided way, clinging to the traits of the spoilt brat. But her antagonism to O'Shea went deeper than the relative blueness of mountains, still nursing her grudge against him for refusing to let her join his cavalcade. The irony of it all was that, a dust storm building up in Sydney, her aunt had taken fright at the coach-station and scurried back to Brighton leaving Ned to make the trip with his mistress – and her father to face her anger as she swept from the coach seething at their insolent 'coachy' and his wretched conveyance that had kept breaking down and spilling them out to walk to ease the load. She would much rather have taken her chances with the wagons and drays, she insisted. Furious with O'Shea, even more furious with the world in general, she had demanded her aunt be sent 'home' – wasn't she always bewailing Ireland's loss? – and Owen had not blamed her. If he did decide to buy Burrendah his sister would join them there without complaint or sail back to Stonemore on the first available ship.

'Coming, Papa?' Alannah slapped her mount to startled life and was off. O'Shea's amused eyes met Owen's.

'Your daughter is in no need of a groom, sir, but I shall ease her down for the mare's sake. We have a saying in these parts: "If a mount has sore back 'tis because of a parson or a lady".' His words died in a flurry of dirt, stones and distance and Owen watched the race with pleasure for there had been few in Ireland to ride like Alannah Moynan and there would be few here. He saw her glance over her shoulder then whip her mount, her hat bobbing on its strings and her hair blowing in the breeze. O'Shea's bare head gleamed a rich blue-black as he reached her and gripped her reins but she fought him all the way, straining as they raced, raising the dust in clouds. Loth to leave the vista before him, Owen lingered for here indeed were the bright burnt acres of O'Shea's mural. On just such a rise as this he had paused beside O'Shea to look over the man's Erins Pride: 'Call it sentiment, call it weakness, but here is my life and history and what heart is in me. My soul if man has a soul.' And his eyes, gazing from under his wide bushman's hat, had held the look of one who had come home. If that wife of his, Owen had reflected, is jealous of anything it need not be another woman, it could be this. Actually, the man was proving different on his home ground, easier, more approachable. For weeks after their breakfast at the

102

Crimean he, Owen, had heard nothing from him. He had simply waited. Finally the man had made his move. He had called, putting Delia in a dither until reminded of her manners enough to serve tea. He had come, O'Shea had explained, setting out blatantly to charm the women, to repeat his invitation to Erins Pride. Alannah had accepted there and then and had even begun to pack, while Con seemed interested enough to inspect guns and ask questions about hunt clubs. There was no mention of works manager or any other post then or since but Owen knew it was in the offing. Now he narrowed his eyes against the fierce light. The riders were flickering about the leafy homestead trees. His horse was restive. Stimulated by the pulsing energy ahead he pressed to it.

Ida Charlton's renowned apple cider and a laden table awaited them. On their initial visit servants and station-hands had stood ranked behind manager Dan, his no-nonsense wife, and their lanky eager-faced daughter Grace bubbling over with the prospect of new faces and young company. But today was intended to be leisurely and perhaps decisive for time was passing and conclusions must be reached. From her first glimpse of Burrendah Alannah had been enchanted, her eyes misting at the familiar sound of Scottish burrs and Irish brogues and the sight of pixie Irish faces. The station-hands were a casual cheery lot but plainly would not take kindly to patronage and one must meet them more than half-way, particularly the Paddys One, Two and Three – O'Hara, O'Rourke and Maguire – all small, freckled, sandy-haired and by some freak of coincidence come out on the same ship. Wizard hunters, trappers and masters of anything that ran, crawled and leaped they were all rogues, Owen guessed, out of range of Dan Charlton's eye – he had known too many such Paddys. Yet scarcely aware that they were doing so, he and his daughter moved closer together under the unfamiliar scrutiny of the Blacks. They must learn to be at ease with these people . . . The homestead was a gleaming white with green shutters, its roof low over verandahs shaded by grape-vines and wistaria trellises with passion-flower entwining the pillars. A fine apricot tree gave shade. Despite the dry summer the gardens were well watered and beyond the unexpected delight of English blooms stretched an orchard of gooseberries, apple, pear and plum with fine hedges of quince. In the kitchen garden the Chinese gardener Huie sang his smiling explanations of melons and lettuce and plump little cabbages. Alannah plodded happily through the lush growth beside her father.

'Huie says Argyle is a great county for potatoes and he grows the best. I shall plant an orange tree, Papa, *there*, near the window where it's sheltered and dry and the ground slopes a little. In a year I'll have my own special fruit.' And moving through the beautifully furnished rooms her voice trembled. 'I like it better each time I come. It's all so beautiful, quite perfect, don't you agree?'

He had to agree. Fine rugs, a grand piano, chaise longues. Cool airy bedrooms opening onto wide verandahs. O'Shea's Erins Pride was comfortable enough but Burrendah was almost too perfect, with an air of fragility about it, a little out of place in this practical and harshly functioning society – how homesick its owners must have been! He sat stiffly in chairs, afraid to ease himself in for fear of the delicate brocade. And if he must have paintings he liked a story, something dramatic, not these wishy-washy shepherdesses. It was with some relief that he went in to great pots of tea and mouth-watering honey scones, Grace beaming at his compliments: yes, sir, the scones were her baking but Annie McKenzie the drover's wife came in for special dishes. 'She's from Inverness, y'see, Mr Moynan.' He allowed himself a stifled belch for he had never thought to savour again the luck of a Highland cook. He drifted happily . . . The place would have a soporific effect upon him, no doubt of it, and he pulled himself up sharply to look about with the calculating objective eye of the man of business. The property did seem as sound as a bell, a secure investment not only for himself – with manly appurtenances of leather chairs and pipe-racks, perhaps even a pool table – but for his children. Conall, sauntering in with Jamie, had little to say but Con was always noncommittal until pressed. At least he did not criticise. But Alannah's delight glittered as she lingered on the hill looking back at the homestead. It was clear she had made up her mind.

'There's something special about it, Papa. I felt it from the first. It reminds me of . . . oh, you *know*.' He did know. It was not their formal rather utilitarian house near the Belfast hills of which she was thinking, it was her aunt's old but perfectly preserved farmhouse in County Down where she had been happiest, the house that perhaps she would never see again – and no matter how exasperated he became with his sister Owen forgave her much for having opened her home to niece and nephew when her own family was off her hands at school. So! Alannah must have her bit of Ireland, and no matter the trouble and cost to himself. Alannah turned in her saddle to O'Shea.

'What is the meaning of Burrendah?'

'It is an aboriginal word meaning "the place of the swan". The Huntlys built the house as a replica of their home on the Swan River in the west, and even set a few black swans in the arm of the Creek we call the lagoon. You'll find them sooner or later.'

'The Place of the Swan – I like it.'

'I find it most fitting,' he said quietly and Owen knew what he meant. There was nothing fragile about Alannah in her zest for life, indeed it was so fierce at times it assaulted, but in the play of light and shade under the tall gums she looked pale, almost ethereal, even a little swan-like, holding her graceful young neck and shoulders proudly erect. The place seemed exactly right for her, planted as a touch of England by homesick expatriates in a country that, to them, remained inhospitable. But he had not brought his family to Australia to languish on some counterfeit European estate; he had come to help them mould a new and satisfying life. Alannah would adapt, perhaps too hastily, for where he moved one step at a time she was inclined to gallop but there would be meaning for her here; she was beginning to love something again. And Con? He flicked the reins impatiently. Con must adapt or be swallowed up by this hearty hardy country and its people. It seemed there remained only the handing over of hard-earned Moynan money in this marriage of Old World coin and the Australian land.

Moll Noakes strode – there had never been any other way to describe Moll's walk – to where Patty stared into the kitchen mirror entranced by a forehead curl twirled about her finger, and slapped the girl's cheek hard.

'An *that* for the smudged tumblers. They're mucky.'

'*Ooooh!*' Patty screamed in her dramatic way and rubbed the mark redder. 'You didn't ought to slap me. Hetty says—'

'Mrs Witherstone when you speak of her, Patty Gearin.'

'—Mr O'Shea don't let anyone be beat.'

'As if y'know what a beating be.'

'I could get work at the Royal Arms, I could.'

'Without a doubt. The Arms' kitchen has always been partial to trollops. But I don't see ye scuttling orf there or anywhere else now young Lorne's come – I warn ye, gal, keep out o' the boy's path or I'll have your hide in strips.'

'He ain't a *boy*,' Patty smirked. 'Not any longer.'

'So I hear tell.'

'I don't have to stay here,' the girl screamed her insistence. 'I *don't*.'

'You can be heard through the House.' Hetty swept in to dump a pile of linen in the girl's arms. 'True, you don't have to stay but few pay as well as Mr O'Shea and you know it. But you won't have his good wages much longer if you don't press the napkins better. Do them over.' She moved her palms slowly up her side hair to secure stray wisps, then smoothed her apron – Hetty's aprons were laundered as often as she said her prayers which was regularly. A scullion, she referred to herself when hard driven, yet clearly not without a certain pride. Hetty Witherstone asked but one thing in return for her drudgery (another word that inspired smugness): respect in her own kitchen; an assertion of authority that was the red rag to the bull of Moll Noakes' temper, for the kitchen of Erins Pride was disputed territory between its long-time matriarch and Rob Witherstone's

106

second wife, reverting to neutral ground only when its master was about.

'An' she's not the only one with her mind on mischief instead of her chores.' Moll glowered at the half-breed girl fumbling with an entrée dish. Adina promptly dropped it. 'Your master brought that from Dublin,' Moll boomed, raising an arm to strike her but Hetty pushed Adina towards the dining-room.

'Finish the table. They'll be in soon.'

'An' none o' your sneaking orf while we sup,' Moll shouted after her, slapping plates about.

'If you keep scaring her so she'll drop everything,' Hetty dared.

'I aim to scare her. Someone should. I've no reason to believe she's different from her no-good brother.'

'She's quite different.'

'Black trash.' Moll wiped her hands on her own voluminous apron. 'I've lived among Indians all m'life an' know 'em too well. Not that I'll have slack from whites neither.'

'I don't hold with laziness anywhere, but it's true, the girls don't have to come out to the stations, they can get work in the town and take their pick of men while they're about it – men with money in their pockets too. Times have changed.'

'Well, gals haven't.' Moll strove to fit the broken pieces together with her strong but restless hands. 'They still want the moon in their laps. An' if y'do your duty, Hetty Witherstone, ye'll not take your eyes orf one of 'em with young Lorne prowling m'kitchen.'

'I can't order him out.'

'Well, I can an' will. He'll be leaving his brats all over the country afore he makes old bones, an' I'll not have his bastards crawling m'floors.'

'That young Ned talks too much, spreading rumours – how do we know what he says is true?'

'I believe the lad,' Moll sniffed.

'You should not speak so of Master Jamie.'

'I'll speak in m'kitchen same as always. What's more, Hetty Witherstone, keep your eye on that half-breed Indian for she sneaks out to hang about Joey Bowes.'

'Joey can take care of himself, I reckon.'

'No man can take care of himself.' Moll swept the china aside with such impatience Hetty glanced at her uneasily.

'I'll speak to Mr O'Shea about her,' she soothed, piling the bread on servers – and I'll speak as plain as I dare about you, Moll Noakes, she vowed under her breath. Something had to be done, for Moll was upsetting too many in a changing and difficult world where life and labour were becoming more valuable. The old convict days and ways – Moll's days and ways – were dying out if slowly, killed off by circumstance, time, and distance from England. A new kind of immigrant, capable, often skilled, with a bit of money in his pocket or the means of earning some, was sailing through Sydney Heads to make a place for himself, while the native-born were growing up to look upon a distant Britain as something unknown, unregretted and unlamented. Australia was aggressively, if slowly, growing up.

Moll drifted out to the porch, the third time in ten minutes, and stood where she could see beyond the trees and the gates to the road. Her eyes were still good. She knew Brick and his guests could not be home just yet but her impatience overflowed and buffeted her about, tiring her as so many simple things wearied her these days. Though she would never admit it, minute events shook both her mind and body to an alarming degree. Hetty bullied her to rest but when had she ever rested? Besides, she was not old, not by a long chalk, and had always been strong; a little heavy these days, true, and she lost her wind easily but what of that? She had her headaches of course but they came and went as they had since Brick up and married the widowed Raunie Merrill without word or warning even to herself, his foster-mother. She had kept her counsel over the marriage at the time as she had kept it since, never a word of reproach or even comment, certainly no questions for Erins Pride was his home, his true place, and he was entitled to peace within its walls and on its soil. And so far as Moll Noakes could arrange it, peace he would have.

Even so, time had not eased her bitterness at her life-long plans for her foster-son being foiled abruptly, and deliberately she was convinced, by a gipsy slut – and slut still for all her finery and mannered ways as O'Shea's wife. From the beginning, Raunie Lorne as she had been when tumbled off an immigrant barque and up to the Pride kitchen all of seventeen years ago, had set her sights on O'Shea and, by tricks only she would know – witchcraft too, Moll was certain – had finally brought about her marriage to him. Moll did not blame Brick for he was a man, and though stronger than most, still male, and a man must have his way and his women – the creed of Moll's world – but to *marry* the wanton! The event had ended finally and for ever hope of real power for O'Shea, not the power that came from money – he would always have that – but the precise and privileged power of the still-influential military and the sterlings of the legislature and landed gentry. Even those of the latter class who had become accustomed with time to his convict-aboriginal ancestry with a shrug of what Brick called *laissez-faire*, and were willing, albeit a trifle uneasily, to overlook such social shortcomings, had baulked at accepting his wife – their own wives had seen to that! A woman of dubious beginnings, a woman thrice married, of liaisons including that brazen open affair with Major Merrill, a woman of gipsy blood to boot. The situation was impossible. It simply would not *do!*

So the O'Sheas lived their luxurious but circumscribed life among the commercial and mercantile classes, the barons of shipping and goldfield hostelries and stores and mines and what existed of industry; shrewd ambitious money-grabbing *nouveaux riches*, a surprising number from that nether world into which O'Shea had been born but which she, Moll Noakes, had spent her life helping him escape.

Through Raunie, Moll knew – though not precisely how – the most carefully guarded secret of Moll's life, Brick's aboriginal ancestry, had been proclaimed to the world. A secret that could have remained hidden for ever but for the plots and counterplots of an adventuress. The prestige and privilege that Brick would have gained through his marriage to the Merrill daughter had been denied him, for with the same malevolent stroke Raunie had broken the heart, mind and body of the girl who would have smoothed Brick's rough edges and guided him into the highest echelons of the colony – and beyond it perhaps. The bitterness of Barbara Merrill's death – though Moll had met the girl only once – had never faded even if Brick refused to speak of it. Moll Noakes never forgot.

With an effort that made her head ache she shook off the past to deal with the present. At least Raunie O'Shea – how it stung to have to acknowledge the woman as an O'Shea – did not come to Erins Pride. But she haunted it in the shape of her son, a boy whom Moll detested and distrusted as she did his mother, suffering his sojourns with a bad grace and often open protest. This handsome insolent young buck whom she had delivered one gusty day in a corner of the Pride's old kitchen distracted the men from their work, dallied with the maids (slept with them too, Moll suspected) and wandered the country like a native in search of his tribe, walking in as bold as brass when it suited him, ready for the next mischief. Brick had lived and roamed as freely, but for survival, to build a life; besides, there was no cruelty for cruelty's sake in her foster-son. But if ever a bad end loomed for anyone it loomed for Jamie Lorne, Moll would swear to any who would listen. The irony of it was, the lad thrived.

The road was still empty. Time to don the hated bombazine Hetty shamed her into wearing before guests. Moll straightened the further detestation of her starched cap and with a reassuring rattle of her keys turned back to the House. Whatever the Pride's guests had been served at Burrendah, Erins Pride could, would and must do better.

The riders were ravenous and sat long over the great bowls of mutton broth, the roast meats, the apple pies and clotted cream, with the best from the Pride's cellars. Because it was her duty and because Brick insisted upon it Moll sat at one end of the long table, always uncomfortable and always

110

disconcerted by what she saw as the Pride's splendours, for she remained the peasant she had been born and anything more civilised than a sea-chest and her old iron pots represented luxury in her stolid and ritualistic life. Brick was for ever making changes, what Hetty called 'sprucing up'. The old House was enlarged by verandahs and guest-rooms and proper servants' quarters, and a separate dining-room with silver and pewter on its sideboard and fine china and cutlery inside it. The withdrawing-room was impressive with wool and kangaroo-fur rugs and heavy with cedar, for O'Shea had furnishèd with the pick of the wood before the forests thinned out down south. There was even a pianoforte that nobody played but all prized. There were wondrous farm implements in the paddocks and mysterious new machines in the sheds. The rebuilt kitchen boasted big pantries and new pots and pans which Moll accepted with resignation but with a certain suspicion; she would die rather than admit what all knew, that she was only truly at ease pottering about her worn kitchen table of scrubbed colonial pine that she stubbornly refused to relinquish. But she did her best with what she saw as the myriad minute frightening details of entertaining, 'city affectations' as she dismissed them – coffee after dinner to the gents in the dining-room and the ladies in the withdrawing-room, then tea for both when they joined up . . . Her head often spun with so much to remember. Now, speaking only when spoken to and briefly as behoved her place and her duty, she summed up the family who would most likely buy the Huntly place. The father, even if a cotton miller, was clearly a gentleman, dry-humoured and speaking seldom but straight to the point, conjuring the right words out of awkward silences. Moll liked that. The son was of no account, a flash young swell absorbed in Jamie's doubtful pursuits – birds of a feather there! But the girl . . . Though her clothes looked new they were unfashionable (Moll went more often to Goulburn these days; besides, Daisy Elston over at Wiena was for ever decking herself out in the latest). The girl was as outspoken as her father, a bit too free in her manner and speech for Moll's taste but she would settle, they all did in time. And there was something else about her, something vaguely familiar, a similarity to some other area of life, some other time. To someone . . .

'The country's water-obsessed – by the lack of it I mean.' Conall grew grandiose and argumentative at the dinner table, throwing in *bons mots* picked at random from his newly acquired knowledge of country *mores*. He polished off his wine and waited for his glass to be refilled. But this time O'Shea ignored it.

'Drought is a terrible thing,' he warned. 'Four, five years without rain and we not only dry up, we burn. True, we hanker after rain, fret for it, watch for it and the churches pray for it – but just enough, never to flood. There are great rivers out there—'

'That should be dammed.' Jamie thumped his glass in a hazy alcoholic enthusiasm and spots of red wine stained the damask.

'And who's to build the dams? You might ease up on your hunting and fishing and make a start at Narriah. Then go on out and tackle Oorin. And while we're on the subject of hunting, no more 'roo culling for a while.'

'But they're knocking the fences about. Getting at the green shoots too. A rifle shot only scares 'em off for a time. They're back in waves squatting and chewing.'

'Even so, I'll not have wholesale slaughter.'

'An old man 'roo eats as much grass as a sheep.'

'Not quite.'

'Oh yes. And will travel a hundred miles for good short grass.'

'Spend your seemingly endless leisure scaring them off in other ways. Ease up on the hunts, Jamie. It's an order.'

'You give orders, not reasons. At least, not sound ones.'

Alannah toyed with her food, letting the voices play around her, for if the nightly arguments were not over kangaroos or possums, they were concerned with precisely when to put the rams to the ewes or the proper fattening-up of hogs, all flowing on and out to the withdrawing-room. She escaped in her imagination to Burrendah. It was something more than the beauty of the place that drew her back, it was space and light and a promise of freedom in a serene world of her own that had set her to understanding Burrendah's people as she had come to know by proximity those of Erins Pride. Moll Noakes, rigid at the table's end, was forbidding but Alannah felt she had made a good impression there. 'Work-horse' Hetty, as she dubbed herself along with even more intriguing epithets, was easy to talk to, provided one followed her about as she struggled to hold her own against Moll, made plans for the day with Belle Carmody and Cissy Ryan, or scolded her stepdaughter for picking out notes on the pianoforte when she should have been dusting it. The stockmen and drovers remained elusive, sweating, clanking creatures, riding off or in to eat gargantuan meals, argue over nightly card-games, blame the upper classes for social ills, and women in general for their past and present misfortunes. The blackboys, splendid stockmen and boundary riders, moved silently and eternally on the edge of things. The only one she had come to know and felt she could depend upon was Joey Bowes. When he could be induced to talk she felt she met with his approval.

How different from 'home' as her aunt persisted in calling Ireland, a country still beloved but fading in her mind as some long-ago faraway playground-prison. It was rarely that she dwelt on it, perhaps when rummaging through her jewel box and fingering her rosary, a 'Galway' rosary of amber beads and specially-made silver tubular crosses, a beautiful seventeenth-century thing, very Spanish, that had come to her from her mother, bringing back vignettes of childhood after her mother's death, when she had endured daily Masses and dark warnings and the always pressing sense of Derry, a city that had never known religious peace. She would have been swallowed up by the Cassidys and Derry but for Con breezing in as a shout from another world, with his scepticism and mischiefs and lack of seriousness about anything but his own needs, urging her to the sanity of rebellions, if small, like hiding out for two nights to explore the countryside until hauled back by outraged Cassidy uncles. Young, secretive, desperate years of great divisions and joyous comings-together to query and question and devise answers until drawn finally into adult argument, her father the centre of interminable discussions on the Order of the Nuns of our Holy Fr. St. Dominick and whether she should go to Drogheda or Dublin. Her father and Dublin had won (no doubt with Aunt Delia in the wings somewhere) and she had been packed off to the boarding-school at Cabra to austere white beds and looming crucifixes and chants and drifting whispers . . . 'We pray for the rooting out of the Protestant heresy!' The monthly Rosary: 'for the extirpation of heresy and the spread of the Catholic Faith throughout Ireland'. Sometimes in her dreams she would see Con burning at the stake and would awake, shaken. She had never dared examine her father's fate! It was enough that his visits, along with Con's, drew her back if temporarily but always happily to another life.

But even more than her father and Con, County Down had saved her. She lived for holidays and her escape to Stonemore where there were dogs and fine horses and Anne Carney's pleasant room as her own, and her watchful, severe, yet in her way fond, aunt with her list of Protestant rules: modest demeanour and high collars and good manners and Bible readings of sins and punishments, and hymns and clean hands and quiet deadly Sundays when only the humming of bees broke the silence – rules that did not bother her a jot for Con was always there urging her to break them. How strange that divided life seemed now yet somehow she had managed to come to terms with it: mothers worried to their graves and beyond over a girl's soul and its waiting stage of grace called chastity. A boy's virginity was not so important, he was expected to lose it early, but ah, the warnings against the loss of her 'most precious possession'. Why was it valuable? What exactly was 'it'? How she had ached to ask – and did, finally, to be met with horror and no answers.

There was something of the escape from grey Dublin to sunny – or it had always seemed so – Stonemore in her life at Burrendah. Pressures were here, but different stresses, ones she could see and hope to resolve. At Calua or Wiena, drinking tea with some gentleman of the cloth, she would parry questions she did not wish to answer and not feel guilty. Gone the duties and compulsions of high walls and nuns' habits rustling at her side and the threat and fear of Hell both Catholic and Protestant. If Hell lurked around Burrendah it would look faintly ridiculous threatening her sprawling acres. She moved freely, physically and in her mind that had been toying for some time with an idea, a decision. She would ride astride – why not? More, she would have breeches made for herself, even if she only wore them around her own place. Let them talk! The Old World she had known and, to a large extent, suffered, was fading fast. Here at her Place of the Swan – and she was determined it would be hers – she would live, do, think, exactly as she pleased.

Moll Noakes, letting the arguments drift about her, the only way she had ever known of dealing with the inexplicable volubility of educated folk, felt suddenly and unbearably tired but managed to keep her eyes open and her back straight until the diners retired to the withdrawing-room still arguing and the girls could busy themselves about the tables. Trouble was, she dozed at odd and awkward times, plying her needle, or in her chair as now at the dinner-table, rousing to feel guilty and angry with herself. Tonight she could not fight her malaise. Ashamed of her weakness but helpless before it she slipped off to her room, locked her door behind her, removed her stays with a sigh of relief, rubbed her tormented flesh and sank on her bed to fall into a heavy but, so often these days, troubled sleep.

'It's the keys that's the awkward part, Mr O'Shea. We know she hides them when she feels poorly, afraid we'll take them from her, I suppose.' Between the polishing of silver and counting of cutlery and pulling out and pushing in of drawers, Hetty had manoeuvred the talk to embrace Moll

Noakes as O'Shea leant against the wall by the dying fire – fires started early in Argyle County – cracking nuts. 'The awkward thing is, we must search for them pretending we're looking for something else, for she fusses if we press her about her keys. And if we don't find them we must wait till they're at her waist again. She tires quickly too and locks herself in her room, to sleep we think for we can't rouse her, or she refuses to answer, pretending she's not there – but she could be dead, sir, stretched out, toes up so to speak. She's all mixed up and sick and stubborn about it. She needs a long rest.'

'I'll have duplicate keys made. She'll never know. You should have told me of this long ago.'

'Maybe so. The thing is, she has her place and the rest of us ours.' Primly and firmly, knowing her place and making sure he knew she knew it. 'Another thing . . . the days are gone when the girls will take basting as she calls it, for they yell their heads off at a mere slap of the wrist. They'll hit back too. I manage the girls without beatings, always have, as I've managed Rob's girls since they were small, getting Jane decently wed and Lottie into service at Calua and Fay learning to nurse as fast as she will do anything.'

'I told you to put her to work in the schoolroom. She has a way with children.'

'And fill her head with primer stuff? No girl of mine – for she is mine since her father wishes it so – will waste her time on book-learning.' Her voice took on its righteous and faintly martyred air. 'She'll learn to take the rough with the smooth of service as I've done, and as her mother did, till the right husband comes along. Though I don't hope for much in that direction for she's nigh eighteen and without the looks of her sisters, and from all I've heard, her mother.' Affording to be generous with the former Mrs Witherstone safely in her grave. 'She's not robust, never was, too dreamy altogether with a head full of notions. Now she wants to sing in the music-halls when she can't even hold a tune!'

A nut cracked sharply in Brick's fingers. He felt an unexpected and, he knew, unreasonable antagonism towards the woman for her almost joyous dedication to his affairs.

116

Trouble was, he needed hard-working, managing, critical Hetty and reflected on the curious fate that made this plain busybody of a woman so easily accomplish what pretty dead Betsy had been unable to do for the man she adored – provide him with sons. There was only one area where she had been unable to influence her husband, his stubborn clinging to Erins Pride – Rob and Moll Noakes were alike in that dedication. Rob had refused the Maneroo run, and indeed, everywhere else. If there were anything coming to him let it be put by for his boys with a bit of a dowry for Fay when she married. So he, O'Shea, had sold his old stock station on the Maneroo, added to Narriah, and bought into Oorin with Joey in mind together with Rob's sons when old enough. He stirred to an ominous silence and realised he was expected to answer some comment or question. He took a chance on the always potent subject of his foster-mother.

'Moll has always had her moods.'

'They're worse. So are her tempers. I don't like the way she looks and acts some days.'

'She'll never leave here. Not from choice. Erins Pride has been her life.'

'Her stubbornness makes life hard for us all.' Hetty straightened the silver service on its great tray and placed the candlesticks just so. 'Heaven knows I'm not after her place, Mr O'Shea. I've enough to do with my own work. It's just that someone must speak out. And I'll speak out about other things too. I don't approve of nor do I encourage Adina setting her cap at Joey every time he comes by. It's time you knew of it if you don't already, for I can't see *I* have the right to forbid the pair meeting, if Joey wants it that way, I mean. And he must want it for they do meet, and that's when anything can happen.'

'I don't fear there's anything between them.'

'Not yet, maybe.' Her pause was meaningful. 'But even then I'd not be too sure it's my place to interfere.'

'Does Rob think it his place?'

'Rob only says what he says about a season: good or bad, 'twill pass. But Joey's a man, sir, fully grown and should be marrying, with young Grace at Burrendah exactly right for

117

him, but he hangs back. As for Adina, when he's away she's like something not there. And when he's due back she knows even before we know that he's coming and she sort of . . . well . . . goes off to meet him, if you know what I mean. And when Mrs Noakes threatens to send her away, why, she looks like she'll die; indeed at times she's like something already dead so we let things go on as before. But begging your pardon, sir, and I must say it, it's *you* should take a hand in things, for half-breeds take things hard, inside I mean, as if they know they don't fit in and nothing they can do is going to be much use.' Holding her head high she met his eyes frankly for everyone spoke easily of his antecedents, a circumstance of life at Erins Pride. 'I can't help feeling sorry about it all for Adina's different from her brother, she really is. Indeed she's too submissive and I'd like to take a switch to her at times, to give her some backbone. She lets Barney live off her and it's a shame for he's a fine rider and tracker but won't stick to anything. He's like other seasons, the bad ones that don't pass or, if they do, come back to plague us again and again.'

'Any complaints about him lately?'

'All we know is that there's been pilfering at Calua.'

'I'll see into it. As for Adina, I rather think that's Joey's problem, but if you wish, I'll see into that too.' He tossed the shells into a pewter dish, nodded and went out.

Hetty paused in her folding of napkins to watch him go. She had always liked the way he walked, steady and with purpose as if he knew exactly where he was going and why. As masters went he was a good one and, no doubt of it, the Pride lost a little of its heart without his driving force, yet there was something different about him of late as if, incredible as it might be, he was . . . drifting? As if he had achieved everything yet was not content, not knowing, quite, which road to take. Baulked, he dabbled in industry . . . politics . . . his heart really here on his land. Yet when he did come he did not stay long. He seemed troubled where he had never been troubled. Frowning, Hetty smoothed the fine Nottingham lace cloth. How was it possible after all for him to stay with a wife who would not even set foot in Goulburn let alone Erins Pride?

She shook off her introspection. Thinking made her uneasy. Made her head ache, too. Besides, she had no time to dwell on old dead tales or fret over the colony's bizarre couplings; hers to get on with her job, for everything fell on her shoulders with Belle too often poorly, too timid to stand up to that show-off of a Marty, and Cissy with too many children and always another on the way, and Patty flirting with each new hand, and Fay for ever dreaming . . . She slapped the napkins into a smooth pile with the satisfaction of a job well done. She knew her duty. She had done her duty too in speaking up about Joey, about Adina, about Grace eating her heart out over at Burrendah. She smoothed her hair up and her apron down. Now for her kitchen, yes, *her* kitchen no matter what Moll said, to plan tomorrow's baking. No matter what happened – birth, death, treachery, love, hate, jealousy, disaster of any kind – the world waited to be fed.

Chapter Six

THE SUMMER was at an end. The night was fresh and cool and the mêlée of the day had settled as if held down by the dark. Only a faint flavour of dust played about the mouth and teased the nostrils as Brick left the House and strolled from its glow into the shadows then into the black, pausing now and then to scent the earth, drawing Erins Pride through his senses and making it one with him. When he had breathed it in and communed with it he flung back his head, braced his legs and stood firm, eyes wide to the universe. The sky above Erins Pride had always been a special sky to him and if there were immortality it would be *there*, above his own soil. He traced the friendly familiarity of the Southern Cross that no matter where he was he found and followed. Now, gazing wide, he lost himself in his own universe, absorbing the lights of stars seen and unseen until direction blurred and vanished and he was in space, timeless and without direction, floating . . . whirling . . . He swayed and clutched at a tree, shaking his head to clear it.

But it was not only vertigo that had shocked him to reality, it was sound, muted but distinct from the intermittent laughter from the men's quarters where Jamie and Con spent most of their time. His head jerked to the rustle of a possum – not that, sound beyond the animal. He listened closely. Nothing close by until argument filtered, for a brawl seemed to be developing in the huts. He moved on increasing his pace; Jamie and young Moynan must learn to wipe their own bloody noses. He didn't like their too-swift companionship but then he liked very little Jamie did of late. He passed the office, then the schoolroom, the latter serving as concert hall, and chapel when needed. The growth of Erins Pride over a decade displayed itself in the well-stocked store, the workshop, the enlarged shearing-shed and a new dairy. The cottages – once wattle-and-daubs – housing the Carmody and Ryan families made soft patches of light over the grass but even without light his senses were attuned to the night and the bush; so soft, so certain, so *native* was his tread it never crowded out his hearing. He paused. The odd little sounds seemed to be following him, dying then resuming so softly he was forced to listen for them. He moved on to pause by the orchard to light his pipe, drawing upon it until it lit up his face. A scurry, and his eyes that could see anything caught darker shadows against the dark banks of trees and shrubs. He stood smoking a while then walked on slowly to the coach-house and stables.

As he expected Joey was grooming an already well-groomed Glenora, a favourite task, his tools – curry-comb, brush, mane-comb and sponge – arranged neatly to hand. The stable-boys had gone and the place was warm and redolent with the rich odours of straw and dung and oil. Only one lantern burned. Joey, with Bowes tacked on for no better reason than that it was a name, had grown into a tall skinny young man with the same pale fine hair moving quietly, competently, and with a certain homely charm about his dedicated existence. He spoke seldom and smiled rarely but when he did either it was usually directed as an eager pilgrim at the object of his devotion – O'Shea. The waif of Regent Lodge had simply transferred his allegiance from his dead mistress to the man she had loved, and O'Shea's word had become not only law but inexorable law. Brick was always acutely and rather uneasily conscious of the fact that Joey had been left to him in trust, for behind every word they exchanged, every nuance, Barbara Merrill stood watching over their shoulders.

'It's time those horses were broke.' He spoke lightly in an attempt to set the right mood: it was always difficult to converse frankly with Joey. 'Take the boys tomorrow and round 'em up. There's a likely colt or two I'll send through with the stock. And cut out anything suitable for the Braidwood fields, we've a market there.'

'Yes, Mr O'Shea.'

'One of these days, we'll chase the mobs that roam between the Lachlan and the Darling. They foul up the wells and waterholes so we'll thin 'em out a bit.' Joey said nothing and Brick drummed his fingers on the rail. 'Maybe you should have seen Oorin for yourself before this—'

'Too much work to be done around here.'

'There's work to be done everywhere . . . But you know the essentials of the place: modest as stations go out there, but a share of the thousand head of cattle and some twenty thousand sheep building up on the home and out-stations means you'll get a fair start. Blackett has agreed to stay until you arrive but he won't wait for ever.' He paused but Joey was silent. 'You can breed sound large-framed sheep with heavy fleece out on those plains. Make good use of the saltbush, it grows well after the rains; I've seen it so high and thick over the One Tree Plain no stock should starve. Healthy feed if you add a little dry stuff.' Still silence. 'You understand those rams I'm putting in, don't you?'

'I – think so, sir.'

Brick slammed the rail so hard it shuddered. 'Think is not enough. And how many times have I told you, don't "no sir" and "yes sir". Is it so hard after ten years to call me simply O'Shea if you can't force yourself to call me Brick?"

'I can't do it – sir.'

'At least don't stand off looking eternally grateful. Who knows, you might have had an easier and more profitable life without my patronage.' He paused, baffled. 'You want this run, don't you?'

'I don't rightly know.'

'Why don't you know? You're not taking much of a chance.'

'It's not that.'

'What then? You've had plenty of time, too long I'm thinking, to make up your mind. You can't drift about waiting on me and mine for ever, doing odd jobs, picking up skills where you can.'

'It's all I've ever done, except in service to Miss Barbara.'

'Miss Barbara's dead and your servitude with the Merrills

long over. And you've more than served your time with me. You must live for yourself now. Don't you want to marry?'

'I've thought about it. As all men do.'

'Then think about it again and seriously. I don't know how you've drifted as freely as you have with Grace Charlton's eyes always on you.'

'Grace?'

'Yes, *Grace*. I can't think why you hesitate for she's always hankered after you, everyone knows it. But if she's not to your taste, well, there's that black-haired lass in at the Royal – Lucy, isn't it? I hear she took quite a shine to you. Or take your pick of the district, there are plenty of women about now – but marry, Joey. Marry. You'll need a wife down there. There are great empty stretches where a man alone can go mad. They have.'

Still no answer. Joey was standing staring out at the night as if . . . listening? Seeing? Brick snatched up the brush for he hated friction between himself and Joey and of late it had been growing. As he smoothed Glenora's silky coat Joey turned back, startled, and perhaps a little ashamed at not knowing what to do. Brick stifled anger for it would be useless. Joey had never known what to do.

'Change must come. And it's not happening only to you. Most likely there'll be new folk at Burrendah soon.'

'I've only known Erins Pride and Birubi, since Regent Lodge I mean.'

'Regent Lodge is a school for Catholic theologians – and *that's* change. The whole country is moving on.' He paused. 'Even Adina's moving on and she grew up here.'

'Adina?'

'Adina Cook – and don't echo so. She's going on seventeen, late for even a part-native girl to wed, and she's worth more than a place in my kitchen. Now that fencing's going through Billy Warwick has been made boundary rider at Wiena and a house goes with the job. He's asked for Adina. The Elstons will treat them well. A suitable match in everyone's eyes. Parson will be through shortly to marry them.'

Joey turned to look out at the night again, drawn suddenly and urgently to its deep and pounding life. A night as soft as Adina's eyes, as sweet and yielding as her breasts would be – how certain he was of that – round and full yet soft to his hands and there were times he could scarcely bear the thought for he had not yet touched a woman, not even one of the native women the men used and all he knew of their couplings was what he heard around the stations and he didn't like a lot of what he was told. He could have Patty Gearin if he wanted her, he knew it. And other girls seemed to like him. Grace liked him – he'd been teased over Grace for years – pert and pretty Grace as they said of her except that she was not pretty and only pert enough of late to snap at him. Trouble was he never thought of Grace as he thought of Adina cradled in his arms, part of the soft warm nights. Grace was meant for wifely things, a hard abrupt girl, not soft like Adina – ah, how yielding Adina was as she followed him through the brush, caressing him, drawing him into the shadows, coaxing and whispering, sometimes crying softly when he drew away. Adina had become part of his nights, so often in bed with him – yet not there at all.

Watching Joey, Brick's hand clenched on the brush and he steadied the horse so sharply Glenora whinnied and reared slightly. Don't, Joey – *don't*. I know the soft moist skin of them, that yielding native embrace and the net they can weave around a man's loneliness and need. I know their cloying submission, the giving, *giving*, until a man becomes satiated with so much giving, saturating him until it is part of him, a habit he cannot break. You will, in a way, become tainted by so much giving so that you will become cut off from your own all-judging world outside your passion, that world in which, whether you like it or not, you must strive to please or go under, a world you cannot deny or flout, only try to appease. For no matter how you try you cannot deny it or get away from it; it's always there with its immovable and unchanging rules, a world you have no hope of conquering or even entering while you belong to that other Black world. Make your choice and hold to it, Joey, for either world, black or white, is better than that dim lost world between the two.

Don't live that bitter battle, choose one or the other and gain at least something. He spoke quietly but urgently.

'Don't touch her, Joey.'

Joey turned slowly as if dragging himself back into the shallows from mysterious unexplored depths where he had been treading water. 'I never have, that's the trouble.'

Brick let out his breath, patted the stallion, threw down his brushes and left Joey standing for he could do no more. But as he walked back to the House he heard the faint but distinct sound of a woman crying somewhere deep in the growth. He did not stop or even falter. Joey must make his choice.

Joey stood stroking Glenora. Then his hand stilled and slid slowly from the horse as Adina came out of the shadows, a shape not so much moving as shimmering towards him, and as she came into the lantern glow her black hair shone soft and curling and her dark skin glowed as if alight. Her breasts were indeed full and rounded under the straight cotton shift. He was not certain what he would do as she paused before him. He did not have to do anything. She turned out the lantern, clasped his hands, opened his arms and crept within them to rest her head against his chest. He could feel her breasts straining and moving against him; they would be silky as chocolate cream, he knew it. His arms came up and around her, loosely at first then urgently. She moved gently but provocatively within his hold and he could scarcely bear it. She took his hand and with a gentle sensuous movement drew him into the dark and the smell of straw and grain and polished leather and the sweat of restless beasts. She turned to him. Soft urgent murmurs, a long sigh, heavy and sustained, then nothing but the faint faraway intermittent reminders of a world outside.

The fire blazed. The room was almost too warm but neither Alannah nor her father seemed to notice, already warmed by the excellent dinner, then by the stimulation of talk round the small table littered with wool samples. Rob Witherstone had answered questions in his slow Lincolnshire dialect that had not changed in his fifty-odd years, the only difference in his appearance deeper lines in his lean face and, if it were possible, a sharper sparseness of frame. He moved with the same dogged purpose, heightened by the fact that he was a fulfilled man – he had fathered three sons. He nodded to O'Shea as the latter entered, and continued his talk with the somewhat amused condescension of the countryman to outsiders, doing what had to be done and no more. 'As for the crops, we've had good follow-up rains and the soil's right for wheat sowing next month. We have every reason to expect good harvests.' He talked of sorghum and oats and lucerne, and the flocks eating their way up from the south by the 'long paddock', the grass strip beside the road, fat and healthy after summer pasturage on the lush high plateaux. 'If thou art uneasy over any particular matter, Mr Moynan, call upon me at any time.' Finally he had jammed his hard-bitten pipe in his mouth, scooped up his wool, nodded all round and was gone. Alannah did not open the pianoforte as was her habit; she felt too restless to play, much less sing, tonight. She flung herself in the chair opposite her father where he sat twirling his empty glass and staring into the fire. He had been abstracted, watching the door, for Con had not come in after dinner; he seldom did but he knew tonight was important. O'Shea too seemed preoccupied, grating the decanters in choosing liqueurs. Eager and excited, she leant forward. 'There's so much to learn, Papa, I don't know where to start.'

He roused to smile at her enthusiasm. 'You can start by accepting seasons upside-down from Europe. In any case, you will not be required to practise wool-classing.'

'But I want to know all about it. I want to know everything now that we are to buy Burrendah.'

'Now as to that . . .' He shifted in his chair. 'There are many things to be considered before we make a decision.'

'I made my decision long ago.'

'Indeed, you've made your feelings quite plain over the past weeks. For one thing, if your aunt does decide to stay in

Australia it is only fair she has a second chance to view the property.'

'She'll love it, you'll see. It was such a scorcher that day in Sydney it scared her half out of her wits. But now the weather's wonderful.' She ran her hands up and down the chair arms. 'I will have Burrendah, Papa.'

'You *will?*'

'You must know how badly I want it!'

'Con must have his say.' He was always stubborn over Con.

'He loves it too, I know he does.' Springing to her brother's defence, not only from habit or to soothe her father but because she was certain O'Shea was listening; he seemed always listening and watching and, as a family, they must not appear uncertain and vulnerable before him. 'Just look at him these past weeks, seldom off a horse.'

'Scarcely an indication of his devotion to a property.'

'I will have my Place of the Swan, Papa.' With a new hardness to her voice. 'And I will have it now.'

He looked up sharply. 'What exactly do you mean by that?'

She sprang to her feet. 'I'm not going back to Sydney, not for a day or even an hour. I brought everything with me – everything! I decided before I left Brighton that if I liked Burrendah, and I expected to do so, I would stay on. I hate Brighton and won't live in it again, not even for your sake.'

'I had no idea you felt so strongly about the house. But there are other houses. We could find one you liked.'

'I will not go back.' Her voice trembled with fervour. 'I've nothing to go back *for*. If you must go, for the business side of things and to settle matters with Aunt Delia as I suppose you must, I shall stay here and watch the wonderful things that happen after rain – it's magic, it really is.' He was staring at her as if she were mad and her words came tumbling. 'And if you still refuse to buy Burrendah, well, I shall manage somehow. There is Mama's money coming to me—'

'Don't talk nonsense, girl, you don't inherit till you're twenty-one.' Sharply, for there was something almost feverish about her. 'You've fallen in love with a house, instantly,

127

the way you do everything. Admittedly, it's a fine house but we can't purchase simply because of an attractive residence. There's the overall property to be considered.'

'We've explored every inch of it and can't fault a thing. I thought you wanted me to be happy . . .' She moved restlessly about the room. 'I *know* we can all be happy at Burrendah. And Brighton will be taken over quickly, you'll see, lots of people like it. Don't stop me, Papa, *don't*.'

He placed his glass on the small table and stood slowly. 'There are matters pertaining to myself that will necessitate my keeping a house in Sydney.'

'Matters?' She frowned. 'What matters?' But he hesitated, hands behind his back, as if about to pace the room. O'Shea moved to his side, liqueur in hand, and there was something about them as they faced her that set her on the defensive. 'Mr O'Shea, you must convince my father that the Huntly place is exactly right for us.'

O'Shea placed the liqueur beside her father's empty glass. 'All I am certain of, Miss Moynan, is that it was exactly right for the Huntlys.'

'I expected your support.'

Owen made a sharp movement. 'I am not giving up Brighton.'

'But when we do need to go down there are hotels aplenty.'

'I shall need a town house and Brighton will be admirable for my purpose.' So! He had not only reached the Rubicon; he was about to cross it and was achingly aware of O'Shea's eyes on him. Drat the man! While his daughter's eyes were rebellious, even hostile. But there was no turning back.

'What purpose?'

'If I do decide to buy Burrendah – I repeat, *if* – I shall not be able to join you. At least, not for some time.'

'But why *not*?'

'We shall discuss my reasons at length later. It is enough to say here and now that circumstances I did not foresee when we arrived in Australia have altered my plans.'

'What plans? You do not *say*.'

'Then I say now. I have decided to assist Mr O'Shea in a business venture.'

'If Papa will not explain then you must, Mr O'Shea.' There was something almost frantic in her plea.

'A matter of business you could not be expected to understand, Miss Moynan.'

'I understand a great deal about my father's life. *And* his work.'

'I see I should have prepared you but until tonight I was not certain . . .' Owen floundered a little but recovered to meet her eyes. 'I have made up my mind.'

'Your father is an engineer, Miss Moynan. And an expert on textile manufacture.'

'But he left all that behind in Ireland.'

'It seems I have induced him to come out of his premature retirement. I am attempting to set up mills for worsted in this country.'

'I don't give a fig for your mills,' she flared.

'*Alannah!*'

'A pity,' O'Shea said smoothly. 'I hoped you might find them interesting. If your father consents to work with me we can make great strides but it will entail close attention to my Sydney works as well as a good deal of travelling to establish a mill in the north, preferably at Newcastle. I have gone into every eventuality.'

'I see that you have.' Her voice trembled with anger. 'I'm surprised you haven't already installed servants of your choice at Brighton and decided what furniture will stay and what be sent to Burrendah, as well as deciding what my aunt feels about the move. Have you worked out Papa's daily menus?'

'Do not be impertinent,' her father snapped. 'You forget you are a guest in this house.'

'But I won't have it,' she throbbed. 'Decisions have always been made between us as a family and now everything is spoilt just when I was so happy. Whatever you say and do, Mr O'Shea, and whatever Papa says and does, I won't go back to Sydney, not even if I have to camp out in the hills. I can't bear the kind of social life I'm expected to live in a city. I don't do the right things, or say them—'

'We will discuss such personal aspects later.' Owen cut off

her words sharply. 'Meanwhile it will be best if we postpone the purchase of the property until I can be with you, at least from time to time.'

'But we could lose Burrendah.'

'There are other sheep stations.'

'I want this one. And I will have it, Papa. I *will!*' So savage in her determination that O'Shea said hastily:

'Since Miss Moynan is determined to stay, sir, and now, perhaps I can set your mind at rest. As well as excellent management at Burrendah I put Erins Pride at her disposal. Witherstone will ride over regularly to see all is well, immediately if there should be urgent problems and, when he is away, Joey Bowes. Ashby, my clerk-secretary and general factotum, is trying his luck on the fields but he'll make a clumsy digger and I expect him back any time. Meanwhile, Carmody has a bit of a head for figures—'

'I can see I won't lack keepers,' Alannah broke in.

'Helpers was what I had in mind.'

'I shall make my own arrangements as to servants, Mr O'Shea.'

'Scarcely practical since you do not know this country as yet. A sheep run in Australia is not the rural farming of County Down. It certainly entails more than housekeeping in a Belfast suburb—'

'Must you be overbearing as well as patronising?'

'And must you be rude as well as stubborn, Alannah?' Her father cut her off brusquely. He knew she was digging in her heels and he wished he'd taken a switch to her early in life. And yet . . . there was something appealing in her eagerness and determination to build a new life. If only Con . . .

'Your Place of the Swan, as you call it, is something of an anachronism here.' O'Shea spoke smoothly and reasonably. Too reasonably. 'It is an Old World dream built by lonely expatriates, and gives such as yourselves a distorted picture of outback life. A sheep station is not a European farm—'

'Then I'll soon learn the difference, won't I!' She hated him standing there lecturing, attempting to manipulate her as he manipulated her father, exploited her father, she was sure of it. The man would not be permitted to arrange *her* life;

130

she would learn to run her own place, and run it well. She could ride to match anyone, she could cook, she would learn bush nursing and all to do with wool and crops and her own livestock. She would improve her marksmanship. She would even join one of their brutal bloody kangaroo hunts if it were necessary to prove herself. She turned her back on him. 'I have only one regret, Papa. I cannot make personal farewells to my friends.'

He looked puzzled. 'What friends?'

'Simon in particular.'

'Simon?'

How obtuse he could be at times. 'Simon *Aldercott*. How could you forget when you see him so often.'

'Not often. There was some discussion between us when I recommended him to the shipping house, again when I referred him to the master at that academy – I understand they are keeping him in mind. Yet again, when I introduced him to Mr Cruise. I believe he is giving his sons evening instruction in the classics.'

'Those dreadful boys who pelt cats with peach stones? I cannot believe Simon would be satisfied with that or, even if he is head clerk, some horrid shipping company. Assure him I shall miss our interesting talks and will answer his letters promptly.' Why was she babbling on about a man she could not abide? And growing angrier still at her father's bewildered expression. Besides, there was something about O'Shea's broad back that fuelled her resentment. 'You are perhaps acquainted with Simon Aldercott, Mr O'Shea?'

He turned slowly. 'Should I be?'

'Since you seem to know the identity of everyone who comes and goes in this colony I assumed you would at least have heard of him. If not, I feel it would be to your advantage to meet such a well-educated gentleman.'

'There's your answer then: I do not move in well-educated circles. Certainly I meet few you would call gentlemen. You are wise to cultivate such a paragon for you'll not duplicate his like about here. Your closest male prospects would be the Elstons but they're as wild as their father with Wiena

131

mortgaged to the hilt. There are the Creeveys, of course, rich but mean—'

'I spoke of Simon because you seemed in need of clerical help, but only as a stop-gap for him for I'm sure Papa can help him to better things.' She took a long deep breath for she was doing it again; haranguing this man and her father over a stiff-necked boring pen-pusher who didn't mean a thing to her. But how dared this man O'Shea compose his impossible list of 'male prospects' as he called them. She wanted to run from him. Yet needed to stay, with an urge to beat him at something. Anything.

'Clerks are ten a penny in the colonies so a man for my job must be an all-rounder. He must travel the back-country, not for the faint-hearted I assure you, to supervise not only financially but in every aspect my properties, enterprises and investments in this state and Victoria, and now my investments at Moreton Bay.'

'Simon could turn his hand to anything,' she promised recklessly, 'provided of course he should be interested.'

'Oh, he'll be interested when he learns I pay higher wages than most. However, if your young man—'

'He is not *my* young man, he is a family friend, is he not, Papa?' Ignoring her father's stunned expression.

'Your family friend then . . . cares to present his credentials to your father in Sydney we will consider his application, assuming of course he is not too gentlemanly to take orders, along with his salary, from an aborigine?'

Her eyes blazed. How exactly like him to raise an issue she had not even considered; she seldom did, it was he who could not seem to forget his aboriginal blood. She snatched up the poker and attacked the fire. It spurted and the angry flare matched her mood. She itched to slam the poker down on him and, oddly, at the same time, hard across Simon Aldercott's inoffensive unsuspecting back. Hating Simon, hating O'Shea, hating her father just then for he seemed in league with the others, she threw the poker down to see it glance off O'Shea's boot with such a clang he drew back. She wished she had broken his toes. His whole *foot!* And to her horror gave a faintly hysterical giggle.

132

'Go to bed,' her father ordered sharply. 'You're tired.'

'I am not in the least tired.'

'Then go to your room. Mr O'Shea and I have private matters to discuss.'

He was angry as much as he ever showed anger, dismissing her as a naughty child. But, enjoying her rebellion, she stalked out on a wave of elation leaving them to their nightcaps of brandy and water and their plotting and planning, for nothing they could say or do would stop her settling in to Burrendah here and now. It was on the same wave of elation and rebellion that she wrote to Simon Aldercott and it was not until much later, recalling her letter, that she realised she had written a much warmer one than she had intended.

Through the crisp clear days of that change of season Alannah rode to Burrendah past crops that were looking good; green was everywhere and the ploughed soil awaiting the wheat was rich and dark. Her feelings for her Place of the Swan did not falter, though her confidence as to her ability to run it efficiently even with competent help did waver from time to time. But she was careful never to show hesitation, or let Con's indifference or, as she regarded it, her father's desertion daunt her. She saw little of her father who was off with O'Shea or Rob, or in the workshop, or out inspecting farm machinery and implements, not avoiding her exactly yet not seeking her out. He argued with Con a great deal which made her uneasy over her brother's intentions. 'You always get your way in the end so why ask my opinion?' Con would brush aside her queries, and it not only saddened but frightened her that they should all be moving along disparate paths. But whatever happened she would not be swerved from hers.

O'Shea preserved a scrupulous politeness towards her as she was careful to do towards him, though formality crumpled when he presented her with a small cream mare of her own. She had no reason to refuse his gift, indeed found she could not, and promptly named her Mourne. Nor could she find an excuse to refuse his offer to try out her mount, and in riding the roads and tracks of Argyle at his side she came to know the land through his eyes: its often exotic flavour, its wild and sudden changes, the dark coming down so swiftly, the rhythm of its days and nights. She saw him against his true background, that of the bushman, involved in fiery arguments with his men, or breaking up fist fights in dealing with what appeared to be urgent dramatic crises yet turned out to be no more than part of the day's work. She saw him accepted in the district as one of those settlers who had dug in early, a squatter of time and standing as well as wealth, and never heard open criticism or allusion to his forebears. They would pass the time of day with diggers on their way to the Braidwood fields. They passed China Men loping south to the Adelong fields, oblivious of the chill in their loose blue trousers and jumpers and umbrella-like hats, bamboos across their shoulders suspending their mining gear. They rode to Wiena to meet George Elston (fancies himself as the county lady-killer, Hetty sniffed), his fluttery fashion-plate of a wife, Daisy (her men are spending her money fast), sons Hal and Roy (they'll ride you down if you get in their way), and spoilt daughters (too many servants eating up Wiena's profits and if it weren't for my Rob the place would be bankrupt), to ride home in the evening calm tantalised by scented spirals of smoke from burning-off, the sound of frogs and crickets along the Creek and the squeal of small things she could not name. They discovered the swans beyond the tall rushes sailing gracefully over the pond known as the lagoon. Rising suddenly in flight they were surprisingly awkward in stretching out their long necks and flapping their wings to show a white trim of feathers beneath. There were wild ducks gliding tamely to take sudden darting dives for pickings. In those luscious heady April days Alannah found the world of Burrendah all she wanted. She nursed a deep satisfying sense of having come home.

Yet there were aspects of it that disturbed, cutting into her neatly rounded-off days like the nick of a knife. One day she made a detour with O'Shea and Hennessy, the latter leading a spare horse, to the camp of the Fish River natives and their

134

ramshackle lean-tos with unkempt women and dirty men with husky coughs. Mangy wolf-like curs with much in them of the native dog – the warrigal – wandered about, grubbing and rooting in the dirt beside naked tumbling pickaninnies. It looked a squalid and meaningless settlement, going nowhere, with an air of doom about it. It depressed her, and feeling a little sick she longed to turn back.

'It's not populated as it was ten years ago; they're scattering.' O'Shea put out a warning hand. 'Don't let them too close, they're none too healthy. *Yuena!*' he called and went off with a Jen to find the head man, or king, seeking news of Barney Cook, Adina's brother, for he'd been seen running from Calua's store and O'Shea meant to lock him up out of trouble – at least he couldn't get the drink for a while. Hennessy had wandered off and she waited alone, reluctant to dismount, while the women pointed, jabbering, soaking their sugar bags and drinking the dirty sweetened water with much giggling and flashing of stained teeth – at least they were good-humoured. It seemed an age before Brick came up from a hut leading a sullen but good-looking young half-caste. Alannah avoided the liquid expressionless eyes as Brick roped him about the neck, hoisted him on the spare horse and roped both to Hennessy. She was horrified watching them ride off.

'Must you rope him like an animal?'

'He's lucky he's not chained as was the custom. He'll stay put until after his sister's marriage for he'd stop it if he could. Billy's objecting to his sponging on Adina.'

'I'm sure Adina doesn't see it that way. She frets over Barney.'

He laughed shortly. 'Is that what you believe?'

'Well, she just sits about—'

'They all sit about till you kick 'em in the rump and send 'em packing.'

'But surely if they were handled differently—'

'How do you consider these people be handled, Miss Moynan? Come, I'm interested for if you're going to live among them, and you are, you must have definite attitudes otherwise they'll know and you'll be in real trouble. What you don't understand is that Barney doesn't really resent me for this, he just decides to give in for a while, it's easier; then when he thinks I've forgotten about him he takes off again.'

'He should be treated with kindness. Given a chance.'

'He's had many chances. He's healthy and strong with enough education to work at many tasks but he won't do it. He'd rather steal food or the money to buy it. He drinks too much. He's been in the lockup twice this year and I'm tired of bailing him out. I'm weary of chasing him up too. His father was one of my best hands. And his mother was well thought of.'

'There may be sound reasons why he doesn't settle.'

'Laziness for one. I can't help my people if they won't help themselves.'

'They're not *your* people.'

'Have you forgotten? It doesn't do to forget.'

She was shocked. This knowledgeable confident ambitious man, part of the civilisation she knew, blood-brother to Barney Cook? Aeons separated the two, the gap so wide one would have thought it unbridgeable. Too angry for coherence she babbled, a little breathless at keeping up with him as they walked their mounts from the camp to the road.

'They are *not* your people, they are nomads. A stone-age people. Savages.'

'True enough of my grandmother. She would stop at nothing.'

'But you can't expect Barney to be . . . well . . . responsible. Not as others. Not as you.' Her face flamed. 'I mean, you can't expect Barney to fit in.'

'So I "fit in", do I?'

'You know what I mean. You don't have to *try* to fit in. It's not important to you. You don't care.'

'I don't care?' His fury was sudden and terrible. 'It doesn't matter? So! I've played the fool more expertly than I thought or are you too naive, too stupid perhaps to see that if I hadn't told myself it didn't matter I would have gone mad? It seems I've become too clever, so cunning I can convince everyone I've accepted my lot simply because my rebellions are so trivial and harmless as not to embarrass. I confront the world with the justifiable little explosions, the trifling outbursts, the interesting understandable ones because they are just enough to arouse pity in women and patronage in men, while the deep dangerous rebellions lie safely buried, so deeply they ferment – and God, how they ferment.' He threw back his head laughing, a hard and terrible sound on the deserted road and she wanted to run, to gallop off yet somehow could not. 'I can only allow myself to vent bitterness on a pariah fly.' His stockwhip curled as a sliver of red-brown against the blue, its red silk tip gleaming, and Alannah's eyes fastened on the black speck in the dust, a flattened blowfly. Then something even fiercer and deeper took hold of him and grew until with all the strength of his powerful body he swung the whip around and about his head in great circles, hurling it at the helpless earth, at bushes, at the tall gums till they shivered over her head, leaves shimmering and fluttering and scattering around her. He went on slashing and beating and thudding until all was chaos about him and he was spent. And she too was spent watching his violence, feeling it as if it were actually against her. Perhaps it was against her for she was the other world. She shuddered. She had been frightened of him many times but never so sharply as now. But he folded his whip calmly and rode beside her, silent and remote as if the heart and will had been flogged from him to leave him lonely and desolate. She could not bear it and put out an impulsive hand. He did not notice her gesture and she drew back hastily, appalled at herself. They rode home to Erins Pride in silence.

O'Shea was riding down but her father and young Ned would travel to Sydney by coach, and even this gave Alannah a sense of her father hurrying off to some mysterious existence he did not attempt to discuss with her. At least Con was settling into his room to display his guns and shined-up boots and new clothes tailored in Goulburn. He talked enviously of Melbourne tailoring and what he'd heard of the city, a city he meant to visit before long. His restlessness disturbed her for he seemed more than ever

137

transient. They all three moved in a state of near-suspension
with little to say to each other and welcomed the small
diversion of Adina's marriage. In a white dress Hetty had
made for her, clutching a posy of Huie's choicest blooms,
Adina Cook laid her hand in Billy Warwick's and made her
responses so softly few could hear her. Joey was nowhere to
be seen. But next morning O'Shea rode in to Goulburn and
brought him home, for the first time in his life in a drunken
stupor, inert across his saddle. Two days later she stood
watching O'Shea, her father, and the reluctant Ned disappear along the road to Goulburn and the Sydney coach
with a loneliness so intense it took all her strength and
courage to turn and stroll down the slight hill to the
white-painted, green-shuttered house glinting in the morning sun. But it looked a friendly house, she decided with a lift
of her heart. A happy house – or she intended it to be. In any
case, as her aunt would remind her, she, Alannah Moynan,
had 'made her bed'. She felt a small tremble of excitement.
For the first time in her life she was in command of her own
home. Even more important, in control of her own life. Her
step quickened.

Because it was the weekend they had camped overnight
north-east of the old Government township of Bungonia,
towards the caves and the rugged country of the Shoalhaven
– Hal and Roy Elston of Wiena, Burrendah's Paddy Two,
Hennessy from the Pride offloading his Saturday drafting to
Jimmy Ryan (Hennessy would contrive anything to join a
'roo hunt, particularly a forbidden one), Jamie and Con
Moynan. Con's head swam, stuffed with Hennessy's bush
lore, a monologue of facts but chiefly fable, related with a
wealth of Celtic gesture and in dramatically ominous tones
lightened, if one could call it that, with his malicious Irish
humour against candlelight or lantern glow, preferably to
the far-distant note of the curlew, eerie and, to Con, strange.
'Leave the small stuff, man. Don't waste toime or shot from
your foine gun on the warrigals. Save yeself and your horse
for the big reds and greys.' Con had accustomed himself to

skinning on the spot: with the body of the 'roo still warm, Hennessy would make quick expert cuts with his sharpest knife, take the 'roo skin in both hands, put his foot on the animal's neck and strip off the hide, tail to head, with one deft pull, leaving the quivering pulpy flesh for the dogs. The Blacks stole the tails so they must be well guarded until taken home for soup, the sinews for sewing hides and harness, wounds too if there was nought else to hand. The tough grainless kangaroo leather was valuable as was the fur for coats and rugs. The men had many and personal idiosyncrasies in their bagging of kangaroos and most wouldn't risk flying bullets, but Con had polished and primed his precious gun until it sparkled under the autumn sun.

Now they thundered in the chase – the big 'roos, dogs, horses, each sweating rider urging on his dog with shouts and whoops of excitement. The young 'flying does' were swift but the older ones and those carrying young were soon hard pressed by the dogs, and here and there a doe would stoop and let her young from the pouch to hop for cover like some skinny vertical rat. The horses were racing their hearts out, even so they could not keep up with the dogs. The large powerful staghounds, and others resembling greyhounds only taller and heavier, were all fighting-fit and catching up on the great kangaroos despite their thirty-foot leaps over fallen timbers, fences, anything in their paths, propelled by their great tails, the thump-thump of their powerful hind feet striking the ground like drumbeats. Nearing the slopes the mob was splitting up over the flat scrubby uneven ground, making for cover, crashing into and through the brush, the greys merging with the vegetation to the exasperation of the Elstons for they must be bagged before they hit thick bush. Horses, dogs, kangaroos and men formed one mad glorious ecstatic mêlée; branches came crashing, leaves and vines entangling as man and horse struggled to keep up with the dogs and the dogs with their prey.

Con rode madly and wildly, half blind and breathless with excitement, a little confused (though he would never admit it) by the savage ritual that to the others was as natural as bubbling kangaroo-tail soup over a campfire. He couldn't distinguish men or dogs or even the big greys, only hear the thrashing about and the wild barking and voices shouting and urging, and see shapes and shadows moving between trees. He pulled up sharply, for Hennessy's greyhound Digger had bailed up an old man kangaroo, a big grey, a huge beast baulked and dangerous because hedged in by a waterhole then the swamp behind it. Rearing up over six feet in height it was kicking savagely with its hind feet. Someone – Paddy Two, Con thought – was creeping through the brush with his stirrup-iron poised. Hal – was it Hal? – gripped his stockwhip butt at the ready. But a yell from above made him look up, blinking. Jamie balanced on a rock ledge, shouting down, at him Con thought though he couldn't distinguish words. He stumbled off his horse. Jamie was shouting again. What was it the men had told him round some campfire, or had it been in their quarters . . . A 'roo is easily killed with a light blow on the right spot on the back of the head. The right spot . . . What exactly was the right spot? He couldn't remember if they had told him, he was past thinking in this mêlée; he could only feel, sense, hear and smell the overpowering sickening odour of animals and men. He took a firm grip on his rifle.

Hennessy's dog was game. He went straight for the 'roo's throat for once he took firm hold he would grapple savagely to throw the beast. But the kangaroo caught Digger and ripped the dog's front leg and shoulder almost off, and the screaming and writhing of the bloody pulp of an animal was so earsplitting and awful, Con screamed with it – shoot the dog, Hennessy! *Shoot!* Hennessy loved his dog, all the men loved their dogs, but Hennessy must shoot his own mangled animal for the dog was going mad. But where were the firearms? He couldn't recall who had carried guns. Tormented by Digger's screams and half-demented with rage against the great savage beast of a kangaroo he plunged forward, raising his gun.

His rifle went spinning and the world whirled madly around him. The 'roo had him in an embrace, its terrible claws digging into his shoulder. With almost a loving gesture the beast lifted him bodily while Con shouted and squirmed,

140

his legs kicking helplessly. Through the nightmare, and shouting from somewhere, he felt the animal rip his breeches from waist to below his knee and he was staring down at his own flesh hanging in a long strip, blood oozing and dripping. In shock he felt nothing, not then. But ahhh . . . now the pain was there and he was shrieking, sick at the dreadful bloody mess of his body. The beast was half dragging, half carrying him to the waterhole, to drown him in its mire and his own blood and he was making sounds, a terrible stupid gibberish. A shot – was it a shot? – from a distance. A great distance. A long way off . . .

Chapter Seven

'I HEAR Archy Mead almost turned handsprings at his first taste of your honey scones. He bought up the whole batch at the church fête and him so careful with his shillings – and rightly so,' Ida added smugly.

'Archy Mead couldn't run from an overweight hippo let alone turn somersaults,' her daughter scorned.

'He's well-nourished, no more. I hear he's not only expanding his saddlery in Goulburn but buying one in Yass. Any girl with a head on her shoulders would set her cap at him rather than burn up in the saltbush with a shilly-shallying Jack-of-all-trades who can't make up his mind if it's Monday or Friday.'

'I'll have Joey Bowes the minute he asks me.' Grace's pillow-thumping from the linen room grew violent.

'Mead?' A long pause and Alannah, attempting to read her letters in what she had hoped would be privacy, knew her aunt was about to put her foot in things – again. 'I do believe that's the portly little man who tripped over my cabin trunk in that dreadful debacle at the coach-station – and I've said it before and I'll say it again, I never did hold with coach depots in public-houses.'

'Mr Mead can't help being long-sighted.'

'He can help being too mean to buy proper spectacles,' Grace pursued, sensing an ally in her mistress's somewhat quaint little aunt.

'He won't make old bones. Working with leather is bad for the lungs. You don't want your girl widowed young with a mortgage and a family to support alone, do you, Ida Charlton?'

'I'm sure you're a well-meaning body, Mrs Carney, but I'll ask you to leave my daughter's future in my hands.'

'In mine, Ma. In *mine.*'

'You're not of age, Grace Charlton, so get about your business.'

Further argument was lost in Grace's clatter as she escaped to outdoor chores. Alannah swept up her mail and retreated to the verandah, cold with the winds off early snows but where it was sunny and certainly more peaceful. The morning, as most mornings now, rang with the discord of women; even the hearty cheerful Grace was snapping at heads, particularly Joey's when he did come by which was precious seldom for a courting man as her mother constantly reminded her. Delia Carney's voice had grown uncomfortably shrill in laying down the law, particularly to Ida Charlton who was a law unto herself, since arriving with her best mantle under a layer of dust, wearing her most accomplished air of martyrdom and encumbered with so many bags and boxes it had taken two strapping lads to bring her out from Goulburn, to be met with the shock of her nephew's accident. For the first time in her cosy imperious life Aunt Delia was baffled and baulked by a country and people who would not behave as she expected, and perhaps never again, Alannah suspected, would she be her precise decisive self. Further, there had soon surfaced an even deeper reason for her agitation: her brother – *your* father as she began alluding to Owen – had engaged a housekeeper, a draper's widow from Hackney, even if it *were* Hackney proper and not Hackney Wick – Eveline Purdue precise as to the difference – with nary a reference pertaining to housekeeping and only something from an emporium where she had sold gloves! This . . . *person* . . . had been installed at Brighton even before she, Owen's own kin, had been decently out of the door. 'But I have made my bed and will lie in it,' she had assured her niece, selecting the most comfortable room in the house and beckoning Grace in her wake with her well-trained crook of finger, 'even if I expire in it as I undoubtedly shall, prematurely of course.' Why could not Alannah have made her life in Sydney among respectable citizens instead of among ex-convicts and Blacks wandering the bush, and Chinese the roads – foreigners!

And she had threatened to take the coach straight back to Sydney if not ship to England at her first sight of Alannah in her working garb.

'I'll give thanks in my prayers that Sister Monica is not here to see those . . . those . . .' Words failed her.

'Breeks, Annie McKenzie calls them.'

'As for the prioress—'

'I wear them only about Burrendah, Aunt. Skirts elsewhere.'

'But you ride astride, Alannah. *Astride*! Like some Jezebel. People are talking. And what your father would say I cannot bear to think.'

'I hope he would say I'm being practical. I'm certainly comfortable. People will get used to the idea, you'll see.'

'You've changed, and not for the better.'

'Yes, I've changed,' Alannah agreed quietly, 'but whether for better or worse I cannot tell. Nor do I particularly care.'

She made a further attempt to finish Simon Aldercott's letter: . . . 'My decision to accept O'Shea's offer was not a hasty one, even after your father's assurances, for it was difficult for me to see how a man of O'Shea's reputation, and ancestry, could make a suitable employer.' Alannah almost tossed the letter aside.

'Nor did I look forward to travel between his properties – I am a scholar not a farmer – but not even in my most fevered imaginings did I picture anything as desolate and abandoned by God and man as the country I have traversed these past weeks.' Dear God, she thought wildly, had O'Shea sent him off, green as they put it, wandering the backblocks simply because he didn't like the cut of his frock-coat? The man was quite capable of doing so. 'Shortly after you receive this I shall be at Erins Pride (I admit to finding the name slightly ostentatious). It will still be upcountry living though I have been assured the place is more civilised than most and if one so delicately reared as yourself can face life there then I am prepared to accept my lot knowing you will be close by. Australia is rich indeed in its courageous and capable women, and your brother must surely appreciate your womanly support in his work . . .'

Con's work? Now she did throw the letter down, feeling anything but courageous or capable. Even when Simon was at his most affable he succeeded in irritating her; why, even in pique, had she suggested O'Shea employ him? She must have been quite mad. But since it was she who had set wheels in motion she had no choice but to try to establish good relations all round – and Burrendah certainly needed good relations all round. Yet how was she to explain Con's absence and ensuing silence; he had been gone two weeks already without explanation or a goodbye. On his previous jaunts with Jamie – if he *were* with Jamie now – he had at least left a note, arriving home with rough and bearded men who pillaged the larders and fought with the stockmen so savagely Dan Charlton had knocked heads together to quieten all down. But when she reproached her brother he only laughed or sulked or complained of his lack of money which meant, usually, he was gambling at the Goulburn pubs or at poker with Hennessy and his cronies. He was not only bored, he was broke, he insisted, and she had given him from her own purse, aware she was making a mistake in indulging him, but if she tried to reason with him he grumbled that he had no taste for working the land, he had been forced to the place and all knew it. She dared not caution him further about his drinking; everyone drank in Australia, he argued, the heat set them off. His injuries at the 'roo hunt and ensuing fever had laid him dangerously low for weeks. He had lost much blood and it said a lot for bush doctoring that he was even alive when they brought him in. Nursing him back to life in those first terrible days she had needed all her strength and patience in dealing, not only with him, but with her aunt's distaste for Australia swollen to hate.

'A savage country. Savage men and savage beasts.' Delia Carney was beside herself.

'There's nothing gentle about an Irish hunt,' Alannah reasoned.

'The place is unfit for civilised living. As soon as Con can travel your Papa must take us home.'

'To Ireland?' Alannah stared at her, aghast. 'Burrendah is

my home now. But you're free to sail any time you wish, you know that. Meanwhile, Papa is not to be told of Con's accident. Papa can do nothing here. Con is recovering.'

'I've ordered that mischievous, nay, evil young man from the house.'

'I say who comes and goes about Burrendah, Aunt Delia.'

'But he's the cause of this catastrophe. I won't have him hanging about Con's room, disturbing him.' Refusing to be soothed she hovered about her nephew, interfering with Ida's work and bullying Grace. Worse turmoil broke out when the usually reserved Rob stamped through the house to pin Jamie to a wall with a steel-like arm across the boy's chest.

'Move a muscle, lad, and I'll tighten my grip. Thee took young Moynan on that hunt with the lad knowing nought or little about the game.'

'He swore he was a good hunter,' Jamie gasped.

'In Ireland perhaps. There's a difference.'

'I shouted at him not to dismount.'

'He was not prepared for the kill. I've talked to the men – and don't take out thy temper on them for they said nought against thee – but thou knowest, as all good bushmen know, one must approach a bailed-up 'roo with a waddy in each hand, poke the left one at the beast and when he grabs it finish him off with the right.'

'Everyone knows that.'

'Not young Moynan apparently. It was not explained to him. He owes his life, not to thy care but to Roy Elston's markmanship.'

'I shouted down at him. He heard what I said but he always goes his own way. And take your hands off me, you bogland peasant.'

'I thrashed thee as a child and I can do so now.' And he sent the boy thudding against the wall. Jamie shouted obscenities. Rob slapped him down again. 'And *that* for language before ladies. Now get thee on thy horse, thou art coming home. And no more sneaking off, I'll be watching thee.'

When Con was finally up and about again he was pale, too

thin and with a scar he would carry all his life. His aunt fussed in feeding him up on broth and oatmeal, and her special honeyed milk which he promptly threw to the pigs. Then one morning he was simply not there and his abrupt disappearance transmitted itself in unease to a household already at loggerheads over many issues. What was happening to the life she had come here so confidently, even joyously, to live? Alannah wondered. What was happening to her aunt, aimless where she had never been so, unsure of herself, seeking tasks about a house where she had no authority or even contentment, out of her close familiar world into this alien one and making a bad fist of the change. Nor had she, Alannah decided, expected to be so daunted by these nonchalant, self-sufficient, cruel – yes, cruel – country folk. There was a violence, though subdued and all the worse for its jocularity, beneath the surface of these people with their 'near enough is good enough' and their amused condescension, even contempt, for the new chum.

'You starve your dogs,' she had protested to Paddy Three – Maguire? Yes, Maguire – as he squatted painting emu eggs from Jamie's last sojourn on the Black Soil Plains as souvenirs for Mrs Elston to take to England.

'They won't work if we feed 'em up.'

'You keep them chained in the open in bitter weather.'

'To toughen 'em up, Miss. To toughen 'em.' Laughing as if she were daft. 'If such upsets ye ye'd best sail back to the Emerald Isle.'

'I'm not sailing anywhere, Mr Maguire.'

'Then keep away from the tail-docking and other such matters, for in thruth 'tis a bloody business making the lambs' tails fly and us spattered with blood frum head to toe like butchers.'

'If you're painting those in your leisure time, which I hope you are, get on with it.'

Now she stirred to riffle through her letters. She had thought that to read her mail would soothe her but it was having the opposite effect. She took up her father's letter.

'. . . I think of you constantly, my dearest daughter, likewise of Conall but he has not written and you mention him so seldom I feel he is finding Burrendah dull – or wholly absorbing. I hope it is the latter. Your aunt will have mentioned, perhaps, my housekeeper, [Mentioned? She had talked of little else] a necessary adjunct since your aunt decided to shoulder her responsibilities which she calls 'making her bed'. I deplore this long separation as much as you do but for the present it is unavoidable. We shall have years together at Burrendah, please God, when I am past working and must sit with my grandchildren about me and watch my son run the property as a prosperous country squire . . .' Con a country squire? She felt a little lightheaded. Besides, so like her father to call any addition to his household an 'adjunct'. 'I am off to Newcastle, a port crowded with men returning from the ill-fated fields up north. It is possible there are mechanics among them, perhaps even some of the operative engineers who came out in '53 on one of Mrs Chisholm's ships. If I cannot be at Burrendah before spring I look forward to having you at Brighton for Christmas. We have made many changes [We?] that might make the house more acceptable in your eyes . . .' She put the letter aside. It was June. Even if he did come she felt he would not stay long, and her anger as usual centred on Brick O'Shea for she was convinced if it hadn't been for his interference her father would have settled comfortably into country life. She needed her father. She certainly needed someone . . .

'Miss *Moy* . . . *nan!*' Grace's sing-song meant Joey Bowes had made his promised detour. She was riding out with him to meet the last of the flocks coming from the south after a spell at the Gamble station, escaping kitchen turmoil for a few hours – but with a more urgent reason in mind; though it was only days since she had spoken with Joey he might, just might, have heard something more. But beyond his greeting he was silent, even withdrawn as they rode towards the hills. She hesitated to force him on the defensive for she had come to depend on him when Rob was away, preferring his quiet competence to Rob's polite but taciturn company. It wasn't until they paused for tea amid the sprouting green that she said casually:

'I suppose no news is good news but I hoped you'd have something fresh to tell me.'

'I promised to send word if news come through, Miss.'

'I know, but . . .'

'Still nought. Except – but it can mean nothing.'

'There *is* something then?'

'Only that diggers came through yesterday from the Adelong with talk of trouble down there with the Chinks. But there's always trouble with the Chinks. And it doesn't mean your brother is even there, let alone mixed up in their fights.'

'But it's possible – is that what you mean?'

'If he's with Jamie it is, for Jamie goes looking for trouble. I guessed he was up to something when he wriggled out of going with Rob. He's been too quiet of late, too willing to take over. 'Tain't like him to pitch in willingly if you know what I mean. And where Jamie is, your brother is like to be these days – and best if he is really, for new chums can lose themselves out in that country.'

'And Barney could be along?'

He laughed shortly. 'If Barney Cook loses himself it's by choice. Best Black tracker in these parts. New chums often take him along for he knows a way over any mountain or along any river you can name; even Jamie takes him along if he's planning something special.' Gulping the last of his post 'n'rails.

'Don't they care at Erins Pride?'

He looked uncomfortable. 'They're used to Jamie going off, y'see. Besides, Mrs Hetty's too fussed over Mrs Noakes, she's poorly and they've sent to Goulburn for a doctor.'

'Then Rob Witherstone must go after my brother.'

'Rob won't be back inside weeks, Miss. He might have to go a long way for the thirty head of fat stock he's after.'

'I want my brother back, Joey. I need him here. I need—' She broke off, aghast at the name trembling on her lips.

'No one can do anything about Jamie but Mr O'Shea, Miss Moynan.' He stared into his mug seemingly absorbed in counting tea leaves. 'Leastways, he tries.'

'Then he must go after them.'

He looked shocked. 'The master only comes through for the shearing, on his way south – unless there's something important.'

'This is important.'

'He won't come, Miss. He can't. Not with his mill and his stables and school and all else down there.'

'I shall insist that he come. A letter won't do, the mails are too slow. And if he should be out of town a telegraph message could just lie about.' Remembering Birubi's careless luxury and Raunie's inquisitive eyes. 'You must go down, Joey. You'll find him, I know. You seem to know his movements and his haunts better than anyone.'

'I can't go, Miss.' Looking startled then miserable. 'I must stay close to the Pride when Rob's away. Them's orders.'

'Then I give you further orders – and will answer for them.' Stubbornly, and recklessly perhaps, for after all Con was a grown man and able to look after himself – but was he? She strove to push aside the disturbing haunting vision of a gun in her brother's hand. But she did not argue further for Joey had grown sullen, resentful, she knew, of any possible alteration to his beloved daily routine.

A week later an incident occurred that clinched her resolve. A couple of 'old hands' – except that they were not old but strong and vigorous-looking men – confronted her as she came up from the kitchen garden. The younger pushed a letter into her hands.

'Man down near the Fish gave us this for Miss Moynan, mistress of Burrendah. I reckon you're the one?' At her nod his bold faintly bloodshot eyes travelled over her, trim in her breeks, but she stared back for she would not be intimidated. 'We come out of our way to bring it but he said you'd make it worth our while.' The letter was sealed but stained and thumb-marked. Ripping it open she checked the signature – yes, it was Con's. 'Could do with a bit o' scauf,' the man added.

'Some baccy too.' His companion hawked and spat too close to her feet.

'You'll get both at the house,' she snapped. 'Tell them you've spoken to me.' She was anxious to be rid of them for there were too many runaway felons and disgruntled gold-seekers wandering the roads. And bushrangers coming down out of the hills.

'Could do with a lot o' things,' the younger grinned.

'You won't get anything idling here.' Still they took their time in riding off, laughing together at some secret joke.

'Alannah,' she read, 'I'm going south with the kid.' Con had always called Jamie 'the kid'. 'Don't fuss if I'm not back before spring. You've hands galore to run the place. I can't bear the boredom of your fancy doll's-house any longer.'

Doll's-house? Was that what she was making of Burrendah? Con must see it so. She needed to talk with someone and who else but Hetty, for the letter concerned the Pride as well as Burrendah. She must risk Hetty's irritation. And if she should need a further excuse for her visit there was always Simon Aldercott whom she preferred to greet at the Pride rather than have him ride to Burrendah causing gossip. She would go today, now! She packed a change of clothes, gave no explanation to her aunt other than that she considered a few days at the Pride would be good for her, and set out in the soft evening light.

She found Erins Pride in a sort of limbo, as if awaiting direction, certainly impetus from some outside source. She was shocked at the change in Moll Noakes, this plump, suddenly old woman slumped awkwardly in a chair by the fire, her hands gripping its arms tightly, breathing heavily as though from some terrible exhaustion yet conveying a determined if confused energy. From time to time her hand wavered across her forehead then pressed to her left temple, and she kept rubbing her arm. It was clear she was in great distress and Patty and Belle Carmody crept about looking scared. Hetty made a show of heeding Alannah while tackling what seemed half a dozen tasks at once – her 'multitude of sins' as she often alluded to her duties. Finally, she shrugged.

'We can't do anything about Master Jamie, Miss Moynan, until Rob arrives.'

'Jamie?' Moll twisted herself about slowly, and painfully it was clear, to stare at Alannah. 'The devil's spawn, that one. I knowed it when he was born, I know it now and I knowed it in between. He's a bad one, like his mother.'

'You must not speak so of the mistress.' Hetty was not only shocked but angry.

'Mistress, is it? I'm mistress here.'

'Mrs O'Shea is mistress of Erins Pride wherever she may be and you know it. You should not gossip so, certainly not before the girls as you do. And the hands. I've heard you.'

Moll gave out something resembling a cackle. ''Tis not gossip, 'tis gospel truth. O'Shea's wife has been trouble since she was spewed from a fever ship in a devilish red dress to set her cap at men with her wicked witchy ways.'

'No witchcraft, I'm sure.' Alannah attempted to soothe. 'Unless you call great charm, witchcraft.'

'Charm? Aye, she'll charm you. She'll wind you about her little finger stopping at naught to get her way.' She leant forward, her face contorted. 'Moll Noakes knows the heart o' her so never trust her, gal. She will use you as she did Miss Merrill, bless the poor soul. She lost her will to live, y' see – ah, she did that. She would never have been thrown from a horse even in a storm—'

'No sense in going over the past,' Hetty fretted. 'I'm always telling you so.'

'He was set to marry her, see, but there were words written on a bit o' pasteboard years afore by Brick's young mother – black blood there but only meself to know of it an' I'd sooner have cut m' heart out than blabber it to the world for I'd spent m' life hiding the truth. But when Maddy lay dying and meself not there to stay her fears she wrote the truth, a reminder, see, knowing I were the only one on the station could read. But I never knowed o' that scrap o' paper for it were stolen an' lost down the years till it come into that wanton's hands an' she passed it to her lover who hated O'Shea—'

'If you must blabber that old story tell the truth of it. And you can't because you don't really know it.'

'I know it.'

'All anyone knows is what the world knows – that a bit o' pasteboard with faded words saying Mr O'Shea was a Black was set before the Governor by Major Merrill at a public dinner. An old scandal and none now to care.'

'I care.'

'What can it matter how it came into the Major's hands. Or who was the cause of it?'

'She were the cause of it.' Moll's fists beat an urgent restless tattoo on the chair arms. 'She waited her chance and took it, she a gipsy and he a Black, making them twain in her scheming mind. An' in the doing of it she broke the heart o' the gal he was to marry as if she'd used poison on her. Or spells. Wicked witchy spells, I say.'

'Did Mrs O'Shea take a knife to Miss Merrill?' An exasperated Hetty brandished one before throwing it down with a clatter. 'No, she did not. Did she use a pistol against her? No, she did not. And you talk too much and too often of spells and potions and witchcraft. Nor can anyone be blamed for a broken heart for who really knows how or when that happens – except that you're breaking mine as I stand here rolling pastry and trying not to hear your evil words.'

'I'll speak m' piece as I've always done. An' I'll speak it now. If I could do for that hussy I would. If I could get m' hands around her throat I'd twist it like I'd twist a chicken's neck.' Moll had almost twisted herself out of her chair in rage and excitement and Hetty pushed her back none too gently.

'She's been making such threats ever since I can remember.' Hetty shook a doleful head at Alannah. 'It must come out, you see, so we let her talk. But we don't tell the master for we don't know what he'd do.' She set the soup tureen on the table with an exasperated thump. 'Where *is* that doctor?'

'Won't have no sawbones.' Moll was agitated again. 'I'll see him into his grave. And I'll see you into yours.' Her words were becoming blurred and slurred and Hetty looked alarmed.

'Hush. Oh, do *hush*.'

But Moll pushed her aside, struggling to her feet, to stand trembling, seeking footholds. Hetty rushed to support her but the woman shook her off again, shuddering in a kind of spasm.

'*Patty!*' Hetty shouted. '*Belle!*'

Moll staggered, stood quivering like an old tree in a storm then fell, striking the floor with a sickening jolt. Patty rushed in to be ordered off for Joey, for anyone.

'It's what I've been afraid of, the lightning stroke,' Hetty gasped, supporting the woman while dashing cold water over her head and face. 'I've seen it coming. I've seen such before.' Joey and young Richie managed to lift the unconscious woman and carry her to her bed where Hetty mopped her off and packed her about with blankets and pillows while all stood about in awe. Finally she pressed fingers to Moll's pulse. 'Not dead but near it I'd say. How long she'll stay in the coma who can tell? Liniment to the spine and mustard poultices to the feet and what more any doctor can do I don't know. But whatever happens it's us will bear the brunt of it.' She sniffed. 'And when you come right down to it, who else but Hetty Witherstone?'

Indecisive and helpless, the men drifted back to their work, all except Joey whom Hetty ordered to stay close. Simon clattered in – he clattered a great deal when nervous – solicitous but as helpless as the others and he too soon drifted off. Watching Hetty transfer Moll's keys to her own waistbelt Alannah found something significant, almost symbolic in the gesture as the end of one matriarchy and the beginning of another.

'Mr O'Shea must be told,' Hetty pronounced. 'He'll not forgive us otherwise.' And Alannah grasped her opportunity.

'Send Joey down. He can explain about Jamie and my brother.'

'Mr O'Shea is not likely to come for your brother, Miss Moynan.' Tartly.

'He must come. My father can't wander this country looking for Con, any more than I can.'

'Mr O'Shea's not likely to come for Master Jamie, perhaps not even for Mrs Noakes, but at least he can tell us what to do. In any case, Joey's here to attend to the Pride's affairs.'

154

'And Burrendah's. Mr O'Shea made that clear, remember?'

'Are you ordering Joey down?' Hetty's manner was distinctly cool.

'Someone must go and Joey's reliable. I'll answer for my decision.'

'If you say so – I suppose. All the same, I wouldn't be in your shoes if Master Jamie and your brother walked in here before the master arrives – that's if he does decide to come. Well then, Joey Bowes, you heard?'

'If it's an order, I heard.'

'It's an order.' Alannah was determined, ignoring Hetty's hostility. She would deal with that later. 'And you'll go by coach. By the look of Mrs Noakes there's no time for riding down.'

'I'll try Parramatta first. Mr O'Shea often stays at the Sheaf when passing through.'

He was respectful and helpful but still reluctant. Nevertheless he would carry out her wishes to the letter. Hetty smoothed Moll's skin with a damp cloth. 'Can she hear us?' Alannah whispered.

'It's not likely.'

'Is all she said of the Merrills and Mr O'Shea true?' Alannah was troubled, uneasy somehow, for even if Raunie O'Shea had shattered Brick's prospects in life, his early youthful ambitions, by causing the death of the woman he was about to marry, he had not only made Raunie his mistress but he had married her. What a bond there must be between them!

'Most of it, I reckon. Even so, we mind our business about it. Rob knows more than most but he lets it be, it's an old story and all tell it different. It's just that Moll needs to talk it out for whatever touches her foster-son touches her; they've been together all their lives. She hates the master's wife, we know that. And hate can kill, as I keep telling her. Never let the sun go down on your anger, I say, the Good Book don't approve.'

She was beginning to sound too much like her Aunt Delia for Alannah's taste and she decided not to stay another night. Nor would she come to Erins Pride until Hetty was friendly again. She felt isolated, a little lonely, wanting her own place, her Place of the Swan. She warmed to the sight of Simon Aldercott hastening from his classroom to wish her God-speed. At least she had one uncritical unquestioning friend.

She rode home with the sun warm on her face. Nearing Burrendah she left the road as she often did and eased Mourne along the tracks, then the sheep-walks over the rise and fall of the little slopes where sheep moved, heads down, or by hollows where they clustered in the long shadows of trees so still they resembled painted beasts in a world locked in the deep silence of late afternoon. Near the homestead cattle slouched in the lush byways and fringes of the Creek. As always, she paused on a favourite rise for her first glimpse of her Place of the Swan, a sight that always warmed and welcomed her, then took the wisp of path beside the waterway. The sharp little wind had dropped at the going down of the sun that made long yellow patches over the grass. She alighted at her favourite spot – the spinney, as she called it – where she often strolled or sat to watch the Creek gurgle over the stones in the shallows. The world had a cool stillness about it and there was an infinite peace in the dull green slopes and distant smudges of purple hills fronting a sky streaked with the rich red of sunset. She slapped Mourne to graze and parted the willow fronds that trailed the lush grass carpet and stood in the sweet cool of seclusion broken only by the murmur of water over stones or the sudden flight of a bird. This had always been an enchanted place to her, reminding her of favourite places in Ireland, and she felt as she had sometimes felt when walking abruptly from the familiarity of an Irish lane to some haunting circle – in Ireland one expected such. It happened. But one did not expect mysterious, even faintly sinister corners in this sunny, wide-open country, certainly one did not expect pagan places of uneasy spirits. It was as if the sun had gone behind a cloud where there were no clouds and a cold bleak wind was coiling about her and she shivered . . . Yet she stayed, enthralled, held by the magic of it. She could not move. She did not want to move. Her eyes grew hazy, looking out at far-off things and her lips moved, whispering to whoever . . . whatever . . . might be there. 'Bring Con home. Bring him home.' Then, abruptly, she was back with the sky still bright through the shimmering fronds and Mourne nuzzling and cropping the sweet grass, and the strange cloudy moment was gone as the dream it must have been and Burrendah was along a bit and sunlight bathed her. She shook off her strange bewildering mood, a little ashamed of it, for this was not Ireland, this was Australia with no piled-up centuries of mysticism and barbarism. This was a new, bright and promising world.

But moving out from her coppice, letting the fronds trail behind her, she froze. A man stood watching her, a dark bearded man and though he was some distance away she recognised the younger digger of some days before. She had thought him gone along with his mate, and the shock of his presence in this solitary place – her own private particular place – as if barring her way consciously or otherwise, made her move towards her mare. But the man moved with her and towards her and she felt threatened yet strove to set the feeling aside, for the house was nearby and this was her land and she must not show alarm, only authority and decision.

'What are you doing here?' she called.

'Camped along a bit. By the stream.'

'Who gave you permission to camp on my property?'

He gave a derisive little laugh, pushing aside the ferns and brush as he came closer. She took a firmer grip on her whip, not much of a weapon but it reassured a little. 'You're a new chum,' he sneered, 'so wouldn't know the ways o' the road.'

'You will leave here at once.'

'Will I now?' Still he came on. 'Women didn't ought to roam the bush alone for them that does is asking for something though they might not know it.' He looked flushed and she knew he had been drinking.

'I'll wander my own land as I please.'

'And it pleases ye to wander near m' camp, eh? I can see that. You look hoighty-toighty enough today in your skirts an' all but I reckon you're no better than y' should be.'

'Get out of my way.'

He laughed again, unpleasantly. 'Ye can scarce blame a man for thinking ye've the habits of a goldfields tart when ye wander about showing yeself off in breeches. Tight ones at that.' He put a heavy hand on her shoulder, squeezing it till his fingers hurt and his flesh burned through her clothing. His hand slid roughly down her arm, ripping her blouse.

'Take your hand away,' she gasped, wrenching free. He slapped his open hand across her mouth while his other arm slid around her waist to pull her hard against him. He pressed his body against hers. She freed her mouth enough to scream, crookedly and faintly, but he cut off the sound.

'Nought to scream about. Ye'll like it, ye'll see. Be still now,' he growled for she was struggling violently. ''Twill hurt less if ye don't struggle.'

She fought him but he was too strong for her, dragging her down with him into the bracken. She could only gulp and gasp behind his hand, striving for breath, tasting the dirt and sourness of him, drawing in the sickly sweet stench of his body. His free hand clawed at her clothes, baring her breasts and he was over her, nuzzling and mouthing them. She twisted herself about in her disgust and managed to scream again, a useless scream for they were too far from the house to be heard. He was swearing, mouthing threats as well as obscene talk. He hit her a stinging blow to the cheek. She lay stunned but roused when he began dragging at his own clothes. She must have kicked him for he grunted, baulked long enough for her to grope for and grasp her whip and hit out in panic. Awed perhaps by her ferocity he backed slightly, crouching, hands up against her fury. But he made for her again. He was strong and vicious as he spreadeagled himself over her and she could scarcely breathe under his weight. She could not fight him much longer, she knew it, when mercifully he was dragged from her.

'Y' bloody fool, didn't I warn ye? Do y' want to be strung up? And m'self along with ye? Y' stupid bloody fool of a galah!'

Now they were fighting each other. And could kill each other for all she cared. She ran wildly through the ferns, her legs torn and cut by bracken, her hair loose, clutching her torn clothes about her. Bleeding and horribly dishevelled she scrambled up on Mourne and galloped home to her Place of the Swan.

With Paddys Two and Three, Dan rode along the Creek but all returned to say they had found nothing but the remains of a camp fire. Their concern was as sincere as Aunt Delia's was noisy and Ida's angry as the women bathed and bandaged and imposed impossible restrictions – she was not to ride out alone in future! 'See what comes of dressing like that hussy, George Sand?' her aunt scolded. But she was wearing her skirt, Alannah protested uselessly for despite their outrage she had the feeling they were condemning her for having somehow brought the situation about – by her boldness, or arrogance, or she might even be exaggerating a little in their eyes. The men looked ill-at-ease. They'd never had trouble of this kind before; diggers on the road looked grim, even menacing, and could certainly be bold, but a man knew he'd get the term of his natural life if he touched an unwilling woman, particularly a woman of standing. But the man had tried to rape her, she insisted, and even Grace looked shocked at her frankness. He would set the troopers after the pair, Dan assured them, but men on the road were usually good bushmen and once in the hills it would be almost impossible to find them. Alannah cringed at the idea of the police for even now the tale would be spreading. She had managed to get herself into an embarrassing situation, a new chum fool. A fine pioneer she was turning out when women managed to survive alone hundreds of miles from their neighbours. All the same . . . She grew stubborn. And very determined. Next morning she saddled Mourne and rode for miles. She would go where she pleased and how – in her breeks if she wished it – and be damned to Australia and its people!

The Southern Alps were packed tight with snow and it was very cold but the wind had dropped and the world around him was clear and still as Brick paused, enjoying the sun on his back, before riding down to Burrendah. He had ridden up to the Pride for he wanted Glenora on the journey down with Moll, a trip that would not be easy no matter how carefully he arranged it. The problem of transporting a hapless helpless woman immersed in liniment and poultices with little hope held out of even partial recovery, would be immense. He had already set plans in motion to take her down by hired coach, Fay Witherstone along as nurse, and himself and Richie as outriders. He had sent Joey on to Birubi from Parramatta where the youth had found him horse-trading at Andrew Donald's stud. He had pledged Joey to secrecy over Moll Noakes' illness as well as over Miss Moynan's demands, arming the youth with letters to Mrs O'Shea and Mr Owen Moynan, discreet letters, for the less either knew of the real reasons for his trip inland the better. Raunie would fuss at his sudden departure for Erins Pride but his promise to bring Jamie home would mollify her, at least for a time. He had no intention of chasing after Jamie, certainly not after young Moynan – playing down the youth's disappearance to his father as a harmless prank for he needed Moynan in Sydney, not racketing about Australia chasing wayward offspring. As for Barney Cook, he could spend the rest of his life in gaol for all Brick cared. A pox on all three! He had come for Moll and Moll alone – until he had found the stock-money gone.

He had gone to Joey's desk to store George Elston's fifty pounds, the man eager to get fat stock at five pounds a head, and had passed over the bags of small coin kept for incidentals, groping at the back for the canvas bag usually stuffed with sovereigns. The bag was there but less one hundred pounds. He had stormed through the Pride, irked by his lifelong but now misplaced trust of unlocked cupboards, doors, cash-boxes and bags, and his insistence on one rule and one only; money taken and spent to be done so openly and known to all. Aldercott had been quite properly horrified at such casual handling of coin outside his fine copperplate entries, while Hetty had frowned.

'It was all there when Rob left, I saw him hand it to Joey. There's been no cause to touch a penny of it.' She met his eyes reluctantly and he had cut off speculation firmly.

'If Joey made no mention of it then he knows nothing.'

'It's that Barney.' She was always stubborn and often venomous over Barney Cook. But one name, one certainty kept running through Brick's consciousness: Jamie. Jamie had stolen the money, he was convinced of it, and a terrible anger was driving him to find the boy. But curiously, unjustly and unreasonably he knew, his immediate anger was directed not against his son but against Alannah Moynan for confronting him with the situation; more, for in a way creating it; worse, for driving him down to Burrendah homestead on this chill morning to where she stood in her flimsy gown, only a shawl clutched about her against the cold, against the world, against him . . . At the sight of her standing waiting his hostility grew until it almost choked him because he knew she was waiting for him and it was a terrible thing to know for it must not be. Even more terrible than his vulnerability before her was hers before him; it laid her open to his temper, his will, his assault if he so wished it. She had no defence against him and the knowledge of it was driving him mad.

There was something about Brick O'Shea that daunted Alannah so that she did not move forward to greet him. But neither did she move back though it was colder than she would have expected had she thought about it at all. She had sprung from bed in her warm room pausing only to draw a shawl about her before slipping out to the verandah – and, incredibly, there he was. Unexpected and wonderful. But he was not smiling, indeed there was something in his face that made her shiver with more than the cold, and because she did not know what else to do she began to mouth banalities.

161

'You look . . . weary.'

'Weary?' His breath made tiny gusts of vapour as he hitched Glenora roughly to her verandah post. 'What else? I've had precious little rest since you arrived in the colony, Miss Moynan, and even less since you took over the running of Burrendah.'

'That's not *fair!*' Reeling a little from his savage blast. 'You came because of Mrs Noakes and not because of my brother, I know that: most certainly not to please or help me. But since you are here the least you can do is look for Con. He doesn't know this country or its people.'

'He seems to be learning the ways of both quickly enough. And you should have acquired knowledge enough by now to seek him out for yourself.'

'You actually expect me to wander the country?'

'Why not? It seems to be a habit of yours. But if you plan to go far afield I advise you to learn how to protect yourself against all comers, for they'll have you down in the bracken before asking what's for supper – oh yes, I heard of your "episode" as it's called, embellished and embroidered so you're even with child in some quarters.'

'How dare people gossip so.'

'You can scarcely blame 'em – wait, I don't give a damn if you wear pantaloons or a clown's garb or those breeches you're famous for, but simple bush folk look at things differently. This is not Ireland where passions are rigorously submerged and where such as yourself can wander any-where, sacrosanct under rules set down by generations of your class. Besides, Ireland doesn't have goldfields packed with men of mixed habits, race and ideas. This country has grown any-old-how, without rules to speak of, a raw place where women have always been scarce and men need them so much that social taboos, at least in the bush, have largely been dispensed with. Men will do almost anything to get women and have lost their fear of prison; too many have seen the inside of too many to care. A woman must know how to look out for herself without fuss or complaint and the first rule is not to go asking for trouble—'

'I'll wear what I please and go where I like, certainly on

my own land.' She was trembling and not only from the cold. 'Why . . . oh, *why* is it always like this? I came out as I do every day, hoping to see you here, not stopping to think or dress or anything, and there you were and I was glad because you had come. *Glad*—'

'Don't you dare cry,' he throbbed. 'Not one tear, do you hear?'

'Don't shout at me. And don't wake the house.'

'Why not? I'm up and about.' To her dismay he began stamping up and down, his great boots thumping while she stood transfixed, staring at this madman roaring away at the world – or was it really at her? 'We've no place for women who cry their way through crises – and button up that thing you're wearing,' he stopped dead to thunder at her. 'If I should go on your mad mission it's to find Jamie – Barney too to get him out of my hair – but I haven't the time or stomach to wander the Adelong looking for your brother. He can tumble down a mine shaft and rot there for all I give a damn.'

'I've not asked you to wander the Adelong. I don't even know where it is.'

'Then why bring me here? God damn it, I have machines arriving from England, wagons bogged on the way up from the coast, trouble at my mine, my cook has walked out of my pub, my gem store has been robbed, and an acting troupe has managed to lose itself in a sandstorm in country where it had no business to be. And if that's not enough, my crops up north are nigh eaten out by a 'hopper plague. But I know I'll not get a moment's rest till I haul your brother back to be coddled and spoiled by his womenfolk. Well then, I'll get him out of my hair too, for good I swear it, for if he gives me trouble I'll string him up and account for the deed later. And the way I feel about the Moynan clan right now I could string you up along with him, and your father for begetting you!'

He paused, breathing heavily, staring at her, devouring her, she felt, and she tried to draw her nightgown about her throat but there was a button missing. Buttons should not be missing; it seemed suddenly and terribly important that they were not. His eyes moved beyond her to her open door and it seemed to drive him to further excesses. He threw down his whip in a terrible blazing fury while she stared at him in amazement.

'Do up those buttons or I'll have my bit of fun here and now on your doorstep. I've energy enough for *that*. Do you hear me, girl? Do up your gown!'

Chapter Eight

'BIG BORU McConickey!'

Brick O'Shea shouted into the crowded confusion of the Fighting Cock, misty with steam from drying-out clothing and smoke from the roaring fires. There was a sickly stench of sweating unwashed bodies. Teutonic voices boomed, French phrases skipped and Californians outshouted each other. A tipsy sailor, jumped ship and as far from the sea as he could get, danced a hornpipe to someone's out-of-tune accordion. From the back rooms, grandly called parlours, blasts of song swamped all else to die abruptly or slur drunkenly away. In one corner drunken diggers were knocking the tops off champagne, sherry and porter bottles and swilling their contents into a great wooden tub. A digger fumbled off his boots then his apologies for socks and sank his feet into the mixture, his companions following suit.

'*McConickey!*' O'Shea thundered.

A slumped-over digger, head down on the counter, lurched upright, staggered, grinned stupidly and threw a matey arm about O'Shea's shoulders. In no mood for jovial drunks Brick slammed him to the wall, the man's arms shattering glasses on the way. An unmistakably Irish head (despite his mixed parentage) shot up from behind the counter and Big Boru drew himself to his full five-feet-two for which he compensated with a zealously guarded reputation for roguery, a fierce vocabulary and the body-guard of a huge Highland barman dubbed MacHercules. Earsplitting Gaelic oaths were directed at the stunned customer before Boru swung from his shoulder without a chance of connecting. His victim, swaying at the bar, sank to the floor. Brick stepped over him, grasped Boru by his

165

neckerchief and propped him up before him. The man's eyes popped and his flailing arms sent another stack of glasses flying.

'Holy Mither, Mr O'Shea. Oi'm losing m'stock.'

'All cracked and chipped so good riddance.' Brick released him to slam a coin on the smeary counter. 'Sixpence. Plenty for your private store so bring out your best.'

'Ah now, Mr O'Shea, 'tis a shilling a nobbler on the Reef. All over for that matter.'

'Sixpence. Your best and be quick about it.'

Boru's ugly wizened face fell but he obeyed, if reluctantly, shielding his bottle as he set it on the counter. Brick held it to the light, wiped a salvaged glass on his sleeve and slopped in the spirit. He poured it down his throat with equal abandon. 'Now then! Have you seen my son?'

'Young Jamie?'

'He could be travelling with a young Irishman.'

'Frum the ould sod, is it?' Making a furtive attempt to slide his precious bottle out of Brick's range if not out of sight. 'There are so many, Mr O'Shea.'

'You'd not forget this one for he acts the landed gentry. Barney could be with one or both – and don't pretend you've forgotten Barney Cook.'

'The nigger with the sister with the tender smile?' Boru assumed a beatific expression as he wiped the counter with a filthy rag. He had been cook at Wiena until chased from the cookhouse by the butcher's cleaver, brandished by shearers infuriated by his practice of serving soup made from calves' heads while selling the mutton at a profit. ' 'Tis not loikely Oi'll forget her.'

'You'd best forget her. She married Billy Warwick.'

'Indade? 'Tis a shame then for I fancied that black bit of a colleen.' He gloomed. 'Y' see, Mr O'Shea, 'tis not so much the black skin of 'em that makes a man think twice, 'tis their wailing look, something in the eyes that gives ye the creeps and 'tis a shame for we're arl brothers and sisters under the skin.'

'Stop talking bloody rot and answer me.' To Boru's dismay Brick filled his glass again. 'Have you seen Jamie?'

166

'By the Holy Cross Oi've not sighted the lad. Nor his Oirish friend.'

'If Barney's about say so for I swear I'll have the truth.'

'Sent him packing yisterday,' Boru ventured hastily, slapping the cloth about in triumph as if he'd kicked him out personally. 'Can't have trouble at the Fighting Cock with gintlemen favourin' me with their patronage. There's a party of squatters in m'best parlour this minute, exclusive loike.'

'I heard them, exclusive like.'

'And others of real education, gintlemen with fancy shined-up boots, talking poetry and writing letters on fancy paper with them new founting pens – and wondrous wee things they be.' He dragged one from his pocket, thought better of exposing such a novelty and thrust it from sight again. 'No use for poetry meself but—'

'Use for the trinkets remittance men are fool enough to carry about, and with Barney competing you'd have trouble getting your hands on even a plug of tobacco. You'd dub him in for half a peg, I know that, but I want the three together if possible.' Somehow Boru had managed to stopper his whiskey but with a swipe Brick knocked the stopper loose again. 'The truth now, for you'd sell your own mother if you could make a profit on the deal. Have you seen Jamie and his Irish friend?'

'By the Holy Cross—'

'Don't waste your oaths on me, you Irish bastard.'

'Now there's a darty lie wherever y' heard it for m' mither and faarther were wed before m' very eyes, dragged to the altar by Father Timothy himself with all Ballylickey and most of Bantry Bay come over to see. The good faarther set the matter roight an' that's a fact.'

'The truth,' Brick boomed.

'Oi've not set eyes on the lad nor his friend and three Our Fathers and three Hail Marys if I lie.' Sweating like a pig he crossed himself and drew the rag about his sweating neck before blowing his nose in it. 'Ye could troy the grog shop a mile along the river. Even better, Queanbeyan.'

'I came through that way.' Near Queanbeyan there had

been much talk of youths leaving their mark in camp brawls, gambling for high stakes and causing resentment by bouts of lavish spending, though many spoke indulgently of the one called Jamie who laughed, win or lose, and was always ready with drinks all round. But brows creased over the quick-tempered Irish youth who brandished his pistol with a reckless abandon, such a fancy weapon it was a wonder it hadn't been stolen. Brick cursed young Moynan as a boastful blunderer with a genius for making enemies – yet did not doubt Jamie would be urging the other on, not in so many words but by his assurance in a world he knew well. Jamie thrived on sensation and drama and would partake of both wherever they could be found or engendered. 'Bring Barney in,' Brick added curtly. 'You know where he is so don't lie about it. Meanwhile, tucker and a bed.'

'Oi've a nice cut o' beef down the hall,' Boru hedged, intent on his bottle, 'with linen on the table an' arl. I keep a woman for the niceties.' His hand crept out to close on what remained of his spirit, his lips moving in silent prayer.

'And a single room.'

The man looked scared. ''Tis an honour you do the Fighting Cock but Oi've not a pallet left this night.'

'Find one. Clean at that.' Brick upended the bottle and finished the dregs. He would sleep in a bed tonight or his name was not Black Brick O'Shea. It had been hard travelling from Goulburn through Bungendore to Queanbeyan, weaving, climbing, dipping again to save an hour or so of light to explore backwaters. Luckily the rain had been light and fitful so he had managed his average of six miles an hour, spelling Glenora as little as he dared while mingling with the flotsam and jetsam of the creeks flowing into the North and South Fish Rivers. The men were strangers and suspicious, but he had squatted beside them in the mullock as they twirled their muddied cradles or gulped stewed tea, arguing in their goldfields lingo – a blackhaired youth and a young Irishman? A Black called Barney? If he knew the fields now he'd know the Irish were ten a penny, and black-haired vagabonds almost as cheap. But the darky . . . There *had* been a nigger causing trouble and his name

168

could have been Barney. A big Swede had trounced him for filching his gold dust, then someone's jack-knife had disappeared, and food from the tents, with the nigger blamed for it all. Then there was that fracas over the revolver . . . Brick downed his bitter tea and left them to their arguments; at least he had a lead. He'd taken a chance on leaving a valuable horse, even though stabled and in the charge of a well-bribed groom, but Glenora needed feed and a warm place instead of weathering it outside his window – if he should get a window – with the reins twisted about his wrist as he slept. Tonight he would risk horse thieves. Tonight he would sleep in a bed if he had to kick everyone from the pub to do it.

Boru wiped the bottle's emptiness with tears in his eyes as he might wash a corpse for a wake. 'The only spare is in the General's room for which he's paid, Mr O'Shea, an' he'd make the very de'il of a fuss if I even put m' hand on his door.'

'I'm not partial to drummed-out half-pay younger sons shipped to the colonies for the family good.'

'Nor I.' Boru was virtuous and indignant. 'Army gits the blown meat an' the creaking cots. But the General has the lingo of the gintry with tales of the wars to keep the men around the bar, an' money to spend, an' a foine watch to flash, a snuffbox too though what he wants with that I cannot tell. And he has a fist as thick as a tree – or MacHercules here – to protect himself an' his gewgaws. 'Tis not worth m' hide to argue with the General, Mr O'Shea.'

'I can make a fist too.' Brick picked up his pack. 'Is it the General's room or your own?'

'Ye wouldn't loike mine, Mr O'Shea, 'tis a hole in the wall an' bang against the privy. Ye'd git no sleep at arl, at arl.'

'Then it's the General's.'

' 'Tis himself won't loike it but first along the back hall.'

'A good table now,' Brick warned. 'Fresh meat or I'll ram it down your throat, maggots and all.'

'Fresh killed, sir. I saw to it meself.'

The food wasn't at all bad but he was too weary to eat much. As he pressed his way to his room MacHercules stood goggling at a bag of gold dust dangled over his head by the now clean-footed, pink-legged diggers. 'Good pay, Mac, for the loan of your muscles. The stuff's good and rich so take it in with the compliments of the house, no explanations given, none asked – they're too far gone in there to ask questions. But if they press you, tell 'em we celebrate a strike.' Aided and abetted by the drunken diggers the tub of foetid liquor wavered and tilted its way to the back parlour and the equally tipsy squatters. The General's door squeaked as Brick let himself in to rum-soured air and snores like tumbril drums. He felt for the empty bed. Too tired to light a candle and search for lice he sprawled on the stretcher, boots and all. In any case boots were safer on one's feet. With his pack for a pillow and his revolver tucked beneath it he turned over to sleep.

He was awakened instantly and fully as was his way by a parade-ground bellow, to stare up at a dripping candle and a pistol held too lightly by a big fellow, obviously the General, in crumpled nightshirt, bull legs quivering as violently as his hand – no 'younger son', this! The pistol trembled and the candle dripped as the man swayed, half asleep, probably still drunk, mumbling largely incoherent threats. But Brick caught 'snuffbox' and 'watch' and with a wary eye on the gun he directed it towards the open window and collected his possessions. 'I believe I know the thief. Your snuffbox could be in the creek by now for I doubt if he knows what it is, but he has an excellent knowledge of timepieces. Put that thing away, be quiet, and wait.'

Confused, and assisted by a strategic push, the man sprawled on his cot again to snore his head off. Brick climbed from the window and crept to the back of the inn amid the refuse and smell of urine and horses' dung and bodies sprawled all-which-way. Here and there someone would stir to stare sleepily or drunkenly or both, then turn over dragging his neighbour's blanket with him. A dog barked, setting off other mongrels, as Brick moved silently towards the creek, for if Barney were hiding it would be where the scrub was thickest. A shadow darted and he was in pursuit, knowing his quarry, running as swiftly as the wily darting

170

creature before him. The shadow stilled to lose itself in darker shadows. Brick waited. The shadow darted again and he sprang. A tussle and he had pinned Barney Cook against a tree.

'Hand over your loot, Barney, all of it, don't hide a thing or you'll be in worse trouble. You disturbed a victim, a big mistake. Everything, Barney, or this will speak and you won't like it.'

The half-breed's eyes rolled at the sight of the revolver. All guns were magical but O'Shea's was unequalled in its power and all knew it. Barney coveted O'Shea's revolver yet would not touch it for it carried O'Shea within it and could be fatal. Barney Cook's life was waged as a battle between his desires and his fear of O'Shea's powers, and he stood stiffly as Brick went through his pockets, dragging forth the watch, the snuffbox, a pair of cufflinks and a signet ring. Another pocket was stuffed with coins, more wealth probably than Barney would possess over his lifetime.

'I'll return this stuff and say nothing of you if you tell where Master Jamie and young Mr Moynan are headed.' Barney turned his head away but Brick dragged him round to face him. 'Talk or you'll be back to gaol.'

'They're around, boss.'

'When did you last see them.'

'Three . . . four days.'

'When you ran out on them?'

'They have fun round Queanbeyan. Laugh, make friends, spend money. Plenty money.'

Brick tinkled coins. 'Is this some of it?'

'Jamie give me, I not take, not this time, boss, so 'elp me Gawd.' He raised a solemn right hand.

'If you didn't steal from them why did you run away?'

'Me come here.'

'Where you're less likely to run into troopers, eh?'

'Me come back to river.' He was indignant but dignified. 'Him Yealanbidgee River.'

'The old excuse of sentimental walkabouts around your ancient tribal grounds has worn thin. It's wearing thin all over the country.'

'I go home to Pride, boss,' Barney wheedled.

'You do not go "home".'

'I stay here then? This my country.'

'Nor will you stay here. You'll help me track those two without a wasted step or go to gaol. And this time you'll stay there.' Barney feared O'Shea but he feared gaol more: if he did what O'Shea wanted and quick all would be well, it might even bring rewards, but you could never please a gaol. You did what a gaol wanted and quick but you stayed there all the same. 'Were they making for the Adelong? Answer me.'

'They go after fun, boss. All time, fun. Fun on the Reef.'

He would be taking a chance but, he felt, a slight one, for these days all life went west to the Adelong fields. Jamie and Con Moynan could be well ahead but would be lingering around inns and homesteads and native camps, taking their time. By crossing the Cotter, then the Brindabellas and the Goodradigbee River, keeping the Bogong Peaks far to the south in perspective, he could follow the creeks down into Tumut. He'd save days.

'We'll cross the Range,' he ordered Barney. 'The shortest routes all the way.'

'Hard going, boss. Plenty rain about.'

'There'll be rain whichever way we go but it's not heavy enough yet to soak the ground. And even if it does you know every inch of that country, the inches I don't know. And you're a good fisherman. Plenty of cod in the rivers.'

Barney knew it was the end of argument. Even so, Brick tied him to a tree and went back to wake the General and slam his trinkets into his surprised hands. But tipsy as the man was, he was devious enough to try to claim ring and cufflinks until Brick hinted at the police. 'And keep a still tongue over this business or I'll spread the word that "Lieutenant" is engraved on the watch; you'd have some explaining to do. The room is yours, "Lieutenant", if you're even that. You're welcome to the place; it stinks.'

He scooped up the man's blanket along with his own and returned to where Barney slumped against his tree. He covered him and stretched out close by. But he only dozed, stirring to stare up at the stars, drawn by his old childhood sense of disembodiment. But he wasn't alone in the black space for a face came and went, a face with Alannah Moynan's rebellious eyes. Then, oddly, it became Barbara's face . . . He rolled over trying to sleep, struggling with the idea of Barbara-Alannah. Damned fool, he cursed himself, at forty-eight coveting a young girl. He was a madman becoming more lunatic, wanting to laugh out loud at himself lying under the trees with a vision of Alannah standing on Burrendah's doorstep waiting for him . . . He should not, must not, centre his thoughts on this young impulsive untried girl, this virgin of a girl, no matter how she invaded and troubled his nights. Yet, how avoid her? Alannah Moynan was possessing his life. Possessing him. Finally, mercifully, his restlessness died a little and he slept.

The Reef at Adelong was booming. Everywhere batteries reared their awkward ugly heads. Brick guided Glenora through the slush and confusion of Camp Street, an arrow path between steep hills where tents clung precariously to the slopes, a street lined with trading huts and eating houses, bark-and-slab humpies and inns swarming with diggers, the gangs who worked for a wage in the mines and the drifting penniless pickers scrabbling from field to field, wandering up into the hills seeking the last of the alluvial, fighting it out for leftovers with the Chinese who scavenged from abandoned holes and mullock heaps, breeding suspicion and hate, fouling the water and fighting their faction fights with razor-sharp knives and iron pikeheads on sapling poles, while drawing about them the worst of vagabonds, male and female, yellow and white.

At Tumut, O'Shea had heard an irate hosteller threaten to set the troopers – if he could find them – on the trail of an Irish youth for shooting up his gaming tables. Not that someone wasn't always shooting up his gaming tables but never as recklessly or with such arrogance; an Irishman trailing a reputation for destruction, particularly in his cups. Further, Brick had recognised Con Moynan's watch –

flourished nightly around the Pride's dining-table – displayed by a digger with a red beard, and had paid what the rogue demanded; whether the fellow had won it at cards as he insisted mattered not, for Con, and doubtless Jamie, had passed by. But there was no sign or sound of them in the inns and eating-places of Camp Street and a hunch, more, a foreboding sent him riding back to Lower Adelong and its settled respectability of fruiterers and smithies and pinafored children and the domesticity of women keeping house. Glenora needed spelling so he decided to send Barney into the hills to reconnoitre, with instructions – and Barney knew better than to disobey – to meet him at the junction of the creeks; ten . . . twelve miles of crossing and recrossing water as the road climbed into the black-timbered range, a world of hawks and crows and tumbling falls and great gums and ferns and mist and cold. And now, rain. The silent, faintly mysterious, menacing, scrabbling world of the Chinese. But he had time only to brew black tea over his fire before Barney rode down upon him, excited, eyes popping and, Brick could see, scared.

'Big yabber this morning, boss. Chinks.' Barney hated the Chinks.

'I told you to keep clear of them.'

'But white men too, from all over. They swear to run Chinks out of Adelong, out of whole country.'

'How do you know all this?'

'All run through bush, yabbering. All mixed up, boss, fighting each other. All fight each other.'

'How far did you ride?'

'Two . . . three miles. Road up there on hill best. See far, far down.'

He had no real reason to believe that Jamie and Con were involved in what sounded an all-out mob war but it was worth a try, so they climbed the track grandly called road leading up and away from the creek that, swollen now, went tumbling and singing in the gorge to their left. As they climbed they lost the sound of it, and only steep paths winding down through the jungle of ferns towards tents with smoke coiling about them and the distant sound of pickaxes, indicated human life. Here on the road they were alone in a damp and eerie world. One mile . . . two, and Brick paused. Far to their left mountains glowed blue and purple in stray shafts of weak afternoon sun, but around them the mist had become a drizzle and the wind over the ridges was cold. Magpies dipped, black with glints of white, and the only sound was the wailing wind and the mournful cry of crows. The desolate manless silence pricked at them and Barney's eyes became melancholy with his longing for warm fires and walls, even at that moment, gaol walls – at least they would keep him warm. Barney hated the cold. He pointed towards the Tumbarumba Road.

'Smoke, boss. Big smoke.'

Big smoke there was, covering a wide area and sifting through trees to hang and mingle with the rain. Too much smoke for a camp fire or, in this damp, bushfire. There was something about it, lazy, heavy and ominous-looking, that made Brick spur the horses and climb until they came out suddenly into a cleared patch, only large trees left standing. What was left of the camp was blackened and charred, a terrible desolation of smouldering fires and tents hacked to pieces and stores scattered, hunks of meat and broken rice bags and dried fish and tea trodden into the mud. Dogs rummaged in the mess and the caw of crows was a lonely sound. There was something uncanny in the stillness and solitude. Brick turned over the body of a Chinese covered in bloodied mud. There were dead whites too, for this was a white men's camp by the look of the store boxes and gear. A lone figure with a shocked Oriental face moved out from the bushes, gesticulated, then became threatening. Brick aimed his revolver. The Chinese fled.

They turned to face a curious little procession straggling through the trees: a group of white youths, dirty and dishevelled, armed with spades, pickaxes and bits of paling, some arguing, others brawling with faces aflare with violence. A directionless mob that stopped dead at the sight of O'Shea and Barney in the background. The violence died to sullenness when Brick raised his revolver. They possessed no firearms that Brick could see in a glance for his eyes had scarcely moved from Jamie, head down, leading his own horse and another piled with what looked like muddy blankets. Jamie raised his head, stopped dead and stared back. The dark red stain seemed to be spreading and with an oath and a swift movement Brick whipped the cloths aside; yes, it was Con Moynan, or what was left of him for he had been torn apart by knives. Hacked to death by the look of it. Sickened, he covered the corpse, grabbed Jamie and threw him to the ground. The others stood frozen.

'They murdered him!' Jamie screamed. 'They *murdered* him!'

'Stop that caterwauling,' Brick thundered. 'Who murdered him? This lot?'

'No. Chinks, with whites along. They came down on us early, in the dark, and broke up camp, thieving and burning.'

'Did they use firearms?'

'They didn't have to, they surprised us. But he . . . Con . . . wouldn't leave well alone. At first he fired over their heads, keeping it up, scaring hell out of 'em the way he does. Then he went after them, maiming, and they turned on him, twelve – more – rushing in to knife him. They kept driving the knives in, out, in, out . . . You know what their knives are like.' He was close to hysteria, shrieking it out to the stunned group, to his stepfather, to the world. 'They kept on stabbing . . . *stabbing* . . .'

'You led him into it. You led him on.'

Jamie shrieked obscenities, a muddy sodden creature huddled in the dirt, hating the world and all in it, hating the dead man, hating the China Men, hating his stepfather. Until now nothing much had gone wrong for Jamie Lorne-O'Shea. He'd always had his way in the end. Now all was wrong. This was not supposed to have happened. But O'Shea, staring over the boy's head, made a sudden move. He wrenched open the youth's saddlebag and dragged forth a bloody scalp with a long pigtail attached. He held it aloft. The lank black hair hung, bits of flesh drooping from it.

'God damn you,' he roared, 'you've been scalping. Don't lie or I'll beat the truth out of this rabble. I've hunted you for stealing coin, among other things, to find you scalping Chinese. Damn you, no one from the House of O'Shea scalps.'

'They knifed him – we had to go after them. We trailed 'em for miles. Caught a few too. I'm not the only one to scalp.'

O'Shea flung the awful mess of blood and flesh and hair far out into the bush, tore the shirt from the frantic youth and brought his whip down hard on his back. Jamie yelled in surprise then in horror and pain, squirming in the mud, attempting to escape the savagery of the whip but there was no escape. He screamed, kicking his heels but Brick did not pause, save once to grasp his victim and force him face down again. The rhythmic flogging went on until Jamie ceased fighting and sank, moaning, his back mangled and bleeding. He lay cursing until his protests died in whimpers. O'Shea stood looking down on him, breathing heavily, getting his own breath. After a while he lifted the boy, flung him across his saddle then turned to the silent motionless gang of vagabonds and adventurers.

'I shall send the police into these mountains. Count yourselves lucky I don't send them after you. Even so, you'd be wise to make yourselves scarce.'

He motioned Barney to follow with the laden horses and they picked their way back the paths they had come amid the smell of death and carnage and desolation, the only life pariah dogs snuffling in the rubbish, and a hawk hanging pendulant in the grey and misty sky.

Burrendah was coming to light. Alannah turned over to the world and lay still, watching the day filter through the curtains. There had been rain but a weak sun was piercing the blinds. She knew she would not sleep again so dragged on a gown and padded to the verandah as had become her habit of a morning. It was cold. She turned to go inside but, glancing back, stilled – Brick O'Shea was riding the road to Burrendah. So unexpected was he that she stood staring, half expecting him to disappear as some image conjured up by her fancy, but no – it was he. As he came close she saw his clothes were badly stained and his boots caked with mud; furthermore, that he was unsmiling. There was something different about him and she waited hesitant, somehow a little afraid. Still silent, still unsmiling, he put his hand under her elbow and gripped it hard. 'Don't waken anyone. Not yet. I must talk to you.' He led her firmly into her little sitting-room.

'There's something wrong,' she said quietly. 'I know it. And I know it's to do with Con.'

'It is.' As she gripped his arm. 'That's right, hold on to me for there's no easy way to say it. Your brother's dead, Alannah.'

A curious lightness crept down her limbs and if he had not led her to a chair she would have staggered or fallen. She sat trying to control the spasms of her body while his voice advanced and receded, drifting about, explaining something . . . Con buried near Queanbeyan – where was Queanbeyan? Troopers sent after his murderers – Con murdered? Bizarrely she wanted to laugh but instead there was the sound of a woman weeping and of course it was herself and she could not stop until something was pressed to her lips and she gulped and fire coursed through her. Mercifully the confusion and sadness dimmed a little, but only briefly for she was trembling again, gulping tears. His arms seemed to be supporting her and she heard herself say clearly, precisely:

'I don't believe you. It's just not true.'

'It's true.'

'*No*. Con can't be dead – not Con. He's done something foolish and is afraid to come home and wants everyone to believe he's dead. He does silly things sometimes.'

'Stop talking so.'

'He'll hide till the trouble, whatever it is, dies down then he'll be back, you'll see.'

'He won't be back, he's dead.' He held her tightly. 'Oh, my *dear* girl.' Did he really say that? She wasn't certain of anything just then. Distracted, she whispered:

'Not Con. Not *Con*. He's all I have of the old days.'

'You have your father.'

'No. He's not here. He's not anywhere . . .' She grew

angry, speaking wildly. 'My father should be here. Why isn't he here?'

'He doesn't know of this. All I told him was that your brother went on an expedition.'

'If my father had been here this would not have happened.'

'It would have happened sooner or later. Your brother went looking for trouble. He found it.'

'You're always so . . . reasonable.' She pushed him away with all her strength. 'Stoic – that's the word. As if you expect awful things to happen.'

'Hate me if you must but don't hate the country. Don't blame it for not being Ireland. Put Ireland behind you. Stop clinging to fairy-tale houses and gardens and coppices to dream in.'

'A doll's-house, that's what Con called Burrendah. He said I was making it a doll's-house.'

'He was right.'

'I'm cold.' She shivered. 'My hands are cold.'

He folded them in his, pressing them, warming them through. He turned the palms upward and put his face to one then the other and the warmth of his breath was wonderful. His lips on her wrists made her skin tingle and she felt as if life was flowing through her again. And because she could not help it she brushed her lips across his bent head. Leaning against him she felt calmer. She straightened.

'I'll manage,' she assured him. 'Really I will.'

She went inside to waken her aunt.

Simon Aldercott held his pen as precisely as he held his back but with his head slightly to one side as was his habit when concentrating on long columns of figures; besides, it hindered the familiar slide of his spectacles that distorted his vision until he replaced them with his usual pat. He moved his ledgers and lists about with hands so well scrubbed there seemed a veil over them like faint abrasive gloves, and his nails were fanatically clean as if from a need to flaunt some badge of dedication before a world he was constantly required to please. His linen was old but fiercely laundered (Hetty's heart ached for all bachelors) while his neckties remained neatly folded through summer heat and winter gale. 'Ye'll be wiping off the sweat with 'em, mate, when the heat really gets to ye,' Hennessy taunted, setting the men laughing. They laughed at him long and often but he could only try to ignore them. He had no intention of letting down the standards by which he had survived an adolescence devoted to pleasing those Aldercotts counting out their zealously guarded guineas for his begrudged but, in the end, thorough education.

Born the son of an Enthusiast shopkeeper dealing in fine cloths, ironically in the shadow of Lichfield Cathedral, he had been 'taken up' by his beaky-nosed vigilante uncles horrified at their younger brother not only descending to trade but Methodism; worse, flaunting Wesleyan habits before decent conformist church-goers by insisting his son 'improve the shining hour' by propping an open book before him on his saddle, and the lad such an indifferent horseman he was for ever retrieving some tattered tome from hedge or haystack. Uncles Nathan, Hubert and Ambrose had conspired to save their nephew's threatened but still redeemable soul (even if his father was past redemption) by offering him a one-way passage to under Capricorn, knowing nothing of the country to which they would ship him but convinced any colony labouring under a convict taint must benefit from an Aldercott (blood *must* tell), who could and would 'raise the tone' of any haunt of evil, at the same time removing an embarrassment from a family that had always voted Tory and embraced Army or Church. So here he was, raising the tone, or attempting to do so, of a colony that persisted in going its cheerful bawdy way, ignoring him but to torment one more impoverished clerk shuttled about the country on his employer's whim, getting the feel of it, as some minion put it. Buying, selling, accounting, acting secretary when required, keeping ledgers and lists and conducting hastily assembled classes of polyglot children in makeshift huts held more or less vertical by some unseen force, he was a Jack-of-all-trades of O'Shea enterprises. Ordered here then

180

there by bushmen with big muscles and bigger hats, scrambling off bullock-drays onto wagons or carts, falling off scarcely-broke horses, even tied to the saddle – where there was a saddle – of wild and fearsome beasts, travelling by river where possible, on foot where nothing else offered, he had embarked on a fearsome trek through the back-country of New South Wales and Victoria, never knowing and often past caring if he were pointed north, south, east or west; struggling through seared and apparently endless miles to be burnt and blistered, bitten by mosquitoes, tormented by flies and ants, confronted by snakes, and birds and beasts he could not name and hoped never to see again; running from mobs of cattle that appeared out of dust clouds like demon beasts or forced to listen to their death moans when bogged in black gluey mud; existing on milkless tea, damper, kangaroo meat and other nauseous flesh he spat out to go hungry; loathing the flat vistas of waterless scrubby plains and appalled by the meandering cracks in the earth that should have been streams, with always the fear that he would be sent north to some worse hell at Moreton Bay. But somehow, anyhow, he had survived to return to his stint at Erins Pride, a Nirvana compared to the deserts where he had thought to die of longing for the green fields of his native Staffordshire, even more, for the neat market town of his birth.

Why had he endured it? Why did he stay? He straightened, pushed his books and papers aside, flexed his fingers for they were cold, and stood to stamp a foot hard for he was a victim of cramp. Thumping his way to the door he opened it wide on the sun as well as the distractions of children at play, men shouting, women gossiping or collecting washing, chimneys smoking from kitchen fires, all the day-by-day domestic life of a prosperous sheep station. He had chosen this little room adjoining the schoolroom as study and retreat for his spare moments, and sometimes his nights, daunted by the big House, but mainly because he could see the gates and along the road a way. Besides, there were cupboards where he could lock away not only his ledgers and letters but his notebooks tabulating his modest savings, even more importantly those personal diaries in which he recorded that secret life wherein he, as it were, unfolded his ties and exposed the flesh of his plans. Or, rather, his dreams . . .

With an occasional stamp on the wooden floor he stood gazing out on the folds of hills where sheep never seemed to move yet he supposed they must now and then. How different from English sheep. How different everything was. He could with some juggling of finances manage his passage back to the mists and soft twilights of his childhood and without the need to beseech the family for one penny, so what, in the end, kept him braving this awesome country? It was the promise, no, not even that, the *hope* of the girl Alannah riding through the gates to smile upon him. Even so, it could still be wishful thinking on his part for there was no reason why she should favour him when the colony was full of men of wealth and position. She puzzled him. But all women puzzled him . . . Did she even notice his efforts to adapt to a country she seemed to love – or at least her own corner of it? Did she realise it was for her that he had finally taken up O'Shea's unexpected and casual offer, through her father at that. Though Moynan had been tactful, even kind, he, Aldercott, had almost refused but in the end had accepted, for when Alannah had left Sydney for her Place of the Swan as she called it, it was as if a light had gone out and he could not see his way. He knew only one thing; wherever she was he must be. Particularly now. Yet no matter how attentive he was he was unable to comfort her in her sorrow for her brother – could anyone? He rode more often to Burrendah but she remained polite and very calm – too calm – and heartbreakingly remote, not only from him but from the world.

The open space before him was centred about the 'big tree', a giant stringy-bark around which most activities seemed to take place. But now the square was empty – no, not quite, for he had been staring at without really seeing the half-breed Adina, wife to Billy Warwick at Wiena; what was she doing here? He recalled that she was often here; odd that, for Wiena was a good twelve miles along the next valley. Yet she often sat there when she was not haunting the kitchen quarters bothering Hetty Witherstone no end. How did she get here? Perhaps she walked, for these people roamed great distances, appearing and disappearing as shadows, popping up again where and when least expected. Perhaps, like a stray puppy, she missed her old home; she did not seem a contented young woman which was sad for she looked quite pretty in her light shift with her black curls shining in the sun. Perhaps she was lonely in that tribal way these people had; perhaps she missed her brother who seemed either in gaol or living off her when he wasn't wandering off – up to no good as Hetty put it. The girl had not moved a muscle, just sat gazing ahead. Perhaps, like himself, she watched the road waiting for someone to ride in . . . Briefly, with the world silent and empty around them as if only they inhabited it, even though they had never spoken directly to each other, there seemed some communion, an unspoken understanding, a yearning for the unattainable that he sensed she too was enduring. In this way they were an alien pair, remote from the life around them, as if born to some other place, even on another planet, not part of the landscape and remote from the aims and urges of its native-born. In their unease, they were less than visitors. They were transients.

Standing in his doorway in his well brushed, too-heavy, too-formal garb he felt he understood this girl, native though she was, as she might possibly understand him and, curiously, though she had not turned her head his way and perhaps did not even know he was there, he did not feel quite so alone.

183

Chapter Nine

'ARROGANCE, YOUR pure merinos as you call 'em, boasting this is the greatest wool-producing country in the world if they can't get their clips down to the wharves. I've seen the Cove there black with masts, mine among 'em, and all sitting about on our butts waiting for wool bogged down for weeks . . . months . . . on your quagmires of roads with the fleece rotting in the bales.'

'Nowt to do but live with the wet, Heggett,' Mason bullied, stimulated by argument as an old hunting dog is stimulated by prey.

'Not much better in the dry as I hear it, with men and beasts half-blind from sandy-blight. Dust, mud and distances are the curse of your goddamned country.'

'Oh aye, but you've a big country too, Yankee. Our river traffic's noan so bad. It's growing.'

'Paddle-wheelers and barges are only good when the rivers run. Build roads, more railways and, while you're at it, get your telegraph through. You're only just connecting up your cities, man.'

'Who's to build roads and railways? Squatters aren't the only ones shouting for cheap labour and more of it.'

'Bring back your felons, then. From what I hear they dragged carts over your ruts and puddles out there as good as bullocks.'

'Under the lash, Captain.' Hugh Whaley filled his pipe with a hard concentration. 'You call yourself Yankee but your talk is all southern gentry. We don't use slaves in New South Wales any longer, at least not convict slaves.'

'Then bring 'em up from Van Diemen's Land.'

'We call it Tasmania these days.'

'The captain talks sense.' Will Purdue burped behind

a flabby hand. 'We need more banks. Certainly more brokers . . . What use insisting we're the greatest gold-producing country on the face of the globe if gold dust lies about in diggers' pockets handy to squander on harlots and whores?'

'And liquor – don't forget the Demon Drink,' Mason mocked. 'Truth is, Purdue, diggers don't trust your banks any more than they trust your fancy investments. They want cheap land, can't get it, so bury their brass in pickle jars or under floorboards where they can reach it.'

'The longer it lies about in pockets – or pickle jars – around Bendigo the better for our business, and your Old Lady of Threadneedle Street can whistle for shipments.' Kurt Herlicht crossed his finely-tailored legs. 'Even so, the country needs a good kick in the rump, it lives too comfortably on its fat. Even those rotten little coastal steamers need scrapping.'

'Those rotten little coastal steamers have served you well, I reckon. Don't see you jolting overland on any bullock-wagon; it's hang the expense and down to Melbourne by Cobb & Co., with a first-class cabin round to Sydney.'

And a first-class table at Brighton, Owen added silently, any night you're at a loose end waiting for O'Shea. He didn't like or trust Herlicht; a clever trickster was the general (discreet) opinion, even if his business acumen was to be envied, and he did wonder sometimes why O'Shea kept him. Perhaps each knew an embarrassing but convenient amount about the other? Which, perhaps, could apply to these other men-of-affairs busily jumping on but seldom off the O'Shea bandwagon? *Not*, he decided, the bumptious Heggett for ever fretting over his cargoes. Maybe the shrewd silent broker, Courtney, who'd just opened a warehouse on the Circular Quay? *Not* grizzled, outspoken, political animal but lazy, Hugh Whaley. Purdue without a doubt: O'Shea had merely laughed at the man's near-slanderous gossip, made a fat donation to his chapel and taken out shares in his coach-building schemes in return for his undoubted influence with the wowser vote. Most certainly the ubiquitous Mason, head stuffed with price structures and women in that order – rumour had it he kept a nubile and budding actress in a house in lower Elizabeth Street – intent on cultivating the political élite, quite prepared to move out to the sand-hills of Randwick, or even down to the Illawarra to win a place in some newly-incorporated council. Owen steadied his glass as Mason flopped in the chair beside him, shaking the small side table, and poked an elbow in his host's ribs.

'Lucky dog,' he leered, his whisper filling the room, 'where did you find the lass?' His chuckle was an assault. 'You'll be lacking nowt there!'

Owen ignored the query as he evaded the man's whisky breath, hoping Maria (Maria in his mind if Mrs Swallow properly before servants and the world) had not heard. If she had she remained composed, directing Effie at the ornate (and expensive) silver service he had bought so recklessly when she had complained of a lack of such appurtenances, for Brighton was becoming almost luxurious under her ministrations where it had been not much more than functional under his sister's. He was much aware of the woman in his house, fascinated by her smooth precision – smooth was precisely the word for Maria with her hair drawn back, no fussy side curls, its fairness setting off her severe black broken only by a lace collar fastened with a cameo brooch. She sat embroidering her little collars under the lamp at night where he could watch her from his study as he attempted to work on his plans or sat with an open book, not absorbing it, too aware of the sensual rustle of her skirt as she bent for her scissors or to the light to thread her needle. Mourning suited her. She had been frank as to her situation when she had called so soon after he had registered with the agency: indeed, yes, Mr Moynan, a great tragedy Mr Swallow drowning in the wreck of the *Dunbar*; only one survivor washed up on a ledge – but not her Albert Swallow. Her landlady had taken her out to the Gap at Watson's Bay that dreadful Friday morning to find nothing of the ship but a spar until broken pieces of bodies – legs and arms – had washed up over the great bed of black rock to be washed out, then in again. Her description had been so graphic Delia had marched from the room, but the woman had continued, unperturbed. Mr Swallow had had trouble disposing of the drapery so they had decided she would sail ahead and prepare a home – but it was not to be. No accounting for the sea is there, Mr Moynan? For a dreadful moment he had thought she would cry – Delia and Alannah were great criers – but no, an emotionally strong woman. References? Unfortunately not as housekeeper, but she hoped he would consider her for she must earn her living and had kept her own house well and felt the need to serve in a gentleman's establishment with a family about her as perhaps he could understand?

He had grown stubborn and determined when faced with Delia's objections: Burrendah's purchase was finalised, she had promised to give the property a trial so there was to be no further argument. Finally, she had bounced off to pack, but for Ireland, Jamaica or Burrendah he did not know nor did he particularly care. He had done his best to please all, even giving young Aldercott a leg up for Alannah's sake (he felt she did not exactly dislike the man) and now, dammit, he would please himself! And it pleased him to place Brighton in Maria Swallow's capable hands. He found her neat, skilful, pleasant, and thrifty when she went marketing, impeccably gloved of course, Effie striving not to swing her basket and Phipps properly in her kitchen bullying Ned about his formidable list of tasks. But, miraculously, everything was done and well. His coffee was brewed exactly as he liked it and served in the fine Meissen (another extravagance) with his evening cognac to hand. He was becoming a little sleek, with time to look around him at his house, to notice how she set artefacts just so, even to the trivia of native flora about.

'I find Australian flowers somewhat . . . harsh, Mr Moynan, but the little pots reminded me of the musk and mignonette sold in London streets in summer. Odd how one recalls such small details.'

'I passed through London, no more, so cannot say I know the city. Do you miss it?'

'Not at all.' Briskly. 'When I agreed to come out for Mr Swallow's health – the warmer climate you know – I

187

decided, even if Mr Swallow did not, to burn my bridges behind me. They were burned for me you might say . . .'

'Too many foreigners these days.' Mason's grating, half-tipsy voice dragged Owen back to hate those thrust upon him. They had exhausted roads and railways and were setting their fangs in migration. 'One can't turn round for foreigners. No offence of course, Herlicht.'

Kurt bestowed one of his distinctly patronising smiles upon the other man. 'I came out with the first rush in '52 – almost a native by now.'

'Germans are hard workers, I'll admit that.'

'Actually, I'm Austrian.'

'Oh? Well, same thing, I reckon.'

'Not quite.'

Mason glowered, confused, and Owen followed the undeviating path of his prejudiced mind – Austrians, Germans, all arrogant bastards. Maria was serving his coffee and as he took it their fingers brushed and he did not care if others noticed. The serving of his after-dinner coffee and liqueur by her own hands had become one of the most pleasant rituals of his day after fighting off the dog-packs of Sussex Street and beggars and incipient pickpockets everywhere. He was acutely conscious of his youth and vigour, troubled by sexual urges he had thought dying if not dead. He toyed with the impulse to invite her to walk out on Sunday, before the world, through the Botanical Gardens and down to Mrs Macquarie's Chair, but set the urge aside for it pleased him to consider her here in his house, his secret, in a way his possession. The situation was beginning not only to intrigue but to delight him.

'Desirée? Plain Dolly, I'd say. I know a Midlands slattern even bolstered up by new stays, a new carriage and a fancy henna rinse.' Nance Mason dismissed the haughty occupant of a passing equipage. Her voice, as strident as her husband's, struggled to assume the confidential tones of gossip. 'But I suppose when all one's got is a hit-and-miss arrangement one's apt to be over-eager. I heard she fell into such a pet when Abe sent up that bouquet to the *prima donna* at the Royal she burst a lace.'

Raunie laughed, but more at her companion than with her for Nance was becoming somewhat gross herself and in a fright to keep her own man, though she was right about one thing; a wedding ring did give some security. Flashing her own, Raunie smoothed her neat waist with satisfaction. Of all social pastimes she loved the promenade and today the crowd afforded some compensation for the distaste she always felt at being obliged to sit a horse. But ride she must if everyone of note did so, and ride she did this clear winter's day along the bridle paths of the Domain, dogged by her hunchback groom, with Government House impressively on its rise behind and ships in full sail passing the security of Fort Denison, to be criticised but, she knew, secretly envied by the women and ogled by the young bucks in their gay waistcoats and gleaming fob-chains, spanking smart in carriages or mincing by on expensive mounts. To add even more colour and style, the military were out. Sydney was on parade, to see and be seen.

To see and be seen was the spice of Raunie O'Shea's life. The nucleus of her world, unchanged and unmarred except by the presence or absence of her husband, was Sydney, with carriage drives to Double Bay or to the South Head to watch a wool-clipper beating out or an immigrant ship in. Shopping along George Street passed a pleasant few hours. She revelled in little dinners, the O'Shea carriage almost constantly on the road from 'the wilds of Rose Bay' as she derided it when particularly piqued or lonely. Leaving household disputes to a suitably bribed Abigail she would often stay with the Masons in Lyons Terrace when Brick was away – and these days he was too often away. The theatre was the ideal venue to see and be seen and, wrapped in sable, she yawned through opera and yearned for the lusty stimulation of the burlesque – but no one of account save young gallants out on the town dared be seen in such places. Instead, she patronised the oyster saloons hard by the play-houses, properly escorted of course. Strolling Hyde Park along 'lovers' walk' on a fine evening towards the

Terrace was very much the thing to do. And since Brick would not countenance a house in town she could only direct her carriage along Macquarie Street, dwelling on her triumphs and ignoring her often despairing life there as Alister Merrill's mistress, arriving home in a temper for Winthrop looked more than ever 'city'.

The Masons were currently *très gai* in cultivating Melbourne horse-breeders, and Silas's neck glowed from too many brandies rather than physical exertion. Raunie flirted with his guests, snubbing M. Lucien as some small balm for Madame's insult in bending to adjust her child's bonnet as she, Raunie, had cantered by. The Misses Romains, old hags both, passed her by without a glance; if only Brick would buy up their insolvent brother's business and put them out on the street instead of laughing. 'What the blazes would you do with a haberdashery?' 'Turn it into a pot-house and make more money.' How dared they look down their noses at her. Hadn't she a richer, more indulgent husband than any woman in Sydney? Had she not a finer house, more clothes and carriages, and a personal attendant in specially tailored livery? After all, who else had a lively little dwarf as slave, even if he were absurd in his possessiveness and his jealousies.

'You know I can't bear deformity,' Nance had shuddered at her first sight of Gondola prancing along on his pony. 'Where did you find such a grotesque?'

'In a Sydney gutter straight from a Venetian one – no, there are no gutters in Venice, a *calle* as they call their streets. He landed here with a circus troupe but got into mischief so they left him behind. He was working in a stables when I found him. He's a wizard with horses – though there are no horses in Venice either – and so nimble he could outwit any thug. Outshoot any marksman too.'

'But everyone *stares*.'

'Indeed they do.' She was delighted. 'He's teaching me Italian words, for that touch of Europe – you know?' Revelling in the Italian influence she had brushed aside Abby's distaste to laugh with Jamie at the hunchback's acrobatic antics. Brick had only shrugged, cautioned them

190

to watch the silver, and warned the dwarf away from Glenora. But today Raunie was a little weary of her flashy groom, wearier still of her own forced gaiety, uneasy over Brick's absence, still piqued at his letter delivered by Joey Bowes whom she had promptly despatched to Brighton to help Jebediah and Ned with odd jobs, suffering him about Birubi with a bad grace. Her longing for Brick was a physical ache; in a way she died without him and she was dying now, for no matter how she crowded her days and nights she wanted to run from the house, any house, seek him out and feel him against her.

'Do look.' Even Nance's whisper was harsh. 'Bridie's new baby. Not a bit like Sam, is he? Just as well perhaps. But it does make one wonder . . . Any news of your wandering spouse?'

'Oh, you know Brick.' Raunie laughed off the query. 'He'll walk in as large as life when he's ready and not before.'

'I'll never understand this penchant men have for communing with Nature. Do you think they're drawn back to ancient fertility rites they've consciously forgotten? Nature isn't always beguiling – it prickles.' She brushed aside a spiked frond. 'It stings too.' Warning away a persistent fly. 'More sensible to leave virgin land to the industrious poor and deal with its produce, as the middle-man, like my Silas, though he's livid at the high wages asked these days. He swears the country has gone to the pack since the convict supply gave out and if he'd been in business twenty years ago we'd be deliriously rich by now.'

'You *are* deliriously rich.'

'Are we really?' She was genuinely surprised. 'Well, who better qualified than an O'Shea to decide financial status? Don't fret over Brick, my pet. He's probably helping your Irish friends settle in.'

'They settled in long ago. And they're not my friends.'

'Protégés then. And I'll vouch for at least one member of that family; Papa Owen definitely improves on acquaintance.'

'So it's Owen now, is it?'

Nance gave one of her deep unattractive laughs. 'A

delightful man when prised from his machines. He'd get my vote if I had one.'

'Vote? For what?'

'The Assembly – doesn't Brick tell you *anything*? Silas swears the man is being groomed for Parliament by way of City Council; it seems that controlling sewerage and rounding up stray dogs is a necessary preliminary.' This time it was a malicious little laugh. 'Rather different, I imagine, from your first years here when every excuse for a gutter was a festering cesspool.' Raunie's hands tightened on the reins but she said calmly enough:

'Why waste precious dalliance time on Owen Moynan? Rumour has it he's enamoured of his housekeeper.'

Nance gave a mock sigh. 'Housekeepers have the advantage of propinquity at all times – and hours. Since Owen is in Sydney about your husband's affairs – along with his own, it seems – it's reasonable he should expect his virginal, at least we assume she is, daughter protected from the rigours and dangers of the bush, and who more experienced at protection of all kinds than your husband? Fortunately, the properties are only a few miles apart as the crow flies.'

'Sheath your claws, Nancy. Brick can take his pick of more exciting females, if he were so interested, than lanky Irish girls barely out of the schoolroom, too gauche to handle their wine.'

'A man is interested in any female who happens to be to hand.'

'Mantua needs exercise.' Raunie pressed in her spurs, her groom leaping after. Nance Mason was a jealous bitch, because Brick ignored her, but she wouldn't go too far in spite, desperate as she was for a coming-out party for her impossible Nicolette – French names were so chic! Hateful Nance. Hateful everyone. But she preserved her façade of gaiety until it was time to spell the horses and gossip and flirt a little under the trees. Seeking diversion among the picnickers and promenaders, her glance skimmed Maxim Werner, waxing ever fatter financially and in girth – but how Georgina Merrill had loved that fatuous philanderer! She turned her back on him, for despite a rich wife he was small

192

fry, to find her eyes held by a pair of deep-set grey ones in a smooth interesting face – Kurt Herlicht. She nodded briefly and coolly; she had no reason to show surprise for it was high time he was in Sydney. Even so, she found his presence, particularly in Brick's absence, disconcerting for there was no escaping his eyes. Indeed, no escape from him at all as he moved towards her openly and deliberately. The same Kurt, his blond hair sleek, his Melbourne tailoring superb. There was nothing of the country yokel about Kurt Herlicht: he was Europe personified, revelling in his reputation as a *bon viveur*, delighting in an audience when devoting himself to a woman, confusing her, putting her at a disadvantage, and so rendering her vulnerable. But attractive as he was and had always been to her, he was simply not Brick and she would never let him confuse her again. She forced her reins on her zealous hunchback, took Kurt's proffered hand and breathed a quiet sigh of relief when she managed to dismount competently if not expertly. Even so, she resolved to take further riding lessons.

'Well, Raunie?'

'Don't call me Raunie,' she murmured, but forcing a smile for there were those watching, particularly Nance, who knew him well – she sometimes wondered how well. 'Certainly not here. I'm Mrs O'Shea to you.'

'I called you Raunie in the old days.' But he had the grace to lower his voice.

'These are not the old days.'

'Unfortunately, no. But we could bring them back.' Ah, yes, the same Kurt, never wasting time on preliminaries. It was years since she had been alone with him like this, for Brick conducted the bulk of his business from his O'Connell Street office and these days, when out of town, through Owen Moynan. But seeing Kurt again, even in a crowd, memories she did not want were conjured up. Who should know better than herself that his compliments were a thin veneer over strong and individual urges – Kurt Herlicht presaged no good for any woman.

'Brick's out of town,' she said abruptly, 'which you must know by now.'

193

'I've been informed.' He gave a tiny shrug. 'His general factotum, works manager or whatever he's called, a worthy, rather stolid but, I assume, well-qualified Ulsterman, set me straight on many matters over rather good cognac. But the waiting need not be tedious for either of us.' She turned away abruptly but he followed. 'The old days, remember?' His voice had the sheen of silk. 'Golden days in a golden town we called them. You used to dance for me.'

'How dare you speak of that here,' she flashed. 'Or anywhere.'

He smiled intimately. 'Why not? "A flash of light red-gold on black, a fiery shadow in the mystery of night".'

'Don't waste your poetry on me.'

'That scrap of verse was considered admirable among Bendigo's *literati* – no, I've not turned poet, I filched it from an aspirate who died of lung fever two days after he struck gold. He wrote minor doggerel but he did work a good claim.'

'Which you doubtless filched along with his verse . . . Naturally, you're staying at Petty's.'

'Why not? Your husband has the reputation of being a generous employer.'

'Not generous enough for the best hotels as often as you patronise them. Or your wild wagers at race-meetings all the way down to cock-fighting. *Or* your celebration dinners. *Or* your peacock wardrobe. Certainly not for what you are rumoured to spend on women. I was a fool, I never cost you a penny.'

'Your husband believes in self-advertisement so if he cuts a swathe so must I. I always found you to be of the same mind. He needs all the publicity he can get in selling the Bendigo store, one reason I'm here, and in drumming up interest in your Hunter Street jewellery. Odd, I always thought that little shop one of your favourite toys.' Surprise must have shown on her face. 'But didn't you know?'

'Of course I know,' she lied. 'I know everything my husband does.' She turned aside, angry and on the defensive for it seemed Brick was becoming secretive, unlike him in matters pertaining to their mutual interests and possessions.

'You could help banish the boredom of waiting,' he murmured, 'by inviting me out to dinner.'

'I am not obliged to ask you to Birubi.'

'Oh come, Raunie, isn't this a little absurd when I remember you as anything but formal.' His hand curled about hers where it rested against her skirt.

'Take your hand away.'

He obeyed but with a lingering gesture. 'Some other time then.'

She ignored the half-query. 'Don't be too sure of yourself, Kurt; after all, you are only an O'Shea employee. Now you had better be polite to people. Brick will expect it – as I do.'

But he remained unruffled and in command of the situation, obviously believing himself in command of her as he warmed to old friends, was affable to acquaintances and charming to strangers. Too sure of himself by far, she decided. It gave her great satisfaction to refuse openly his offer to escort her home.

Gondola's black beady eyes were everywhere and his hand close to his revolver – or rather, Raunie's – as they rode out to Rose Bay. Brick forbade the hunchback to carry firearms but Raunie armed him secretly when he acted groom. Usually when she joined a city riding party she took the carriage in and out, Gondola leading her mount, but today, needing practice, she had chosen to ride. She ignored the polyglot little streets of workmen's residences and servicing shops creeping down the slopes to Woolloomooloo Bay, but on the heights of Darlinghurst, passing the turn-off to where the Regent Lodge of old nestled in its still extensive grounds though pressed upon by development, she put on a spurt. She hated this part of the journey and for some reason always felt particularly aware on horseback. She had managed to forget much of her past but today memories crowded. The Merrills were much on her mind, particularly Alister. Only once in recent years had she been confronted by any member of that family with which her life had been so closely entwined: in George Street she had come face to face with

Georgina Merrill, now Blair, with her youngest children. They had stared at each other, surprised and a little embarrassed but they had not turned away, for of all the Merrills Georgina had been the one with whom she, Raunie, had had some rapport. But she was shocked at the change in the once gay and beautiful girl, the golden hair dull under the dowdy bonnet, her lovely body lost in sombre colours and a heavy cloak, looking the country matron she had obviously become. They talked politely of irrelevancies, a conversational skating on thin ice until Gina's voice trembled:

'I never see anyone from the old days.'

'If you mean Maxim, as you do, he thrives – but he's losing his hair.' She could not resist it. She had never liked Maxim Werner.

'Such beautiful hair.' It was a cry of girlish anguish. But she rallied to give an account of her mother's latest illness while Raunie hid her yawns and avoided the stares of the stolid Blair offspring – when had Eleanor been anything but poorly? Gina went on to explain that she rarely came to Sydney because of her large family but had made the long and tiresome trip through to Port Macquarie to see her father – and here her voice did falter a little. Yet something remained of the forthright girl she had always been and she met Raunie's eyes frankly. The major was still on his property but not making much of a go of it, though Jeremy and a couple of hands did their best. Raunie passed hastily over Alister, reluctant to be reminded of him. Alister Merrill had been the only man other than Brick to leave his mark upon her: a desperate man consuming her in his desperate need, and out of her own need she had returned his passion. She refused to think of him in any other way but as a lean, demanding body meeting hers to create not only sexual pleasure but sharp clear moments of happiness.

She breathed more easily when Darlinghurst and Potts Point were left behind, their only reminder the new St John's Church rising above the trees and scattered dwellings along the ridge of Darlinghurst Heights, and turned down side tracks towards the Harbour. They cantered the beach-front of Rose Bay before climbing the hill and taking the track to the waterfront. It was late and growing chill as she rode up Birubi's drive to stare at a carriage where Joey Bowes and a youth he called Richie were unloading a great many boxes and bags. Joey straightened as she dismounted, prepared to be his polite if wary self towards his master's wife.

'What is all this?' she demanded.

'Baggage, ma'am.'

'I can see *that*, you dolt. And I can see that the valise there belongs to my husband. Is he home?'

'He's upstairs, Mrs O'Shea, attending to Mrs Noakes.'

'Moll Noakes?' The words came out in a shriek. 'What are you babbling about?'

'Mr O'Shea will explain.'

She flew through the hall and up the stairs. The house was silent with not a servant in sight, not even Abby 'poking about' as Brick called the woman's silent glide from room to room about Raunie's errands and commands. '*Abigail!*' she screamed, reluctant to face her husband just then without a barrier, that shield that Jamie usually provided. No answer. '*Abby!*' She pounded the stairtop with her riding crop, her usual summons when servants were slow. Finally Abby did appear from the north-eastern suite, the sunny corner rooms reserved for special guests, closing the door softly behind her. Raunie threw down her crop and gloves in temper, to lie where they fell till a servant picked them up. 'It's as well somebody answered. So he brought her down, did he?'

'The rooms are being prepared now. She's very ill and must have quiet. It was a hard journey.'

'I don't want to hear of Moll's troubles,' Raunie raged. 'And I don't want her here. Where is my husband?'

'Keep your voice down.' He followed Abigail from the room, waved the woman back inside, closed the door on her, grasped Raunie's arm and, ignoring her protests, dragged her along to her own room. 'Get in,' he snapped, 'and don't make a scene. And don't bang the door.'

But she did bang it and loudly. 'Is that all you have to say to me after so long away? Where have you been? And why didn't you tell me Kurt was expected? *And* that you plan to sell my shop.'

'Not now, Raunie,' he protested wearily. 'I've had little sleep for nights.'

'I refuse to have that woman in my house.'

'"That woman", as you call her, is here to stay. She's taken a stroke.'

She stared at him in horror. 'Is she mad?'

'Her mind, sight and hearing are as sound as your dinner bell but she's lost almost total use of her hands, her right hand very badly. Her speech is badly impaired. She must be fed, dressed and bathed and the Pride has no time or labour to care for her properly. She has learnt to take a few steps but she needs expert medical care if she's to improve further. I've engaged a nurse to live in. And Fay Witherstone will stay on, at least for a while.'

'The house will be crowded out,' Raunie wailed. 'And I hate nurses about the place; starchy horrors always complaining of noise and demanding this and that.'

'The nurse will report to me daily. You won't come into it.'

'I can't *bear* it.' She was dramatic and injured.

'You won't have to bear anything. You won't even have to see them. They'll live in the end suite.'

'But that's the guest suite. It overlooks the gardens and the bay.'

'Don't begrudge her an outlook, her eyesight's about the only thing left to her.'

'Everything will be a mess.'

'Nonsense. You have rooms empty all over the house.'

'Who'll do the work?'

'Who always does your work? Servants. Get another, get a dozen. This need not interfere one jot with your fancy existence.' He ran a weary hand through his hair. 'Come now, Egypt, it's a waste of temper to go on so for she doesn't know where she is yet, not entirely, and doesn't really care. If you want to rage against someone rage against your son.'

'Jamie?' she gasped. 'You brought him home?'

'I brought him – wait, dammit!' For she went flying down the hall to pound on Jamie's door. It remained closed.

'You're lying,' she shouted. 'There's no sound. Nothing.'

'*Christ!*' he exploded, striding the hall to pound with her. 'Open up, Jamie, or I'll beat my way in. You might as well face your mother now as later.' Finally the bolt was drawn and Jamie confronted them, sleepy, sullen and looking a little ill. Raunie clasped him in her usual dramatic way.

'I've been so miserable without you. I thought you'd never come.'

Brick thrust them inside, followed and shot the bolt. 'A matter of luck he's alive. But since he's decided to rise from the dead we might as well get all over with now.'

Murmuring endearments, Raunie fondled her son but his cry of pain made her pull back. 'What *is* it? There's something wrong, I know it.'

'What you don't know is this.' With a swift movement Brick ripped the shirt from the boy's back leaving him in his breeches and, ignoring Jamie's groans, twisted him about and pushed him face-down on the bed. Raunie screamed.

'He's been beaten. *Flogged.*'

'He has and so thoroughly he'll carry the scars to his grave, exactly as it should be. You'll listen to reasons, as he'll hear them over again – and if you move a muscle, Jamie lad, you'll get another basting.'

'You did it?' Raunie screamed. '*You?*'

'I did. And without apologies.'

'You had no right to touch him. He's my son – *mine*. You black *baster*, you!' She flew at him, beating at him with her fists, strong in her fury, but he stood unmoved until she sank helplessly beside the bed to crouch, moaning, burying her head against Jamie's side, running her hands over his back, attempting to soothe and heal. 'You've marked him.'

'I have. But his wounds have been dressed. I'm no sadist.'

'Just because he wouldn't work at the Pride. Why should he do the work of menials? Why should you make a servant of him?'

'He's been flogged for more than laziness, not the least of it, theft from the Pride's cash-bag.'

'I don't believe you.'

'He admitted it. He had plenty of time riding down to admit to many things.'

'You bullied it out of him. If he did take spending money it's because you're mean to him. Why do you treat him so when he's your heir?'

'*Was* my heir. He's always had a generous allowance but seemingly adds to it where and how he pleases. I don't like the way he grabs so he'll get nothing from me in future unless he labours for it. He'll sweat it out like my station hands, to be paid like them, otherwise he can go cap in hand to you, to anyone. Stay where you *are*,' he throbbed as she attempted to struggle up. He pushed her down and stood over her, and the silent boy with his head buried in the pillow. 'There's more, much more, and you'll hear me out. Some of those cuts are for hunting Chinese for the sport of blood-letting; even worse in my book, scalping. But his deepest cuts are for being the cause, if indirectly, of a man's death.'

'What are you talking about?'

'I'm talking of young Moynan. He's dead.'

'That *boy*?'

'That boy. Dead because of the recklessness, and viciousness, of your son leading him, a novice, into that rackety world of thieves and thugs, murderers too, that we know so well – and Jamie seems to know even better. Young Moynan was fair game for scum and Jamie goaded him into flashing that fancy pistol of his, goaded him too into taking other men's women, buying them openly and lavishly – oh yes, he's done a lot of talking—'

'I don't believe you.' She pounded the floor in her indignation. 'I don't believe a word of it.'

'He admitted it. Young Moynan was knifed to death and horribly; I haven't seen worse and I've seen a great deal. There wasn't much left of him. Jamie threw that boy to the dogs of this country, both Chinese and renegade whites; for Jamie's an old hand at survival with the cunning to pull back when the game gets dangerous. But he let Moynan play the strutting young squire, fuel for fire out on the mullock heaps. Dammit, you *will* listen!' He dragged her hands from her ears and held them so tightly she gasped and squirmed with pain.

'I've let Jamie rampage this country too long, hoping he'd grow out of his wanderlust and settle to my plans for him, but no . . . He meant a great deal to me once, he was my future, but now he's free to be what he is, a larrikin, a gipsy larrikin at that. Now he'll be a poor larrikin and that's a drab and dingy thing to be. He's disowned my name, now he can disown my money. He won't be forced back to the Pride, he won't be forced to anything for I no longer care what he does or where he goes. He's yours, and both of you can be what you are at heart, gipsy vagabonds. So take your brat, you're welcome to him.' He released her abruptly and turned to the door but she reached out to grasp him about the knees.

'Don't talk that way. You know you don't mean it.'

'I mean it. By God, I mean it.' He wrenched himself free. 'And watch your jewels if you want them for he knows their worth and you may not have them long. He's gambled himself into debt.'

'But I never know where he goes or what he's doing.' Swaying from side to side in a desperate primitive wailing. 'You're the one who finds him and brings him home.'

'Find him yourself if you want him. Or leave him in his back alleys, or in some whore's bed – and speaking of beds, and whores if amateur ones, his child will be born in August. I was reminded of that by grandmother and mother-to-be in Parramatta.'

'I won't keep Dora's brat,' Jamie raged. 'You can't make me.'

'I can and I will.' Brick swept an arm about the richly cluttered room. 'This expensive junk should bring enough to settle your immediate debts with a start for your child. Sell the lot or I'll do it.' As he tugged at the door Raunie scrambled up to fling herself against it, barring his way.

'Don't go. Not like this. *Wait*—'

'I can't wait.' He flung her aside. 'I go to tell a man his son is dead. Would you like to help me explain that your son's stupidity helped him die?'

The slam of the door reverberated. She held her hands over her ears as if to shut out its sound along with her plight and his damning words. She rocked herself in her agony for he meant what he said, she knew it.

'Mama?' Jamie was leaning on his elbow watching her. She turned on him savagely and slapped his face

'*That* can't match the cuts on your back but I hope it stung. This time you've gone too far. You could have had everything you wanted but now you've lost it all. You'll never get the Irish Boy or anything else for he means what he says, I know him too well. You're a fool. *Fool!*' She went mad, slapping him again and again about the face and shoulders. He tried to escape by sliding over the bed and huddling against the wall but she followed, raging at him with ancient gipsy curses and Cockney spleen and the richness of goldfields blasphemy. 'Fool. *Fool!*' He did not hit back or try to run from the room; just crouched accepting her blows and insults until, spent, she sank beside him, moaning, running her hands over his marked back with murmurs and whimpering little caresses. She was utterly bereft.

'What are we going to do? What *are* we going to *do*?'

The slightest movement of his hands seemed difficult as well as painful as Owen opened his daughter's letter for he knew he could not postpone its reading longer. It was brief and as painful to read as it must have been to write:

'It will be best, Papa, if we bear this apart. I cannot explain why I feel this except that I cannot speak of Con, and even writing his name is a painful thing. Do not come to Burrendah, not now. We will write each other but not of Con. Not yet . . .'

He had known the moment O'Shea had walked in that something was wrong, very wrong, and his first thought was of Alannah, for Con had always managed to escape real trouble by sliding his burden on to other shoulders – but not this time. O'Shea had talked quietly and at length, detailing and explaining, and Owen had interrupted him only once.

'You should have warned me. You should have given me the choice of going with you.'

'Perhaps. But it would not have changed anything.' After that he remembered only the final words. 'You want to run, I know it. You feel hatred for the country; for its indifference, its laxity, its savagery. It is a savage country and always will be. But you will stay for it imposes itself upon you. You will do what all do, strive to meet it on its own terms. Accept what cannot be changed.'

He could find no answer. Much later he had walked out of Brighton to wander the city, not knowing or caring where he went. Now he sat on the waterfront of Farm Cove watching the restless little waves slam the rocks, not knowing if it were the same day or if he had wandered into tomorrow. It did not seem to matter. There was only now.

Raunie could not sleep. It was often so now that Brick slept along the hall in the small bedroom adjoining his dressing-room. He had not slept with her for weeks and she was certain the household knew it. She had expected him to get over his mood, as had happened before, and come to her – but not this time. At first when Jamie had stamped off sulking at the sale of his possessions, to stay with Tom Pearson at Potts Point, she had accepted his absence, if temporarily, as clearing the air and the house for herself and Brick. But her husband came and went, polite yet remote from her, preoccupied with Moll, the nurses and doctors, his business associates and interests, in conference she supposed with Kurt, and speaking to her only when necessary. She complained of Moll's presence, she raged at Abby, at Gondola, at Cook and the servants, at anyone and anything to gain and keep Brick's attention, but he remained achingly, fearsomely, distant. Soon he would be on his way south for the shearing then on to distant places she refused even to visit – except Bendigo. She persisted with the subject of Bendigo but he was adamant – he would not take her to Bendigo.

The room was bare and empty and achingly lonely without him. She slid from the bed – she simply could not *bear* it. She crept along the hall to the small room he had made his own. He lay face down on the bed, arms hanging loose each side, asleep or appearing to be so. His remote relaxed pose drove her mad – asleep and unaware of her! She knelt by the bed and laid her cheek against his hand but he did not stir. She reached up to kiss him, whispering endearments, little pet names heard only between them in intimacy.

'Don't quarrel with me. Don't turn from me. Don't.' She trembled against him, running her hands down his shoulders and into the hollow of his waist. He stirred. She went on kissing him, entreating, clinging, begging. He turned over on his back with a long sigh. He was waking to her. She stretched beside him holding him close and at last he turned over. He wanted her, she knew it. Now all would be well.

But it was not well, not this time. It was too quick, too awkward where it had never been awkward before and, unsatisfied, she clutched at him, hating him then for what he denied her. She beat at him in her hunger and love and desperation, then clung to him, entreating. But the response she could always wring from him with insistence did not come. His eyes were closed against her. All was different, all was wrong. He was shutting her out. Her wonderful world of loving and being loved by him was changing, dissolving, slipping away, leaving her desolate. Without him she would die.

Chapter Ten

THE WINTER had wrapped Alannah in a chilly cocoon, but lightly as if the cold were a living and understanding element hesitant to penetrate her sensitive outer skin. She moved in a remote, even dreamlike way, going through the motions of donning warm clothing, eating and sleeping, the latter fitfully. She heard her aunt ask questions but so distantly she felt no urge to answer. She fancied she heard Ida urging Grace to something, then Dan's voice soothing. Sometimes she made an effort to talk with those around her but, oddly, such moments would be interrupted by her brother; Con would actually be beside her and they would be as they had always been, playmates and companions. Then he would be gone as suddenly and she would be back with the sadness, wanting to run and hide in caves but there were no caves and all she could do was saddle Mourne and ride out to the hills, where there was only the empty world to see and know her despair.

But gradually, mercifully, the world and its people came into true focus and she began to watch even the mundane sowing of peas and potatoes as sharply etched and meaningful events. She answered letters of condolence from people she did not know, all about the healing properties of time and patience. She answered her father's safely impersonal letters just as impersonally – but his latest letter was almost entirely concerned with his housekeeper.

'He calls her Maria!' Her aunt slammed the letter face down on the table. 'Your father will make a fool of himself over that woman, you'll see. She's turning his head entirely. A common piece, her hair's too brassy.' She picked away at issues as she might pick at a chicken bone: letters took so long to come out, anything, *anything* could have happened at

Stonemore. Vincent did not write, or his letters were going astray. 'We're so far from Jamaica,' she complained. 'Ireland is far from Jamaica,' Alannah reasoned, but nothing would soothe her aunt, not even cramming already crammed shelves with her own preserves or rearranging already neat medicine chests and pantries. Her resentment, always smouldering against Jamie O'Shea, or Lorne, or whatever he called himself, for her nephew's death, flared.

'Your brother's murderer still goes free.'

'Murderers, by the number of stab—' Alannah felt sick attempting to speak of it. 'He was caught up in a mob war.'

'I'm convinced the police don't try to catch criminals. They haven't even produced the wretch who molested you.' Thwarted, Delia threw her dammed-up energy into the constant arguments over Grace and her 'affairs'. It had always been assumed that Grace and Joey Bowes would marry when he came through in the spring, but nothing had been arranged or even mooted, to Ida's disgust.

'As Mrs Archy Mead you'd be on our doorstep, so to speak,' she lectured her daughter. 'Real handy.'

'I don't even like his name. It makes me think of some sort of stew, or home-brewed drink.'

'Mr Mead is Temperance so never mention liquor in his presence. As for his name it's as good as any other. You could grow to like it.'

'A girl needs to hanker after a man to wed him, Ma.'

'If it's love you mean, the likes of us can't afford it. And plenty get along without it if they have a house and money coming in and a nice little business to work up. Think, girl, you'd have a real house in a respectable street instead of a shack out in the saltbush.'

'We'll fix up the place on Oorin just fine. Joey's real handy with his hands.'

'I don't see him fixing up to wed you. What we need is an old-time matchmaker; everything arranged nice and proper.'

'Work up a business yourself, then. You'd be good at it. But leave me be.'

Alannah found Grace beating rugs as if her life depended

on it, as perhaps it did just then. 'If she don't stop, Miss, I will run orf.'

'No you won't. You'll stick it out. All Joey needs is a good push.'

'He's never around long enough for me to give him a shove, let alone prop him up before parson.'

'He'll be back sooner or later and the banns will be read, you'll see. They don't call you pert and pretty Grace for nothing.'

'That's only because I laugh a lot, as if I don't have a care in the world, keep sort of bright, you know? But there's a bit of mirror in the kitchen and I scare m'self silly sometimes in m' big apron and great boots – but fine for slopping around Oorin if they should last so long – with no time to even fix m' hair.'

'We'll get more help in the kitchen.'

'I'll have no Goulburn flibbertigibbet interfering with my chores,' she flashed, then calmed a little, 'if it's all the same to you, Miss Moynan. I have m' ways, y' see. It's just that no matter what I do I know Joey can get lots prettier girls than me.'

'Wear the dress your mother bought you from that hawker.'

'Great gawky me in frills?' She was horrified. 'I'm waiting m' chance to burn that.'

'But everyone would notice you.'

'I don't want everyone, I just want Joey – though I'm daft hankering after him, I know it.' Venting her confusion and longing on Burrendah's carpets with great savage wallops that made Alannah blink. 'I don't mind rough living, Miss, for it's all I've known since the mine went bust and Mr O'Shea got Pa this place. Everything's so nice here it's made Ma ambitious. I mean, she had her own house in Melbourne which I can't remember and she wants the same for me and that's why I don't answer her back – well, not much.' More hefty whacks. 'I don't care if it is hard at Oorin, I'm used to making-do and I've a green thumb and can bake, and help with the ploughing and reaping and I understand stock and will have a go at anything, even pigs. But Joey's got to speak up, Miss, and he don't so I've figured out why . . . A willing horse of a woman is all most men want in the bush but there's some like Joey what looks for more, some excitement in a girl so he can weave stories and happenings about her in his mind, know what I mean? Joey has the imagination to want something . . . *mysterious* you might say, about a girl, not that I really know what being mysterious means, all I know is Joey wants it.' She paused, a frown between her soft brown eyes. 'But I don't make that happen for Joey, or for anyone else come to that. I'm just plain Gracie Charlton, straight-talking and doing and can't be less. Or otherwise.'

'No,' Alannah said thoughtfully, 'but you could be more.'

'More?'

'There's *feeling*, Grace.' A long pause. 'You could help Joey *feel* with you.'

The girl swivelled her broom about. 'I hope you don't mean what I think you mean, Miss Moynan.'

'Only a *little*. To set his imagination working. And his expectations. Oh, for heaven's sake!' She raised helpless hands. 'You've got to do *something*, haven't you?'

Grace straightened her back, her broom and her hair. 'I have, and that's a fact.' And she attacked her carpets with a new and terrible zeal. But looking back Alannah saw her leaning on her broom, the carpets limp and forgotten on the line.

There were visible touches of spring in the misty green of willows and the small pale blossoms of flowering fruit trees. And yesterday Huie had brought her strawberries moist on their leaves. There were new foals staggering in the rye and the white dots of newly-dropped lambs everywhere – and the wheat was looking good. The world was putting out feelers in green shoots and Alannah's inner sadness stretched to a mere thread, as with exciting new energy she rode with the men to the burning off of grass dry as tinder from winter frosts and a danger, particularly to Calua station over near Marulan. All through the wild morning with the crackle and hiss of flames, Paddy One rushing from tussock to tussock with grass torches while they shaded their eyes from the smoke and glare, tensing for the crash and burst of timber, she found in such crammed, busy and varied days something of the Mourne Festival, that ecstatic urgent fulfilment of the season of fruition.

She had met most of the county at the Easter sports and picnic races at the Old Township of Goulburn, but was happy to meet others as well as old acquaintances at Daisy Elston's send-off. Daisy was sailing with her daughters to spend a year in England, fares paid by her folk in Somerset (she's so daffy about her George she won't see he's packing her off to wheedle more brass while snaring lords' sons for those girls – if there are any left over there for they all seem out here grubbing for gold, Hetty sniffed). Desolate at leaving her 'precious darling' as Daisy startled strangers by addressing the bumptious George, she twisted her hands in her nervous 'tic', tripping up her over-lavish, too-girlish skirts so the children giggled at her frilled drawers. Elston, as always oblivious of her frantic efforts to please him, called her 'petal', enveloped her in great bear hugs and filled the refreshment tent with his booming laughter as his 'boys' rode their horses right through it on a dare bringing it down as a floating cloud in a mêlée of chicken legs and blancmange. With nothing more serious to treat than shock Aunt Delia bustled with smelling salts and proverbs while Alannah coaxed Daisy into showing her Adina's cottage prettied up unsuitably with frilled curtains and Toby jugs.

'She's too quiet.' Daisy patted her side curls before Adina's mirror. 'She's always been quiet but now it's as if she's not there at all. She doesn't seem to hear when I speak to her. And she's so slow about the kitchen. If she's in the family way she won't say, just hangs her head, and I hesitate to ask Billy, he's a deep one. She puzzles us all, the way she looks sort of lost, as if she were fretting, her roundness gone. We're tired of sending Billy to the Pride to bring her back. She can't seem to get over leaving her old home – or something. Could it be someone, do you think?'

Alannah tried to talk to the girl as they sat together by the lemon tree.

'Does Billy beat you?'

'No'm.'

'You like your little house, don't you?'

'Yes'm.'

She gave her beads and a bracelet and ribbons for her hair. The girl thanked her politely but set the gifts aside in a disinterested way. Hetty had lost patience entirely: 'I'll not have her hanging about my kitchen with that hang-dog look, nor will I let her sit there under the big tree plaguing the schoolmaster at his classes. She's pining for Joey and can't have Joey, she knows it and that's the trouble. The best thing that fashion-plate over at Wiena can do is slap some sense into the girl and set her to hard work. Mr O'Shea means Joey for Grace. He'll not force either, of course, though he's getting impatient with Joey, we all see it, Joey not making up his mind about Oorin – but he'll not force him there either. I wish it were shearing-time, and you can see I'm fraught when I wish that work on m'self, but Mr O'Shea should come and look to his people.'

O'Shea's people? The phrase had an archaic, almost feudal, ring though in a sense it was true for big stations lived and worked as self-sufficient worlds. But there were exceptions. Clearly, Simon Aldercott had not become one of 'O'Shea's people'; he was at odds with Erins Pride and most in it, even more sharply at odds with the country, and it bothered Alannah that he might be enduring his sojourn solely for the few times they met. On his arrival at the Pride he had ridden to Burrendah on a formal call, wind-ruffled, struggling with his mount and anxious over the ride back. Her aunt, glad of any caller, had been almost affable, while Ida considered him genteel – after all, he was the schoolmaster – and had bullied Grace into her hated frills to serve tea which from nervousness or eagerness he spilled on his trousers, rubbing the stain so vigorously it made it worse. If only he weren't so *worthy*, Alannah had sighed then and since; so pink-skinned and peeling from his 'inland ordeal' of which he would talk given the slightest encouragement. He watched for her to ride in to Erins Pride, hastening from the schoolroom to greet her, his pupils crowding to the window to giggle, much to his distress. Her visits to Erins Pride had become something of a ritual for usually she would leave her Place of the Swan with the frost heavy on the ground and, making it an easy ride, arrive as morning tea was brewing, sometimes staying over in the guestroom kept ready for her. If it were a weekend he would escort her home, for safety he insisted, and she would be obliged to suit her pace to his hack, finding his apologies for his poor horsemanship embarrassing as well as irritating.

'I have never been entirely at ease on horseback, Miss Moynan, but I have persisted; my father was a rigid man expecting much. "John Wesley", he would observe, "would ride fifty miles in a day every day".' But, curiously, with only herself and the bush to watch his careful painful progress and hear him speak intimately of his youth as he never had before, her impatience lessened. There was a difference, a subtle difference in him, even a hint of decisiveness as if he'd been through some cleansing sacrificial fire.

'I do not believe I could survive such a journey again for I lost all sense of time and place. The desert landscape is mesmeric, with mirages, as if the twisted trees on the horizon floated in shimmering water – but there is no water there.' He looked haunted by the memory of it, and of O'Shea's warnings at their brief and aweful meeting before he had set out. The man had loomed, big, dark and ominous-seeming, a threatening monster of a man stabbing fingers at maps and mouthing names that had a ribald exotic ring – Booligal! Balranald! Billabong!

'You'll cover every inch of it, Aldercott, or go back to your clerk's stool – or to England for all I care. I'm paying for an all-round man to do all-round work and I get what I pay for. I throw babes into creeks to sink or swim, the same with my labour, so stomach it or leave my employ.' Well, he had stomached it – somehow – to return to Erins Pride. And Alannah Moynan.

'Sheep must wander so far for feed they are solitary specks over the land. Emus – Oorin means emu in the native tongue – and kangaroos are so motionless they seem part of the landscape. Perhaps they too are stupefied by the sun burning on a desolation such as I imagined the surface of some outer planet might present, bald but for the saltbush as they call the sparse and struggling growth giving the appearance of human hair, tufts of it left after giant hands have dragged it out by the fistful.' He gave the embarrassed little laugh of a man not usually given to imagery.

'Why, Mr Aldercott, you are a poet!'

'True, I have flirted with the muse . . .' But he was not to be diverted from horrors. 'I do not know how man, let alone woman, can live out there, yet they do.'

'Land-hungry people will go anywhere.' She paused. 'I fear you are unhappy in this country.'

'I try not to be unfair to it for I realise I see it through English eyes, but . . .' He glanced at her quickly. 'Do you not miss Ireland?'

She frowned. 'At first, and sorely. But now it passes through my mind in . . . well . . . vignettes, drifting little scenes, rather like recalling the traits, good and bad, of an old friend. I recall Armagh, though why I cannot tell except that it is a cathedral city of red marble. Remembering Stonemore is easy to understand for I loved it dearly. And I remember one day in Dundalk when I saw a girl in a red skirt and wanted one exactly like it.' She gave a soft little laugh. 'Everyone was shocked that I should want to look like a Connemara cottage girl. Ireland is perpetually shocked you know – but of course you don't for you have never been there.' She grew serious. 'I shall never go back.'

'Never?' He was shocked.

'I do not like to be torn between countries – or people – so I make choices, at times too hastily, I know it, and often wrongly. It is possible I have chosen wrongly in this but that is the way of it.'

'You are very young.' As if that explained her foolish heresy.

'Eighteen is not very young.' Weary of his clumsy efforts to keep up with her, she pointed to storm clouds. 'We must hurry.' And actually enjoyed his confused flurry. 'I fear you are not happy in Mr O'Shea's employ, Mr Aldercott.'

'My stipend is generous enough for some small savings,

and the terms of my employment equally so, but I would not be honest if I did not admit to a certain disquiet. There are areas of my work for Mr O'Shea for which I am quite unsuited, I know it.'

'Then I blame myself for suggesting your employment.'

'You? But I was not aware . . .' He gulped. 'That you gave me consideration at all is most gratifying. And encouraging.'

His eyes said much. He was of course in love with her, or he believed himself to be for men without women lacked comparison, and with a sudden panic she began to talk of everything and anything. Did he consider her father would make a good town councillor? She did not; it would make him lazy. She hoped it would not make him dull. She babbled of Stonemore's fine stables and her end-of-shearing dance, and of her brother's favourite hunters . . .

'It is heartening that you are able to speak, and so calmly, of your dear departed.'

His pious smugness jarred. 'My brother's name was Conall, Mr Aldercott.'

'Indeed, yes. But I thought it might upset you to be reminded of him so soon.'

'It is not *soon*. It is high time I faced the fact that he . . .' To her horror she hesitated. 'He . . .'

'Has passed on. I understand.'

'You do *not* understand. My brother is dead, Mr Aldercott. *Dead*.' There, it was out. 'You are usually eloquent in expression, as a man of education should be, but you disappoint me now.'

'Education?' He frowned. 'I find my particular education inadequate for survival in this country. Cicero and Plato and a classical vocabulary have little to do with a shepherd's life, even less with a shepherd's children. I have studied philology and I find a jargon, a new language, growing out of the upheaval of migration. The Irish has always contained much of the Elizabethan, you know, and I find it blending with that of the Scot and the Cockney not unhappily, so it seems I must be the student here before I am equipped to teach. Surprisingly, I have discovered that I like teaching children and believe I would find satisfaction in assisting

213

young colonials to a satisfying and fulfilled life. To that end I am giving much thought to a school of my own, an ambitious project for there are already a number of academies in Sydney, but I have gained some practical experience and useful contacts – your father for one.' He reddened at his use of the word 'useful', but plodded on, in all ways. 'He has recommended me in various quarters. Further, your aunt informs me she has had some experience as matron at a boys' school.'

'Why . . . yes. I had forgotten. The Antrim Academy.'

'Then I shall be grateful for any advice she can give me. On my return to Sydney I shall seek your father's help in selecting a house, not large but in a central position with rooms suitable for conversion into classrooms.'

'You have left Mr O'Shea's employ?'

'Not formally.' He frowned again. 'So much of Mr O'Shea's business is now conducted through your father, as was my engagement, that my resignation in the same manner might be best. It will require deep consideration. And, I might add, discretion.'

Spots of rain. Clouds were banking up. She could not face guiding him over muddy tracks so increased her pace and they finally loped in to Burrendah, cold, damp and, mercifully, silent. He began to cough and she knew Ida and her aunt would invite him to stay over. At least, she consoled herself, there were women a-plenty to take him off her hands.

It was close to shearing-time when Joey Bowes came home to Erins Pride, preceding his master. He rode to Burrendah unexpectedly one morning, setting Grace agog and the women thumping fruit cakes and scones and great pots of tea on the kitchen table before settling to an exchange of news. He had been working at Brighton as well as at Birubi but he said little of Birubi's master and mistress. Master Jamie was seldom home. Mr Moynan still travelled a great deal but when in Sydney attended many public and political gatherings. Mr O'Shea's mill was looking spanking smart these days, the talk of the town. Ida gave the teapot a vigorous swirl. And where was Richie? Erins Pride was short of hands.

Richie must stay at Birubi till Mr O'Shea ordered otherwise. Dan was interested only in the electric telegraph: surely the capital cities were connected by now? It was tipped for this month. Joey looked blank, accepted his third slice of cake and escaped to the men's quarters. Grace had refused to 'dress up' as she put it, compromising with a fresh apron, but when she met with Joey alone she was in her old shirt and looped-up skirt, her boots smelling of the fowlyard, a bit of the pigsty and a lot of the warm earth. As Joey plodded up from the blacksmith's shop she dumped her loaded vegetable basket in his path with such force cabbages and carrots spilled out into the dust.

'You've brought the spring if you've brought nought else, Joey Bowes. We're short of men this year. Have you made up your mind then?'

'About what, Grace?' Avoiding her eyes by dusting off a bunch of carrots.

'You know about what – Oorin. If you try Mr O'Shea too far he could put someone else in, have you thought of that?'

'I've thought of it. And he could – I suppose.'

'Is it that you're waiting for someone else to make up your mind?'

'That could be – I suppose.'

'You do too much supposing. If you're waiting for me to make up your mind I'd say take the place and quick.'

'You would?'

'I would. And I'd say more; I'd say grab it for another as well.'

'There's not many would take it on, Grace.' Retrieving a couple of cabbages.

'There's some. Me, I've got the hang of it.'

'You've not even seen it.'

'Mr O'Shea wouldn't give you useless land, I know that much. Anyway, all land's good for something and it's time you started collecting your own, and stock, and a house, and crops, and a wife to help all along.'

'You wouldn't want to leave here, Grace,' he blurted. 'Not with your Ma and Pa and such good living.'

'That's for me to say.'

'You wouldn't care about leaving Burrendah?'

'Oh, I'd care. I'd miss m' good stove and water to hand and the shade of Burrendah's trees, but I'd plant things wherever I went and *make* 'em grow. But for me to take a chance on a man he must take a chance on me and with me it means for ever. It's the way I am. If we fail we can't walk back here in an afternoon so it must be boost or bust. So make up your mind and come to me fair and square and say, Grace I'm ready and for it. And when you're ready and for it I'll be too. But you'd best hurry for there are others hankering after me.'

'What others?'

'Archy Mead, for one.'

'The saddler in at Goulburn?'

'The same. Ma's pushing me to take him for the good life he can give me.'

'He's too old for you.'

'But spry – too spry sometimes. Besides, he can afford to keep his sons – daughters too when they come.'

Joey was shocked. 'He speaks to you of such things?'

'And of other matters, why not? A man should put his intentions before a girl and her kin, all fair and square.'

'He can afford to. I've nought to put before anyone.'

'You call your two hands that can make and grow anything, nought?'

'It never rains out in the saltbush.'

'It must rain sometimes, silly, you just wait for it. And you don't sit around watching and waiting, you make ready.'

'No water but what you can save.'

'Rivers flood as well as dry up. You manage.'

'You won't see another woman.'

'I see too many here sometimes. Hear them too. I could do with a bit of quiet.'

'Only scrub and cattle and sheep and saltbush-crystals shining in the sun.'

'I might find that sort of pretty, shining in the sun.'

'I've never had anything of my own, see.' A tirade of words. 'I've always worked other people's land and looked after other folks' things.' He polished the fruit briskly and bent to rearrange the basket. 'It makes a man hesitate.'

'You'll hesitate yourself to a dead stop if you don't watch out. You'll tackle the back-country fine, Joey Bowes, same as I will.'

He straightened slowly. 'You'll really take me on?'

'I'm thinking on it – as I'm thinking on Archy Mead.' Aware she was taking a chance.

'But you're not sure?'

'How can I be sure, you great gook, without *feeling* if it's right between us. I mean, you've taken little notice of me these months, your head full of horses and fencing and the shearing coming up and your pitter-pattering jobs in Sydney and, for all I know, girls. But a man must settle on one sooner or later, mustn't he now?'

'It's hard for women out there, Grace.'

'No need to keep saying it for I never thought it would be easy. Certainly not easy when I bear my own.'

'Gracie Charlton!'

'Don't go on so for you're a grown man and you've seen many born. And I'll bear down so hard they'll pop out in a trice; I've seen how it's done and it won't daunt me. The babes must come and you know it for it can be cold down there as well as hot and I don't aim to have a husband who'll turn from me; there'll be only us to tackle it all and we must turn to each other. But if you're worried if it will be right between us, why we'll make sure now one way or the other.' She took a deep and visible breath at his startled look. 'You've never even kissed me, Joey Bowes.'

'You're a good girl, Grace.'

'Others say that, not I.'

'You've kissed Archy Mead?'

'More or less,' she lied happily, 'for how could I know if it was right with him if I didn't try?'

'Was it right?'

'It was fair.' Warming up to her deceit. 'But I reckon it could be better.'

'I never thought you'd let me kiss you.'

'As a test, that's all, so get that look off your face. But if a kiss is right all else that follows must be, wouldn't you say?'

217

'Seems fair to say it.' There was nothing left to retrieve or stack, nothing to do but stand waiting.

'Then think on this.' She grasped his face between her hands firmly and kissed him full on the mouth, holding the kiss until his mouth slackened and trembled under the hard pressure of her own. She let him go abruptly and he stood, flushed, faintly dishevelled and breathing quickly. 'Are you thinking on it?'

'I am.'

'Well?'

'It was . . . pleasant.'

'Is that all? It's not enough.' She reached for him again but, startled, he backed.

'Not here and in the day.'

'There's only a crow on a stump to see. But if you know of some secret place . . .' It seemed to set him in a panic, and he said breathlessly:

'You'd really take me on, then?'

It wasn't much of a proposal but if he'd said 'take Archy Mead' she would have died. That fumbling hasty boy-girl kiss was a start for he was beginning to see her as she was and to like what he saw. So, no more hated frills and slicked-up hair or flowers behind her ear dropping their creepy-crawlies down her back, all part of the awful prettying-up Ma considered necessary to catch a man. She, Grace Charlton soon to be Bowes, had much to learn as he had, but where they would go they'd have solitude and time surely to learn and to teach. She would never wilt from love like Adina Cook; she would live for love and thrive. She brushed off her hands with a purposeful gesture. Joey backed, turned and ran in stumbling panic. Laughing, she swept up her heavy basket, rested it on her hip and stood braced, legs apart.

'Of course I'll take you, you great gook.' Shouting it to the world. 'You great great *gook*!'

The shearers, working their way down from the Darling Downs, had been dribbling through Burrendah's gates for weeks past. The flocks from Calua and, this year, Erins

Pride, were coming in, moving across the home paddocks as grey worm-like undulations of dust, the dogs working, black specks on white backs as they stepped quivering from sheep to sheep or, snapping, hurled themselves at the flock. From kitchen to yards the stoves roared and the tables groaned for the mornings were still chilly and the men always ravenous. Alannah had no time to dwell on sadness, involved as she was in a bustling demanding world of toil, making its own rules from expediency rather than tradition, a world slowly forcing her back to life.

But it was more than the activity about her that stimulated. Brick O'Shea had come to Erins Pride, and so to Burrendah, and she could think of little else though he spent his time in the sheds or off with the men, his manner to her polite but quite impersonal – yet why had she expected otherwise? The knowledge that he was close gladdened her as it also saddened, for he would soon move on to Narriah, then to Oorin and its out-stations, farther out perhaps, touching remote places with strange aboriginal names not yet on a map. He would turn south again to follow the stock route across the One Tree Plain to Hay, Echuca, then into Victoria to Bendigo, south to Geelong, and Melbourne for the wool sales, taking steamer round to Sydney for Christmas. He would be weeks on the road, riding most of the way, joining the occasional cavalcade, camping out with Overlanders or a wagon train or a string of drays, or a wool clip on its ponderous haul to the coast, making good time in the dry but oozing and struggling through mud in the rain. Heart-twisting phrases trembled on her lips. *Don't leave me. Stay. But if you must go take me with you.*

Bold crazy words that shocked her. She should not be thinking of this bushman more than twice her age, married and unaware of her except as a neighbouring encumbrance and target for his teasing criticism, yet she could not help it. There were terrible moments when she feared he had already left and her relief actually hurt when he sent word he expected her to ride out with him to inspect new fencing between their properties. Posts and rails were going up all over the country, with boundary riders replacing lonely shepherds in the hills. She found it hard to talk calmly of mundane matters as they rode the long boundary line, wanting to go on like this for ever, alone with him, following the tracks and worn-down sheep pads over the slopes, to pull up and lead their mounts to the last of the fence where it dipped into the valley.

'Shearing's late. The men aren't coming in in numbers.' Testing a post he pounded it, irritated. 'I should have brought over some of the German women from South Australia, excellent shearers I'm told. And still no word from Ashby. Perhaps he's struck gold after all. So I'll need Aldercott more than ever. That pleases you, no doubt?'

It was petty and unlike him. Besides, she didn't want to talk of Simon, or even be reminded of him. 'I like riding with you,' she blurted out.

'I know.' He looked up, grinning. 'Because there's always the chance of outriding me. But only a faint chance, Miss Alannah.'

'Miss Alannah,' she mocked. '*Miss Alannah!*'

'Miss Moynan?'

'That's worse. It's school-marmish. I know I look like a bluestocking and a dull bluestocking at that—'

'What makes you think you look like a bluestocking?' Head down he moved along the rails and she was glad for it made it easier for her to answer.

'There's nothing really interesting about me. And I'm certainly not beautiful.'

'There are many things about you that are quite beautiful.'

She said after a time: 'No one's told me that before.'

'Perhaps you've never given anyone the chance.'

'Why don't you call me Alannah?'

'You've never given me permission, Miss Moynan.' It sounded stiff and horribly formal.

'Then I give it now. And I shall call you "Brick".'

'Alannah!' he mocked, his voice rising with a light triumphant ring to it. It was a fluent voice, a silky voice, an Irish voice if ever there was one, and it touched a deep responsive cord in her.

'You called me Alannah once before.'

220

'I did?'

'You know you did. When you told me of Con . . . and warmed my hands.' She heard her own words as if someone else were speaking them. 'You kissed them warm, remember?'

His hand stilled on the wood. 'I remember.' He turned to face her, frowning. 'Do you know how old I am?'

'Forty?'

'Tactful of you. And gallant. I'm not forty. I'm forty-eight.'

'I suppose you must be,' she said quietly. 'But if I were a man I'd want to be forty-eight. It seems a wonderful age to be. Not too young to be ignorant and foolish and yet not old. Not anywhere near old.' Then staunchly: 'But you don't look over forty.'

'If that is so, you have an excuse for ignoring my age. But no excuse at all for ignoring the fact that I am married.'

Stunned, she wanted to run, to hide, for he was implying that she was not only capricious but predatory. Implying other things too. She said formally, 'No one who has ever seen your wife, Mr O'Shea—'

'Now what's happened to your decision to call me "Brick"?'

'—could forget that you are married. How could anyone, certainly one as ordinary as myself, ignore Raunie? She's too beautiful, too fascinating for anyone to ignore. No woman could hope to compete with her.' Words tumbled. 'Or, knowing your preferences, compete with any other woman you've been rumoured in love with.'

'If I've been rumoured "in love" as you put it, I assure you the gossips exaggerate.'

'Is it not true you were betrothed to a Miss Merrill?' She knew she was being absurd, driven by something . . . jealousy? . . . of a dead woman as well as the living breathing Raunie.

'That much is true.'

'So you planned to marry without love?'

'People do.'

'So I understand. Particularly men. It seems they marry for many reasons – position, opportunity, money, power.'

221

'Barbara had no money. But she did have a certain social position and I had ambitions. But there were other reasons – affection, concern—'

'It was to be a marriage of convenience so why not be honest about it?'

'Perhaps because I hesitate to shock your tender sensibilities further. How very young you are, so young you plunge in probing a circumstance that is, frankly, none of your business.'

She bridled. 'If you imagine for one moment that I have any personal interest in your long-ago affair—'

'It was not an affair in the sense you imply.'

'Betrothal then.' Angry, she made a move towards Mourne.

'Betrothal, yes. Wait!' He spoke so imperiously and urgently she obeyed. 'You shall hear me out for in one of your perverse moods you've opened doors long closed. Besides, you want to hear it, oh yes, you *do*.' He took a long and visible breath. 'I cannot remember ever being what is called "in love", and it certainly mattered little where Barbara was concerned; indeed it was something of a relief from . . . well . . . what the world calls passion, an extravagance of feeling that clouds issues and makes a man less than he is.' He made an impatient gesture. 'But how could you possibly know what I'm talking about?'

'I am not stupid,' she flashed. 'Or as inexperienced as you seem to think.'

'No?' He laughed. 'You're as naïve and gullible and untried as a page of Holy Writ.'

'I will not be treated as a silly ignorant woman.'

'So it's woman now, is it?'

'Yes, woman. *Woman!*' Furious, and humiliated for something inside her was throbbing away in an unexpected disconcerting way. No one had used the word 'passion' to her before; she had heard it but only in Biblical text. Odd that, for there was something pagan-sounding about it as there was about the word 'desire' – and there was that throb again. She felt too warm, flushed, and moved her body in an attempt to dispel the disturbance. 'Passion' . . . 'desire' . . .

222

the words pulsed through her mind and body and she wished she understood what they meant, but she was ignorant, she knew it, and was tired of being so, particularly before this man. She knew about love, of course, for love was a respectable and proper emotion. People talked openly of love, hoped for it and went looking for it; one could see it hovering over others and could bathe oneself indirectly in its light and sometimes, if one was fortunate, love found you. She, Alannah Moynan, loved her father, she had loved her brother, but that was paternal and brotherly love. There was more . . . a love that grew out of respect and admiration for some particular man whom you married and had children by and so lived out your well-defined and approved life – married love. But there was even more . . . some feeling that consumed you and the source of it, culminating in a pleasure that changed you because it was exquisite and a little mysterious and shattered you so completely it stayed with you for ever. Could it be that this . . . intensity was actually touching her? She had not expected this singing in her head and all around her and through her when this man came near, despite being exasperated and humiliated by him, resenting him for speaking of things that had not even brushed her, something he understood and had experienced and that made him attractive and to be envied and the centre of things. He knew secrets she did not. He had tasted some flavour of life that to her, as yet, was an unknown quantity.

'All I was certain of,' he was saying, 'was that I needed Barbara. I am not an easy man or a contented one and never will be either, I suppose. All I knew was that I wanted to live my life with her, and the world about me was good because this was so. We could have made it even better. We would have turned to each other and gladly but she never knew it for there was no time or opportunity; or else I avoided making either or both. It was unfinished. Incomplete.'

'There! I don't believe you're half as callous with women as gossip says.'

'Then you're a fool for the gossips are right. Take heed of their warnings and you'll have no excuse for ignoring, along with my wedded state, my touch of the native which you are

223

too polite or foolish to ignore, and my reputation for being too dangerous for a woman to flirt with – silly word, "flirt", but fashionable, I understand, for describing amateur female efforts at seduction.'

'I flirt with *you*?' That he should think she would condescend like some tart or attention-starved wife!

'Aren't you, Alannah? To see how far you can try me? You are, you know, and it's dangerous, for you don't understand what you are about. You consider you're playing a harmless little game, teasing, offering crumbs, when in actual fact you're offering the whole cake.'

'How dare you speak to me so.' Her control snapped and she struck out with her crop so savagely it cut into his hand. He grasped the whip and held it. She refused to release it. 'I seduce *you*?' she raved, struggling for her whip and her supremacy, beside herself. 'An illbred, roughneck Black—' She broke off, appalled, so ashamed she wanted to run, but instead she pounded the unrelenting hand gripping the whip. 'I refuse to ride with you again,' she shouted. 'I refuse to even speak to you. If Con – if my father were here he would not let you treat me this way. He would kill you.'

'On the contrary I believe your father would understand exactly why I must force facts into the open and make you look at them. What are you? Eighteen? A convent-bred eighteen at that. You know nothing of yourself, certainly nothing of men.'

'I know a great deal about men.'

'Have you ever held a man to your body, breathed in unison with him, lost your breath in his?'

'Do not speak to me so.'

'I speak so to shock you, for too much is clattering about in your head, and in your body, beating away at both. I speak so to make you afraid of me, and set you running.'

'I won't run. I'm not afraid of you. Eighteen is not a child.'

He released her so abruptly she staggered. 'A great age! I can give you thirty years, think of that, thirty years of living while you floated in the womb waiting to shriek your entry to the world. Thirty years of learning and lusting in the worst of dives with the worst of women, white and black, roaring through this country taking what was offered and hungry for more. You will never know, or could imagine, a fraction of the practices I could teach you gathered up in those thirty years – or perhaps you could the way you've been flaunting yourself at me, not to mention wandering diggers and innocent untried clerks. You might take to erotic pastimes like the proverbial duck to water.'

'You are an evil man,' she said quietly but tensely, her eyes moist with emotion as she collected her dignity and folded her whip. 'You mock people. You make fun of feelings, young feelings. You laugh at hopes and longings. You are patronising and spiteful, and cruel for the fun of it.'

'Never that. The rest perhaps because I must drive you off with some sense in your skull. Good God, Alannah, think of what is happening.'

'I am riding home alone,' she said stiffly. 'And you will let me go.' He had made her feel bare, as if she were displaying herself naked before him – and there was that throb again.

'I'll let you go. But I'm a fool to do it for if ever a female was ripe on the vine you're that. Even if you don't know it I know it – hell, I know it. So run to some precious pallid male, to Aldercott if you must, who will say the proper prissy things, and do them. But hurry, for next time I'll not let you go. I swear I'll make things between us so that you won't want to go.'

He stood watching her ride off in a dangerous flurry, his eyes never leaving her, knowing that if her horse stumbled and threw her he would die. He felt a wisp of breeze and saw the long grasses shimmer as they burned under the heat of the noon sun. But beneath the trees there were small oases of shade and the grass was green and soft. Ripe on the vine! He ached to gallop after her and drag her from her horse and take her there in the deep close growth and teach her of his body and her own – and felt a little sick. Perhaps the churchmen and the professors were right and such as he would never be entirely civilised, mad in harbouring thoughts of mating with this girl, too young, alien to him, with her feet in another world. Yet his life had marked time since she had become the focal point of it so he had talked madly of mad things to drive her off, to hate him perhaps for he had done it well. Let her dedicated father, her rigid foolish handmaiden of an aunt, marry her off and soon to someone, anyone, to walk sedately and correctly through life, and he would no longer ride to her Place of the Swan to watch the sun glimmer over her hair and the beads of sweat dapple her throat or her eyes mist when she was hurt or angry or baffled and did not know what to do. And to see with his clear experienced eyes the trembling of her fingers because he was close and, though she did not know it, her eyes inviting him as she moved for him and towards him – ah, a wonderful yet terrible thing for him to know before she knew it herself. He yearned, yet had forced himself to draw back. It must not be. For if it were the world would blow itself to pieces about their heads.

Chapter Eleven

THEY WERE coming from Calua and Wiena and Erins Pride, from properties beyond, and homesteads and hamlets in between, for a day of sports and feasting culminating in the woolshed dance, traditional at Burrendah since Charles Huntly's young wife had bestowed the grace of her presence upon the event. The Blacks were camped along the Creek, the Jens in new shifts, twining ribbons in their hair and exchanging strings of beads as they whispered together, weaving favourite spells that the blue skies and velvety nights would hold. The shearing-shed had been cleaned and cleared in case of bad weather but no one would countenance the idea, and the grassy flat before it was decorated with branches and strings of coloured papers and all the Chinese lanterns that could be gathered from country cupboards. For days the children, white and black, had clustered goggle-eyed at the unpacking of great baskets and boxes of pies and cakes and fancy breads and buns, while Grace and Annie McKenzie prinked tarts and squeezed lemonade and piled fruits. Sheep had been slaughtered and hung in the cool-room for the roasting. Alannah, delighting in her new sprigged muslin, opened her trinket box and chose a Celtic cross on a fine chain that had belonged to her mother, to Grandmother Cassidy before her and others back in time, for it was very old, of Irish silver that glinted between her breasts; she had lowered her neckline and Aunt Delia could rage all she wanted, it would stay so. She was conscious of her body in a wonderful but faintly disturbing way and could think of nothing, no one, but Brick O'Shea – would he come? 'I refuse to ride with you again,' she had told him in anger. 'I refuse to even speak to you.' Had he believed her? She had meant it then. And could not understand why she rode to quiet corners of her world to look out over the rise and fall of hills towards Erins Pride, and sometimes cry quietly to herself.

It was a blue and gold, burning-bright day with wisps of cloud feathers on the horizon and a gentle breeze moving the treetops. Simon Aldercott, his tie already awry, marshalled his charges from Erins Pride together with children squeezed into the dray along the road, for no child must be left behind. Patty Gearin hovered for she had decided to set her cap at the schoolmaster, a figure of fun to the hands in his old-fashioned clothes, but a gent all the same. Besides, she liked a man to be a little shy, it was fun bringing him out of his shell, and she let out with a clenched fist at any boy who dared cheek him.

'Your father should be here,' Aunt Delia scolded as if it were Alannah's fault entirely he was not. 'It's his duty to be seen as the master of this property, it is not enough his daughter show herself. I suggested he ride up, a nothing of a ride for a man who rode from Londonderry to Magilligan just to exercise his horse on the sands. He's getting soft in the head as well as body by the sound of things. It's that woman. He's besotted with her. At his age!'

Alannah avoided discussion of her father, and was still reluctant to meet him not only because Con's death still haunted but because her father's life and her own seemed more than ever alien, he with city entertaining that would daunt her, his talk of O'Shea's mill building in Newcastle, his business associates and political aims – or rather, she suspected, O'Shea's political aims. Except for politics it was as if he had transplanted his comfortable Belfast existence to Castlereagh Street, Sydney, but with an added bonus: 'that woman' as her aunt insisted on calling his housekeeper so persistently it was often difficult to remember her name.

The entire population of Argyle County seemed to have jolted through Burrendah's gates since sun-up on drays, carts, horseback, and those living close, on foot. Barney Cook had come out of the shadows to hang around the men who would have none of him so he drifted to his cronies along the Creek. Adina slipped in, shadowed as usual by Billy, to squat under her favourite tree. Bedrooms and privies had been set aside for the pregnant and nursing mothers, the sleeping babes, and the old. Aunt Delia bickered happily with Ida over the setting out of food on trestle tables under the trees. Joey Bowes moved in his quiet absorbed way attempting to create order from the happy chaos, pursued by a vigilant Grace. Rob Witherstone looked unhappy in his unaccustomed leisure while Hetty made straight for the kitchen. There was a clown for the children and swings and hoops and all manner of games in which Simon appeared smothered in small boys until Patty slapped and slammed them to order. Alannah's eyes returned again and again to the road and beyond, throughout the morning of long-jumping and high-jumping, the tugs-o'-war and sack-races and three-legged races. She had always been able to run but now it was bitter-sweet for somehow Con was running beside her, shoulder to shoulder as they used to do until she made a sudden spurt and away – she had invariably won the sprints and he the cross-country races. In the afternoon the elders lounged or dozed off their lunch while the children and the youthful paddled or threw in fishing lines or wandered the Creek banks. The breeze died and they lay about in the cool of the evening but, restless, Alannah could not be still. The day was almost gone and he had not come. Brick O'Shea had not come . . .

'*When over Drumla's tide he'd see . . . the lamp of home . . .*'

Patrick O'Flaherty, father of the newly-arrived family at Calua station, sang in his raw quick plaintive voice that held all the lamentations and wild sweet gladnesses of Ireland – and many of its mischiefs. There would be much singing before the night was out for anyone who could keep a tune would be expected to do so. '*Old crumbling castles, holy wells and tolling spires . . .*' The sadness of nostalgia fell over his listeners touching Alannah quite unexpectedly and evoking a longing for Conall, for her father, for County Down, most certainly for Stonemore – with a deeper yearning she could not, dared not, identify or try to express. She was achingly conscious of time passing and her responses grew a little feverish as energies revived against a background of fat bracket candles and torches and coloured lanterns in long gay strings, with a concertina and flutes and all the fiddles that could be gathered from miles around tuning up. They gathered for the field dances and, though the night was warm, fires were built up on the outskirts for light but even more for friendliness, glowing over the children running about laughing and squealing and quarrelling and coaxing couples into the reels. Alannah moved, farewelling those who must leave early, serving drinks and offering her basket of little rolls and home-made sweets and chocolate for the children, but still he had not come. Brick O'Shea had not come . . . To cheer herself she forced herself to flippancy as fiddles tantalised and Pat shifted from one itchy foot to the other yet hung back shaking his head at her urging:

'Shame on you, Patrick O'Flaherty, that you put your heart into your songs but not your feet into the reels.'

'But the south reels to the pipes, Miss Moynan. The south has the bagpipes, y' see, and meself used to 'em.'

'The fiddles are finer. The fiddles sing. It has always been the fiddles with me, Patrick O'Flaherty.'

'But you'd not be knowing the true sweet call o' the pipes, you frum the Black North an' not used to the dancing.'

'Is that all you know of Belfast?' She stuffed corned-meat rolls into the grasping hands of his ever-hungry brood while his wife sat with her head down ashamed of her man's audacity at speaking so to the mistress of Burrendah. 'Many a Belfast hornpipe I've danced. You've not seen the dancing or heard the music on the streets of Belfast any Saturday evening, more Irish than ever came out of Connemara. Or, for that matter, County Cork.'

'Shame on your aunt, then, for allowing a well-brought-up young lady to dance in the streets with the rabble.' The mocking voice came from behind her muffled by the crowd but she would know it anywhere – he had come. Brick O'Shea had come! To be neighbourly or for good manners or simply tradition or because his people were here: it did not matter, he had come. Her basket trembled as she turned to face him.

'Belfast has no rabble as others know it, Mr O'Shea.' So formal about it but she was trembling so much she dared not speak otherwise. He was holding out his hand for her basket and their fingers brushed and she felt the world was watching, certainly Grace was staring but she did not care, she gloried in his touch. He hadn't taken his eyes from her and her hands moved intuitively to her open collar – a button missing? She did not care if it were, all she cared about was that he was here and she could not, would not, hide her delight. Con had been right, she was a child: grow up, Alannah Moynan, come out from your cloisters, from behind your grilles, and grow up to this man! She lifted her eyes boldly. 'There were times, you see, when Con and I ran off to dance, and for other mischiefs I suppose.' She laughed and then swallowed hard, shattered by the look in his eyes. He was devouring her. 'Among the mountainy people is where you'll see the dancing, in their big nailed boots and jumping three feet in the air and never tiring. Con and I once danced to ten fiddles all night and went home only when the sun rose and even then were not tired.'

'In that case,' he said clearly, but it would not have mattered if he had whispered, she would have heard, 'Burrendah's modest reels will scarcely touch the edge of your endurance.'

'I'll not be dancing the reels.'

'And why not?'

'Without my brother?' She was shocked. 'Con never tired, you see.'

'I do not tire easily.'

''Tis easy to be tricked in the reels.'

'Nor will you trick me easily.' He held out his hand. 'I've danced in Ireland long and well.'

The fiddles were squeals and shrieks of impatient sound – ah, to dance as she used to dance. She could not help herself and put her hand in his. His fingers wrapped about her wrist and with a wonderful lift to her heart and a tingle of her limbs she ran with him to be hurled into the ring of dancers. They stood poised, waiting, tapping, quivering to be off as Hennessy raised his flute and set the beat with a sharp tap-tap

231

of his boot – a born flautist, Hennessy. The other flutes joined in, the fiddles scraped, and they were off.

The fires glowed red and yellow daggers over them as they whirled and twirled to the racing violins. O'Shea was a wonderful dancer, she knew it from his first steps, a big man yet light and secure on his feet. She glimpsed Grace and Joey thumping by, a haze of Joey's light hair and earnest face and Grace's hands firm upon him. Other faces and bodies intruded – Simon intent on his feet in trying to keep up with Patty Gearin – but faces and bodies that slid away, drifting, for she saw nothing clearly, felt nothing but Brick's hands on her and she gave herself up to sensation against a background of throbbing exciting rhythms, remembering loved childhood festivals: the tolling of bells and counting of Ave Marias through the churches of Antrim . . . Playing truant from the nuns' crocodiles through Belfast lanes . . . Vivid mornings at Stonemore . . . The corner shrines of Eire . . . Old men, hands in sagging pockets, trudging Irish lanes to and from the local bar. And in and around and through it the force of the man who swayed with her, smiling as if he were as happy as she. Her body strained in its thin muslin as, lips parted and eyes shining, her heart high in her throat and loving it all, she throbbed to the music. Her eyes clung to his. She had never been as happy as now, never, and she laughed aloud for there was something right in her new joy. Life had changed. Life was different. There was nothing, no one in all the world but herself and the man holding her lightly, but ah, so surely.

Brick's eyes followed the firelight's gleam on her hair to the glitter of a cross, an Irish cross on a paper-fine chain that swung about her throat as she danced, glinting her skin. Such young skin. Her hand was warm and moist in his and the touch of her was almost more than he could bear. 'Alannah,' he whispered, then loudly, '*Alannah!*' to be lost in the wind of movement. Her name was always in his mind, and on his lips when alone. 'ALANNAH!' he shouted, losing it in the music and clapping and the thump of many feet as they whirled to the shrieking sensuous peasant rhythms of the Irish reels. His blood raced and he prayed hers did too,

232

for him. Abruptly the dance was over and they stood quivering, unable to part. Her eyes were wild and gleaming and met his freely and boldly but the crowd rushed them apart and carried her off to sing for them in the Irish – when she had caught her breath, she laughed, startled, looking back at him, pleading with him he knew. He could only follow her bright head to find her seated, hunched, half in shadow, her arms embracing her knees, a blur of white and gold where the firelight flickered over her. She sang 'The Irish Emigrant', the song of County Down, not such an old song but poignant in its story-telling, and she sang it in the Gaelic taught her by Grandmother Cassidy; always the Gaelic with Grandmother Cassidy: 'The worrds do not come out roight in the English,' she would grumble fiercely. 'The worrds do not fit.' All were silent now for the voice was young, sweet and very clear. Aunt Delia had been precise in her tuition: 'Never slide off the notes, girl. I do not teach you to wail at a Connemara wake, I train you to sing in Belfast drawing-rooms.' Her triumphs in that direction had been modest but sweet and now, as she sang, visions were conjured up in the homesick Irish of places they would never see again, hard forbidding places but their own, and when it was over all were quiet, for Ireland, the hard and soft of it, remained and they hunched, subdued, some weeping, the Scots ashamed of the way the Irish, silly sods, went on, and the Blacks crouched on the outskirts close to the fires with eyes like white marbles, afraid of such emotion, brooding on evil spirits of their own. Mercifully, some roused calling for a jig. Then there must, of course, be a hornpipe, and children ran about begging sweets and little rolls and so intent were they all on the dancing no one noticed Alannah Moynan merging with the shadows, at least none but Brick O'Shea whose eyes had never left her, absorbing her as a thirsty man gulps drink, watching her pale shape fade into distance. He slipped from amid the revellers, past the fires, moving down a river of warm dark towards the burning brooding fire that was Alannah – ah, he knew! Pausing at the foot of the slope he let out his breath at the hazy white of her drifting here now there as if she did not know, quite, where she was going. But he knew she was making her way to the willows that hunched to meet overhead and form a barrier between the Creek and the homestead; her private place, her coppice as she called it. He parted matted grasses pungent with the scents of early summer. Ferns teased, accentuating his tension, and only once did he pause at a gust of sound from behind him. He stood till it died away and he was alone again but for the faint lap of Creek water to proclaim there was a world about him. He tangled in willows as if he were swimming through watery fronds and knew he was close to her for he heard tiny irregular sounds. He saw her dim shape leaning against the remains of an old bridge that had crossed the Creek long before Burrendah had taken shape, now crumbled to a bare hint of a wall.

'Alannah,' he whispered, but urgently. Silence until he felt her brush by and his hands went out to grasp and hold her. 'Don't run away. And don't cry so.'

'You had no right to follow me.' She struggled, savage in her pride, but he would not release her. 'This is my own place and no one else comes here. Where I go or what I do has nothing to do with anyone. Certainly not with you.'

'It has everything to do with me. Be still now.' But she strained against him, her palms flat against his chest.

'Why shouldn't I cry? For my father whom I never see. For my brother whom I will never see again. For my aunt if I wish it. For Ireland.' Wild and fierce in her unhappiness.

'You've set Ireland behind you.'

'Not tonight.'

'Everyone's missing some country tonight. It will pass.'

'I don't know where I belong. I thought I knew but I don't. Not really.'

'You're not crying for Ireland. Or because of your father, or your aunt. Not even for your brother.'

'*Yes.*'

'No. You're crying for something else, not what you've lost or think you've lost but what you want.'

'I don't know what I want – I suppose.' It was a plaintive cry of despair.

'You know.'

'I do *not*.'

'Oh yes. And you must put it into words, hear yourself say it aloud. For I must hear it too.'

'Why must you hear it?'

'Is it your Simon Aldercott?'

'He is not *my* Simon.' Straining from him yet towards him. 'I don't want Simon. I want . . . want—'

'*Say* it.'

'It's you I want. *You*. There, I've said it.' Even in the half-dark he could see her eyes wild and hunted and he held her close, knowing that at that precise moment she hated him. 'You should not have made me say it.'

'I had to hear it.' Trembling with her as she turned her cheek against his. Their lips clung, hers tasting of salt yet very sweet. He drew her down to the warm scented grass in the shelter of the old stones. She turned her body wholly and pressed to him with the eager jerky movements of a child, pleading and urgent, yet there was nothing of the child in her violent little caresses. With a heavy drawn-out sigh she held his open palms against her breasts, covering them, and he felt the nipples harden as she bared them to him with a gesture that was entirely primitive, as if she would die without his touch.

'Yes . . . *yes*,' he murmured and buried his head between her breasts, sinking into them as he sank into her yielding body that closed around him and held. She caressed his face, her lips opening to his as he moved his hands over her in love, enchanted. He caressed her in long loving movements, over her shoulders and down the long lines of her back to the curve of her waist and with a long-held final sob that grew into gasps her arms went about him and her mouth became eager and hungry, the way he wanted her. Seeking the depths of each other they passed the point from which they could return. If she could, he could not. If the mind could return the body could not. Finally the mind was still. The world was still. Only once was there human sound: a woman's deep and rasping cry, dragged from the very roots of her to mingle with the gentle lap of the stream and lose itself in the enclosing ferns and willow curtains that sheltered them from the outside world.

She was the first to stir. At the movement of her head, then her naked thigh from his, he opened his eyes to first light. They had dozed through the night in the sheltered warmth of the angle wall, stirring to enjoy each other then sleep again. She pushed aside his jacket, smoothed her hair as best she could, and arranged her clothes. They stood quietly and close, listening. 'They've all gone,' she said. 'Long ago.' They walked hand in hand through the willows and up the slight slope to the dead fires and the litter of the night's revelry; even the Blacks had gone leaving an empty and abandoned world. But a world that would soon be astir.

'Don't come close,' she whispered. 'Not now.' They kissed long and deeply before she hastened to that part of the sleeping house that was her own. He stood watching her until her door closed. It was not until midday that he rode in to Erins Pride. How far he had ridden he could not tell nor did he care, he had given Glenora his head. He spoke little and gave no explanations and no one asked questions. They never did. He fell on his bed and slept as a dead man.

Joey Bowes was decidedly unsteady on his feet and ashamed of his tipsiness for he knew Mr O'Shea would not approve. As for Grace . . . He groaned more at the idea of confronting Grace than at his aching head. After she had finally relinquished him some madness had sent him to join the men and the Three Paddys' store of grog, for away from Dan Charlton they became teasing rip-roaring rogues. One thing had led to another and he didn't know how he came to be here behind the workshop. He groaned with something more than his heaving stomach; Grace would give him an earful if he did not spark up before she was about. As for her mother . . . He blinked, assaulted by the growing light, with no time of heart to ponder Grace or her mother or women in general, a subject that plagued him, for he was forced to run behind the shed again to throw up decently and thoroughly. So intent was he on his still-heaving stomach and getting his breath that at first he could not be certain the two coming up through the brush were really Mr O'Shea and Miss Moynan, hand in hand . . . He decided they must have been out for an early ride until he recognised Miss Moynan's dress of the night before, remembering how fine she had looked dancing by, with a pendant of some sort, a cross he thought, swinging about her throat and glinting in the lights. But she looked different now, sort of dishevelled, unusual for her and the fact disturbed him. They were coming up from the Creek, from the place she called her coppice, her secret private place always left sacred to her own purposes. As he stood watching, they turned to each other and kissed. He shrank back, wishing he hadn't seen that kiss. He wished he hadn't seen them at all for he felt shock and embarrassment, then, for some reason, anger, which made him feel sick again but in a different way. Groaning, he ran behind the shed. Finally he flopped in the long cool grass to try to sleep off his misery and bewilderment as well as his aching head. Joey Bowes was troubled as he had never been troubled before.

Alannah bathed, changed her clothes and prepared to confront the day. It was then she missed her Celtic cross. She searched her room without sign of it. She searched the hall then, discreetly, the house, retracing her steps of the night before, staving off her aunt's happily abstracted queries as to exactly when she had come to bed? As she recalled, Aunt Delia had retired early, remarking it was as well the event was only once a year for she was exhausted by it all. Alannah met the queries with lies: after all, she must learn to lie now, and successfully, and seemed to succeed for Delia Carney trotted off to the kitchen to irritate Ida with questions and criticisms. No sign of her necklet about the house. Then she could have lost it dancing, the most likely time and place, for it had swung on its too-thin chain, the clip loose no doubt: she had been careless of it. But it was past midday before she found an opportunity to stroll the dancing area where the

Blacks squatted, feasting on leftovers instead of clearing up and taking down decorations. She noticed Barney Cook wandering about, but then Barney was always prowling somewhere. No sign of pendant or chain. There was only one likely place left to search: her coppice. Yet, curiously perhaps, she felt reluctant to go down, now, today, for it was Brick's beloved place now as well as her own – but she was thinking foolishly. Childishly! She turned her steps resolutely towards the Creek.

She searched the long grass, she searched everywhere, but no sign of cross or chain. Perhaps it had been picked up by an exploring child, a scavenging Black, or a station hand, to be handed in – or kept as a trophy. She was reluctant to make enquiries, impelled by a sense of preservation not only for herself but for Brick for no one else must intrude upon this her sanctuary, her retreat, now theirs since they had made a world here, a world that must remain untouched, unviolated and safe; she did not even want to speak of this place to others. So what, after all, was the pendant's actual worth? Very little she supposed in money terms. Why not let things be? Though she had valued the cross as an heirloom it was really nothing more than a sentimental reminder of a life that had gone. She turned and walked slowly back to the house. Yes, she would let things be. So far as she was concerned the necklet was not only lost but forgotten.

Busy about the Pride stables Joey paused, arrested by Barney Cook squatting, head down, staring at something in his palm, turning whatever it was over and over with one thin finger. He was about to order him out when the something gleamed in the strong light through the open doorway. Barney looked up and closed his hand quickly – nothing subtle about Barney Cook. Joey moved to him.

'What are you hiding there?'

Barney scrambled to his feet and backed. 'Nothing, boss.'

'Don't call me boss. I'm not boss. And you do have something. What is it?'

'I find, not steal.'

'Show me or I'll bring Mr Witherstone.'

Barney's hand shot open. He didn't want the manager of Erins Pride prying and poking. Besides, he wasn't really interested in his find, it was too . . . different. He knew the Christian cross, everyone knew it through the missions and the churches and those who came to take holy service – besides, he was Christian as his father had been Christian. This was like the Christian cross yet not, and he didn't expect anyone would give him money for it, not even in at the Goulburn pubs, and if he couldn't sell it and quick, he didn't want it. It would be bad luck. All the time bad luck. He put the cross on its broken chain into Joey's hand.

'Where did you find it?' Joey examined it carefully. 'Come on, answer me.'

'At Burrendah, boss.'

'Don't call me "boss", I said. Exactly where at Burrendah? And when?'

'Near Creek, boss. Morning after dance. Cleaning up.'

'Scavenging, you mean.' He paused, then looked up sharply.

'What time the morning after the dance?'

'Sun up long time. Long long time. Sun up there.'

He pointed straight up to the midday sun and Joey gave a sigh of relief. If Barney were telling the truth, and he saw no reason for the fellow to lie about it, it would have been noon before he had wandered off to scavenge for himself, picking up a haircomb here, a ribbon there, a few coins if he were lucky, then to invade Miss Moynan's area of the Creek where no one else went, to find this in the long grass. Joey examined it again: yes, he remembered it swinging about her throat as she danced. It was of silver he thought, heavily engraved, and too weighty for its fragile chain. It was an Irish cross, he fancied – and hated it. He hated everything about it – no, what he felt for it was resentment. And because he so resented this thing he held in his hand he could only threaten the one who had confronted him with it.

'If you tell of this there are those who might decide you stole it.'

'I not steal, boss, I find.' Barney was indignant.

'Then keep a still tongue about it. I'll give it in at Burrendah. They'll find the owner – someone from Calua or Wiena perhaps. Now get out and find work to do.'

He wanted rid of Barney though he felt reasonably certain that, for his own sake, the Black would say nothing. He felt just as certain Barney did not know the bauble belonged to Burrendah's mistress. How valuable it was Joey did not know nor did he want to know. He didn't even want to think about it. Yet it seemed he had assumed responsibility for it. Perhaps Miss Moynan was even now fretting over it, searching the house for it. Even so, he could not, would not, confront her with it. What to do? How he wished he had not seen her with Mr O'Shea for somehow the possession of this, her necklet, was involving him in that association and he knew only one thing clearly: he, Joey Bowes, must protect his master. And, a little for her own sake for he had always liked her and did now despite her – treachery, what else? – Miss Moynan.

He tucked the cross in his trousers pocket but it seemed to burn against his leg. Finally he hid it in the box where he kept his few possessions: fishing lines, a warm scarf Miss Merrill had knitted for him, full of holes now but precious. Shells picked up on a Sydney beach. Books the master had given him when he had learned to read, one on husbandry, another on stone-masonry. A map the master had drawn marking Narriah and Oorin and hills and valleys and plains and deserts and great rivers running down to the mighty Murray. Trouble was, wherever he went, the necklet would travel with him in his mind. He couldn't forget it, as he couldn't forget Mr O'Shea and Miss Moynan walking up from her coppice in the early morning, hand in hand . . . kissing . . . He felt possessed by them. And by the silver cross.

The dust of the last wool-team to rumble through Burrendah's gates had settled and men, women and children were attempting to do the same, still reluctant about the daily routine of early summer. Joey rode to Burrendah to say his

240

dutiful goodbyes but Grace was making it an awkward and sentimental parting, dragging him along the Creek for a Sunday picnic fortified by a basket of meat rolls and lemon tarts and her freshly baked scones. He managed to smother her loudest laments in the chomping of his jaws, wondering idly if there would be honey at Oorin – wild bees? He did not know, and it bothered him sometimes how little he really knew about Oorin, but he consoled himself that Grace would know everything, she would make a point of it. Rather regretfully he declined the scones for he'd already devoured half a dozen. He concentrated on his pannikin of tea, hot, strong and very sweet, while her voice flowed on and over him like the eddies of the stream.

'Mr O'Shea should have sent someone else down. Anyway, Richie's there, though he's never good for much. Fay's there too though she's good for even less. But it just isn't right to separate husband and wife.' Joey's mouth dropped open from surprise, then expectation as she handed him a lemon tart. 'You've got to think of us now, you know.'

'I think of us all the time, Grace,' he managed between bites. 'But orders are orders.' There was something responsible and comforting and final about the phrase for it meant someone else was doing the deciding. 'Orders are orders,' he repeated.

'It's bad luck to postpone a wedding. Now I suppose we must wait until May.' But she roused with her usual optimism. 'But since we'll have nigh on five hundred miles to travel I'm already packin' m'boots, so to speak.'

'Plenty of time, Grace.'

'Time goes. Besides, Miss Moynan's giving me things: sheets and blankets, and cloth to make curtains, and clothes she no longer wears, good clothes mind, no cast-offs. And she says I may choose any dress of hers I fancy so I'll take the one she wore to the woolshed dance, the finest there. And she's promised preserves enough to last us years. And cuttings for a garden. Seeds too. We'll have a rich start, Joey Bowes, thanks to the mistress, and her with so much on her mind. I mean, she must have, for it's as if she's pondering something, something serious, only perking up when she goes riding out in her breeks. She's different of late, sort of closed up, harder to talk to.'

'Pass the tarts,' he ordered sharply for he was getting his second wind. But Grace's mind seemed firmly fixed on the mistress of Burrendah.

'She was different the night of the dance, in her lovely dress and her hair flying and her pendant swinging on its chain, dancing by with Mr O'Shea, laughing up at him. Now she looks sort of lost, as if she's aching for something. Someone . . .' She paused, frowning.

'You shouldn't talk so of your mistress.'

'Why not? Miss Moynan's real friendly. She talks to me a lot – at least, she *did* – of things and people. We talked about you—'

'You talk too much all round.'

'You'll be glad of m'chatter when we're off at Oorin.'

'Not so sure that I will. Anyway, you don't know Miss Moynan, not really.'

'Oh, but I do. I know she's drifting off somewhere – like Adina. Adina was always off somewhere in that odd way she had—'

'Hold your tongue, Grace Charlton.' The last straw was Adina dragged back into his life, by Grace at that. He did not want to be reminded of Adina. Or of Miss Moynan and her pendant. Nor did he want to be reminded of Mr O'Shea. He didn't even want to be reminded of himself and Grace, not now, not yet. 'You talk too much of things you don't understand,' he went on in a rush, 'so stick to your baking and washing and beating of carpets for if you don't hold your tongue I'm like to take some other girl to Oorin – Lucy from the Royal, or Patty Gearin, oh, there's many would jump at the chance, I know that. And you'll not be grabbing at Miss Moynan's things, certainly not that dress she wore to the dance. You'll wear the dresses I provide and you'll work and eat and bed down with me as I say in the house I'll be fixing up. And if you don't like the sound of that then don't come. If we're for each other it'll be my way so you'll quiet down a bit for there are times like now, and times to come, when I don't want to hear you speak. I'm off tomorrow and you'll wait at

Burrendah's gates to bid me goodbye as I ride by. And you'll wait at Burrendah till I choose to come and wed you. And if you don't like the sound of it all, Gracie Charlton, don't take me on. Just don't take me on.'

As he scolded loudly, harshly but firmly, Grace's jaw had dropped open to hang while she stared, stunned by the words pouring from him as if he had crowded them in and saved them up until the exact moment to let them loose. Never before had she heard him use words as he did now, she hadn't realised he knew so many. It not only shocked but stopped her in her tracks and she could find nothing to say to match him as he scrambled to his feet and stalked off without a backward glance. All she could do was take a long deep breath.

'Well!' she breathed. She took another long deep breath. '*Well!*'

It promised to be a hot summer. Though they were barely into November, heat shimmered and burned over the hills. Aunt Delia spent much time on a chaise-longue fanning herself or mopping her cheeks with a damp cloth, a cool lemonade to hand, begging Alannah to stay indoors at least until evening. 'Why do you ride out so often? You'll take sunstroke. This country is not for Celts, one must be born to it, like the blackfellows.' Alannah was not aware, nor did she care if it were hot or cold or night or day, she lived only for her meetings with Brick. Usually they met halfway and turned along the Creek to the lagoon with only sheep and the swans to see them, but she would not have cared if the whole country knew of their coupling, as perhaps it did by now. They did not talk much, there would be time for that later, but ate of each other through the hot lazy afternoons, prolonging their lovemaking till they lay inert and satisfied in a world of their own. So intense was their need of each other they slept uneasily and fitfully when apart. How wonderful it was to love and be loved, Alannah dreamed, not at all as she had been told – what did the nuns know? she scorned in her pride of initiation. She scorned too her

243

aunt's Puritan warnings. And felt more than ever remote from her father: fathers worried about hot or cold winds on you, whether you got enough to eat or had clean pocket-handkerchiefs; fathers told you nothing of life or love as it really was, this feverish longing for one particular man. Perhaps they did not want daughters to know. Perhaps they simply did not know how it was. Possessed, and so, possessive, she refused to spoil their time together by speaking of days to come, even less of the immediate future. It was he who spoke of such matters.

'The North is no longer a dumping ground for unwanted cargoes, including human ones. I have invested in land on the Darling Downs; at present it's out on lease. But if you don't like the idea of Moreton Bay, or even of Australia, there are places in Europe where a man and woman can live together without interference.'

'You'd leave Erins Pride?'

'I'll build another. I'll build a dozen. After all, you will leave your Place of the Swan. All you give up I will replace, I'll make up for the lack of marriage lines.'

'It's not that,' she assured him. Indeed it was the least of her concerns; her concern was with the pang of separation. How would she endure the weeks without this rhythm of loving that had become part of her? Even so, she would not hold him back for the sooner he went the sooner he would return, and their final goodbyes were as controlled as they could manage them, so resigned that she was surprised when, on the morning of his departure, he rode by.

'I must go with an easy mind, Alannah.' He paused before adding bluntly, 'Is all well with you?'

He looked . . . forlorn, she thought. Yes, 'forlorn' was the word, if a strange word to apply to him. He was in a strange mood and she could not let him leave her so. She made light of things. 'Of course all is well. But it will be better when you come again. Hurry back. Just hurry back!'

To Delia Carney's relief Mr Aldercott was to accompany them to Sydney. If Mrs Carney and Miss Moynan would permit he would be happy to make all arrangements, which meant he could ride to Burrendah for little discussions on coach times and baggage lists and calculation of expenditure. Alannah was happy to leave all to him and her aunt. One letter had come from Brick, addressed to Dan: he was making for the Murray, then to Narriah on the Edward and on to Oorin and its outstations in Lachlan country. Though hungry for news of him she found she resented the letter for its detachment, an unreasonable reaction but without him her world was desolate, his whereabouts no more significant than a string of exotic-sounding names. She would have drifted bereft but for Grace's insistence on helping her pack for Sydney. They were leaving for Brighton at the end of the month.

Obsessed as she was with her physical loss the world jarred. Nothing seemed to go right and her depression grew, to culminate one morning when she woke in the dark disturbed by a dream – what else but a dream? But struggling upright, breathless, she was aware suddenly and clearly that what had woken her was not entirely a dream but the continuance of a disturbance, a doubt now confirmed. This was the real world and her body was a part of that world, a body she had trained herself to ignore as an instrument that if well-treated and kept healthy would manage itself. But it seemed that her body was no longer entirely hers; it was managing and possessing her, its rhythm disturbed, its monthly cycle interrupted, possessed by something . . . someone other than her own familiar bones and flesh and blood. A child. Brick's child. Her first reaction was shock, her heart racing until, scolding herself into some semblance of calmness, she breathed deeply and rationally. Why should she be surprised? She had given herself often and gladly, as had Brick to her, in a world of their own making and mating. So: high time, Alannah Moynan, you stopped whimpering for this is a circumstance of your own making and only you can resolve it – at least learn to handle it. She was back with the practical natural world of cause and effect so no agonising, no regrets –

ah, certainly no regrets. She had wanted him for so long, as he had her, and it was done, they belonged. But for all her reasoning she pressed her mouth deep into her pillow to stop the trembling of her lips, longing for him. He would know what to do. What to do? Fool that she was, what *could* he do? What could anyone do? Even so, she needed his presence and he was not anywhere that she knew of and she drifted in helplessness and loneliness. In the still dark her lover seemed lost in some awful isolation she could not visualise and where she could not follow.

She rode more often to Erins Pride hoping there would be word of him but there was nothing. They did not expect letters, Hetty snapped, her mind on Jane's difficult pregnancy. Where, then, could she write Mr O'Shea? Hetty's glance was as much puzzled as irritated and her reply impatient as it so often was with the mistress of Burrendah. Sometimes she did not understand Miss Moynan at all, such a . . . a . . . *persistent* young woman! If Burrendah was in need of help she had only to ask it. Mr O'Shea did not like to be bothered by trifles. Trifles! Alannah didn't dare laugh for fear it would turn to hysteria but she was dogged in her questions to a Hetty just as dogged in her answers. No one could be certain letters would reach Mr O'Shea when he was on the road but Taylor's Hotel at Deniliquin held his mail and forwarded it when possible. Or she could write to his Melbourne bank, but he wouldn't touch Melbourne for some time. Alannah did commence a letter but tore it up – what was there to say? *I am having your child, come back immediately.* It sounded too ridiculous if it weren't so heartbreakingly real. How long before others must know . . . Her father? Her aunt who had beaten her for her first lie, a white lie at that? She moved through her days without energy or interest, unwilling even to discuss their Sydney visit, ignoring Simon's attentions, certainly his air of sublime patience in explaining arrangements. She escaped in riding out to the hills, breaking into a gallop now and then as if in so doing she might leave the situation behind, but it kept pace with her, always there and tormenting. If she were to sit carelessly in the saddle she could catch her shoulder on that branch approaching, the one that hung low . . . She would survive, she felt that, but the child that was not yet a child would surely abort. Her hands loosened on the reins and she sat sideways, slipping a little, but a sickening lurch made her cry out and clutch at the mare. What had stopped her? Why had she pulled back? Cowardice? Or something else . . . the conviction that this was not the way for her? She had no choice but to face the fact that she, an unmarried woman, was to bear a child to a man already married, furthermore, to a man outside her world and background. Even more significant to a man of the aboriginal race – her mind cut off, refusing to pursue that line of thought for somehow the fact had always been a part of him and his personality, now imparted to her. Her problem was to contrive, plot, plan, for her own safety and survival – and that of her child. Calm again, she rode slowly and carefully home.

Chapter Twelve

SYDNEY WAS ringed by bushfires. Hot winds from the inland built up dark and ominous clouds on the horizon to creep over the city in choking blinding dust, sending 'helps' hurrying to slam windows and stop up crevices. The sun pierced the mustard haze to crackle the earth as if it were paper. One o'clock struck from the churches followed by bells from the Shipping over a languid city closing for its hour, with gentlemen puffing along near-deserted streets for their shilling luncheons and working-men to seek shade, any shade, for their dinners. Summer tightened its grip with temperatures already in the top nineties and climbing. Sydney wilted and longed for a 'southerly buster'.

Night brought no relief but darkness. Collars choked and dress clothes constricted and men sweated for even the partial relief of a smoking jacket, a sherry cobbler and a pipe. Even Owen Moynan found Brighton confining, his guests dawdling as much over talk as over their perch and roast mutton, not even Durand's Alley and its fellow cesspools sparking verbal heat. Argument was scarcely more vigorous over the newly-introduced secret ballot, a long overdue advance, Whaley insisted, since Victoria and South Australia had enjoyed it for two years. Enjoy? A man will know nowt of what his friends drop into the ballot box, Mason grumbled. Precisely the idea, Hugh grinned. Mason disliked Hugh Whaley, dubbing him a know-all colonial 'blower'. Owen strove to confine argument to the less heating subjects of commerce or colonial tweeds but argument always settled, finally, on O'Shea's silence. He had never arrived at Hallows station so into what desert had he disappeared? Bill Hallows had sent men out as far and as often as he could spare them, but nothing . . .

248

'These tribal Blacks are all the same, half daft.' Mason smacked lips over his opinions as much as over other folk's liquor. Owen frowned.

'Tribal? O'Shea?'

'Summat must linger, wouldn't you say?'

'Bred out long ago,' Hugh scorned. 'Colour breeds out in the Australian Aborigine, you know that, Mason, or should. Ride out over the sand-hills and see all shades.'

'Know all I want to know about the bastards. Niggers have been causing trouble since we settled the place.'

'You settled nothing. You're a new broom.'

'Other habits stay, then.' He was truculent and florid. 'The Indians up and go walkabout, as they call it.'

'I'd scarcely call O'Shea vetting his lands and property, going walkabout.'

'The man has too much, too scattered. He's lost himself in it.'

'He'll turn up. He always has.'

But he wasn't turning up and Owen was forced to make decisions concerning arrivals from overseas or from Victoria with introductory letters, people he dared not, from a business point of view, ignore. But, deliberately, he off-shouldered the womenfolk to Birubi's mistress, reluctant though she was, to amuse as best she could. At least he could depend on the smooth running of Brighton, even now with the imminent arrival of his daughter and sister; their rooms were ready and waiting, while he viewed with dismay, even some panic, Maria Swallow moving upstairs to the small attic room.

'But it is right, Mr Moynan.' Always formal around the house and before others. 'This is your family.' All he would know now of her would be the rustle of her gown as she served him breakfast, or cool drinks when they were needed and even when not. All that would go on but not the other . . .

He had met Con's death with outer calm but then had come the restless, sometimes sleepless, nights when he would wander the house to pour a whisky, or brandy and water, even in desperation to fall back upon the banality of hot chocolate. He had been carrying a cup of it to his room when a shaft of light had cut across the landing and his housekeeper was in her doorway, her hair braided to her waist, and they had stared at each other, the ticking of the big grandfather clock clear and precise, echoing something within themselves, or at least within him. He had stumbled over the falsehood of an apology.

'I was not asleep, sir. I heard you go down. If there is anything I can do, at any time, you have only to ring.'

He scarcely heard his murmured excuses. She had taken the chocolate, her hand steady where his had trembled so that the cup made tiny slurring sounds against the saucer. She had moved back to place the drink on her bureau and he had followed because he could not help it. She had drawn him in and the click of the door-bolt had sounded almost exultant. With an equal lack of fuss she had drawn him into her bed to scented sheets that were cool and soothing on his bare limbs. Even more delightfully her body had been as cool as it was smooth through the still hot night, plump but not unduly so, her hips and belly softly rounded as he liked them to be in a woman. A soft and soothing body – until the fire had begun, an inner core of heat that burned him up, rousing his own heat to fuse with hers in a delicious fever of sensation. The tantalising promise of that fire had drawn him back, night after night, and now he fretted for her. It was of course time his daughter was here for Alannah needed change, certainly sea breezes, and to talk of many things, particularly her brother, but Maria Swallow had become his sustenance, his food and drink. How long must he wait for her?

As the coach neared Sydney it became a stifling prison of wood and leather. Angry flares of fire flickered along the roadside so that they wondered if they would get through safely. The bustle of the Haymarket came as heavenly relief and as their cab plodded its heavily baggaged way towards Brighton, Aunt Delia dozing in her corner, Alannah roused from her own torpor to admire shops gay with bonbons and greenery and cut-out paper doyleys, for despite everything

Sydney was preparing to enjoy its Christmas. When the cab halted, baulked by wagons and horsemen, she leant out to breathe in the odours of roasted Mocha and spices and heady unidentified scents from beneath shop awnings, feeling an urge to go shopping, not only to fulfil her own needs but that of – she pulled up her thoughts. How naturally she was accepting this baby! Leaving her aunt to complain of stiffness and order Simon and young Ned about as they struggled with the boxes, she hurried up Brighton's steps to greet her father coming along the hall.

'Dearest girl.' He seemed genuinely happy to see her. But Aunt Delia loosened veils and swept off her cape, her mouth a determined pursy-pink as she marched through rooms seeking a battleground from which to vanquish the detested Swallow. Alannah found the woman polite and helpful but with something about her – could 'menacing' be the word? – though never, she noticed, when her father was near. As the days went by she could even feel sympathy for her aunt, for a rapier thrust of a rapier finger across a bureau top or a knick-knack revealed nary a speck of dust, and Delia Carney finally retreated to lose herself in Eveline Purdue's programme of Good Works. But a temporary retreat, Alannah was sure; Aunt Delia was merely 'girding her loins', as she would put it.

No matter how she tried to resume her old relationship with her father she found him a stranger, talking of the Legislative Assembly as if he were already a Member rather than in the process of being groomed for some suburban municipal council. 'Easy enough to get a Bill through the Lower House but Council can be stubborn.' He described minor details of O'Shea's mills as if he believed her to be as interested in the project as himself. He spoke of Con in the same tone as he spoke of markets for wool and showed only a passing interest in Burrendah which saddened her more than surprised for he was, she could see, warmly ensconced in a world he found gratifying and full of promise. He had hoped she would bring news of O'Shea. All Sydney was knocking on his door, some obviously glad to be rid of the man – debtors mostly, he smiled – others demanding a search party be sent out, still others insisting O'Shea would not take kindly to being hunted as a criminal. He wore a signet ring and his thick hair with its touches of grey shone sleekly, he who had despised dandyisms in his son. She felt as isolated from him as she felt from Sydney's social life and dreaded the moment he must know of her coming child. A love child. A bastard, for that is what it would be. Yet he was all she had – and her aunt of course. But she dared not contemplate Aunt Delia's reaction, a woman who had punished her severely for childish evasions and rebellions.

'Have you said your prayers?'

'Yes, Aunt Delia.'

'And studied your Bible?'

'No, Aunt Delia.'

'I'm well aware that the Old Church has always been suspicious of the Bible as a confusing and dangerous book, nevertheless it is God's voice—'

'I don't like those dreadful old prophets thundering at me.'

'Protestant or papish God, that is your choice, but at Stonemore we do not insult the Old Testament. Extra prayers, Alannah. And a reading of Genesis 11.'

'Not all those begats again!'

'Genesis 11. Or you will be beaten for blasphemy as well as insolence!'

Someone, the sentimental Effie perhaps, had festooned green sprigs about pictures and posts, and was keeping Christmas flowers alive with love and precious water. The last few years they had adopted the custom of the Christmas tree but since there were no firs here someone, her father she suspected, had set a native bush in an ornamental tub – so he had remembered. It was only a rather prickly shrub but the best they could do and with the decorations she had brought out in her baggage – strings of coloured bells and wax lights – and with the addition of holly sprays even without red berries she could make the tree look happily nostalgic until Twelfth Night. Her father remarked that she looked tired even making allowances for the heat and the rigours of the journey and he felt a little city gaiety would be good for her. He was certain Simon would be happy to escort her wherever she might wish to go – it was 'Simon' now, she noticed, as if he were actually one of the family. Clearly her father and his friends were pairing her with Simon Aldercott for he was a familiar presence about Brighton, hanging on her father's words, head slightly tilted, face eager, standing, back straight to the empty grate, with the habit of glancing over his shoulder as if hoping for the friendly fires of a Lichfield December. He brought books from the lending library and wildflowers which he went out of his way to pick in suburban lanes. And was so obviously delighted to be her table companion at her special birthday dinner she felt herself being drawn into a situation she did not have the strength, even less the will, to resist. He was kind, helpful, awkward and, no matter how she searched for interesting topics of conversation, ponderous and wearying. But she needed reassurance. Simon Aldercott, despite himself, gave her that.

At last the southerlies came roaring up the coast, shivering women into shawls and men into their great-coats. The wind changed to the summer nor'easters with their clinging biting sting of the sea, and a new energy surged in those pre-Christmas weeks with interesting invitations on the silver salver in the hall, for Sydney was Christmas-gay with ships in with mail and Yuletide delicacies. Country folk were converging on the city and Birubi was opened up for Christmas entertainment, Raunie O'Shea confident that her husband would walk in any day now, hale and hearty. The Moynans and Mrs Carney (the latter a token invitation for Aunt Delia still refused to set foot on O'Shea property), and Mr Aldercott (an afterthought, Alannah suspected) were summoned more than invited to little dinners to entertain spoilt *hausfraus* from Port Macquarie or round from Melbourne, queasy after the sea voyage. Raunie looked more beautiful than ever, Alannah thought, for Jamie was home and filling the house with noisy, raffish-looking youths including a bouncing bully of a fellow everyone called 'Good

Old Harry', all fawning on Kurt Herlicht, O'Shea's Bendigo manager, while they talked fisticuffs or deer-hunting or made plans for race-meetings at Homebush or Redfern. Alannah found it difficult to be at ease with Raunie, particularly when she expressed the wish to visit Moll Noakes. Raunie was horrified.

'I never go near her. Anyway, she wouldn't want me, she hates me, always has. Besides, the nurses are insolent. My house is not my own. Brick must send her to an institution. I shall insist on it.'

'But I promised Hetty first-hand news of her.'

'More fool you. Well, you must do as you please, I suppose. But don't expect me to visit with you.'

Moll's room gave a splendid view over the garden and Harbour. She sat propped up in her easy chair staring out through her wide windows; she would sit so all day, all night too if not firmly led off to her bed. But if she were particularly agitated they would relent a little, prop her up with pillows, cover her with a rug and let her doze a while before her view of the world. Fay Witherstone seemed happy in her routine tasks of fetching and carrying for there were times she could sneak down back stairs to tinkle the pianoforte until discovered and ordered away. Moll seemed to understand Alannah's gossip, nodding now and then, even attempting to speak. Nurse Puttering was anxious to display her patient's improvement by guiding her fingers with a stick of charcoal; they were persevering, hoping the fingers would strengthen enough to write, but the results were illegible and when Moll slumped back, her face blank and body exhausted, Alannah crept out. She could not watch the agony longer. She did not like the old shrew, few did, but who would wish her this living death? She had the uneasy conviction that perhaps Raunie would.

Her father urged her out for little drives and riding parties, and shopping expeditions to jostle with housewives and ginger and lollipop men crying their wares to children whose noses were pressed to windows of dolls and wooden toys. Simon was so anxious to help she loaded him with purchases of nuts and cheeses and dates from the East and fragrant

Jordan almonds. But though her days were filled with people and activity, alone again she would be back with her bizarre situation, too aware of her daily-more-urgent problem. Time, precious time, was passing. So far as she could calculate she was some six weeks pregnant, plenty of time for concealment: but solution? There was a growing nagging terror in her days and nights and she knew terrible moments, her nerves on edge, when she would hold her hands over her ears at the high shrill of the cicadas, or wake in the night to open windows on the still-inflamed western sky. Blessedly she remained physically well, even so she was achingly alone in a festive world, her need of Brick a sickness, an ennui, that made her shrink from others, particularly Raunie whom it was almost impossible to avoid; indeed, the woman seemed to seek her out. Missing Burrendah she wrote regularly to Ida who was proud of her schooling and answered promptly. But she was surprised to receive a letter from Hetty who could read a little but who was timorous about putting words to paper:

'I have been too upset as all have hereabouts to put pen to paper, or rather, let Marty set my words down as I speak them. We have been sad over Adina, poor soul, her body found in the bush, starved to death we think but whether willingly or not who knows for these people can live off the land for a long time; besides there was habitation close by. It was almost as if she wanted to die but we keep such thoughts to ourselves except that Marty is putting mine down, as a priest takes confession you might say, as I've just reminded him – and I'll knock his block off if he alters a word of what I say, and I made him put that down too. I have my own thoughts about Adina for there was a melancholy in her, all could see it yet few spoke of it. Young feelings cannot always be controlled. It's as well Joey is in Sydney and we all agree with Rob that he should stay there for the time being. Since you enquire, no news of Mr O'Shea, it's a mystery all right. Rob wrote to his Melbourne bank, other places too, but no one has heard of him since he passed through Hay across the One Tree

Plain towards Hallows and the Darling country. No one out there seems concerned, but then it's another world as Grace and Joey will discover. Adina's death is a bad start for their marriage, to be in the autumn I suppose, but many have had worse starts and made a go of it.'

Poor Adina. The sadness of that indolent but yearning and loving girl shocked Alannah. But shock became over-whelmed by her own circumstances. She found herself increasingly dependent upon Simon which delighted him, particularly when she consented to drive with him and her aunt to inspect possible venues for his school. She recom-mended Lucknow in Bridge Street, not because she particu-larly liked the house – she found it rather dark and cramped – but she knew he valued its prime location. Moreover, he was anxious to leave his lodgings for his own residence. She was certain her father was financing the venture and, resenting the fact, grew capricious: no, she would not attend a lecture on 'Noble Women in the Nineteenth Century' which, for some reason, Simon seemed to find applicable to herself, but insisted on attending a performance of *Camille* simply because he did not consider the subject proper for a young lady. He bore her whims and changes of mood so patiently it infuriated her further. She could not, it seemed, drive him away. Yet his presence did impart a sense of security, perhaps the only security she had just then for at the back of her mind was the fear – extravagant, unfair, foolish, improbable, yet a fear that nagged – that if Brick O'Shea were not dead he had, quite simply, forgotten her.

Brighton was Christmas-sparkling, the pudding tight in its cloth, the cake iced and decorated. Effie, smart in new cap and apron, was bustled off her feet by Phipps for there was to be hospitality on Christmas Eve as well as on Christmas Day. It was understood without putting it into words that with this coming and going of guests the Moynans would dwell less on Conall Moynan beneath the soil of some lonely valley. Simon, eager to help with the tree, arrived early

256

Christmas Eve in a new waistcoat teetering on the edge of fashion, with what he would regard as a festive air, and clutching a bunch of Christmas blooms which he presented with a ridiculous air of joviality. She felt his eyes adoring her as she passed him the baubles and he clambered about awkwardly but eagerly, throwing strings of little bells over the dusty green branches; how painful if must be, she thought, to scrub one's hands so abrasively and shave so close, to say nothing of his old-fashioned high collars: even so he did not seem to sweat. There was a suppressed excitement about him as if he might suddenly reveal some precious secret as a Christmas treat. She struggled for words. The right words. Leading words.

'I hear you make excellent progress with your school.'

'Academy.' A pause. A satisfied one she felt. 'Indeed . . . yes. Thanks to your father's introductions and influence.'

'And your own credentials, I'm sure. You have decided on a house then?'

'Indeed . . . yes.' The phrase was becoming a monotonous habit. 'Lucknow, as you recommended. A wise choice, for with a minimum of expense it can be adapted to my needs, and of course those of my students. Besides,' he drew himself straighter still, 'Mrs Purdue approves.' Alannah had nothing to say. 'Mrs Purdue is a lady of much influence in the colony,' he added in a tone that held a faint rebuke.

'So I understand. But I feel you underestimate your own diligence in the enterprise.'

'Perhaps.' He rocked gently on his heels. 'It is my conviction that intellectual as well as physical application to an idea, a *cause* shall we say, can be so personally satisfying as to become therapeutic, instilling a sense of well-being in the individual. Pure theory of course, but . . .'

'If it is true then you must enjoy more than usual good health.' She rummaged deeply in her box of decorations, head down, to hide a yawn.

'A slight tendency to the bronchial which I had hoped would be alleviated by the Australian climate, but it clings. However, one learns to overlook trivialities and cultivate a positive outlook. A further theory – if you will bear with

257

me – is that too many nurse inflated ambitions, so inflated as to be unreal and therefore remain unfulfilled.'

'While you contain yours, most sensibly, within the realm of possibility?' She yawned again, for the conversation, or rather near-monologue, seemed to be leading nowhere.

'It has been my experience that retribution overtakes those who distort or supersede such plans as the Almighty has devised for our well-being.' He folded his hands behind his back and rocked again, surveying the decorated room as a cat might view a saucer of cream. 'It is beginning to look like home.'

'Home? Oh, you mean England.'

'Of course – England.' There was a hint of irritation in the clearing of his throat, and his abrupt selection of decorations. 'Miss Moynan . . .' He paused to frown over the unravelling of coloured ribbons. Her control snapped.

'Surely, now that we are trimming a Christmas tree together, you can bring yourself to call me Alannah?'

He dropped the ribbons, from surprise she supposed. 'I had not thought the time opportune . . . but I assure you nothing would give me greater pleasure.'

'Then do so – why not? You seem almost a member of the household by now. My father seems to regard you as so. And Aunt Delia speaks highly of your future.'

'Your father has been kind in favouring me not only with his regard but with practical assistance, and since it was offered with generosity, I might even say with fervour, I was not ashamed to accept it. It will of course be repaid with interest. Now I am hoping you will favour me in a different way, an even more important way. But before I speak of it I hasten to assure you that your father has long been aware of my hopes – and fears – in the matter—'

'What matter – Simon?'

'—and that he is in sympathy with my plans.'

'What plans?' Dear God, Christmas would be over and done with if he did not condense his sentences.

'Hopes would be a more appropriate word. Would that I could be as certain of your approval. And dare I add, your affection.'

258

'Affection?' She looked at him directly and hard for he seemed to be approaching, if haltingly and painfully, the moment of truth. 'What you are trying to say seems to concern me so why speak of Papa?'

'Because my intention was to wait your full year of mourning.'

'I do not support the ritual. I have always found something . . . ominous . . . about it.'

He looked a little dazed. 'But since Christmas has always seemed a happy and auspicious time I am encouraged by the season and its joys to speak to you. I have had many ambitions in life, Alannah – it is delightful to have the right to call you so – but I have noticed that ambitious people are usually clever people, or rather, clever enough to fulfil at least some of the ambitions they nurture. But I am not clever. I have been forced to put hard work and application and that diligence you have been so kind as to credit me with, in the place of superior mental ability.'

'You underestimate yourself – Simon.' Patience, if it took all of Christmas Eve.

'Knowing your love for Burrendah I would not expect you to sever your ties with it completely though I am convinced you are too gently reared, too fragile for the Australian land.'

'I am not at all fragile. I have one of those hardy Celtic frames—' She broke off. Dead God, his face had flamed at her allusion to the human body. 'But what has Burrendah to do with this mysterious matter you find so difficult to put into words?'

'A great deal. If your father had not assured me that your property is in excellent hands and that he is reluctant for you to return to it at least for a time, I would not have the courage to speak, even more so because of my almost complete lack of worldly assets. But now that your father—'

'*Must* you keep talking of Papa?'

'I am in agreement with him that a change would be to your advantage and so I take heart in speaking . . . asking . . .' He paused again and, maddened, she straightened a sprig of leaves so sharply it snapped. He added miserably. 'I am afraid I am making rather a hash of things.'

'It might help if you were to finish your sentences.' She straightened the silver paper star kept for the top of the tree. 'But perhaps it is my fault, I am too impatient.' She held out the ornament, permitting their fingers to touch. She took a long decisive breath. 'Are you by any chance, Simon, asking me to marry you?'

'Indeed . . . *yes*.' His relief was apparent. 'I have felt for some time that of all ladies of my acquaintance you would be the most admirable of helpmeets and companions.' He dared to fold her hand in his. His palm felt soft and sweaty. 'I am not rich or important and certainly not clever but I dare, yes, dare – Alannah – to ask you to become my wife.'

He stood holding the little star, his heart in his eyes. So here was her proposal, her saving proposal, for all she had to do was say 'yes'. Her relief was like a purge. She strove to set aside her unforgivable manipulation of this naïve, oddly innocent young man, yet an eager ambitious young man whom she was learning to deceive with guile. Brick seemed to have left her more than his child, he had given her of his strength and cunning. Don't think of Brick, don't think of anything but the security this man offers you. She gave a candle a little pat, twirled a twig, picked up a length of ribbon and turned with a calculated and tender smile to her suitor.

'I shall be very happy to marry you, Simon.'

There, it was done! She permitted him to draw her close and kiss her, very properly on the cheek, wondering through her mingled relief and despair what it would be like to put her lips to his in intimacy – well, she must soon know. She was doing a deliberate and terrible thing for in this man's inexperience and naïveté, to all intents and purposes, her child and Brick's would be Simon Aldercott's. Furthermore, she would swear before a hundred Madonnas that it was so. Looking into the eyes of this precise, no longer austere young man who loved her, or the girl he considered her to be – virginal, modest, sincere, and of course in love with him otherwise why would she agree to marry him – it hurt to see him so happy. He would be wronged in this marriage yet she must enter into it, she had no choice. She even forced herself

260

to be a little coquettish, a pose entirely foreign to her nature, in pursuing her deceit to the end.

'Am I right in assuming – Simon – that you would like an early ceremony? Please be frank for I know you are anxious to move into Lucknow. I'm sure there is still much to be done.'

'I do not deny that a wife would be a great advantage in promoting and establishing my academy.' Still and always an eye for the main chance yet she could not blame him. 'But I could not ask it of you.'

'You are not impatient for me?' Wide-eyed and unbelievably tender in achieving the correct note of gentle reproach.

He gulped. 'Oh my *dear* Alannah! To begin a new life, hazardous in the beginning perhaps but with much to hope for, with you beside me would be the purest joy. Yet it is not fitting that I hurry you.'

'Not even if I wish it?' The 'wish it' sent him into visible transports. 'It would be quite simple really: a small family ceremony which my aunt would be happy to arrange.'

He cleared his throat. 'Which brings me to another matter. I understand that you – cherish, is perhaps the word – a leaning towards Roman Catholicism.'

'I was raised in the Faith if that is what you mean, but it is in the past. Perhaps you find that strange since it was instilled in me from childhood, but the truth is, the True Faith, as my mother called her religion, never entirely satisfied me. I cannot explain why not. Or why, as time goes by, it satisfies me even less. It seems so far away and long ago, so distant that I am willing to be married in any church or by any clergyman anywhere that might please you.'

The religious significance of this marriage mattered little to her for it was a marriage of convenience, a substitute necessary for survival in the society into which she had been born. Her true 'marriage' was with Brick, their union nothing to do with legalities. Yet she was bearing a child and legalities must be considered; she was simply doing the best she could and doing it with cold-blooded purpose. 'Suppose we leave the choice of ceremony to my father and my aunt, a kind of compromise? But knowing their ways, I can assure you it will be proper, legal, and Protestant.' She gave a quick little laugh but he did not respond; the situation bothered him, she could see that. Then she must coax him out of it, hasten past it. 'Papa will agree to our marriage if it is what I want.'

The 'I want' jolted him out of his introspection. 'Then all that remains is to advise your father. It is right and proper that I wait upon him. I shall do so tonight.'

She was relieved that it was right and proper for she could not face her father at present, even less her aunt. Let them all organise, plan, comment, delight and arrange and she would be grateful for that much. As she put her hand in Simon's her mind raced. Even if all grew more complicated than now, and it very well could, she must contrive, manipulate, plot and plan, persisting in her new career as an expert in deceit. She returned his eager but chaste kiss sealing more of a bargain than he would ever know.

In moving about her duties Maria Swallow had cultivated a sensuous little glide that drew Owen's eyes if also, unfortunately, those of his martinet of a sister and his difficult keen-eyed daughter. But keeping her lover's attention was so important, indeed urgent, that she ignored the women to pause longer than was necessary to pat her hair or arrange her collar or pour Owen's coffee with the ceremony he appreciated while remaining the epitome of the attentive efficient housekeeper. It was only when she locked her bedroom door behind her that a transformation in demeanour as well as personality took place and she spread her rather splendid wings. She would remove her cameo brooch with as much haste as she dared, careful it did not tear her collar, for she loathed the confinement of clothes; her modestly contrived gowns were gestures of propriety, no more. The brooch meant nothing to her other than being the only thing of value Albert Swallow had ever given her. It was a handsome piece and, intrigued, she had shown it to a jeweller who had thought highly of it. She had always had the feeling that Albert had reserved it as a sort of prize for some deserving

262

strumpet who might come up to scratch without much trouble. Well, she had come up to scratch one furtive desperate night on Hampstead Heath, gaining nothing from their bleak coupling but a savage squirming on his part and concealed disgust on hers, her price for his attempt at copulation then and in the future being marriage. In this he had come up to scratch in rescuing her (though ignorant of the fact) from the debt-besieged artist who was about to turn her out of their squalid room. But she had paid for Albert Swallow's ring on her finger by frustration with and subjection to his cruelties, so well hidden in their bedroom savagery that they were able to present the united and respectable front required for the shop with residence above that he had inherited. It was agreed among their fellow traders that the Swallows were a decent couple sadly unblessed with issue and would be missed when they emigrated to a climate necessary for Albert's health. In fact he had violated a young woman in some luckily distant borough, husband and wife knowing it was only a matter of time before he would be apprehended, so emigration was hurriedly arranged. The sea had freed her from Albert Swallow and her past, at the same time providing a new country in which to please herself. There was excitement in the knowledge. Owen Moynan pleased her and would please her more if she played her cards right. She intended to do so for her hold on him was secure enough sexually to weather this temporary halt in their relationship; even so she devoted herself to making his need of her even more urgent. She had brought him to her bed simply and deliberately and only she knew how desperately. She would bring him to marriage if not so easily, just as deliberately and desperately.

She ran her hands down her fine silk stockings. Her thighs looked and felt like others though more shapely, but only she knew their constant hunger. She undressed slowly as she liked to do and, naked but for the stockings, turned her body to one side then to the other admiring it in the swivel mirror, appraising her tall, full, heavy-breasted frame, a youthful body and unmarred, which always prompted surprise when she studied its contours for it was a body that had been much used and, at times, abused. She was big-boned, as some venomous male had once taunted her, a term she did not like for it intimated heaviness and that she was not. She preferred 'voluptuous' which her artist lover had used when posing her – but she preferred not to remember those poses which could be intriguing some London bordello if they had not suffered from rising damp in the miserable room in which she had left both paintings and lover. She ran her hands down over her breasts to flatten them, then released them abruptly to spring back – she was young enough for firmness. She moved her fingers in symmetrical motions into the curve of her waist, out over her hips then forward to linger over the vee of pubic hair then back over her full thighs, a caress she particularly enjoyed. How innocent, how strangely untouched a woman's body could look, its urges and potency concealed between the hips giving the appearance of negation, of passivity, nothing intrusive to proclaim that it had ever been touched, even less, maltreated, its responses hidden and dormant until roused. Except that she was not dormant, never quite; something always seethed within her outer shell of composed virginity. Virginal? The Milly Bolton that had been? In the privacy of her room she could laugh and did, for she had thrown chastity to the winds early and eagerly as so much excess baggage. Owen Moynan actually believed that he summoned forth the strange tormenting flame that had driven her to excesses with squalid violent men, suffered bitterly yet ecstatically in a procession of squalid violent rooms from Dover to Boulogne, from Calais to Portsmouth, and areas of Whitechapel she refused to dwell upon.

Owen Moynan would satisfy her sexual needs and more; she would see that he did. But her needs were not only sexual. This handsome, slow-talking and, she suspected, slow-thinking, stolid man had enough of the world's goods to make life comfortable. She quite fancied herself as an alderman's wife, even more so as the wife of an MLC, that epitome of outer respectability and a not-impossible goal. But her manipulation of her lover would be easier if the daughter were married off and the suspicious busybody of an aunt diverted – she would see to it! She dipped a cloth in a basin of warm water and began to sponge herself, smoothing her body hairs until they hung limp, a defeated look. She laughed again. Milly Bolton defeated? Never. She had made this neat and pleasant house a home for a man who needed one and in so doing had made it a refuge for herself. The crudities of her experience in satisfying her bodily needs would be a closed book, such needs now to be satisfied by this man, still young and at this moment fretting for her. There would be a challenge in creating new and subtle needs in him, and so in herself. With slow undulating movements she loosened her long blonde hair. It was beautiful hair, shining and well cared for and lay silky as a fan around her shoulders. She stretched her body slowly and sensuously, loving the movement. The night was warm and she slipped naked between her snowy sheets. Abstinence was imposed upon her as well as her lover. They must wait for each other – but not too long.

The Yorkshire Lad was a waterside tavern ideally situated for dubious pursuits, boasting high stone walls enclosing a courtyard open to an inlet of Harbour water lolloping against a jetty with slimy stone steps that saw much coming and going of the 'fancy'. The Lad, as it was dubbed, catered for bare-knuckle fights where other pubs on the outskirts of town favoured ratting or dog-fighting or cocking or bull-baiting. Tonight the attraction was Bully Butcher, a negro from California down on his luck on the fields who had drifted back to Sydney to pick up a purse where he might. And tonight the purse was good, for though his eyesight was poor and he'd been punch-drunk for years he had weight, his right was still deadly, and he would fight till he dropped – Bully Butcher was a killer. His opponent was whipper-sharp Irish Pat, cunning, devious, game as a cockerel and, though he couldn't match Bully in muscle and bone, so quick on his feet he could worry his opponent down. He had won his last two fights, so betting was brisk about the roughly marked ring, the colours wobbling on a stick under a crooked lantern much the worse for drunken target practice, its light shaded, for despite a well-bribed constabulary the Lad's publican didn't believe in courting trouble. Excitement mounted as Bully's powerful stripped-to-the-waist frame gleamed with the sweat of the seventeenth round, still deadly though blundering a little after the still side-stepping but tiring Irish Pat.

'He'll kill that skinny bit of old sod when he catches up with him,' Good Old Harry groaned. Why did he keep listening to Herlicht's 'certainties'? Because Kurt was not only definite and deadly – but Kurt held his IOUs. 'Irish Pat's a bloody mess.'

'Drawn his cork, that's all.' Tom Pearson felt he could afford to comfort a bit for he was anticipating a couple of hundred on a Bully win; London was expensive, at least the way he liked to 'do' that city. He'd pressed Jamie to sail with him but Jamie disparaged Europe. 'What's over there but gargoyles and old stones? I like it here.' Tom winced as Irish Pat snuck in a 'facer'. 'Niggers have thick skulls,' he asserted, to console himself.

'All skulls are the same.'

'Want to bet on it.' He swaggered a bit. 'Bully trains on gin. Keeps his ginger up.'

'Well, the Blue Ruin's getting to him at last. He's losing his wind.'

'A few bouts left in the fellow yet.' Kurt Herlicht never shouted or even seemed to raise his voice, but all heard. 'I'd like to get him to Bendigo for the Easter Fair. They're spoiling for professionals around there, even ageing ones.'

'You'll have a hard time prising even expenses from O'Shea. He's buried his money-bags.' Jamie needed to take out his mood on someone, anyone, for Irish Pat was down again and he cursed Kurt Herlicht under his breath. It looked as if he and Good Old Harry would be walking home tonight.

'Up with your mawleys, Bully,' a woman screeched from a dark corner, 'or Irish Pat'll put the teeth in.'

'He's only got three and they're loose,' someone yelled back at her. Kurt moved to where Jamie leaned against the stone wall.

'You haven't seen the Irish Boy for some time. We've made improvements. Come down for a spell. After all, it is your pub.'

'Not my pub. And the way things are going it's never likely to be.'

'Bendigo might change your luck in many ways. It's always been a lucky town for you.'

Jamie gloomed. Maybe he should get out of Sydney for a while. Birubi was impossible at the moment with Raunie alternately fretting and complaining about O'Shea's absence no matter the 'front' she displayed for her friends, and making a hell of a fuss over every five pounds he managed to wring from her. He had to get money somehow. Right now he couldn't raise travelling expenses to Bendigo, which meant Kurt would have to stake him. But once in Bendigo Good Old Harry had a string of poker-playing cronies to cook up sporting events and little dinners at the Shamrock as well as being good for loans when they were flush, not pressing you to settle up. Not like Kurt . . . Oddly, for he'd never done so before, he found himself edging from Kurt Herlicht. It wasn't exactly what the man said, it was the smooth yet deadly way he had of saying it. He seemed to be waiting for an answer to his observations. Jamie roused.

'Who leaves Sydney in midsummer to stew inland?'

'I do. I can't wait around here any longer for O'Shea to turn up. If you can't come down with Harry soon, see you get down for Easter. Always something doing, you know that. Your luck could change.' He left the youth to mull over the idea and wove between noisy groups to where Good Old Harry was kicking the water-butt in rage and excitement, shouting his stupid head off for Irish Pat to murder Bully Butcher which the Irishman hadn't a hope in Hell of doing. 'The old sod's tiring.' Harry chewed his fingernails. 'Anyway, he hasn't the reach.'

'Get Jamie down to Bendigo, Harry,' Kurt ordered bluntly. 'Any way you like. Just get him down.'

'Why?'

'For old times' sake, if you like.'

'He hasn't a penny, except what he wins now and then.

O'Shea cut off his allowance. Sold up his things too, left him in rags.'

'Pretty expensive rags,' Kurt observed drily.

'This to be a favour to you, I take it?'

'If you like.'

'One favour should beget another, I say. In this case to the tune of fifty pounds.'

Kurt frowned. Good Old Harry wasn't quite as stupid as he acted. He took out a wallet and riffled through its contents. 'This the one? Harry Ventril, IOU, fifty pounds—'

'The very one. Fifty bloody pounds.'

A roar. Irish Pat was on his back and looked like staying there. Kurt repocketed his wallet, then took out a fine Havana. Good Old Harry was nothing if not dependable; rip one IOU to shreds and there'd always be another. 'You'll get that IOU in your hands the moment Jamie's on the way. You know I won't renege because I know you'd talk your silly head off over it not only to Jamie but to the world. It's yours to tear up as soon as Jamie ships out of Sydney. A bargain?'

'I don't seem to have much choice.'

'Not much, Harry, not much.' Kurt didn't offer Good Old Harry a fine cigar. Any cigar. He never did to those in his debt.

Chapter Thirteen

IT WAS understood by the few carefully selected guests that the small family wedding of Alannah Moynan and Simon Aldercott, celebrated by an Anglican clergyman as the most sensible compromise that could be managed, was a modest affair in deference to the tragic death of the Moynan son and brother as much as to the young couple's eagerness to open their academy. The honeymoon at Parramatta consisted of walks beside the river, drives amid rural cottages and cows, innocuous conversation around the boarding-house dining-table, and polite but thorough consummation of their nuptials in the big double-bed in the pleasant bedroom overlooking the equally pleasant garden. At the end of their week the young Aldercotts returned to Sydney to finalise the move to Lucknow which still had a tang of paint and disinfectant about it, its largest room converted to a classroom with a second room in the process of renovation for what Simon and an eager Aunt Delia hoped would be a rash of applications. Alannah was resigned to her aunt's management, and to playing her own part as the respectable adjunct of a respectable young schoolmaster, and masked her true feelings as she had learned to do over many issues in her longing for the winds, the swaying grasses, above all for the quiet secret corners of her Place of the Swan.

Her marriage had not been such an ordeal as she had expected. She found her husband considerate to the point of fussiness in his eagerness to make her happy, even more considerate if it were possible in his love-making which was as she had anticipated, affectionate but moderate and at all times decently controlled, for which she was silently grateful. At least she did not shrink from him while she seemed to satisfy him; if he wanted more from her he did not demand it.

Physical passion, the intensity with which she was now so familiar, did hover sometimes behind his caresses and occasional playfulness but did not break over her, and she was thankful for she knew she could not meet it with the explosive tearing *giving* she had known with Brick. So the first weeks of their marriage drifted over her, as they did her husband for all she knew, like a tepid bath taken in a dimly lit room, her role one of duty, companionship and, when she could not evade it, a pretence of love, a role lived in silent incredulity and a certain horror at the success of her deception. At an appropriate moment she would tell him of the coming child and he would be pleased in his mild and amiable way and never query or wonder – why should he – and she would push to the back of her mind her longing for a man who seemed to have vanished from the face of the earth.

But soon after they had settled in, Owen Moynan received a letter from Kurt Herlicht in Bendigo detailing facts sent on from Deniliquin: O'Shea was at Hallows station recovering from injuries received when thrown from a brumby and left by his renegade Black to die of a shattered body. He had been found by a lone native who had sheltered, fed and watered him through fever. Luckily, others had chanced by, one man with a knowledge of bone-setting, who had saved O'Shea's life. But they were rogues on the run and would not risk carrying him to safety so abandoned him, until one had relented enough to send help. O'Shea had been carried on a makeshift stretcher to Hallows . . .

It was of course the talk of Sydney: O'Shea tossed from a horse, even a wild one? Incredible. But O'Shea's wife was jubilant; hadn't she insisted her husband was indestructible and would return as large as life and with tales to tell? Alannah paced rooms or lay wide-eyed beside her sleeping husband for the blankness and bareness of the letter. Brick was alive, he would get well, she felt that, and there was relief in the conviction, but what now? She had made several attempts to tell Simon of the coming baby yet something always held her back and though her pregnancy was not evident she as so aware of it she wore wide skirts and full cloaks and moved from revealing lights to evade the all-knowing and all-seeing eyes of women, as if by thus covering up, her situation did not exist. She felt particularly self-conscious in Raunie's company but it was impossible to avoid the woman; for good or ill they had become part of each other's existence.

But her carefully built up and artificial world was shattered abruptly and sharply. She had driven out to dinner at Birubi with her husband and father to fête the newly-landed daughter of a wealthy ironmonger as well as a London singer soon to be launched at the Victoria, but in the beautiful ante-room under the sparkling chandeliers they felt a shimmer of excitement beyond the importance of such guests. Silas Mason lumbered over to explain.

'O'Shea walked in today – aye, *walked* – and insisted the dinner go on as planned. Came down by coach after a stay at his Goulburn property. Promises to be an exciting evening. Our hostess is hopping mad at noan having been warned – but what lass knows O'Shea better, eh? Or should.'

Alannah's initial impulse was to run but she knew there was no escape; in any case Brick would have heard of her marriage by now. There was indeed an air of anticipation with Raunie tapping her fan and watching the stairs, for dinner had been kept waiting overlong. Alannah was making an attempt at conversation with Nance Mason when she heard Brick's voice behind her.

'I flattered myself the fatted calf would be killed for my benefit but I understand we have nuptials – of a kind – to celebrate.'

·Ah – he knew! But she would not be intimidated and turned to face him calmly. He stood poised in the doorway, his eyes seeking hers, probing, and she shivered slightly but met his gaze directly, praying he would not see her heart in hers. His evening clothes were, as always, impeccable, even lavish, as though he had made a deliberate and exaggerated gesture to the occasion, but he was thinner, burned almost black by the sun, and there was the trace of a limp as he crossed the room to her father.

'We have much to discuss later, Moynan.' He turned abruptly to Simon. 'Ah, Aldercott! I hear through my usual back doors that you are planning, or should I say plotting, to forsake my employ. Take care, sir, you do not find yourself out on a premature limb for it seems you've plotted successfully in other directions as well.' He cut off any reply by turning with a brisk little bow to Alannah. 'Miss Moynan.'

'Aldercott,' Raunie corrected sharply. 'Mrs Simon Aldercott, as you very well know.'

He shrugged. 'Old habits die hard. Or perhaps I find it improbable as well as distasteful to accept my erstwhile clerk as the lady's consort.'

'An excellent clerk,' Owen bridled. 'Indeed, more than a clerk in his management of your affairs in your absence with great skill and application.'

'No doubt. I agree it must have taken more than ordinary efficiency to sweep a convent-bred young woman off her feet so suddenly, one could even say hurriedly. But then, the generous hours I extend my employees could only have helped his courtship.' He motioned Belmont to refill his glass. It was clear he'd already had a good deal to drink.

'We must go in.' The snap of Raunie's voice matched the snap of her fan. 'Dinner's waited too long.'

'Or perhaps it was, simply, the summer moon,' Brick added.

Don't, Alannah yearned silently. *Don't!* Just give me the chance to explain. How shall I get through this dinner, my dearest dear, and how will you? People are staring, not understanding, and how can they be otherwise? Raunie manoeuvred the subdued little procession to the dining-room to sort all out with place cards and surface pleasantries.

'Unlike you to keep a captive audience waiting,' she goaded her husband. 'All Sydney's breathless to hear of your adventures.'

'If they can digest their roast beef garnished with accounts of foul meat and water and the setting of my shattered leg without even a tot of rum to batter me insensible, I'll congratulate them on strong stomachs.'

It was indeed a nightmare of a dinner. Brick evaded

questions as if he didn't hear them, as perhaps he didn't, ignoring the strangers at his table to cut, bite and probe the muted attempts at conversation, pitting himself against Raunie's growing anger, Owen's bewilderment and Simon's resentment. Alannah sat dying slowly but, incredibly, eating, drinking, smiling and talking while certain the food would soon choke her. There was a devil in the man driving him to feats of sarcasm; every gesture, every nuance, she knew, directed against herself. If only they could escape to thrash all out between them but there was no way they could be alone – not yet. They were trapped in a cage of warmth and colour and open human hostility. He drank heavily yet his control showed no signs of breaking though often teetering on a razor's edge of malice and obscenity while she sat tense, struggling for control against his fury that she feared would explode in their faces, consuming her. But his control did not quite fail and as the charade progressed through the hesitant questions of guests and his bitter scarcely-veiled accusations, she almost welcomed a denouement as some relief in the tension. By pushing himself and her to the edge he had become a fearsome stranger and she realised with a shock how little she really knew of him and his life, so much of it lived out before they had even met. All she knew was that she had stopped the world with him one magical evening, driven by her loneliness and loss, intoxicated by atmosphere, above all by the closeness of this fascinating man who had filled her thoughts and life for so long. Rightly or wrongly she had loved him, did love him, and would love him again: they were committed, was she not nurturing the result? But now his flagellation of himself, and indirectly of her, went on and on and they had no remedy but to sit eating too much, the men taking refuge in wine, the women glancing uneasily at each other, confounded, often horrified, yet intrigued, while she floated in the eye of the storm, aware of the tumult around her but sealed in her cocoon of understanding. Raunie's voice cut across her husband's, by now no mean feat, in detailing her plans for an easy descent to Birubi's beach by the cutting of rock steps connected by little paths, all embellished by border shrubs and gardens and statuary of the Roman kind so much in vogue, perhaps a small fountain, and seats here and there on the way down, and a bathing-box on the sands beside the boat-house, all to be ready before summer's end for she was planning picnics. Joey's marriage would have to wait, she was kidnapping him, assured he had training in stone-masonry.

'Emotionally,' Brick rasped, ignoring her, 'women are as tough-hided as armadillos with an inborn capacity for deviousness—'

'It has been too much of a scramble down with baskets and rugs and cloaks.'

'They arrange their faces in exquisite masks and brim their eyes at will so expertly that if a man dares utter a word of reproach he bruises them for life—'

'I shall put everyone to work, from stable-boy to gardener.'

'—meanwhile proceeding with their plans with all the steel-like strategy of a battalion at war.'

Raunie turned on him. 'You're drunk.'

'Intoxicated.' Flippantly, with a mocking inclination of his head. 'Drunk, never.'

'Drunk.' She spat the word at him. '*Drunk!*'

'*That* is a reflection on my ability to cut capers without interference from wife or spy which, damn you, Egypt, has come to mean the same thing.'

'Don't call me Egypt.'

'Why not?' There was malice in his tiny smile. 'There have been a few intimate moments when you've actually begged to hear it. Do you really imagine Sydney doesn't know of your humble, not to say doubtful beginnings, along with your expensive habits and whims? I'm rattling family skeletons, oh yes, so why not add a few of your own? Come, Egypt, list your reasons for hating Erins Pride, even here on these walls – no? Then sulk all you want for its likeness not only stays but is to be enlarged.' He turned savage. 'One must destroy to rebuild – an old adage – so I'll make a start.' He swept up his glass of wine and threw it at the mural, following it with a second, scattering great smears of claret to trickle down the vivid blue and green and gold. Raunie sprang to her feet.

'You stupid drunken fool.'

'Drunk if you like, but stupid never. Come, you've wanted to destroy this symbol of your servile poverty – as you see it – ever since it was painted here.' He grinned at the silent bewildered guests. 'And now I suppose enough transgressions have accumulated for me to apologise to your guests.'

'*Our* guests.'

'My apologies, Miss Moynan.'

'Mrs Aldercott.' Simon clattered to his feet. 'My wife, sir.'

'So I am told.' Brick gave him a mock salute. 'Duly wedded. And bedded I presume.'

'I refuse to subject my wife to this . . . *this*—'

'I have never found your – wife as you regard her, willing to let others speak for her; she's usually most voluble in argument.' He paused. Don't speak, Alannah warned herself, not here, not now, don't make things worse! 'No? Then hear me out, Aldercott.' He leant across the table, seemingly dead sober. His voice was cold. 'I dislike furtive couplings, particularly among my employees, for it has been my rather popular habit to make a gala occasion of a marriage; call it a quirk of philanthropy if you like. Your more-than-shaky association with me should have warned you to await my pleasure instead of staging what appears a drab arrangement of some haste – with the future prospect of starvation not only for yourself but for your spouse. It is to be hoped you have friends.'

'My wife will never starve, Mr O'Shea.' Simon's voice was equally cold.

'Ah – but nor she will. I was forgetting. As I understand it she's something of an heiress, a fact that obviously has not slipped your mind.'

'You will excuse us, Mrs O'Shea?' Owen folded his table napkin.

'No, Papa – *no*. We must not leave this way—'

'This is a serious matter.' He stopped her protests with a firm hand. 'Nothing secretive or furtive was ever intended, O'Shea.'

'No? There was not even a rumour of this pairing when I left Sydney.'

'I was not aware that my family's domestic arrangements were required to be displayed for your approval along with my professional skills?'

'We cannot stay in your house.' Simon stood firmly beside his father-in-law, angry yet dignified.

Brick waved an exasperated hand. 'Oh, sit down, man. Women keep. This one will.' He spread his hands in mock despair. 'Come, you should be accustomed to my ways by now. Part of your job.' He turned the wine decanter upside down, shaking the last drops on the Nottingham lace spread. 'More wine,' he shouted. 'Where *is* that flunkey?'

'You don't have to remind people you're a roughneck,' Raunie snapped. 'They know it only too well.'

He held his empty glass high. 'Here's to my straight-talking, straight-from-the-shoulder wife who can bring me back to earth with a thump quicker than anyone in this world. I'll have your hide, Belmont,' he thundered.

'No wine, I said.'

His fist struck the table. 'Wine, damn you. And damn Belmont. And every other flunkey in my employ.'

'No wine,' she rasped.

He sent the chair crashing to drag Belmont around by the collar. But the man remained unperturbed, his eyes querying his mistress. Raunie thrust herself between the men.

'Damn you, I said no wine.' The back of her hand struck him sharply across the mouth, and from surprise perhaps he backed. Her rings must have cut for there was a tiny bead of blood on his lip. He pulled her close. She struggled and her hand closed about a table knife. Forcing herself back she held it to his chest, digging in. He laughed.

'What the hell do you think that could do?'

'You can take it from me, but if you do I'll find some other way to make you walk off your moods and your liquor. You've been too long in the backblocks. My house is not a shearing-shed or a slaughter-house. I'll keep a civilised table here if it's the last thing I do.'

The stunned guests sat frozen until Brick snatched the knife and threw it at a small table so hard it quivered in the wood. With a mock salute to his guests, then a special one to the Moynans, he blundered out, curiously at odds for he never blundered. But they heard the crash of a terrace chair as he meandered his way to the garden. Raunie finished her wine calmly before she rose from the table.

'We shall take our coffee.' Once again the gracious hostess, she led the women to the withdrawing-room, easing tension with a word here, one there, smiles and much inconsequential small talk. The men joined them almost immediately so with the same easy grace she arranged herself at the pianoforte to soothe with music and song. But running her hands over the keys she did not feel so confident of dispelling the effect of the awful haphazard scene just gone, for Brick had acted strangely: she knew his moods and had never seen him quite like this – why? His leg didn't seem to bother him unduly. Bad luck at cards? A horse unplaced? A deal lost in business? Or, perhaps, the wool hadn't brought what he expected. But these were normal regular annoyances that he took in his stride. Perhaps Jamie . . . But no, there had been no time or opportunity for them to clash for Jamie was with the Pearsons most of the time and about his usual pastimes – Richie had seen him at a bare-knuckle fight. And for the time being perhaps, with Brick in this unpredictable mood, it was best Jamie was away. No, Brick's fury was directed towards something of unusual importance, something of which she was as yet ignorant. She began a song of rural pleasantries and the room forgot O'Shea and his inexplicable tempers in the beguiling cadences of her voice.

Certainly, if he wished, they would take their leave, Alannah murmured to Simon, but Papa seemed to be enjoying himself; besides, she could not leave without her usual visit to Mrs Noakes, the woman looked forward to company. She was so decisive even in whispers that her father's slightly puzzled eyes followed her as she slipped from her seat by the door; could this new maturity be induced by the worthy but bumbling young man who, despite his faultless book-keeping he, Owen, assisted solely for his daughter's sake? Life was full of surprises! Raunie,

raising her eyes along with a trill to the mirror above her
head, caught the shimmer of a woman's skirt round the
garden door. A blue skirt. Alannah Aldercott's skirt. But her
voice did not falter and her hands on the keys were firm and
sure.

As Alannah whispered his name Brick turned, a flicker of
outline in the darkness. The distant music and the tiny lap of
water on the rocks below seemed to fill the night as they faced
each other.

'None of it helped, did it?' she said calmly.

'What did you expect? My blessings with the soup?' he
throbbed. 'Why, Alannah? In God's name, *why*? It would
have saved trouble all round if you'd told me you meant to
marry the fellow all along.'

'Because it's not true. You'll know that when I explain—'

'How can you explain this travesty of a marriage?'

'*Please* – they'll hear.' She drew him further into the
shadows.

'Why shouldn't they hear that with me out of the way you
off and married Aldercott – of all men.'

'Haven't you talked enough?' Her anger spilled over. 'In
your eyes it was all so simple, a circumstance to be neatly
resolved when and how you chose. You would continue on
your way at your pleasure while I waited here for you to
arrange our lives in disposing of all and everything in your
way – the ideal happy-ever-after solution. Life doesn't fall
into place like that. It didn't with me.'

'I blundered somewhere along the line. Like some simple-
minded oaf of a shepherd boy devouring his first woman.
You came to hate me and I can understand it, I suppose. I
took you too well and too soon. I haven't learnt much about
women after all, have I? At least not convent-bred maids
who view the world through imaginary rose-tinted windows
high above the ground of reality, pining for men to strew rose
petals in their paths before venturing a chaste kiss or two –
life isn't like that either, Alannah. Men are not like that.
We're sexually impetuous bulls, we're meant to be, or we

believe we are, and women just have to put up with us. I needed to bind you to me then and there and I thought I had done so.'

'We *are* bound – you don't know how much.' Her words came tumbling. 'My first thought was to find you and blurt it all out but you were lost somewhere, I couldn't find you and you couldn't know what that was like; it was as if you were dead. You could have been dead. All I could think of was how to manage. I almost threw myself from a horse once. To kill us both—'

'Both?'

'—but I couldn't do it. So I took the only way open. Simon was there wanting to marry me so I cheated him, and I'm still cheating him and will go on doing it, pretending your child is his.'

'God in heaven!' He moved towards her so sharply she heard the crack of a branch and felt leaves scattering about them as he grasped her. 'I wouldn't have left you if I'd known.'

'There was nothing to know – then.'

'I'll never leave you again.' He held her tightly. 'It won't take long to set my affairs in order. It might be a bad time for you, in fact it will be, but it must be done.'

She stiffened slightly. 'Simon is my husband.'

'Don't say "husband".'

'You don't seem to understand. I married him.'

'He accepts your story?'

'He will.'

'You mean, he doesn't know of the child?'

She gave a tiny desperate laugh. 'One can't hide pregnancy for ever.'

His arms dropped away. 'When it comes to guile, no harlot could contrive a more dishonest nest for herself. This is *my* child—'

'You couldn't give it a name. You couldn't marry me.'

'No,' he said slowly, 'but I couldn't marry you that night in your precious coppice at your precious Place of the Swan. And you knew it then.'

'I wouldn't be the first woman to commit a foolish act,'

she said wildly, and wanted to die. He was coming through this much better than she. But she felt enclosed, trapped, desperate to beat her way out of the net closing about her, and run. He was trying to force her to conclusions she could not make, not now, not yet. After all, the child was within *her* and didn't seem to have anything to do with him, or with Simon, or with any other man.

'Foolish?' His voice was cold. 'Is that what it was? Foolish?'

'I didn't mean it so.' She took his face between her hands and covered it with wild and urgent kisses. 'I didn't mean it.' She clung to him, whispering, whimpering a little. 'I'm crying, I suppose, because I'm only nineteen but feel ninety at this moment. When I'm twenty-nine perhaps I'll do better. At thirty-nine I might manage, don't you think? But now, I'm just doing the best I can.'

He said slowly: 'When I heard of your marriage I began counting all possible reasons why you might have turned from me. I took a long look at every male trait girls like you are taught to avoid. Other women? There have been many but I've never denied that. My age?' He gave a tight little laugh. 'A fact that can only get worse. Other reasons – my background, my "touch of the tarbrush" as some call it that may or may not disturb you, I don't know—'

'It disturbs *you*. You pass on the disturbance.'

'Is that the way of it?' He was thoughtful. 'Even so, it's more than that. The underlying reason as I see it is the gulf between our worlds. I've never lived by your taboos, I wasn't even aware of such conventions when I was your age, or any rule but that of expediency. But your world of smug hypocrisy controls you and if you're afraid to take a chance with me against it what can I do? What *can* I do, Alannah?' He held up her face. His eyes were two light points. 'You were happy with me, weren't you?'

'Very happy.'

'Then there's no argument, not really.' He held her tightly. 'I thought I would never want my own child, but I do.'

She drew back. 'But I'm married to Simon – now *you*

must listen. I married him because my child had to belong somewhere.'

'My child too and I'm damned if I'll let it belong to that sanctimonious pen-pusher.'

'You keep insisting what *you* want,' she throbbed, 'but it was I who had to make the decision. I grew up, oh yes, and quickly. I don't stamp my feet any more. I don't cry – well, not often. I don't have tantrums, not childish ones. I get angry in a proper grown-up way.'

'You will only grow up when you shout to all and sundry that you are bearing a child to a man already married but who loves you and will care for you and is ready to damn the world and all in it for you – isn't that enough?' Her silence seemed to drive him mad. 'It has to be enough, and it will be enough – for you, for those sycophants in there gorging on my food and wine and waiting for the next sensation. Well then, they'll get sensation, here, now, tonight—'

'If you do that,' she gasped, 'I shall deny it.'

'What good will that do? In due course my child will proclaim itself.'

She gripped something, the tree, to steady herself for he had put into words the thing that was always there. 'Don't you think I've considered that?'

He buried his face against her throat. 'No, don't look like that – I can't see your face but I know how you look and I can't have it. I won't get my way by threats, by blackmail. The truth is I have never seen an aboriginal child darker than the darkest of its parents and I have seen many over this country. It cannot be more pronounced than I.' She broke from him and they stood a little apart as if to get their breath and ease tension. She made a desperate little gesture.

'I'm tired. So *tired*. Weary of thinking, lying, planning and contriving. I need rest and time and peace, yes, peace to consider my child – *my* child.' Savagely. 'I'm the one who had to make the decisions, too many and too quickly, so quickly I cannot know if I made the right ones. This baby is not Simon's but the odd thing is, it doesn't seem yours either, not here at this minute, only mine. It doesn't really seem anything to do with anyone but myself, not even you. So you must leave me be to get my breath and face what I've done and must do – I had to do *something*, don't you see?' She seemed close to hysteria, leaning against the tree. 'No more. Not now. Not *now*.'

His hands dropped away with a gesture of helplessness. What was he to do? What *could* he do? Drag her, a woman approaching confinement, from house to house, country property to country property, among strangers? It would be bizarre, and of course cruel, and he could not do it any more than he could humiliate her here and now in his house – Raunie's house – for the child must not become a pawn in this game before it was even born. She must have what she wanted and needed, safety and comfort, at least until the child was born. Then it would be *his* comfort and safety he would offer her and be damned to the world. He straightened.

'I suppose I can see – at least I'm trying to see – but I can't and won't stay on the sidelines and watch this masquerade. I shall leave Sydney with the always convenient excuse of "watching over my farflung Empire". But there's the future, and I swear by anything or anyone you choose that I'll have you both, I swear it. So get your tears over while I'm gone for if this hasn't changed your life it has mine, the difference being that I know it and face it. You've done the planning, as you complain, so now I'll take over. There's a new state forming up north – oh yes, it won't be long – and we can become part of it unless you know of a better place under the circumstances. But I won't hide, nor will I allow you to hide for ever. For a time, if you must, go back to your lies and pretences. But there'll be nothing, no superfluous chit-chat between us, Alannah, until I come for you. And I'll come, make no mistake about it, and before long at that.'

He did not touch her again and she felt as if a cold wind had blown over her, over them both, and she could not bear it. With a queer desperate little run she pressed herself to him and kissed him wildly. He held her off. 'Go then. Now. *Now*.' Still she hesitated, poised, until he turned and blundered off into the dark, disappearing amid the paths and arbours of the slopes. He would clamber down and pace the beach, or sit the night through somewhere, hating her – why should he not? She had failed him, lost him perhaps? Maybe, she pondered in her misery, real courage comes with age while the youthful taking-of-chances is an impulse, a bravado born of nothing more than impulsive ignorance. In time she might be different and know that safety and security are not the most necessary and important things. But here and now she was barely nineteen, and had made a bargain, a marriage of convenience, to cushion herself, and her child conceived outside that marriage, from a world of savage reprisal. Moving away from wherever he was out there with a tiny gesture of sadness and despair, she turned back to the warm and glowing house.

Brick turned Glenora down the track to his Neutral Bay house – odd perhaps but he'd never given it a name, it was known simply as 'O'Shea's house'. The trees and ferns crowded and he could only guide the horse by glimpses of the beach glowing whitely against the blue water where a ferry was moving out and rowboats plodded in the lazy afternoon. Neglect screamed around him and he grew angry at Benny Brack who spent his time fishing or wandering the bush to the nearest inn, but whom he was loth to turn out; besides, there was nothing to steal, for when Raunie had refused to live here he had emptied the house of valuables, locked it and left it to the birds and weeds. Yet he could never bring himself to sell it for he had built it to found a marriage and a dynasty. He would give Alannah time to recover from the birth and for the child to grow a little, then no more lies, no subterfuges. He had never given a fig for public opinion – why should he – and she must learn to do the same. In that night in her coppice, and since, she had thrown in her lot with him. He didn't want any other kind of woman. As for Raunie, he owed her nothing. She had always taken what was to hand and turned it to her will and wants. Raunie would survive.

He strolled restlessly through the tangle of shrubs and native flowers, the ivy he had planted long ago curving about the classical pillars. Memories drifted . . . and through the shimmer of leaves and vines, faces: Barbara's face the day he had first brought her here, each with a growing awareness of the other, a tension between them, the right tension. But, fool that he was, not wishing to frighten her, he had hesitated, respecting the virgin, and had done no more than put his lips to her palm. Fool! How he had cursed himself since for she was dead suddenly and shockingly, mangled and bleeding, staring up at the world, at him – it was he who had closed her eyes. What had driven her to saddle Kumara and ride out on such a night? Had she simply slipped from her saddle or was she half mad with a sickness of the spirit, a malaise, a conflict so extreme she wanted to die? She had known of his black ancestry then, before he had known it himself, revealed to her, viciously he knew, by her father, the man who had hated him and whom he had hated in return because of everything they were and wanted, the opposing extremes of Australia, making them implacable enemies. And between them a Barbara loving them both – was that the way of it? He would never really know. Nor would he know the answer to his final query: Barbara had loved him, he knew that, but would she, finally, have married him?

A twig snapped beneath his feet bringing him back to his surroundings. All that was history, dead as Barbara was dead, and what remained of the Merrill family scattered. And in the play of light and shade another face drifted, a girl's face, like Barbara's yet not quite so, the face of a young woman he wanted badly – and he laughed aloud, scattering birds, for there was something wry about it. Brick O'Shea, a man of forty-eight, cutting off his past as if it had never been to plan his future with a young girl, awkward, naïve, oh yes, a girl who often exasperated him, a spoilt girl with whom he lost patience yet a girl with whom he had thrown in his lot and would do so for the rest of his life. Wherever he went and whatever he did he could not put her from his mind or his body. She was part of both.

Leaves scattered under stumbling footsteps that cut off abruptly as he stepped out from the shade. Benny Brack was a twisted weasel of a man, clutching a jug of rum. Brick snatched the spirit and threw it far out into the water while the fellow's desolate eyes followed its path. He winced at its plop.

'This property is to be sold so get out your tools and start clearing and cleaning up or you'll be back on the streets where I found you, you drunken old lag. Do you hear me? Get to work.'

'Finneas says Jamie rode in, this morning when we were out looking for him, packed a bag, gave Gondola a thrashing for getting in his way, and rode back towards town.' Abby paused. 'It's my guess he's taken steamship south. I sense it.'

'Oh, you and your intuition! Jamie wouldn't take ship anywhere without telling me. He'll be back. He always comes back eventually. Probably needed more clothes, something special for one of the Pearsons' dances . . .'

'Tom Pearson sailed for England and it's not likely Jamie would stay on at Pennine House without him—'

'I won't listen to your gossip. I'm weary of it. Get out and leave me alone.'

Abby slammed the door as hard as she dared, and she dared a great deal. Alone again, Raunie regretted her temper for Abigail was all she had now that both Jamie and Brick had gone. It was not her husband's sudden trip north that disturbed her greatly – he'd been doing wild abrupt things all his life – but his physical retreat from her that terrified for without him she drifted, full of longing and hurt and the fear of losing him for ever, and with a terrible jealousy of what or of whom she could not be certain, his new deep absorption in – what? A woman? Other women had never bothered her for they came and went. But what if one particular woman was to stay, to possess him as she, his wife, had always possessed him? There was terror in the thought. Dear Gorgio God, she prayed, forgive me my sins whatever they are but let me bear Brick's child, then he will never leave me. Though he denies it he must want his own son and he's married to a woman who cannot conceive. She always returned to that bitter thought: she was barren. She could use the word to herself, torment herself in private. Something must have gone wrong at Jamie's birth, some twist, for she had not conceived to Kenneth Merrill, or to Alister, Kenneth's father, or to Feli the gipsy – a brief episode but long enough – or to Kurt Herlicht. She had never wanted children to these men but more than anything in the world she wanted to conceive to Brick – and she was barren. Barren!

Another circumstance of this day nagged at her. She had gone driving about town, as she sometimes did when Jamie was away, missing him, sending Abigail in and out of hotels and lodging-houses and restaurants. No Jamie. But driving home, bored, despondent, she had roused to stare from the carriage at Alannah Aldercott walking up the steps of the discreetly placed consulting-rooms of Doctor Bains, an obstetrician newly arrived from London. Every woman who could afford him was rushing to consult, hadn't she done so herself only last week to find him no better than other doctors with the same bland and useless advice: no apparent abnormality . . . cold baths alternated with warm . . . plenty of fresh air . . . long walks . . . And there was that freckle-faced country girl full and rounded after barely six weeks married.

She sat very still. Alannah Aldercott rounded with child and only six weeks married? Yes, rounded, despite the fussy gowns and full cloaks she had taken to wearing, styles that did not suit her. Fuller in the face too. Well now! But it was incredible, laughable, that Alannah could have been driven by uncontrollable passion to roll in the hay with that passionless clerk? Yet if not Aldercott, who? The girl knew few men and none intimately that she had heard tell of. Besides, there was nothing of the flirt about her. But undoubtedly there had been a lover before her marriage.

Her fingers tightened on the lace spread. Hitherto insignificant details drifted through her mind: the surprise, more, the shock on Brick's face as she had told him of Alannah's marriage. Alannah's awareness of him when he came into a room. Chance remarks: 'She rides like . . .' Did he actually see something of the dead Barbara in Alannah? Yes, there was something that reminded one of Barbara Merrill, both ordinary and rather dowdy and out of place in hothouse surroundings. The way they moved, their speech, Alannah more volatile, but the things they said that other women did not. Both a little secretive, seeming to inhabit some private world of their own devising, with that baffling, maddening, dignified withdrawal as if from lesser mortals.

Her hands picked restlessly at the lace spread. She would go mad lying here. She slid from the bed so violently the lace tore and it pleased her for she wanted to tear away at things, at people, at Alannah Aldercott with all the romanticism of eighteen – no, nineteen now. She wanted to tear away at Brick with his experience and deadly charm that affected women so strongly . . . How, where, could it have happened? Not in Sydney for Nance Mason would have known, Nance knew everything. At Erins Pride? She doubted that. Then it could only have been at Burrendah, the girl's precious Place of the Swan; Brick had been there in October. 'Fortunate they are only a few miles apart,' Nance had teased. Then Alannah's unexpected, hasty – oh, yes, hasty – marriage to a man she did not even profess to like. Everything coincided, even to Alannah slipping out into the garden the night of the dinner-party to join Brick. Suspicion became conviction, then hate for Alannah Aldercott, even more, for the child she was carrying.

Her moan was a long-drawn-out animal sound. She ran to the mirror. Her hair was as black and thick and shining as ever, her face unlined – or was it? How did others see her? How did Brick see her? She searched her face for lines as she seldom did, always reluctant to face the passing years, but now she fumbled for her rouge pot and dabbed at her cheeks. The result did not reassure. She needed stronger weapons. Something she could not control had happened; an intrusion, a threat, a new life mocking her, growing, a part of Brick but not of her. She hated the child and wanted to destroy it, *needed* to destroy it, for she could not live with even the idea of it. She did what she usually did when baulked and baffled, she destroyed. She swept clothes off the bed and chairs, her brushes and combs from the bureau in her terrible rage, the sound of shattering tearing and crashing blending with her despair. Abigail pounded the door with anxious queries but she ignored the woman, intent on herself. Alannah Aldercott was to bear Brick's child and she wanted to tear away at the girl. But just as much at her own body for its inadequacy in denying her what Alannah could so easily provide.

Breathless, she paused at last and forced herself to calmness. Her body had always been her ultimate weapon; she must nurture it, care for it, and never harm it. It could not bear a child but it had other uses and she would employ them to their utmost to win back her husband and lover. Whatever it cost her or others, to win him back and keep him, that cost must be paid. Brick was hers, had always been hers, and she would never let him go.

Chapter Fourteen

'STRAIGHTEN UP, Joey, and try Matilda's peach pie.' Miss Moynan – Mrs Aldercott now, but he could never think of her as anything but Miss Moynan, preferably as Miss Alannah – was smiling and holding out a loaded plate.

He was glad to straighten up though he was behind with his work and it bothered him for he liked working at Lucknow, stocking the woodpile, tending furnace, keeping the classroom shipshape between the setting in of paths amid the little gardens, all with the comforting chant of the boys at their lessons. He liked working at Brighton too when Mr Moynan was home but was wary of Brighton's housekeeper when he was not and if it weren't for Effie winking at him as she cut lettuce he would somehow avoid going. But he disliked working at Birubi, particularly now that Mr O'Shea had gone away without leaving orders for him as he usually did, and he dreaded the job of making the steps down to Birubi's beach with no real help to be expected from Old Samuel and even less from Finneas who hated being taken from the stables, and Richie useless at stonework, and young Ned over from Brighton only when he could be spared. Besides, he suspected Mrs O'Shea's strange hunchback, always peeping at him from behind pillars, of carrying tales. But Mrs O'Shea was impatient for him to begin work. His old odd sense of being possessed by women plagued him: Mrs O'Shea, scorning and criticising as she had done since the old days at Regent Lodge when the kitchen had credited her with the evil eye . . . Mrs Swallow watching over his shoulder as he worked about Brighton . . . Grace, impatient to wed him and 'don her boots' and start the long trek to Oorin. Grace had never been easy, not like Adina, but he didn't think of Adina these days, he could not, it was too painful. As for Miss Moynan – Mrs Aldercott – she seemed different of late (Grace had been right there), sometimes looking past him as if she didn't see him at all. He licked the crumbs from his fingers, watching her stroll among the plaster cupids and dolphins waiting to be set around the minute fountain, pausing to listen, he supposed, to the murmurs from the schoolroom. She did not smile so often these days. She seldom went riding; she did not like riding about Sydney, she explained, it was not the same. Altogether she bothered him for there was something else, something to *do* with her that nagged, tormenting him: her silver cross. He would sometimes unwrap it from the scrap of linen in which he carried it about in his pocket, afraid to leave it in his box in case it should be stolen, an unlikely event but he felt responsible for it. He would stare at it, smoothing and polishing, feeling in a way a thief, wanting to return it yet not daring to do so. Something always held him back; the vision in his mind's eye of herself and Mr O'Shea coming up from her coppice in the early morning, hand in hand . . . kissing . . . And she had married Mr Aldercott. There were times he almost hated her and, because of her, Mr O'Shea. That was the worst of it. He didn't want to hate Mr O'Shea.

She had reached the back wall. As she turned she met his eyes and he looked away in confusion but she strolled back, smiling. 'Go round to the kitchen for another slice. Matilda baked plenty.' She paused to run her hand over the curve of a plaster dolphin. 'Do you miss Erins Pride, Joey?' He nodded dumbly. 'And Grace of course.' He nodded again, slowly. 'I miss my Place of the Swan, dreadfully.'

'I know.' Embarrassed, he picked up a slab of stone and examined it carefully with his sticky fingers, not looking at her for he had the awful feeling that though he wasn't close enough to see her tears, he knew she was crying.

There were moments when Alannah, with a sense almost of shock, pondered the incongruity of her association, for it could scarcely be called friendship, with Brick O'Shea's wife. But the fact that it was not she who sought contact seemed to make the bizarre situation more plausible, certainly more acceptable. It was Raunie who arranged their social occasions, often sending her carriage in to Bridge Street to await Alannah's pleasure so that her invitations became difficult to refuse, particularly as she found she needed diversion from a life that did not, after all, involve her closely. Though loving and devoted to her slightest expressed wish Simon was absorbed in his curriculum and the cultivation of solid citizens with growing sons. Moreover, he and her aunt had achieved a quite unexpected rapport, particularly since he had decided to take a few well-connected boarders. He had raised no objections when Delia Carney had moved in, to select a cook-housekeeper and maids, compose menus and rules, decide fittings and furnishings, and bombard his always-respectful self with advice as to the proper selection of a proper assistant-master. Aunt Delia Carney had clearly found her niche in life, seemingly absorbed by her self-established role of Lucknow's nurse-matron, and no longer talked of returning home, while Simon was delighted his wife was relieved of 'tedious duties' as he put it, for he seemed to regard her as a fragile porcelain ornament. Alannah found herself no more in demand and about as half as useful as the handsome plaster matron (chosen, chastely garbed, by Aunt Delia) propped against the wall waiting to be sealed to the centre pedestal of the pool where carp glided and sported. She was left with much free time that city attractions, even if she were interested, could never absorb.

Simon had been delighted with her news of the baby and she had hastened to draw him in firmly to her inner world of pregnancy – what an actress she had become! Yet how easy it was to hoodwink a man, at least this man, and she gave thanks to whatever dark deity was watching over her schemes that he was so unworldly and inexperienced. When was the 'happy event'? – clichés to the last. Well, it could scarcely be earlier than September, now could it, but there *was* this tendency in her family to premature birth, and the way she was feeling if not looking – yet – it promised to be a big baby. He wanted to proclaim the news to the world but

291

she stopped him with calculated sweetness; not even her father or her aunt knew yet and she wanted to enjoy her secret with her husband a while longer, would he not indulge her in this? Flattered, he had promised, and she knew he would keep his promise and for this she showed him added consideration and attention, filling her days with activity and their nights with as much response as she could manage. Indeed, she welcomed his attentions in an effort to blot Brick entirely from her mind and body, living out her contrived, dishonest and secret existence in the only way she could keep her safe corner of the world in which her child could be born and accepted by this man who asked no questions – why would he doubt her? He loved her in his boyish, naïve, often aggravating way, overlooking her moods, her sometimes hesitancy, her sharpness those times she missed Burrendah the most – its abrasive talk, its involvement with people and life, even its cruelties, most of all her crisp morning rides to Erins Pride – missing it so intensely there were moments she felt she could not bear Sydney another day. But Burrendah seemed to function equally well without her! Though they would have no reason to suspect her deceit, her courage ebbed at facing her father and aunt with the news and she laced herself as tightly as she dared and lived for the day, refusing to consider what she would do when Brick returned, as of course he would. It was all she could do to deal with the now.

In this strange lull of waiting Raunie O'Shea became not only an amusing and stimulating companion but a retreat, an escape. Even Simon in his glowing new contentment, and sense of achievement no doubt, made no objection to their companionship, while her aunt grew expansive if not entirely forgiving when inundated with Birubi's choicest blooms. As for her father, Raunie would stop the carriage before Brighton's gleaming door-knocker to shimmer through its rooms in her peacock clothes, trailing perfumes, witticisms and smiles, coaxing Owen from his study so charmingly he never hesitated to set aside his blueprints or plans to listen, even to respond in his faintly austere way to her flirtatious overtures. Her gaiety was as infectious as her generosity was overwhelming when selecting rings or brooches at her toy of a shop – since it was to be sold over her head why not help themselves, she would laugh, and press a mother-of-pearl fan or a fancy comb upon Alannah. She complained incessantly of her husband's latest excursion: he had based himself in that awful smoky port of Newcastle, to build another mill or seek more land, or labour, she never really knew what he was up to these days. He might even be on his way north. But if he thought she would live in that steaming tropical jungle of swamps and cannibal Blacks — oh yes, they ate people in the North – with convicts wandering the bush as well as the streets, he was mistaken. She simply could not convey to Alannah what her company had meant these past weeks with that sick old woman upstairs and nurses answerable only to Mr O'Shea as they kept reminding her so insolently, and Jamie off again, this time without a word – what wandering men she had!

'Everyone says I spoil my son and perhaps I do but he *is* only a boy. The odd thing is, Brick was even more indulgent of him than I when Jamie was a child, promising him the world. Brick hates his gambling, but Jamie can't help being a gambler, after all I'm one.' Her laugh was infectious. 'But he hasn't my luck at cards. I'm lucky at love too. I must be, for I have Brick – well, most of the time.'

'You must have some idea of Jamie's whereabouts?'

Raunie shrugged. 'He hasn't written, but then he seldom does. I only know he's left the Pearsons' Pennine House – Tom Pearson is on his way to Europe. Jamie's wandering some goldfield, I suppose, he can't seem to live without excitement. Or he might have gone south to stay with Good Old Harry – funny how names stick — Ventril. Harry was in Sydney over Christmas, you know. He's always writing to Jamie to join him in Bendigo. The Ventrils kept the Princess Royal pub there when Jamie was growing up and he and Harry got into mischief together – as I suppose they still do – until the Ventrils bought a sheep property near Ballarat. But the family keep permanent rooms in Bendigo.' She wandered the room, twisting her hands together, uneasy, Alannah could see. 'After all, why should Jamie stay around here with only that old woman upstairs sitting staring at nothing, hating him as she hates me. I can't understand why you bother to visit such a dangerous old hag.'

'That poor sick old woman dangerous?'

'She'll revive, you'll see. She'll go on living just to plague me – but why are we talking of Moll Noakes when there are so many interesting things to speak of – and do. For instance, is all well with you?'

'Quite well.'

Raunie gave a tiny, meant-to-be-understanding laugh. 'Under the circumstances, I suppose.'

'Circumstances?' she hedged. But her hands trembled slightly as she placed her cup carefully in its saucer. She must accustom herself to probing, and the giving of suitable answers. She couldn't go on hiding her child for ever, indeed it was wonder questions hadn't been asked before this.

'Oh, come. I saw you going into Doctor Bains' rooms and after all he is an obstetrician. I think you're wise for they say he has all the latest European ideas.' Aching to tear away at the girl's fair skin and right through to the child – Brick's child – so tight and safe and untouchable within her. How would she bear it when the child was born? How could she bear to watch it grow? How would she endure its mother using it as a weapon, the most potent weapon any woman could use against another? She, Raunie, was Brick's wife, but it would not be enough to hold him when his child was born, and the conviction that he would leave her for this milkmaid-mother was more than she could bear. Yet somehow she kept her voice light and impersonal.

'When is the "happy event", as the world calls a woman's travail?'

'September.' Without hesitation for she had rehearsed her answers to such questions many times without considering exactly how she would spin July to September – how else but the usual excuse of premature birth? There would be the doctor, of course, but she had chosen a new arrival to the colony who did not know, or care, she presumed, the date of her marriage.

'You didn't lose a moment, did you,' Raunie laughed, in awe of the girl's control.

'I assure you we were properly wed before we bedded,' Alannah insisted with the right amount of flippancy. 'After all, with so many chatelaines protecting my virginity how could it be otherwise?' She strolled to the window to avoid the woman's eyes and, she hoped, further questions, by guiding the conversation beyond the brightness of the day to the littered lawns and ring of picks and grate of shovels. 'Are they chipping away the entire cliff?'

'Joey insists it's a difficult job but I don't believe him. He's taking his time to annoy me. The men are lazy and sullen because they want their usual work so take their cue from him.'

'But why should Joey want to annoy you?'

'Because he hates me. He always has and, without Brick to stand over him, he lags. You can't trust Joey Bowes.'

'I've always found him an excellent worker.'

'What can you know about him, really? Brick took him in and made a pet of him and these waifs expect the world from their benefactors. Joey's shrewd. He's always been a parasite living off the fat of the land, doing what he pleases when Brick's away.'

'He does the work of three.'

'All a front for Brick's benefit. He's treated better than other menials—'

'Joey's not exactly a menial, certainly not in Brick's eyes—' She broke off. She had spoken Brick's name in intimacy but if Raunie noticed she did not comment.

'He's a menial when I'm in charge.'

'He's been a good friend to me.'

'Oh well, if you want to make friends of a servant . . .'

'I make friends with whom I wish. And perhaps I had better go.'

'Oh, Alannah!' Laughing it off. 'Don't let's quarrel over Joey.' So contrite in her most engaging way that Alannah felt a little ashamed of her anger. 'There, the breeze has come up. Let's walk about and see how the work is progressing, it might spur the men along. I promise not to say a cross word to anyone, particularly Joey. Come?'

She was so persuasive, so irresistible, her black hair

glinting in its jet-spangled net, playing with the strings of her hat, that Alannah felt a little gauche and rather unreasonable when she should be grateful for the friendship of this lovely generous woman who was guiding her through a situation she could scarcely endure – and never mind the odd twisted ethics of bearing a child to this selfsame woman's husband. She tried to put the circumstance from her mind as they strolled the lawns fringed by gardens and, in turn, by a wall of shrubs bordering the cliff face before it sloped gently then more abruptly to the beach; watching the chipping and cutting and setting-in and taking out and lifting, coughing a little in the fine dust, Old Samuel and Finneas doing their best on the orders of a distinctly uncomfortable Joey. The men nodded to Alannah, but kept their heads down, daunted as always by the determined calculating critical eyes of the mistress of Birubi.

The project she had initiated in a moment of pique was assuming great importance in Raunie's eyes, not only as a means of proclaiming her authority in her husband's absence but for deeper reasons. She was obsessed by what she saw as not only Joey's hostility but the lassitude of the men, and could not keep away from the terrace to urge them on, fretting, asking questions and impatient of Joey's plodding answers. One morning she waited till Old Samuel and Finneas were working lower down the cliff before delivering her ultimatum: all to be completed and ready for use in a week, to be precise by next Tuesday. Tuesday? Joey looked aghast. Impossible, Mrs O'Shea. She grew angry. Nothing was impossible. She had already sent invitations to a celebration picnic, all was arranged, and if he had not let the men laze their time away she would have no need to hurry them now.

Uneasy, Joey grew stubborn. He was expected at Lucknow on Sunday, to begin work Monday on the schoolroom desks, the boys off on an excursion and the schoolroom empty. A couple of days at Lucknow and he would be back to finish here. You'll finish all here before you leave, Joey Bowes, that's an order. He stood shifting from one foot to the other, running his hands down his soiled breeches in awkward little movements as if she might shake hands with him and he must be ready.

'But it's the mortar, Mrs O'Shea. Old Samuel and Finneas aren't used to it.'

'I don't care how you mix the stuff, or how you use it, just get the job done.'

'But they're heavy steps, twelve of 'em, some chipped out of the rock face itself, others cut from blocks and mortared in, deep in, Ma'am, the only way it can be done. Each step takes planning y'see, before cutting and setting in just right. And mortar's awful slow-drying stuff.'

'Then you must work into the night, with lanterns.'

'But it's what we're doing now, for young Ned hurt his leg and can't move fast and must rest a lot, and it's holding us back – we're one less you might say. Then there are the gardens and paths and rockeries and the fountain to be set in and the seat halfway down. A mighty lot to do yet—'

'Everything will set in a wink in this weather. In any case, I refuse to change my plans so get more help if you must, you're responsible, and if you don't please me in this you'll make Mr O'Shea angry. Very angry. All finished and ready for use before you leave here on Sunday, understood?'

He dared not argue further. Besides, how could he be certain she was not simply passing on Mr O'Shea's orders? He wished Mr O'Shea were here – how he wished it. Miserably he watched her go yet was glad the ordeal of trying to talk to her was over, at least for now. Nothing else for it, they must work even harder, right through the night if need be, Ned with his bad leg, and Old Samuel and Finneas tiring easily and wanting their beds. But better that than Richie hindering and spoiling the job; fit only for mustering and branding, that one! Even if they should finish up by Sunday – and a miracle it would be – he would be uneasy. What more could he do without angering the mistress further? A warning of some kind . . . A rope barrier across the top step? A clumsy awkward device but at least it would make him feel a little better, as if he were really doing his duty. He began to harangue the men at their work. And to drive himself almost to distraction.

Raunie paused at the cliff edge above Birubi's beach to survey the finished work. No doubt of it they were strong-looking steps, combining with rockeries and little paths and artificial handholds as well as natural ones to make a gentle safe descent between the rock faces. The toy fountain flowed off in a miniature waterfall, and the brightly painted seat looked inviting. She ran her hands idly along a rope – a rope barrier? Joey's final hindrance. But now Joey was out of the way. There had been a few bad moments yesterday when he had started to argue again but she had simply ordered him off to Lucknow. He dared not refuse, he knew it. It had taken much planning, and not a little expense which she could ill afford, to contrive an empty, or almost empty, house: the housemaid and kitchen and scullery maids with Richie in his cart, Cook and Abigail Luff grandly in the curricle, with Gondola on his pony, all jolting off for a night at the music-hall with spending money from the mistress as a special treat. At first Abby had flatly refused to go, consenting only when bribed with a room overnight at a public-house, no less, for all knew without putting it into words that once in town not one of them could be coaxed or bullied home before the morrow – nor would Abby try, for she loved the town, seldom saw it, and would spend the night her own way leaving them to their devices until she rounded them up the next morning. Fay Witherstone had complained bitterly at being left behind but Puttering could not spare her; besides, there must be someone around to help the daily 'tweeny'. Birubi was empty but for Nurse Puttering and the unhappy Fay in the eastern suite, and Old Samuel and Finneas in their room over the stables. In any case, the servants were not permitted near the lawns and terrace, except Old Samuel to garden and the housemaid to pick flowers when needed; the area was private to family and all must abide by the rules. Raunie knew full well she would be safely alone until midday on the morrow when they would come straggling back. And even if by chance they should make their way home tonight it could not be before midnight. All was quiet and deserted but for ships in mid-Harbour and the soft March breeze tantalising trees and shrubs. There had been a little rain early and it could be damp underfoot but the sky was clear, it would be a fine night. It would be a fine tomorrow. She sat at the plateau edge in the shelter of the trees for a long time.

On the fine edge of darkness she emerged from the house wearing boots, a dark skirt and blouse under a dark cloak, and carrying her old carpet-bag. Always careful of her hands she wore old riding gloves. Removing the rope she stuffed it in her skirt pocket then turned to survey the house, in darkness but for soft outside lamps and a faint glow from the stables where Finneas and Old Samuel would be sleeping off their hard labours. She had decided not to risk a lantern even though her task must be completed before the moon rose and, in any case, she could move in darkness as the gipsy she was. In the shadow of the trees she removed her cape and stuffed it in her carpet-bag, slung the bag over her shoulder and, tucking up her skirt, began to move down carefully and methodically for she had familiarised herself with every inch of her own gardens over the past days. She kept to the trees and shrubs so that even if there were stragglers on the road, which was unlikely, or fishing boats in the Bay, she could not be seen. She trod softly and selectively, avoiding soil patches where she might leave footprints and keeping to the grass. She had never lost her gift of stealthy movement and, light as a cat, picked her way down the barely defined little path beside the steps, past the top step, then the second, for both, she had discovered, had been chiselled out of the rock face itself. Below the third step she paused for breath. She moved on to the fourth step and balanced just below it by wedging her body firmly against the rock face. She removed her gloves and stuffed them in her skirt pocket along with the rope for now she would depend largely on her sense of touch.

She groped in the carpet-bag for a small hammer and a chisel and began to work on the step, chipping away beneath it, digging under and in, slowly and very carefully cutting out the dirt and soil and mortar, dependent not only on touch but on instinct and her sense of what she was about, for if she chipped too much too soon the step would not hold until the precise moment. She worked on skilfully until she sensed rather than heard the faint jar of rock against rock and paused: enough. Precisely enough. The step did little more than hang suspended and would stay balanced just so, she was sure of it, for there would be no more rain or wind. It was a perfect night.

She moved up to the third step, balanced herself again and repeated the process until she felt the step move slightly – if this one did not give under a light tread the fourth would, she was staking everything on that. She felt the sting of a cut on her finger but ignored it for she could not, must not, stop till all was complete. There was a faint light in the eastern sky – but still time before the moon rose. She was tired from concentration more than physical effort and glad it was almost over. She stuffed the tools in her bag, tucked up her skirt and moved carefully from grass patch to grass patch to the lawns. Wrapping her cloak about her and keeping to the trees she slipped inside the dark and silent house.

She was a long time at her wash-basin. The harsh soap stung, eating into the cut, but she washed it clean until it smarted. She flung the bar of soap to the back of the great wardrobe, then her skirt and blouse, both damp and muddy, and her cloak and carpet-bag – she would dispose of everything later. She creamed and smoothed her hands. There! The thing was done and all she must do now was make certain no one came near the steps, more importantly, that no one put a foot upon them; but she was not unduly worried, all knew the garden area was sacred to the O'Sheas. And tomorrow Alannah would come to her picnic, except that there would be no picnic – Richie had been sent about with notes of apology. A postponement to all but Alannah Aldercott. Tomorrow Alannah would come for Alannah had promised and Alannah kept her promises. To make doubly sure the carriage would be sent in early. Raunie threw herself on her bed and lay wide-eyed, elated and excited. It was done. Finally, she slept.

All looked splendid, Alannah assured Raunie as they strolled the now cleared and lushly tended lawns bordered by native shrubs contrasting with English blooms. Her cheerfulness was forced. She had not really wanted to come today for she felt a little tired and her feeling of lassitude had been enhanced at finding Raunie alone and apparently inconsolable at Jamie's continued absence and silence, leaving her long-awaited celebration ruined for the lack of himself and his young friends to carry baskets and rugs and set up the deck chairs, more importantly to amuse her guests when they became bored. She had been so disappointed she had cancelled the whole thing, not able to face questions, certainly not from Eveline Purdue and her like. Even Nance would have been a trial. She had wanted only Alannah for Alannah understood. Understood what? Alannah had frowned. Why, how she, Raunie, felt about things . . . Brick always off somewhere. And now her son wandering parts unknown and leaving her with her beautiful picnic spoiled.

'Nonsense,' Alannah had laughed. 'Nothing's spoiled. We won't allow it.' To cheer herself even more than the other woman. 'I shall admire everything just as if Nance and Eveline and the rest were here to argue over details. Where shall we begin?' She coaxed Raunie to walk with her while she admired the rockeries and paths and the precious steps, even the awful statues peeping at them from behind the shrubs with their dead white eyes. Raunie cheered up considerably. She would entertain more often for Jamie, it might keep him home. She would give a grand beach party for the Regatta, with gentlemen rowing round from Double Bay to help with the arrangements – what a spectacular sight *that* would be. The breeze ruffled Alannah's skirts and tingled her skin as she stood gazing down-Harbour, past the ships and little boats and over the virgin bush with only a few scattered roofs in their shields of trees. How beautiful it all was . . . Even so, she found more beauty in her Place of the Swan – how she missed it. If only Simon were as fond of country life as herself. But his life's work was here, immersed in the gentle realms of the scholar. The clear greeny-blue water seemed far down, farther than usual, some illusion of distance, or else the contours of the cliff had changed. She felt a slight vertigo and drew back, surprised at herself for she had never been timid of heights. Nor did she suffer dizziness; she was, according to Doctor Bains, as fit as a young race-horse. There was just something different about today.

'I'm so *glad* you're here,' Raunie gushed, and Alannah shrank a little for she hated over-effusiveness. Besides, it was unlike Raunie; she, too, seemed different today. 'My first guest. That's why I want you to be the first to use the steps, even before I set foot on them myself.'

Alannah looked startled. 'Now?'

'Why not? I've waited a long time for this . . . well . . . ceremony, if you like. Do, Alannah. Please do.'

She was so eager, so gracious, standing there smiling, begging in a way, the breeze fluttering tiny tendrils of her black hair, that Alannah could not help but respond. 'If you want it so, why not?' She moved to the first step then paused for Raunie was leaning forward and pointing down with an almost childish excitement.

'Do look – crocuses. The early autumn ones of that creamy yellow I adore.'

Alannah leant forward. 'I don't see them.'

'*There*, see? Tucked under the bank below the third step. I must have a bouquet. Do you think . . . I mean, we couldn't both manage on the one step, we'd tangle.' With a tiny giggle.

Alannah laughed back. 'If you want them so much, I'll try.' She took a step down.

'Further down yet.'

Alannah bent forward. The scent of earth was wonderful, cool and a little damp and she stood breathing it in. But still she could not see crocuses, only rock faces and steps. But further down was a tiny rock-garden sheltered by the cliff. Perhaps Raunie meant there . . .

302

'See?' Raunie was pointing again. 'There where the rock face curves under. You must move down.'

Alannah took the third step and bent forward. 'Are you certain—' Her words cut off as the horizon tipped towards her in a great swaying arc. She teetered on a knife edge then the edge went and she heard screaming, her own screams, as her hands went out clutching at rock but grasping air. There were other screams behind her and her hands burned and seared, scraping the rock, catching on shrubs and spikes as she lurched into space, thudding against rock in a terrifying series of sickly jars to her body. Pain, terrible pain, as she lay conscious but twisted. Pain through her head and down her body to her toes. Dull heavy sickly pain . . .

Doctor Bains' eyes travelled over the silent little group waiting at the bottom of Birubi's stairs before coming to rest on Simon Aldercott. 'Your wife has a chance,' he told him, shrugging into his cape. 'A good chance, providing she is not moved, as further loss of blood could be fatal. As it is she will take a long time to recover; there is shock as well as injury, for she fell so heavily it's a wonder she's alive. She has a fractured scapula which will heal by itself but her hands are badly torn.' He paused. 'I am sorry about the child, but I did all I could.'

'Child?' Owen turned to Simon who looked uncomfortable but who met his father-in-law's enquiring glance frankly.

'Alannah wanted it kept secret a while longer – a whim, I suppose. I indulged it.'

'Her prerogative of course – and yours.' Owen recovered his composure with difficulty. 'Even so, if we had known perhaps we could have persuaded her to take more care.'

'Alannah had every care.'

'You may go up, Mr Aldercott, but only for a few minutes.' The doctor was busy and brisk. 'And only yourself for the next few days. I shall send a Nurse Brough.'

'The house is full of nurses. And servants.' Raunie could be silent no longer. Simon turned to her.

'Your husband must be told of this, Mrs O'Shea.'

'I have no idea where he is.'

'He can be contacted through his forwarding address at Newcastle.'

Her chin rose. 'I see no reason to bother him. Every care will be taken of Alannah.'

'Nevertheless, I believe Mr O'Shea will wish to know since this happened in his house. In any case I wish him to know so if you do not telegraph Newcastle, I shall.' He did not look at all wispy, nor did he stumble or fidget with his coat lapels as he usually did. Still she fought him.

'Everything possible is being done for Alannah. No one could have foreseen the carelessness of workmen. Joey Bowes will be punished, and severely, I assure you.'

Simon did not argue, just turned to walk the doctor to the door where Owen Moynan joined them, frowning. 'Young wives,' he murmured uncomfortably, 'have moods, have they not, Doctor? Perhaps at such an early stage of pregnancy my daughter needed time to adjust to the idea.'

'Early?' The doctor frowned. 'Your daughter's pregnancy was well advanced, sir. Indeed, any further advanced and this accident could have cost her her life too. She was over four months I would say.'

Owen stared. 'But surely you are mistaken?'

'I am an experienced obstetrician, Mr Moynan, with long experience in London hospitals.'

'Of course, but—'

'I give a medical opinion, no more. Complete rest for your wife, Mr Aldercott, she must not move a finger. Indeed, I doubt that she could. I will call tomorrow and each morning thereafter until she is out of danger – unless of course I am sent for earlier.'

Raunie had no choice but to offer Owen Moynan, Simon Aldercott, and Mrs Carney (groaning, but what else could she do?) rooms in her house but to her great relief they decided to ride or drive back and forth from town. Bored, she left their tiresome comings and goings to her servants and the nurses, with Abigail, as usual, the intermediary. She delayed informing Brick, hoping Simon would forget but, if he were prepared to do so, Abby was not.

'Are you out of your mind? The girl's lying up there near death. What do you think your precious O'Shea will say and do if you don't let him know? Bring him back for your own sake for if you don't the husband surely will. He means it.'

So she reasoned and goaded and bullied until Raunie telegraphed Brick's Newcastle bank that Mrs Aldercott had met with an accident at Birubi – no more, no less. If he came hurrying back her last doubt – if she had any – would be dissolved. Alannah slept long or, awake, lay pale and listless, seldom speaking as if it were too much of an effort to know who came and went about her bed. A patient Simon managed to get a little food down her throat, surprising everyone with his decisiveness concerning her welfare. Her shocked and badly sprained body would take a long time to heal, all knew it, but Raunie fretted to have the girl out of her house, off to Lucknow or anywhere else she chose. Oddly perhaps, she had not thought beyond ridding herself of a child that threatened the security of her own life and love. In any case, sickness of any kind depressed her and so far as she was concerned the episode was over. But when Brick telegraphed that he was on his way, and by coach, she felt uneasy. She did not know quite what to expect.

'Get it out – every step and stone of it. Throw it all in the Harbour. Flatten everything – steps, paths, gardens and those obscene bits of plaster. Get rid of every blasted rock or I'll string you all up and give you a taste of the "cat" and be damned to the consequences. No one goes down to that beach any more. Get everything out. *Out!*'

Braced by the withdrawing-room windows but carefully out of sight, Raunie shivered at the cold precise steel of Brick's voice as she had shuddered often over the past days, the only curb on his fury a reminder from Nurses Puttering and Brough that the invalids must have quiet. Then he would tramp the shore or ride off to town, returning at unlikely hours to rouse the house if need be and shout all over

305

again like a man demented, urging his men to fresh efforts. She had been afraid many times in her life, of hunger and cold, of being alone, of the idea of growing old, but never so afraid as she had been since he had stalked in to probe answers to his questions and rage at the servants, and Joey – she had thought he would kill Joey Bowes – and at herself for not informing him sooner. He had seemed quite mad, his interrogations savage and persistent, but the servants were dogged in insisting they knew nothing, absolutely nothing about the steps or the new paths or the statuary or the new gardens for they were forbidden the terrace area. Raunie had loudly and publicly denied Joey's story of warnings, certainly of any rope barrier – would she have risked her own life as well as Mrs Aldercott's if she had been warned against using the steps so soon? She had trusted Joey. They had all trusted Joey. Again, Joey must have misheard her concerning picnic guests, she had invited only Mrs Aldercott, her dear friend, to be the first to set foot on the steps, a ceremony of a kind, was that so wrong? Still Brick shouted and bullied and probed until the maids crept about stunned at the awful thing that had happened to a guest in the house. As for Raunie, she could have dealt with Brick's physical violence but his leashed fury struck terror in her. She had only done what any wife had the right to do, rid herself of a child fathered by the husband she adored. If she, Brick O'Shea's wife, could not bear him a child no other woman must do so. She could not understand Brick's persistence for he seemed in torment over a creature unformed, unknown and unseen. The terrible thing was that he did not sleep with her, he did not even seek her out. On his visits to Alannah he would close the door firmly behind him, shutting her and everyone else out, and his secrecy – their secrecy – taunted her, driving her to near madness. At least Joey Bowes was out of the way. He had gone striding down the drive after a terrible scene between himself and Brick, sweet music to her ears, and where he was now she cared not a jot. Yet still Brick raged in his bitter dogged obsession to, as it were, wipe the slate clean, and had gathered up his men from the stables, the gardens and the workshop, to rip out the paths, easy enough, but the steps remained firm. Now they were hacking at them with picks, tearing them out in jagged pieces, bit by bit, while he stood over them in a baffled frenzy, Old Samuel getting the worst of his tongue.

'Get them out, man. *Out!*'

'Y'can see for y'self, sir, they won't budge.'

'If the two down there on the beach broke loose, why not these?'

'I dunno, Mr O'Shea, I just dunno. These are packed solid into the rock face, part of the cliff itself as y'might say – which some of 'em are. Our lime makes hard mortar, sir, and it beats me how even one came loose under a woman's weight, a light-weight at that.'

'There's very little mortar on those down on the beach.'

'I can't explain that, sir, but mortar ain't the whole strength of these steps for Joey had a way of fitting 'em in: cutting 'em to shape as he thought best then wedging 'em a certain way, and that's why it's so hard to move 'em now, I reckon.'

'Chip them out then. Hack them out.'

'It's what we're doing, sir, but it will take time.'

'Out of my way then, you old fool, let me at it.' And he sent Old Samuel sprawling, a man he had never struck in his life, and began tearing at the rock with his bare hands like a man demented. Old Samuel picked himself up to stand watching the violent futile display until O'Shea paused, physically beaten. 'Not one of you will leave the job till it's done if we have to cut away the whole rock face,' he raged on.

'We might come to it, Mr O'Shea, that we might.' Old Samuel paused to scratch his head, then add thoughtfully: 'It's as if the two down there were different like, not really part of the job at all, separate as you might say – and it's odd for we all worked on the steps and set 'em in the way Joey showed us. Don't it seem odd to you, Mr O'Shea, when you really think on it?'

Raunie saw Brick straighten to stare at the old man and she let the curtain drop knowing fear such as she had never known before. She wanted to run, to escape, but there seemed nowhere to run, no escape at all.

Chapter Fifteen

'AND DON'T forget y'breeches, y'dirty old lag. We've lice enough in the beds. Crawlin' up the walls too!'

Joey turned over with a groan on the hard apology for a bed, tormented by the wrangling from other rooms as much as by the snores, mumbles and grumbles of his unseen companions in the rundown room of one of the worst (but cheapest) lodging-houses in the Haymarket, hard by the slum of Durand's Alley; worse after all than trying to sleep in a doorway or in a rowboat drawn up on the beach or behind wool bales with the rats, to save his last coins for food. A fear had grown that the police were after him, on O'Shea's orders, and he had decided to make his way to Erins Pride, somehow, anyhow, for the Pride was his true home if he had a home at all where he would be given sanctuary, at least by Hetty. How to get there? He had no money to hire a horse or pay coach fare or even to take the train as far as Parramatta. Nothing else for it but to work his way with some bullock-team or a family travelling south, weeks on the road perhaps but he had no choice. He had grown a little mad these past days for nothing like this had happened to him before, not even in his hazardous street existence before Miss Merrill had taken him in. He had been banished by the man he had thought his friend, and was suffering through hurt and disappointment to a terrible anger such as he had never felt, or wanted to feel, certainly not for Mr O'Shea. But the strange and awful anger would not go away, worse, it was growing and it scared him. Mr Moynan had not blamed him for the accident, not really, at least not openly. 'Don't dwell on it, Joey, Mrs Aldercott slipped.' Even so, his voice had trailed and they both knew, miserably, dumbly, that the rock steps had broken away.

But how? He had made them very strong with good mortar so, despite his warnings born of caution and his sense of duty, his always-pride in a job well done, how could Miss Moynan's light tread have sent two steps crashing down? The angry snores around him added to his torment as he tossed on the narrow cot, longing for sleep. And why had Mrs O'Shea lied about his warnings? Why had she lied about her arrangements for her picnic? About the rope barrier? He supposed, after all, he might expect anything of her, but that Mr O'Shea should have believed her was the thing that shattered him; a man who had always been his friend to believe that he, Joey Bowes, would be careless? He had been banished like a criminal and the shock was changing him into something he had never been for every word Mr O'Shea had raged against him burned in his brain:

'Mrs Aldercott is very ill. She has lost her child and you are to blame.'

'*No.*' It was dragged from him. 'I would never hurt Miss Alannah. Never.'

'The steps were wrongly, or badly, set in, that much is obvious, and they were your responsibility. If you left the doing of them to Old Samuel, or to Finneas, or both, you are at fault. You can't blame them.'

'I have never blamed them. I warned Mrs O'Shea about using the steps so soon. I even put up a barrier – a rope.'

'What rope? What barrier? No one knows anything about that. I want no more of your evasions, your lies.'

'I have never lied to you.' Shocked, he became inarticulate and could not speak easily of it. It was the end of his life, his world. 'You know it.'

'I don't know it. Look down there . . . two great stones broken away. It's a miracle both women were not killed. You have done a criminal thing.' Shouting in his fury. 'Get out. Go to the devil for all I care.'

Joey had left to wander a city he no longer knew, with his mind picking away at terrible things, wandering the unfriendly ribald areas that were all he could afford, seeking escape from his thoughts, some retreat where he could hide and lick his wounds as it were. He longed for Erins Pride. He even longed for Grace and her hard common sense. There were times he felt he was going mad and he would take out Miss Alannah's silver cross and stare at it, wishing he'd never taken it from Barney. Yet though half-starved and without shelter most of the time he made no attempt to sell it; it belonged to Miss Alannah and he was responsible for it and would wrap it hurriedly, hide it and try to forget it. Yet he could not get away from it, it burned in his brain, as Mr O'Shea and Miss Alannah burned there, coupled, hand-in-hand, kissing . . . Somehow the memory of it made them his enemies, in some devious way the architects – though they did not know it – of his misfortune where they had once been his friends. His hardworking, hitherto secure life with Mr O'Shea was in chaos, shattered since that terrible day when Miss Alannah – as he would always think of her – had almost died and he was blamed, and he would become angry all over again. Work was his life, work was all he had, but now his work was no more since his banishment from Birubi. He was once again a waif, a street boy, and the hurt and anger the knowledge engendered was eating him up. He groaned and, unsleeping, angry tears pushing behind his eyes, stared up at a ceiling given over to the rats he could hear yet mercifully not see in the even more merciful dark.

The steps were finally gouged out and chipped away, leaving the cliff face a scarred and pitted thing. After its wave of feverish activity Birubi became a silent house in which the servants and nurses moved mutely about their duties and Raunie waited for Brick to come to her. But he did not come. On his brief visits he would sit at one end of the great table drinking stolidly, speaking only to order food or demand liquor, his eyes brooding on her and, when he did speak, ignoring her questions. He would visit the invalids alone, and his remoteness, his secrecy as she saw it, almost drove her mad, until as suddenly as he had come he would be off again and she would brood, convinced he was sleeping off his head in Susie's House or, more likely, Julie's, or in the arms of some Cypriot in an Elizabeth Street bordello. She longed for Jamie to lighten her mood but Jamie was nowhere. Her only relief was when Alannah decided to return to Lucknow. Now Birubi was hers again, hers and Brick's, and they would have a chance to resume their comfortable, intent, absorbed life together. But still he did not come and she fretted, and lost her temper, particularly with Gondola who followed her about, his eyes scarcely leaving her, and who took her beatings mutely and meekly. She felt he understood: perhaps he had suffered so much in his life he did not even feel the sting of her little whip. She was lonely and desolate. To win back her husband, her lover, her love, was becoming more than a goal, it was becoming an obsession.

Alannah left Birubi on impulse for she could no longer bear the house; she felt its unease through its very walls. When Brick came to her their attempts to talk were stilted and awkward and they would fall silent, their feeling for each other only in their eyes. They could not talk about the lost child – not yet. They could not talk about each other – not yet. She overheard his violence against Joey as all did and she felt a revulsion, a distaste for this man she had loved, did love, and would always love, afraid of what he might do for there were times he seemed capable of anything. Better, she decided, to regain her strength at Lucknow with her aunt and Simon to fuss and Matilda to nourish with her splendid cooking. But once 'home' – she could not yet think of Lucknow as home – small things irritated, the drone from the schoolroom setting Simon, infinitely patient, to closing doors and keeping voices down which made his work difficult. In any case, Lucknow was become her aunt's busy province which gave her time to dwell on many things, in particular her Place of the Swan. She waited impatiently for Ida's letters with, she hoped, news of Joey Bowes. But Ida had not seen or heard of Joey. Nor had Erins Pride. If Joey were not in Sydney then where was he? Grace was sulking. She, Ida Charlton, would give the fellow a good piece of her mind when he did turn up! Alannah was convinced Joey was still hiding in Sydney brooding on his ill treatment. She could not leave it so. She would insist her father and Simon search for the youth. Joey Bowes must be given a home.

On his visits to Lucknow, Owen tried to talk frankly to his daughter of the past, of Belfast, even of her lost child for he felt it was time she spoke of it. Certainly they must talk of Conall . . . But she remained abstracted, too quiet, avoiding his questions, avoiding him, avoiding even her husband, he felt, and wondered as he often wondered exactly why she had married Simon Aldercott. Had he, her father, inadvertently pushed her into it? Had Delia? Did she really love the man? He doubted it. It was almost as if in marrying Simon she had avoided something else . . . someone? But his mind slurred from the pertinency of the query. Perhaps it was, simply, that she needed a new environment since she had never cared for Brighton and did not seem overfond of Lucknow – perhaps a pleasant villa at Newtown, or farther out at Stanmore with large grounds where she could keep a stable? He studied her closely as she leant back in her garden chair. She was too thin, too languid – would she ever be the Alannah of old? Yet what exactly had been the Alannah of old?

'It's not good to brood, girl.'

'I do not brood, Papa. It's something that has happened and it's over. Many women lose unborn children.'

'You miss Burrendah, I know.'

'I expected to do so.'

'You can visit and often now for the coach service is much improved. It even goes on to Yass.'

'Simon does not care for country life, though he does try.'

'He wants to make you happy. Are you happy?'

'Simon is a devoted husband.'

'I'm sure of that, but it does not answer my question.' He paused for her answer but she remained silent. 'Your marriage happened so suddenly, too quickly I have some-times thought.'

'Simon was anxious to open his school – academy, as he likes it to be called.'

'Was that the only reason?'

She looked at him with candid eyes. 'What other?'

His eyes were equally candid. 'I have sometimes thought there may have been a deeper reason; that you might have been on the rebound as it is called, from some other attachment.'

She laughed. 'Surely you're not considering those awful Elston "boys", who are not boys at all?'

'No, not the Elstons . . . Is there anything you want to tell me, Alannah?' Hating the questions, this delving into her life, thoughts and feelings, but certain phrases persisted. 'Your daughter's pregnancy was well advanced,' the doctor had said. 'Over four months.' Looking surprised at his surprise. Advanced pregnancy . . . when she had been married only two months and a bit? It meant only one thing, of course, she had been pregnant on her marriage, her reason for haste. He had considered the matter at length and it did not so much shock as amaze him. That proper pious young man? His daughter, steeped in the fear of God and Sin by the Spanish Dominicans? Women did not easily cast aside the dictates of the Church unless under the stress of a stronger emotion. Was Aldercott the one to inspire it in her? He thought not. But if not Aldercott, the man she had married, then who? He tried to cut off his mind at the 'who', for whatever had happened and with whom, she had borne the situation and he must respect her strength and her privacy. But the question haunted him.

'I am worried about Joey,' she was saying. 'No one seems to know where he is.'

'A difficult young man, I have always thought.'

'But a good friend. At least he has been so to me. But he seems to have vanished, which is not like him at all – I mean, he has such a sense of order, even more of loyalty. I thought he might have made his way to Erins Pride but Ida writes they have not seen or heard of him.'

'Mr O'Shea ordered him from Birubi.'

'I can't believe that.'

'It's true. The gardener they call Old Samuel swears to it. He didn't like the episode nor, it seems, did anyone else. Joey left and no one has heard of him since.'

'I cannot let Joey be blamed for something that was not his

fault. Joey would never be careless, I'm sure of it, so we must find him and give him a home. You must search for him, Papa. Simon will too if I ask it. Promise me you'll enquire about town?'

'Of course, if you wish it. I shall do my best.'

Joey was more than tipsy, happily so, laughing because it was expected of him with the bullockies who had forced his drunkenness upon him. He was acting the 'good mate', laughing heartily at the bad jokes of the loud-mouthed MacHearn who had promised him work as far as Goulburn and who insisted on sealing their bit of a bargain by drawing him into his noisy circle, to regale them all with the horrors of the wet and broken wheels and trouble with the goddam Blacks and the same with bushrangers, and bushfires and floods and other disasters they could expect along the road. Desperate to be out of Sydney, Joey laughed when he was expected to laugh and often when he was not, until MacHearn had fallen flat on his face and they had dragged him away to sleep off his drunkenness. All Joey could do, the men warned, was hang about the Sevastopol pub where the team would be drawn up before leaving for the inland. A day, maybe two, but knowing MacHearn, it could be three. They had wandered off cheerfully, leaving him to the hazards and hunger of the streets. He shivered, not with cold for it was a fine warm night but with a new loneliness. He had been given hope when given a job, now both were in limbo. He was afraid to wander far. At least from the beach he could keep an eye on the public-house on its George Street corner. Finally, he wandered down to sleep in the lee of a fishing boat, a rough shelter but better than the Haymarket lodging-house. It seemed that his boyhood skills of survival had been lost with time. He longed for the open road. Most of all he longed for Erins Pride at the end of it.

He stirred to a voice and opened his eyes to the glare of morning and a face peering down at him. The face wore a disapproving expression behind a pair of precise spectacles slipping down a precise nose, all topped by a precise bell-topper. Mr Aldercott pushed up his spectacles and reset them with a precise pat.

'You can't go on lying here, Joey, the police will pick you up. And I can't stand about with sand in my shoes. On your feet, lad. Mrs Aldercott has been worried about you. You're lucky to have her concern. I spoke to a pedlar who seemed to know you and advised me to search the beach.'

The muffin man. He had given him stale muffins from time to time. In struggling up he cracked his head on the boat. He was stiff and rather damp and there was sand in his hair and clothes. He felt utterly miserable, and ashamed of his woebegone appearance. Not that he minded Mr Aldercott, he never had, he was the schoolmaster; besides, there was something of the shy diffident boy that he, Joey, had once been, still was perhaps, the part of him he abhorred and tried to overcome yet could not, quite – except with Adina. He had been different with Adina – but don't think of her. *Don't.* He couldn't face Miss Alannah. He couldn't go back to Lucknow, or Brighton, certainly never to Birubi. He wanted to run, to escape them all, everything here, but instead stood brushing himself down, a little fuddled, still a little drunk he supposed for he'd lost all sense of time. He didn't even know what day it was.

'Strong drink won't help your situation,' Mr Aldercott admonished sternly as if scolding one of his class. 'Stop being sorry for yourself and come home.'

'I have no home.'

'Lucknow will be your home. And you will be independent I assure you, for there is much work to be done about the place.'

'I'm not going back to Lucknow.'

Mr Aldercott gave an impatient sound that sounded rather like 'tush, tush'. 'You must understand one thing, Joey, you will not be permitted to wander this city as a vagrant. Mrs Aldercott will not have it. And, though I cannot pretend to understand Mr O'Shea's . . . methods . . . I'm certain he would not allow it.'

'I don't care about Mr O'Shea.'

Mr Aldercott looked distressed. 'That's not like you, lad. But perhaps . . . I fear I am being remiss for you must be very hungry.' He frowned. 'It would be best, I think, if we gave you a wash and a tidy-up and some breakfast before Lucknow sees you.' He narrowed his eyes to gaze across the great width of the Circular Quay. 'There is a tavern over there that looks more respectable than most. We will risk it. Come.'

Joey was indeed hungry, so hungry he did not argue and trudged after the schoolmaster, glancing along the Quay towards George Street and the Sevastopol public-house on its corner but there was no bullock-team as yet. No offsider, Will. Certainly no MacHearn. Still, he could keep watch, and if he saw the team ambling up he could run off and hide till Mr Aldercott became weary of searching for him. He devoured his second pork pie while his companion sat opposite nursing his topper and doing his best not to be noticed. How he must love Miss Alannah – he, Joey Bowes still could not think of her as this man's wife. He did not want to consider her so – and he did a curious thing. He took her silver pendant from his pocket, unwrapped it and set it on the rough wooden table.

'This belongs to Miss Alannah – Mrs Aldercott.' He forced it out. He did not seem to be speaking consciously; another voice, a strange voice had taken over. Mr Aldercott peered at the artefact.

'It does bear a resemblance to a piece belonging to my wife.'

'It's hers all right.'

'How did you come by it?'

'She wore it to the woolshed dance at Burrendah.'

'Last October? What are you doing with it now?'

'I took it from Barney Cook.'

'The blackfellow? Did he steal it? You'd better tell me, Joey, for the fellow has a reputation as a thief. As a liar too.'

'Barney says he found it at Burrendah.'

'If that is so why did he not return it?'

316

'He says he was afraid someone would accuse him of stealing it.'

'I see. That's entirely possible, of course, all the same . . .'

'He was hiding it – or trying to – when I took it from him. I knew it belonged to Miss Alannah.'

'Why did you not return it to her?'

'I didn't think she would wish me to.'

'Why not?'

'Because Barney says he found it the morning after the dance in the grass near her coppice – as she calls that part by the Creek where the willows grow so thick.'

'Yes, yes, I know the area. But I can't recall Mrs Aldercott going down there during the evening. She was busy attending to her guests, and singing – dancing too. I remember her dancing the reels with Mr O'Shea.'

'The reason I didn't return it.'

'What do you mean by that?' Joey felt feverish. His head ached. A terrible burning anger was driving him. It was at that moment he saw MacHearn and his team lumbering along the Quay. He stood poised. 'Answer me, Joey.' Mr Aldercott's voice was cold as well as precise. 'What exactly do you mean by that?'

'I saw them,' Joey blundered. 'Mr O'Shea and Miss Alannah, the morning after the dance, very early, coming up from her coppice. She was wearing the same dress she wore the night before . . .'

God, what was he saying? What was he doing? Words came rushing, angry words, malicious and terrible words, not against this man staring from him to the silver cross then back to him. Not really against Miss Alannah . . . MacHearn was manoeuvring his team around carts and carriages in billowing clouds of dust. 'I'm not going back to Lucknow or Brighton or Birubi. I don't want to see Miss Alannah . . . I never want to see Mr O'Shea again. Don't you see? They came up together from her coppice in the early morning, hand in hand. They kissed . . . Don't you *see*?'

He shouted it at the man staring up at him. He shouted it at Miss Alannah. He shouted it at Mr O'Shea, once his friend and now his enemy. He hated Mr O'Shea. But most of all he hated himself. He turned and ran.

There was a thudding in his ears ... deep in his head ... Brick opened his eyes to realise the thud was not part of his dream but outside himself, outside his room. There it was again, an imperative knocking on his door. Alannah worse? He shook his head in an attempt to clear it – fool, Alannah was at Lucknow. He had come in late the previous night weary of searching for Joey, cursing Joey for a fool, cursing himself for a worse fool in losing his temper with the lad, to throw himself fully dressed on his bed to sleep long, but a troubled sleep, as was not his way. Wincing, he slid off the bed to balance until dizziness passed. The knocking resumed. He opened the door on the scrubbed visage of Nurse Puttering, not quite as starched and imperturbable as usual.

'I overslept,' he murmured a little sheepishly. A formidable woman, Nurse Puttering.

'Nigh on twenty-four hours straight should be enough for any man so I'll not apologise for disturbing you, Mr O'Shea. Besides, I consider the matter not only important but urgent.' She gave a distinct sniff at his dishevelled appearance. 'I suggest warm water with a squeeze of lemon to clear the system, then a cold sponge-bath. Meanwhile, I have no wish to impart confidences in the hall.'

He stood back hastily for her to pass into the room. With another sniff at its disorder she clasped her hands across her starched midriff. 'It will be best if you close the door against careless ears – but only with your assurance that my visit will not be misconstrued in any way.'

Stunned, he managed a solemn reply. 'You have my promise to resist temptation.'

'Then you may close the door.' She was equally serious. 'What I have to say concerns Mrs Noakes.'

'She's worse?' Moll's illness had become a matter of routine, Puttering reporting each morning when he was at Birubi, the doctor calling once a week, more frequently if needed, and anything Moll might intimate that she wanted, to be instantly provided. All the same he had been lax. At first he had dropped in to tell Moll the news of the town, read letters, and impart gossip which she loved, but he had been diverted, obsessed with Alannah – and with himself.

'Not in a physical sense. Indeed, she had been making progress, seemed more settled, even content at times if such could ever be said of her. It's simply that . . . well . . . she's behaving in a rather unusual manner. As you know, she's usually docile and attentive when I speak or read to her but in the past few days she has been restless. Most difficult, I might say.'

'There's been commotion about the house. She could be aware of it. Or the heat could be upsetting her.'

'It's more than that. She's trying to convey something to me, I know the signs. As you know she gave up attempting to speak but is now trying again, yet still without success. She is also attempting to write, words I think, and if I try to distract her she becomes agitated. Today as I held her hand I could feel her fingers moving in an excited way. She actually made letters which as set down have no significance for me but might convey something to you. The point is, she is under stress, great stress and, apart from the fact she will exhaust herself, she is becoming impossible to manage. You must come, Mr O'Shea.'

'Of course. As soon as I change.'

'Now, sir. *Now*.'

He followed her without a word, and meekly. There was never any denying Nurse Puttering.

Moll was sitting awkwardly in her comfortable invalid's chair by the window that gave a wide view of the Harbour and part of the lawns and cliff below, straining to stare out at her particular view of the world. She lived for her familiar place at the window and struggled as best she could against leaving it for her bed. She turned her head slightly at Brick's approach, her eyes glimmering on him, her hand moving shakily but, he knew, with determination to grasp his. He was amazed at her urgent imperative grip. Her lips quivered, her mouth moved, dribbling a little at one corner and he

319

wiped off the saliva, saddened more than embarrassed at her helplessness. She was agitated indeed.

Was there something she needed? Oysters? Shrimps? New clothes perhaps . . . A bottle of stout? Perhaps a drive out; Richie would help him carry her down to the carriage. Her arm moved stiffly, then her body, towards the small table at her side that held newspapers, a water jug and tumbler, books, notepaper and sticks of charcoal. She gripped the charcoal firmly and jabbed the paper, leaving stabs of black, stabbing at something already written – letters. Rough distorted letters but letters all the same. He studied them closely then turned to the nurse.

'She might be more at ease if we were alone.'

Puttering nodded. Actually, a sensible woman. 'I shall be in my room when needed.'

An R . . . and A . . . a U . . . all running into each other before sprawling off into gibberish. But the meaning was clear to him. 'Raunie?' She nodded. 'I won't listen to mischief concerning her, you know that,' he warned.

She leaned forward to look out over the water again, moving her fingers backwards and forwards, then her hand from the wrist in a fanning motion indicating, he decided, something outside the house. Something important. 'The Harbour?' She shook her head in denial. 'The beach?' Another shake of her head. 'The cliff?' This time a nod while she stabbed a second squirl of letters. He looked closely. L . . . O . . . S . . . with something that could be a T.

'Lost? You've lost something?' A vigorous denial. 'Raunie's lost something? On the cliff?' Her denials came thick and fast and he was baffled. She was attempting to write again and he held her hand, letting it move freely under his own. She managed a distinct O. Then an E. 'Loose?' was the best he could make of it.

Her nod was violent and her face so flushed he feared for her but, after all, what more damage could she do to herself. Loose . . . The word meant little coupled with 'Raunie'. She was pointing out of the window again, curving her fingers over and down. He noticed other letters stabbed on the paper: S . . . T . . . E . . . 'Steed?' 'Steam?' 'Step?' A violent nod at the latter. 'Loose steps?' Her nods increased. But she would have heard Puttering and Fay discussing Alannah's accident, and was dwelling on it, bent on mischief. He refused to indulge her. The steps were no more, ripped out, thrown in the Harbour, gone for ever; even so they hung about. He wished he'd never heard of them and the rest of Raunie's decorative nonsense leading down to the beach. He should not have allowed her to embark on such a project, for steps had been devised that had loosened at a woman's light footfall. Loosened . . . 'Loosened?' Her nod was ecstatic. She stab-stabbed at the word 'Raunie'. She threw aside the charcoal and moved her body about, jerking it from side to side as if pulling, dragging, loosening something . . . Was she, incredibly, horribly, trying to tell him that Raunie had loosened the steps?

For a dreadful moment, staring down at this nodding, grotesque, evil old woman, he wanted to kill her. Could he believe her? She hated Raunie and had hated her from the first moment the girl had set foot on Australian soil almost twenty years ago. But Raunie hated Moll so which of them was he to believe? his foster-mother to whom he was bound by childhood ties, or the woman to whom he was, or had been, bound by worldly needs, conspirators working together with mutual aims, bound by love – of a kind. It was unbearable that he must accept her as deliberately setting out to murder an unborn child – yet possible, for someone must have tampered with the steps, moved them perhaps when still wet. If Raunie had done this thing to Alannah's child – *his* child – then lied cheerfully and pragmatically about so many aspects of it, he would be entitled to revenge and he would have the truth if it took him the rest of his life. But Moll was exhausted, that was clear. Passing Puttering's door he banged on it for her to resume her duties. If Raunie had planned murder – and it *was* murder – he was quite capable of killing his wife.

Raunie was dressing for dinner at the Masons', taking Abby as duenna. The carriage had been ordered, she had bathed long and luxuriously in her hip-bath and was making a careful selection of an evening gown for she needed diversion, even a flirtation or two. She had almost decided on a gold with flounces when Brick flung open the door.

'Get out,' he ordered Abigail, 'and don't argue. And don't bother to get into that thing,' he warned his wife, 'you're not going anywhere.' He kicked the door shut after the silent Abby and forced Raunie into a chair.

'You're hurting me,' she complained, the cut on her finger smarting under his grip.

'Did you have anything to do with Alannah's so-called accident? I want the truth.'

'What do you mean, "so-called"? And why do you keep on about those wretched steps.'

'Did you meddle with them in any way? Answer me.'

'How could I meddle with rock steps?'

'You can do anything you want once you put your mind to it.'

'Why can't you let it all be?'

'I can't let all be. Those broken steps caused the death of an unborn child. My—' Mercifully, he stopped, for she could not have borne to hear him say 'my child'. But she made no recognition of his hesitation. 'And almost caused a woman's death. They could have caused yours, did you consider that? Probably not, for you never stop to consider the result of your schemes—'

'You're mad. Quite mad. You must be. Why should I want to injure Alannah? *Why*?'

'I don't *know*. There are so many things about you, still, that I don't know.'

She realised she must tread warily, never admitting or revealing in any way that she suspected Alannah's child of being his, for if she did it would proclaim motive on her part. The circumstance must remain a secret between them for the rest of their lives. Who had planted suspicion in his mind? Alannah? She doubted that. Joey Bowes? Brick would no longer listen to Joey. Owen Moynan? Scarcely. Some other who might possibly have glimpsed her that night, moving across her lawn then between the shrubs to move down the steps . . . Perhaps returning to the house? Improbable, for she had been so careful in ridding Birubi of lights, of curious occupants, of all and everything that might possibly damn her, but it was not impossible. She said hurriedly:

'You've listened to gossip about me – lies. You know how people hate me. Alannah hates me – oh yes, she does. Joey hates me. Moll hates me.' She paused. Moll . . . Could it possibly have been Moll Noakes, crippled and doomed to her room, sitting at her window day and night . . . She had not, perhaps strangely, considered Moll Noakes, not wanting to be reminded of the woman in her house, but Moll could move a little, Moll could swivel about in her chair, lean forward – and her eyesight was still good. It was possible that Moll had seen a woman's figure moving through the darkness and had decided it was the mistress of Birubi. Moll could not speak – but she could make marks. Could she have conveyed enough to arouse suspicion in Brick's mind? Someone certainly had. Moll hated her for what she saw as the spoiling of her foster-son's career, blaming her, Raunie, for producing out of the rubbish of an old sandalwood box, carried through the years, unknowingly, by the native girl, Inar, until it came by devious means into Raunie's hands – a warning message from Brick O'Shea's long-dead mother: 'Moll . . . never let Brick know he is Black.' But it was Alister who had picked the scrap of pasteboard from the rubbish and used it against O'Shea, grasping his chance to destroy the man he hated for his power in the colony, for being a native-born radical, for being everything he, Major Alister Merrill, nephew of and Military Secretary to the Commander of the Forces in New South Wales, despised. Again, for being the man his daughter wanted to marry. Above all, for being a quarter-caste aborigine. Alister Merrill had revealed Brick O'Shea to Barbara and to the world, but Moll Noakes would blame her, Raunie, for the denouement until the day she died – and hate her for it.

'Why do you keep on about those stupid steps. They've gone, finished.' Her voice softened. 'And why do you treat me this way. All I want is for you to love me – why are you spoiling our life together? Forget Alannah and think of me – of us. Kiss me. Stay with me.' She drew his face down and pressed her mouth to his but he did not return her caresses. He drew back and loosened her hands.

'If I don't get the truth of this business from you, Raunie, I'll get it from others, remember that.' He went without another word.

She sat a long time curled up in her chair. She had failed with him again. He was still too immersed in events here at Birubi. But where could she go, certain he would follow? And what believable excuse could she give for leaving Birubi just now? Jamie . . . Jamie could be the answer, as Jamie so often was. She could follow Jamie south, reasonably certain he was in Bendigo, or at least about the district, and Brick would follow, and in her house that she had always loved, that Brick had loved, in the town where they had been happy, the town where he had married her, she would win him back.

But Bendigo, Victoria, was a long way even by sea then coach, the best part of a week's journey – and she hated sea travel. Well, then, she could stay over a few days in Melbourne – why not enjoy herself? Abby would arrange everything well and comfortably, jumping at the chance to see her precious Kitty at the end of it. Brick would follow her if only to punish, but when he came she would have him to herself, her own again, and she would shut out the world and revive the old magic between them, soothing his fury and his doubts. He would, quite simply, become hers again, she was as certain of that as she was certain of her name. In that house he could not, would not, resist her.

Despite his contacts and his own wanderings about the city Brick had learned nothing of Joey Bowes and had decided, finally, that the youth was working his way back to Erins Pride. It was as well perhaps; he had kept Joey too long in Sydney. In time he would make his peace with the youth, marry him off to Grace and see them on their way to Oorin. Once settled, Joey would make a go of the place, for if he lagged, Grace would take a hand as certain as night followed day. Brick was weary from more than physical activity for behind Raunie, Joey, Moll, Jamie, all the side-issues of politics and business, behind everything in his life, was this undefined unexpressed division between himself and Alannah, a lull in their relationship. She was remote from him. They were never alone together, always divided by others. She was not yet quite strong, he knew that, but he longed for the place, time and opportunity to will her alive, to give of his own vitality and need. There was no going back, he knew it, she knew it. They had come too far together to retreat.

Weary of his room at the stables, bored with Hugh's deliberately cheerful monologues, he was glad to be home. Birubi seemed deserted; no sign of Belmont though he'd rung for him repeatedly. No sign of Raunie either – but Raunie could wait. He bathed and, refreshed, wrapped himself in a towel and went in search of a fresh gown. He seemed always searching for a dressing-gown – what happened to his things? Since Jonathan had been discharged, Belmont had taken on the duties of valet but the man had too much to do: a rum bunch of servants he had; he'd like to get rid of the lot and start over, and would when he got around to it. He jerked open the doors of Raunie's great wardrobe with impatience, for sometimes, inexplicably, his clothes got lumped in with hers. He rummaged through the clutter, throwing aside a pair of riding gloves, damp, a little muddy and mouldy-looking – what on earth? . . . He dragged forth an old skirt. A length of rope fell from its pocket. Rope? A dark cloak, and a blouse, both damp and muddy. Next came Raunie's old carpet-bag, a broken thing he hadn't seen in years. It was heavy. It rattled. Tools bulged – a chisel, a trowel, a hammer – all with dried mud adhering. And something else. Mortar.

Mortar? He studied everything closely. These were Raunie's clothes, no doubt of that, damp and muddy and a little malodorous as if they'd been tucked away so for weeks. There were traces of mortar on everything. Mortar! With an oath he threw the garments across the room to land where they might. Raunie had tampered with the steps, he knew it now, it was quite clear to him. She had dug away beneath them, chipping and digging and gouging until they hung, waiting for Alannah to step upon them. Raunie had known – or guessed – that he had fathered Alannah's child and had planned it all; deliberately, cleverly, she had weakened the rock steps to cause the girl to abort and, he was certain, without a qualm at perhaps killing Alannah in the process, then had lied about it all to him and to everyone else. He had tangled with a savage! Yet, hadn't he always known it? He wrenched open the door and blundered along the hall.

'*Raunie*? Where the devil are you? Answer me.'

Nurse Puttering appeared in Moll's doorway to stare, horrified. 'Mr O'Shea! Even though this is your own hall—'

'Don't be absurd, woman. You're a nurse. Besides, I am not naked.'

'And please lower your voice, Mrs Noakes becomes restless at loud noises.'

'Where's Mrs O'Shea?'

'Mrs O'Shea?'

'My *wife*. You know my wife, don't you?'

'I am not accustomed—'

'Dammit, woman, do you know where she is?'

'If you mean at this precise moment, no. All I know is that she left Birubi over a week ago. Almost two weeks, actually.'

'The hell she did! Where did she go?'

'It is not my habit to pry into the movements of my employers.'

'Then send Luff to me.'

'Mrs Luff left with her mistress. So, thankfully, did that odd unpleasant little hunchback.'

'Where did they go?'

'To the wharves, as I heard it. With a great deal of baggage. Mrs Luff spoke of taking steamer – but I do wish, Mr O'Shea, you would go and garb yourself decently.'

'The *Thistle*? The *Shamrock*? Come, woman, which steamer?'

'I believe, the *Rose*.'

Melbourne. She would dally in the city a while, she could not resist it, then move on to Bendigo with the excuse of looking for Jamie, using Jamie as an excuse, a shield, knowing full well that he, Brick, would follow her for she had made no real attempt to hide her destination. She would wait for him in their Bendigo house and when he came would use every trick in her book, and she had many, to weld them together again. Well, it would not happen so. He would follow her because he must, but not out of love. He would follow her for revenge.

'Get Belmont to pack me a valise.'

'I am not a servant, sir.'

'I am riding into town to try for a passage south. Shipping's heavily booked from now until Easter but I'll find something, anything, so long as it floats. Find Belmont or you pack for me, and don't argue over it, woman. I'm in the devil of a hurry – and in a foul mood. Move, Puttering. *Move!*'

Chapter Sixteen

OWEN SLID rather than turned over from the body of his mistress. Leaving Maria was like cleaving his way out of the cloying sweetness of honey where he had swum at will for as long as he could without drawing breath, exploring warm oozing depths that seemed to seep as some sweet drug through his veins. Her belly was still and relaxed now and she breathed evenly, but her eyes were closed and he felt she was still drawing upon him. He was never quite free of her – he did not want to be free of her. Could there be more between them? He thought not.

Her eyes opened suddenly and wide, fine eyes that became distant and dreamy and rather strange as if turned in upon themselves when absorbed in lovemaking. But now they were clear serene eyes, as refreshed and renewed as her body, a body that never exhausted itself no matter what feats she achieved. She had great reserves of sexual passion, or perhaps she drew upon his to make the whole, one the half of the other. She turned her head and met his gaze with a lazy little smile then flung her arm over her head to rest her cheek against it, her underarm hairs still shining with the sweat of her exertions. He put his mouth to the hollow, he could not help it, she stirred him so easily. It was only when they parted to return to the privacy of his or her own room, moving as a wraith through the dark and silent house, Phipps, Effie and young Ned with the unspoken rules of usage discreetly in their quarters, that he viewed his domestic world with a certain disquiet. He supposed the kitchen gossiped, all servants gossiped, it was the price one paid for comfort, but such tensions would be intensified if he became an alderman like Mason, more so if he aspired to the office of MLA or MLC. What would be permitted him socially as

328

O'Shea's works manager, sometimes business manager, adviser, overseer, and explorer from time to time, would not be permitted in the world of politics. One must be devious enough to appear blameless no matter what one performed behind closed doors.

Maria brought her arm down slowly and placed her hand, fingers spread, on his groin, and her touch, light as it was, burned. Her fingers tightened, pressing into the hollow between his belly and thigh, and he caught his breath. She had many such intimate caresses that he had never before experienced with a woman; now he could not do without them. Yet there were times when they confronted each other, coerced into argument, suffering verbal crosscurrents so potent he wondered sometimes if she deliberately stirred up conflict. Her hand was exploring and he stirred under it. Marry Maria? He recoiled slightly and felt her hand still for she must have sensed his faint withdrawal. Marriage? His one marriage had been brief, but in the beginning, happy with the romantic aspirations of youth until Mary had not so much broken from him as slipped away into sickness, an emotional weakness fed and heightened by her bigoted kin. A wife no longer a wife but a nun-like creature, a holy woman, retreated to the realms of, if not quite phantasy, a concentration upon Eternity. In Mary's eyes the enjoyments of the flesh had become pagan indulgences, a betrayal of her prime love of God. He had not been able to live with Eternity. Most certainly he could not now for Maria was flesh that adhered to his, demanding of him, and he lost himself in her, seeking and gaining what all men craved, the deep throbbing core of the living female.

'Your daughter,' she said, caressing him again – she always said 'your daughter', never 'Alannah' – 'does not seem at ease when she visits Brighton. She is not happy.'

He stilled her hand sharply for he found something obscene in bringing his daughter even verbally into their bed, and of late she had shown an eagerness to do so.

'Alannah assures me she is perfectly well. She certainly has a great deal to make her content,' he said brusquely though regretting his harshness. He regretted it further when she slid from the bed, drew her peignoir about her and seating herself at her dressing-table picked up her hairbrush. She usually wore white in the privacy of their rooms which, for such a worldly woman, seemed an anomaly but it merged superbly with her fair hair and fine skin to give a luminosity, an effervescence of light. She began to brush her hair, her usual one hundred strokes and he counted with her, silently, fascinated by her graceful movements. Feeling relaxed, he stretched . . . Now that they were detached even temporarily, talk was possible even though stilted, perhaps because he did not want further analysis of his womenfolk. Maria and his sister had disliked each other on sight, he knew that; after all, it could scarcely be otherwise. But Alannah?

'Your daughter misses her Place of the Swan, as she calls it,' Maria pursued. 'It is her true home. That is apparent when she speaks of it.'

'Her husband's business is in Sydney.'

'But I understand Mrs Carney manages the Bridge Academy with great aplomb.'

'My sister supervises its domestic arrangements, that is all.'

'It's only that I'm sorry to see such a young girl unhappy.' She paused and he shifted impatiently. 'Mrs Carney,' she went on, 'does not approve of me. She wishes me out of your house.'

'Brighton is my home. If my sister wishes an establishment of her own I will see to it but I believe she has found the answer to her particular needs at Lucknow.'

'Far be it from me to comment upon your family, Owen.'

'Then do not do so – please.' But he had noted the 'Owen'. Lately she had called him so when they were alone and, in a way, it made things more reasonable between them; there had been something a little bizarre in cohabiting with a woman who punctuated her responses with a polite 'Mr Moynan'. Her hair gleamed under the brush and he could not take his eyes from it. He enjoyed watching her at her toilette.

'I feel I must, for both our sakes.' He did not answer and Maria knew she must move carefully. Of all men she had bedded with, Owen Moynan offered her best prospects yet; even so, in or out of bed he was no fool.

'I decide who comes and goes about Brighton.'

'Comes – and goes?'

'An unfortunate turn of phrase, I'll admit. You do not go, Maria, you are here.'

'But if I cause dissension, even unwittingly, to those dearest to you . . .'

'You are dear to me.'

'Yet . . . I am uneasy over my position here.'

'You are Brighton's housekeeper.'

'Housekeeper – and your mistress.' Her brush moved in long slow rhythmic strokes. 'I have had letters from England,' she lied.

'I had not noticed.'

'Sent care of my former landlady, the only address they had for me in London.'

'They? I understood you were quite alone in the world?'

'Not entirely, it seems. I had forgotten distant relatives who run a small cottage industry of lace-making; a maternal grandmother brought particular skills from the island of Burano in the Venetian lagoon. The family have offered me a home should I wish to return to London. I have always been clever with my hands, you see, and would attend to all making and mending as well as other diverse duties. They are well placed in Camden Town.'

'You would go back?' He could scarcely breathe. 'I thought you were happy here.'

'I have no real home so must consider my future – as you, of course, must consider yours. Should you become involved in politics you will be expected to live differently. I hear that politics in this country can be savage.'

'I am – or was – expected by my employer to enter politics but I confess I find that world, or what there is of it here, of no great interest. I am not a political animal, I do not feel an urge to dedicate myself to the manipulation of strange faces in the street for what is called the "country's good". I am politically lazy. Perhaps I am lazy altogether. I know only that I am an engineer and will always be so. A machine is

331

complicated yet exact and not to be tampered with on an individual whim for it simply will not work. It is certainty in the unpredictable chaos of life, each unit responsible for a particular activity making the interlocking whole. Everything in its place—' He broke off. He was talking like a ponderous fool. What could she possibly care for machines?

'Like your household servants.' But she smiled at him in the mirror to temper her words.

'I do not regard you as a servant, you know that.' He knew she was counting strokes, as he was; he made it seventy-five. 'I have decided to install the greenhouse you advised. As you say, it could lessen the heat and glare. Again, now that I entertain more often you need extra household help. That will please you I think?'

She put down her brush and turned slowly on her stool. She believed firmly in the slow drip of water on stone but enough for now. Talk could instil useful ideas, but also doubts, at the very least ruffle feathers and she dared not ruffle Owen's too vigorously. But she had planted seeds . . . She gave a tiny mental shrug. Who would have thought that Guido's ecstatic translation of his letters from Italy where his womenfolk spent their days, and most of their nights it seemed, leaning over the lace-making frame, would some day serve her well? Worth her weary hours of posing for his excessively bad sculpture. She shook out her hair. It shimmered, dazzling Owen. He loved to feel it coil about his body as he held her. She stood up and her gown parted. She let it slip to the floor. Her full, splendidly curved body was smooth and unblemished and he found it, as always, irresistible. He held out an urgent hand. She walked, naked, to the bed.

'Time to take stock, Mason, of what you have to show for your investment of that scrubby allotment out on Randwick Heights. A fight with your five fellow-aldermen over what to do about a potholed road meandering over sand-hills full of lizards and snakes and swamps; it will take you half a day, man, to crawl up that murderous stretch beside the racecourse. Anyway, I can't see your lady wife leaving Lyons Terrace to join dreary legal dignitaries, and merchants hard-pressed to write their own names, not even if you build her a mansion to tower over the rest. And speaking of mansions, you'd better start flogging your grain – or do a fiddle. Swot up on the law too. Those wily legal eagles will wipe the floor with you.' Whaley paused just long enough to look about impatiently for their coffee.

'Got the only gravel pit in Sydney out on those hills,' Silas boasted.

'Waverley will grab that.'

But Mason had the satisfaction, if not of vanquishing Whaley – who could, the man was ubiquitous and persistent – of seeing Purdue's head shoot up. Trust Purdue to consider a bit on the side, even from gravel. He brooded. This celebration of his election to the first municipal council in Sydney had fallen rather flat since Whaley had muscled in on it; at least his scruffy old hat wasn't in evidence even if his scruffy old suit was. Not that the Café Français was exactly the Australian Club, too much the haunt of racketing young swells rather than be-whiskered merchants arguing over shipping and politics, with gold thrown in for good measure, but he favoured its billiard club, and the food was dependable, it had to be, the place served eight hundred dinners a day. Besides, there were other aspects of it he favoured . . . He selected a cigar. He was not enamoured of Randwick and its windy sand-hills but at least he'd beaten Moynan to Council – if such had been Moynan's intention, one never quite knew, the man puzzled with his air of indifference, never seeming to hurry yet always falling on his feet. A shrewd bastard, he'd give that in . . .

But he, Mason, had pulled off his election even if he'd had to grease palms to do it, and a sense of power was like fresh blood through his veins. Even if O'Shea had got a man in – not Moynan, was there bad blood between the two? – but Hoxton, a boot and shoe manufacturer of George Street. It was rumoured O'Shea had gained prior knowledge of the day the Municipalities Bill would receive assent by the Governor and had seen the petition of seventy signatures was ready to lodge precisely the day after. Heggett called O'Shea 'that cagey knowing cove' . . . Mason shuddered. At least he'd been spared the sea-cap'n's booming criticism and aura of stale bilge water, and with a bit of luck the savages of the Solomon Islands who seemed partial to spearing marooned seafarers into their cooking pots would do the same with Heggett before long. No alderman on his way up could afford to associate with the dregs of the wharves as well as the land. Yet . . . the man was right about O'Shea being cagey. O'Shea was also secretive; off again, this time it was said, chasing his wife. Well, marry a temptress with the soul of a harlot and a man asked for trouble. Chasing the son too, no doubt. The three blundered over the face of Australia as arrogantly as the gipsy mongrel lot they were.

The tight male circle – Purdue, Moynan, Courtney who seldom spoke but heard everything, Whaley and himself – stirred to the trays of coffee and liqueurs and the apologetic smile of the friendly hostess: a slight mishap, gentlemen, but she felt sure they would understand and forgive? A whiff of Ashes of Roses, well, Ashes of Something, he, Mason, should know for he kept her well supplied with the stuff and, regretting his deliberate avoidance of her seeking admiring eyes, he blustered:

'Got to start somewhere in politics.'

'You call the municipals, politics? All you'll be doing is gabbling over what dirt to shovel out to fill the potholes of the one who's greased the most palms.' Whaley's cynical tones always rubbed Silas the wrong way. 'Oh, I'll concede you're ponderous enough to draft by-laws, assess property values and strike rates but you're too impatient to think it all through. Rome wasn't built in a day.'

'What's bloody Rome to do with Randwick Council?' he blurted, uncaring if the woman did take offence at his bluntness; after all, when all was said and done, she was but a servant.

'Councils waste good brass.' Purdue peered into his cup as if he expected the Devil to pop out. 'Roads find their own level, like water. What's a few potholes between friends.'

'As long as they don't block your own door, eh, Purdue? Anyway, you get yourself on every committee around.'

'Different kettle of fish. Must cultivate civic pride.'

Mason frowned into his own cup. He couldn't abide Turkish coffee and she knew it. Aggrieved, he topped his Havana. He had no plans to build on Randwick Heights for he had Nance to contend with. She'd prodded him for City Council but he was lucky to have gained what he had and she could climb on his bandwagon or not as she chose, plenty more fish in the sea. But he shifted uneasily. A man's wife was a man's wife and a man's wife must be *seen*. Macquarie Street? Too academic. Potts Point? Too crowded. Elizabeth Bay now, some elegant places going up there . . . The hostess's skirts brushed his knee and the annoyance of having been served Turkish dissolved. Somehow he'd manage to keep an edge in here . . .

'The sixties will see the changes.' Whaley, drat him, was off again. 'A decade of growth, the sixties, you'll see. It's starting already, the sorting and sifting; they're tramping the roads to the North with their blankets and cradles, dolly pots too though they won't need to go down for the quartz yet, the alluvial's thick on the ground.'

'Queensland – as it soon will be – is welcome to the drifters. It might even get them to do some real work for a change. They're so frantic for labour up there they petitioned for Separation on the proviso convicts would be sent out again.'

'Won't have convict scum here. Ship out the whole blasted Rocks, holus-bolus, that's what I say. Sailors swear they can hear the din of it three miles out to sea, and smell it at two.'

'You get good rents for your rotten lean-tos down there, Mason.'

'Good enough for that Irish rabble; a booze-up each night and a fight to finish off. Anyroad, rates are on the up with too few to do the paying. Must have a settled population for trade with summat over for expansion. We need the third this state lost to the first Victorian rushes.'

'They'll not be back. Men settle where they've grubbed to spend their gains.'

'We'll not get true voting power under our system.' Whaley grabbed the floor again. 'We're stuck with the diehard sterlings, in on property qualification, dumping their backsides round Select Committee tables for the recognition, as they see it the prestige of getting themselves invited to Government House, that sort of thing. They drone on, saying nothing. Talk's cheap.'

'South Australia had the right idea: all men of full age entitled to vote after six months in the colony.'

'Adelaide had no felons to foul it up and could start from scratch. Even Tasmania had the sense to get rid of its Vandemonians to the Victorian fields and bring out steady settlers from home.'

'This state lacks "nong". Too much *mañana*.'

'Too much what?'

'*Mañana* – tomorrow. You know, put off till tomorrow what you don't want to do today.'

'Too many Paddy's,' Mason grumbled.

'I thought *mañana* was a Mexican word.'

'Spanish, actually.' And who dared argue with Whaley on Europe?

'Queensland can pitch in and help pay the public debt.'

'With sevenpence in its Treasury? Bowen goes in minus police and civil service, with Lang's Scottish settlers demanding the world, Government Men doing the same, and only sevenpence in the kitty. Literally.'

'Diggers came to the Victorian fields mainly from Europe and America, petty tradesmen and factory hands eager to start shop or factory with their savings.' Turning his back on Purdue's financial trivia to Courtney's receptive ear, Whaley picked away at the old perennial, Protection. Always a good fall-back, Protection. Courtney was a good fall-back too. 'New South Wales got the rural workers.'

'Bog Irish! I shipped out to be rid of that lot and what did I get? Irishtown.'

'Curious . . .' Purdue concentrated on staring out Moynan. 'It's Protection to the last ditch with you, Moynan, but you're no manufacturer, you're a landowner.'

'Give me time.'

'So that's the way of it, eh? Well, if you plan to build your own mill, Wilson paid fifty pounds a foot for his land. And MacDougall shovelled out twenty thousand pounds for his one acre. Land's booming. Why not make a play for O'Shea's mill now the man's on his way out.'

'Is he now.'

Purdue made his usual attempt at a chuckle. 'Who'd know that better than yourself? Give the matter thought, Moynan. You'd be in on the ground floor so to speak with a nicely set up mill leading the way in woollens. There are those, you know, who consider that mill more yours than his.'

Moynan looked cryptic. He invariably looked cryptic, an expert at fence-sitting and, Purdue had long ago decided, a handy cove to have on one's side. They were silent, sipping coffee and liqueurs. Cigar smoke drifted. Whiffs of perfume tantalised and Mason brooded again. With luck and a bit of expertise he might just manage to keep his pretty *danseuse*, whose name he could never remember, in her Elizabeth Street rooms – and keep his options open here. Why not? After all, a man couldn't be expected to give up everything for the public good.

Effie refused to enter a papish church, even if this was a cathedral, and emphasised her refusal with nervous thumps of her basket against the railings. 'Me ma would turn in her grave, Ma'am. "If the tykes won't come into ours," she always said, "we'll not set a foot in theirs." And she never did.'

'You're not always so devout, Effie. I didn't notice you sacrifice a thing for Lent, certainly not Phipps' lemon sorbet.'

She ordered the girl to wait. She couldn't tell why she had dragged her through Hyde Park, or even why they had struggled across College Street's dust and drays, for the girl was chapel, born and bred. Only a few hunched figures knelt at prayer as she genuflected and crossed herself, from habit, the old rituals lingering as Ireland lingered in wisps of memory. Australia possessed her now but she could not quite cut off the old as her father seemed to have done. This great cavern of stone was the stuff of bare cells and pious intense women and her own lonely knowledge that she was different in her assimilaton of the teachings of the Church, distilled over the years to yearnings and longings for what she could not as a child put into words but had found, finally, in Brick O'Shea, her lover.

Her footsteps echoed down the cool stone. The scent of massed lilies was overpowering. Incense drifted. She lighted a candle for Conall, her beloved brother, but did not dwell on him any more than she dwelt on her old life. She could not, would not, return to the rigidity of thought and body that the Church demanded; she had been touched by life and love – so why had she come here? She suffered an unease, a despair of the spirit she supposed, that desperation that Holy Church made promises to ease if not dispel. Or was it that within these quiet walls she had hoped to know herself well? Simon had decided to take her to Burrendah, her Place of the Swan, with sacrifice on his part, for her sake, to make her happy, to complete the marriage as he put it. Complete the marriage . . . The phrase not only haunted, it terrified with its finality. To complete the marriage.

She seldom saw Brick and rarely spoke with him. They yearned across dinner tables or passed each other on bridle paths, or exchanged trivialities in groups at garden parties. There were households between them: servants and aunts and papas, husbands and wives. Sometimes she woke at night feeling for him beside her, to convince her they were still, if not physically, emotionally entwined – but were they? Only once did they touch and that briefly, standing close but among others at a benefit for the Benevolent Asylum. Their eyes clung and their hands brushed but he had said bluntly: 'I know, Alannah, don't you think I *know*? But there'll be no more furtive couplings between us for I did you harm once; I had to leave you and I'll not leave you that way again. No secret meetings in squalid bedrooms of isolated inns, or slinking in shadows under Domain trees like the town youth—'

'It would be something.'

'Not enough. It will be out before the world with us. What

338

are you afraid of? The world doesn't really care about two people of little account in its machinations. Life has this vast indifference . . . No matter what we plan or where we go the world doesn't care, not in the end. The world goes on, bypassing us.' She was expected to merge with the empty bright chatter and pale tea and cucumber sandwiches and the vista of white sails skimming the sparkling blue of the Harbour, and tried. How she tried. But he was different, he did not have to try. And there was an even sharper difference about him now, a new energy, a drive – or his old drive back. He was moving away, off somewhere, without her. And of course he had the right . . .

She'd forgotten her rosary, or rather had not thought of it, yet here it seemed necessary and proper. She should not have come, she felt odd and out of step. Australia, she thought irritably, was an out-of-step country, everything blurred, distorted, where in Ireland all was the same, except religion, and even then all was Irish. Perhaps she had come today to be part of something, to know herself better for what, after all, was she? a girl who loved the wind in her face and the freedom of her own lands. A girl who loved to dance wildly, and sing as sweetly as she was able of free and happy things . . . A girl with a great need of a man she could not possess honestly and completely . . . A girl who could bear children – but here she cut off her mind. A lanky freckled Irish girl with no great skills, a girl of little account, nothing at all really, so why should Brick go on loving and wanting her. Yet he did. And the truth was, if he did not she would die.

Her parasol clattered to the floor and the bent heads raised and lowered without expression. Sunshine pierced the stained glass. Effie would be restless and likely to get into trouble waiting about. Besides, it was getting late, and Papa . . . With a flurry and no regret, certainly no solution, she moved out into the sun.

Owen strolled down George Street towards the Circular Quay, taking his time for it was a beautiful day. In March, the nor'easters eased and in the lull before the south-westerlies took over there were days such as this, so clear and still they dreamed. But more than the weather made him dally for he'd woken that morning with an absurd cringing from the simple ceremony of taking tea with his daughter and sister. He had postponed their meeting week by week until finally Delia reminded him, sharply, that he dashed in and out of Lucknow (Dashed? He'd never dashed in his life.) with scarcely a word to his womenfolk. Her small neat mouth seemed permanently set in disapproving lines as she quoted the hodge-podge of gossip fed her by the detestable Eveline. Why didn't she ask outright if Maria Swallow were his mistress for the query was behind her most innocuous remark? He had rather expected her to sail for Stonemore when Vincent wrote he was returning to Ireland for a spell, but it seemed she was vexed with her favourite son. He could just as easily have come out to her in Australia but he had countered the suggestion with the doubt he could locate such an outlandish country! Vincent Carney had never been Owen's favourite nephew. But he, Owen, rather suspected that the long trip home daunted Delia as it daunted many. Perhaps the reason so many immigrants stayed to become disgruntled citizens was that getting 'home' could be as terrifying as 'coming out'. Eventually Delia had pushed him so far into a corner he had promised tea today at Lucknow, and since the weather was fine, no doubt in the pleasant side garden under the blank stare of the Roman matron on her plinth above the carp darting like jewels, and surrounded by the paths and gardens Joey Bowes had so meticulously fashioned for Alannah.

Nevertheless he took his time for as well as Delia's hostility, he sensed that the deeper processes of his daughter's heart and mind were rigorously kept from him. She rarely came to Brighton; Maria was right in that his women did not care to confront her. Alannah sat across tables smiling politely, or brushing his cheek in hellos and good-byes, or murmuring nothings as they moved about alien rooms. Perhaps today there would be time to talk for he had left the mill early now Quigley had it well in hand. He was lucky to have found Quigley, by chance as things happened, hobbling on a twisted ankle from a fall down a shaft and consoling himself by quaffing ale on the verandah of a Maitland pub. A mechanic from Sheffield, he wasn't averse to starting life over in Sydney and had become the mill's right hand. Together they had made changes for O'Shea left all to them, too much, but the man no longer seemed interested. There was always that about O'Shea: achieve his immediate goal and move on, this time it seemed back to his beginnings, the land, deserting a mill famous for its products despite others opening up in Victoria. With better roads, coach-lines teaming up with the railways and a growing river traffic, all reaching out to embrace small settlements becoming towns, stores were opening up with tailors coming out of the woodwork or, rather, up from the mines to open workrooms. A nation of shopkeepers and capitalists, Whaley the observer and philosopher was wont to pronounce, apropos of nothing.

Owen dawdled, with an occasional swing of his cane. Most shops now had plateglass windows, with smart awnings where previously the rain had dripped down one's collar. Sections of George Street were paved, laying some of the tormenting dust, the city's curse. Now the quieter business section of solid banking-houses, auction rooms and merchants' offices. He crossed Hunter Street lined with exclusive little shops – O'Shea's had brought an excellent price and his mind boggled at the man's worth in hard cash, enough to buy all Moreton Bay if he wanted it. To a whiff of Harbour breeze he turned into Bridge Street, wider than most, its bridge over the Tank Stream long gone, its houses set back in large grounds of trees and shrubs giving a faintly rural air to the fast-growing commercial city. On the northern side tall buildings cast shadows over the picket fences and gardens of domesticity. At the top of the rise tight-packed houses marked the long line of Macquarie Street. Though resigned by now to the empty niceties of the coming 'tea' he still opened Lucknow's gate reluctantly. He did not like the house and suspected Alannah felt the same; its rooms were small and though it faced north it lost its sun early to the opposite buildings. Irrational of him, for Brighton was small and cramped yet Brighton suited him admirably. He was, he knew, being unfair, for Lucknow had been neglected for years and Simon had already improved it, making use of grounds large enough for sporting activities and the keeping of a stable; besides, its location was ideal. He, Owen, was not only unfair to the place, he was unbusinesslike for the Bridge Academy was achieving an enviable reputation not only in Sydney but throughout the country.

He found Simon in his study, between classes, writing letters. Small sparse rooms were Simon Aldercott's insignia in life with what seemed the same ink-spotted desk, bookcase and cupboards, the only difference here being a portrait of the Queen and a bad — Owen knew it was bad for it was overly-heroic and brutal — interpretation of the Battle of Balaklava above his head as he worked. Since the man had left O'Shea's employ he and Owen seldom met outside their brief weekly discussion of loans and interest payments and a report on the school, and today he seemed glad to see his father-in-law, responsive beyond his usual good manners as he put down his pen and got to his feet.

'I'm glad you came early, sir, for I hoped for a few words before your tea.' He paused, frowning. 'Alannah, I believe, went into town but I'm sure she won't be long. We see you so seldom these days.' Sounds penetrated: someone was reading Shakespeare in the toneless voice of the uninterested. The combined scrape of slate pencils jarred. 'I have made a decision, Mr Moynan. I am taking my wife to Burrendah.'

'Excellent. It's time she paid it a visit.'

'Not just a visit, sir. To make it our home.'

'Indeed? I admit I'm surprised.'

'No doubt. But Burrendah is where Alannah is happiest. She does not complain but I know she dislikes living in Sydney. I shall assist in the running of the property but shall also tutor in Goulburn — a small advertisement, I think, would be best.'

'You will ride back and forth to the town?'

His smile was gentle. 'If necessary. But perhaps a light trap . . . Who knows, I may open an academy, for Goulburn

342

has grown with improved coach services. There is even talk of the railway though no one really expects that for many years. I shall of course open a school on the station for the young children, as I did at Erins Pride. As for the Bridge Academy, that will stay for the present; I have an excellent assistant in Mr Portman. I do not know how Mrs Carney feels about the move but it will be discussed at length—'

'My sister does not like the back-country as she calls everything five miles from the city centre. She regards the bush as akin to the Gobi desert so I do not believe she would move, even for Alannah. Certainly Alannah would not wish a reluctant aunt.'

'I realise this can mean the upheaval of a family. Even so, I believe it best for Alannah.'

'She has agreed?'

'Not . . . exactly. She is still surprised, I think.'

'You spoil her.'

'It is not to my advantage, sir, to have an unhappy wife.' He paused to pick up his papers. 'But I must not monopolise you, you came to see your womenfolk and Mrs Carney has been preparing for days. You will excuse me? My class is waiting.'

Owen felt oddly rebuffed – but then, marriage had its barriers. The garden table was set with fine china and Delia's embroidered cloth, and flowers in a vase he was sure to upset, all the awkward domestic impedimenta dear to her sense of social decorum. The fountain tinkled and the carp sported and the sun was bright, too bright, and he wished he were anywhere but here but he must see it through without serious mishap, verbal and otherwise. His sister sat bolt upright in one of the rigid chairs she affected, her small neat shapely feet barely touching the floor, jabbing her needle into her embroidery with such savagery he expected her to stab her finger. Wickedly, he rather hoped she would.

'It is unforgivable.' Jab-jab. 'After the difficulty of bringing us all together Alannah goes off on a whim. I don't understand her, Owen.'

'You never did.'

'And you do? I think not.' Jab-jab. 'Effie's lost herself I

343

suppose, a useless girl but I couldn't spare Lizzy today. But more likely, Alannah's wandering that cavern of a cathedral, catching a chill – they build them massive to impress, you know. She married Protestant so why she goes to St Mary's at all I cannot imagine. It surprises me they even let her in the doors.'

'Perhaps they would not if they knew of her sin. On the other hand there's always Absolution. A soul back in the bag, so to speak.'

'You take everything so calmly. Worse, lightly. You always had a difficult disposition. As a child you quite devastated Mama.'

'I consider myself an equable man.'

'Only when things go your way. When they don't you wait, convinced that if you remain detached from what you don't like it will go away.'

'It often does.' He paused. 'As to Alannah, Del—'

'Don't call me "Del".' Jab-jab. 'You know I hate it.'

'— you know what the Jesuits say: "Give me a child until the age of five and I'll show you the man" – woman too, I assume.'

'Do not quote me papish theology, or philosophy, or whatever you call it. All is not well, not *right*, with Alannah's marriage. I *feel* things. Mama always said I was psychic.'

'Nonsense. You have a gift for peeking round corners and listening at doors unseen.'

'This latest idea of hers of returning to Burrendah . . .'

'It is her husband's decision.'

'But she's settled so nicely here. Cosily. Permanence is part of being a wife, of building a nest. A family.'

'She could not help that unfortunate accident.'

'One disappointment should not stop a woman's natural urges. I have only her welfare at heart and you know it. As I have yours. And Simon's.'

'Which continues to surprise me considering your suspicions of him on board the *Elizabeth Anne*.'

'I always recognised possibilities in Simon Aldercott, even though he is Wesleyan, and I prefer not to be reminded of the voyage out; the sea daunts me.'

'From sailing "home" as you call it?'

'I admit that facing such a journey is one reason I have stayed – but only one. Alannah, yourself, and poor dear Conall are and were my kin and though the country has been a trial at times with its mosquito plagues and dust-storms and that merciless sun burning down and I've sometimes regretted not joining Vincent in Jamaica—'

'The sun burns mercilessly there too.'

'I saw it as my duty to hold us together as a family. I do not forget my nephew—'

'Nor do I.'

'—and will not break my vow never to set foot in an O'Shea establishment.'

'A wasted vendetta. The O'Sheas survive.'

'The O'Sheas are not the only intruders.' Jab-jab.

'If you mean Maria Swallow, say so.'

'Very well, I shall. People are talking about you and that . . . person. Your daughter will suffer because of it; you seem to have no consideration for her at all. Or for yourself. Certainly not for me.'

'Enough.' He slammed the table so hard the cups bounced, she missed a stitch and jabbed her finger so painfully the blood welled. He thought she would cry more from rage than hurt but she preserved her dignity by wrapping the finger, surely absentmindedly, in a table napkin. 'Alannah suffers nothing,' he went on angrily. 'She does not even notice. She is obsessed with other matters.'

'What matters?'

'Matters that are entirely her affair so I'll have no questions or prying or interference in her life – or, for that matter, in mine. Come now, Del, you're free to sail "home" any time you like but if you *do* stay you'll do very well with the Academy and your precious Purdues and your charity committees – quite a court. Not to mention excellent servants. And myself to call on.'

'For how long?' she sniffed.

'What do you mean?'

'You're planning something, I know it. I hear things. It's as well I have Eveline,' she added crossly, slamming her embroidery into her work-box and snapping the lid. 'If it weren't for her I would know *nothing*.' She got to her feet with an indignant little bounce. 'I must see to the kitchen. Lizzy will have trouble keeping the scones hot without burning. And the cream can so easily go off. Really, nothing seems to go *right* any more.'

The tinkle of the pond was the only sound as he wandered the paths. It seemed a day for strolling. He had girded himself for this trite annoying social occasion and his daughter was spurning it and him. But the gate clicked behind him and she was sweeping off her wide-brimmed hat (she hated over-decorated bonnets) and her light cloak with breathless apologies as she held up her cheek for his kiss. Her skin was moist to his lips. And there was something else, some exotic flavour about her . . . Incense.

'I am sorry, Papa. There seemed more bullock-teams than usual on the roads. And of course I had to let Effie off at Brighton.'

'Besides, prayers take time,' he teased.

'Aunt Delia's been complaining, I see. The fact that I enter a church, even a Roman one, should please her.' She looked about her with satisfaction. 'It *is* a nice garden, isn't it? Joey did everything splendidly. I'm glad he's back at Erins Pride, he was unhappy in Sydney. And I hope he and Grace are soon married.'

'From what I hear you could be in time for the nuptials.'

'So Simon's been talking too.'

'Fortunately – since you did not care to inform me.'

'Nothing has been decided yet. You know I love Burrendah but Simon's work is here, he would give up so much.'

'He might gain more. In any case, make your choice and abide by it, Alannah. Do not become one of those women who are never happy anywhere, for such a one is a heavy load on a husband. You must be happy somewhere, sometime. Your aunt frets that you are not a happy wife. Are you a happy wife?'

'I cannot answer such a question simply.'

'Why not? It's a straight question so why not a straight answer?' He had spoilt this girl, he thought irritably. He had let her speak and live too freely, indulged her too often when she was intense, too emotional, too *young*, all the imbalance of youth making her vulnerable. Yet in so many ways she was mature.

'I have no straight answer. Everything's . . . muddled.'

'Don't you think I know that there is something . . . someone? Yes, someone. And that I feel responsible in agreeing to your marriage knowing you were not in love with Simon – no, you were not, and are not now; not that excitement that should be there, a bond that nothing can break. Why did you marry him?'

'There was a reason, an urgent reason and I shall never be sorry for the reason. When I am old I shall remember the reason so don't try to make me regret it for you will not.' She was impassioned, but pathetically helpless in her attempt to explain and he could not help her. 'I've learned so much, Papa,' she struggled on. 'I've learned that sometimes two people brush each other, just two, where a thousand others contact signifying nothing, but one chance encounter can cause such . . . havoc I suppose you could call it, that nothing is the same again. Nothing.' She was not looking at him. She stood, turned away, clutching the stone wall and he saw her fingers white from the pressure. She was emotionally roused and it more than bothered him, it frightened for he had never seen her in quite such a heightened state. How much did Simon know or guess? As much as himself, he supposed, with no real evidence. Did Simon suspect, as he her father suspected – *more* than suspected – that he had not been the father of her child and so had only a tenuous hold upon her? There were no more children; it was as if she cringed from the idea. Was Simon taking her from the influence of another because she was faced with a terrible choice and he hoped in so doing to lessen her turmoil, perhaps even to dissolve it? And then it crashed into his mind, he could no longer hold it back: though Alannah deny it to her death he knew and faced what to him had become fact, that Brick O'Shea had been and perhaps still was his daughter's lover.

Rage such as he had never before experienced shook him and he wanted to wreck the innocent hapless things by which he was surrounded: the tea-setting, the flowers, the statuary, the gardens, and scatter all to the winds, for through action he would hit at the man who had seduced his daughter – and he cringed at the silly, over-dramatic expression for no man seduces a woman who wants him. But because Alannah wanted O'Shea he, her father, needed to humiliate the man, destroy him . . . O'Shea had become his enemy for the man had lain with his daughter. And because O'Shea was not there to strike he raised his hand to strike her but she turned abruptly. Her eyes widened, wild and horrified.

His hand stilled and lowered. He could not do it. He knew, and who should know better, that sometimes desire for another becomes so intense, so desperate, it cannot be stilled by reason and if not satisfied will self-destroy – as it was with himself and Maria. With a helpless hopeless gesture he placed his hand over hers where it rested on the stone wall. It was a gesture of compassion. He could not hurt her further. Besides, who was he to throw the first stone?

Chapter Seventeen

'WELL, RAUNIE? I see you haven't lost your sense of the dramatic. You always could give a wicked interpretation of a *prima donna* at the height of her score.'

Raunie ceased her pacing of the hot little parlour and turned on Kurt Herlicht with an angry flick of her fan. 'I telegraphed from Melbourne so what kept you? You know I hate to be kept waiting.'

'I decided to give you time for tea.'

'To give yourself time, you mean. Anyway, I'm weary of stuffy hotel parlours. And bored with corned beef, cabbage and jam roly-poly in dreary restaurants. I hope the Irish Boy can do better.'

'Much better. We feature French cuisine these days. Hannah McKee and her Scotch broth belong to rougher times. Actually I've discharged the woman but she refuses to go. You can send her packing.'

'I want nothing to do with Hannah McKee.'

Voices clashed from the street. Kurt flung up a window on Abby directing the old digger she'd hired to load their baggage, her instructions punctuated with swipes of her parasol at the town urchins harassing Gondola as with shouts of 'valegia!' 'capelliera!' 'pacco!' he flung his mistress's valise, hat-box and parcels on the cart. 'I see you've found Isaac – or rather, I'd say he found you. Always out to make the odd shilling, he works around the Irish Boy when we're busy.' Then angrily, 'What possessed you to bring that rogue of a groom?'

'He makes a fuss when I try to leave him behind.' She had forgotten how Kurt and Gondola hated each other. 'He would have followed me, he's devoted.'

'Until he finds a circus – and the sooner the better.'

'He can work in the stables.'

'I'll take a whip to him if he causes trouble.'

'I'll not have him beaten by anyone but myself.'

Kurt slammed down the window. 'Your duenna ignored me as usual.'

'Abby dislikes you.' She found Kurt's little shrug as daunting as ever, very much the same Kurt whether in the formality of a Sydney drawing-room or quaffing ale in a miner's tent. Aware she looked anything but her best after her turbulent journey round the coast to Melbourne, then overland on a road that didn't seem one whit better than it had in the old days despite Cobb & Co's well-sprung coaches, she gathered up her things – then set them down with a thump. Let Kurt wait on her! He was, after all, an O'Shea employee.

'Something urgent must have forced you to make such a trip in the height of summer,' he mused, 'or else you've gone quite mad. And if it was your aim to surprise me you've succeeded.'

'I want my house, Kurt. And I want it now.'

Mercifully, he did not argue, just picked up her cloak and scarves and held open the door. But she knew she made a mistake in her smile of thanks, for Kurt Herlicht was always quick to take advantage of a warm response. She caught her breath at the hot north wind but Abby sat perched amid the boxes behind Isaac, her parasol at the ready, Gondola on the hack bowing right and left to the jeering teasing boys. The phaeton was highly polished; doubtless Kurt made use of it in driving out his current visiting actress for there were roads now instead of tracks. She hoped her house was as well kept. The dying sun beat on them like a furnace blast as they turned from the Shamrock Hotel along Pall Mall and out towards McIvor Street. People stared but she recognised no one and felt a little depressed. The town, officially Sandhurst but always Bendigo to those who had thrown in their lot on the fields, was much changed: solid-looking buildings, many of stone, and attempts at parks, and trees growing again in the raped and raked-over valley. She marvelled at so many women and children about and admired fine-looking theatres

350

and the flagged path fronting well-stocked stores shaded by awnings. There was woodblock paving in most streets and land sales were being advertised with enthusiasm. Not a trooper in sight. And where were the packs of scavenging dogs that had torn away at anything and everything? And the tents . . . The clusters of canvas, bark-roofed lean-tos and shanties were being swallowed up by neat weatherboards in neater gardens. But hotels still abounded.

Leaning out she saw a circle of old women, dogs, children and a gaggle of maidservants about a wild-looking man haranguing them from a box, his white hair blowing in the wind and his old pugilist's face sweating with evangelistic zeal as much as with the heat. She gasped.

'It's Sweet Jesus!'

'The same. Still struggling via Leviticus for his own salvation as well as yours. And mine, I suppose.'

'"And if any man's seed of copulation go out from him, then he shall wash all his flesh in water and be unclean until the even,"' the preacher shouted above the giggles of the maids. His voice trailed and his rheumy eyes widened as he stared after the phaeton. Raunie drew back.

'He recognised me, I'm sure of it.'

'He's not likely to forget a woman who moved heaven and earth and the town elders to run him out of town.'

'He's a festering hypocrite of a drunk and all know it. Smells like a bearpit too.'

'Part of being a prophet.'

'He was always half mad. Just keep him away from the Irish Boy,' she fumed, fixing her gaze on an imposing stone church replacing the rough canvas where she and Brick had married.

'Still no laws against street preaching.' He paused. 'Come now, Raunie, tell me why you're here.'

'You are to address me as Mrs O'Shea at all times.'

'You didn't object to "Raunie" in the old days.'

'I did not come to Bendigo to see you, not in the way you seem to think. I came for other reasons. One was to see my house.'

'You have so many residences the town is bound to

wonder why you've become sentimental over a place you've not set eyes on in years.'

'I never forget my house here.'

'Even so, there must be more urgent reasons for your visit. I assume it is a visit, no more?'

'I've come to find my son.'

'What's Jamie done to bring you after him so urgently.'

'After him? That sounds as if you know where he is.' He said nothing and she prodded. 'Well? Do you know? If so, you must tell me.'

'At this moment of time – no.'

'What do you mean by that?'

'He stayed, briefly, at the Irish Boy rather than at the house but moved on to the Ventrils at Ballarat. He rode back last month with Good Old Harry's crowd of young rowdies, all loaded with dust in more ways than one; bags of the stuff swinging from their saddles. Someone had made a lucky strike, perhaps all had; either way it was a bonus for the town for they spent with gusto, most of it at the Irish Boy, before taking off again for God knows where.'

'You should not let him gamble, certainly not at the Irish Boy. You know it makes Brick furious. Nor should you encourage his drinking.'

'Don't carp, just be glad he has gourmet tastes; French champagne is expensive enough to limit his intake. Besides, who am I to command the son of the house? For all I know he might own the Irish Boy by now.'

'If Brick had deeded it over you'd be the first to know, you make a point of knowing everything. But Jamie will never get the hotel. Brick's disowned him.'

Kurt laughed. 'How often have we heard him threaten *that*!'

'This time he means it. He's cut off his allowance too.'

'Well, it doesn't seem to hamper the boy for he sported sovereigns by the fistful. You know what he's like; he always manages to borrow something to tide him over till his next win. Seemingly he has friends in all quarters, a wild egalitarian with the habits and tastes of the gentry yet at home with the rabble, at least when they kowtow to him

which they do for they seem to like him lording it over them –
perhaps because he does it with panache. Even so, I suspect
that while he's hobnobbing with the lower orders he's
despising them, precisely as you do.'

'He's not wild. Not really. Just young.'

'You see him through indulgent eyes.'

'He'll change. Grow up.'

'Why didn't O'Shea come to drag his stepson home?'

'I didn't come to talk of Brick. You must find Jamie for me.
You live here and know everyone.'

'Sometimes I wonder why I do live here.'

'Because the pickings are good. And for many other
reasons I imagine.'

'As you have reasons for coming. I'd say you'd burned
your bridges behind you which means you're in no position
to give orders to anyone, much less myself. If you want help
it will be on my terms.'

'Then I'll get help elsewhere,' she flared.

'From whom? Sweet Jesus?' he mocked. 'There aren't
many left from the old days, Raunie.'

'And don't call me Raunie – as you've reminded me, these
aren't the old days.'

'And as I've reminded you, we could bring them back.' He
placed his smooth, well-manicured hand, not at all the hand
of a man who had started out as a miner, on her knee and
squeezed it. She brushed the hand aside. But her annoyance
dissolved as he eased the phaeton round the corner. The
Irish Boy stood a little apart on what had been the outskirts
of town when she was last here; now solid-looking estates
were developing about the sprawl of the hostelry, one of the
most famous on the Bendigo fields, with its valuable position
on entering the town from the east. Her heart gave a great
thump at the sight of the white-painted double-storeyed
house tight against one wall of the hotel but set back within
extensive gardens leading to an orchard of pear, peach, fig
and pomegranate. It all looked a little dry and wilted and the
shutters needed painting but it was still the imposing house
that had been the talk of the town when Brick had first built
it. She wanted to run up its path, but, conscious of Kurt's

all-seeing cynical eyes she alighted calmly, while the cart followed them round the corner hugged by jostling boys trying to strike a bargain in its unloading.

The tang of tobacco pervaded the rooms. His clothes hung in cupboards and the sideboard was littered with dirty glasses – he had clearly made an effort to tidy up but with no time to erase all signs of occupation. There were women's clothes about too. She swept a mess of books and papers off the dining-table. 'How dare you make my house a saloon? A bawdy-house too by the look of it.' She bundled up the female garb and threw all from a window. 'Pick it up as you go if you want it.'

'The hotel needs every room. It seemed a waste to leave the house empty.'

'You'll move out today. Sleep in a stable or under a tree for all I care.'

'There's plenty of time.' He eased himself out of his coat, skimming his revolver over the table with a complete disregard for its polish, then sprawled in an arm chair. Kurt Herlicht had always had style, one of his great attractions, and could even lounge with grace, but now there was an over-assurance, a bold laxity about him that made her protest angrily. He frowned. 'You've changed.'

'Where you're concerned, yes. You will not walk in here unless I send for you. If you have anything of importance to say concerning Jamie – and I expect news of him promptly – send a message and I will meet you in the town, not in this house. I'll take all the keys now but as I'm sure you have copies I'll have the locks changed. Meals are to be sent in. Send a locksmith, and return my carriage today. And I'll need live-in help.'

'Which all sounds as if you're planning a long, and lonely, vigil. No entertaining at all?'

'I'm here to find Jamie and take him back to Sydney.'

'And if he should refuse to go?' Her answer was to hold out her palm. With a mocking gesture he dropped the keys into it. 'You know, I refuse to believe O'Shea would allow his wife to wander these fields alone. My guess is that you've left him. Have you?'

'No. But if I had it's no concern of yours.'

'It was my concern once – and could be again. So! If you insist on living in some remote and rarefied sphere I warn you you'll find it a solitary vigil. I never found you a woman to bear loneliness well.'

'I have Abby – and Gondola.'

'An Italiano vagrant dwarf and a conniving shrew? Hasn't that virago picked the bones of the O'Shea menage yet?'

'Abby and I understand each other.'

He shrugged. 'In any case, I have ways of getting around bodyguards.'

'If you or your henchmen try to force your way into my house Brick will kill you and you know it.'

'There are hundreds of miles between us and your husband, even if I were afraid of him which I'm not; you know it, as he knows it. Besides, I won't have to force my way in here, all I need do is wait.' She raised an angry hand to strike but he gripped her wrist and drew it down, slowly but strongly. 'I'm more in awe of your newly-acquired propriety than of O'Shea. We work for each other, that's all, he serves my purposes as I his. Actually we hate each other's guts and all know it. But I don't hate O'Shea's wife.'

'Don't talk that way.'

'You'll soon tire of waiting,' he murmured with that soft beguiling tone he could assume in an instant, a tone well remembered and once enjoyed. 'The days are long and the nights longer and you'll send for me and soon.' Despite her resolve her heart leaped. A rogue, a tease, but she needed to laugh and Kurt could always amuse her, Kurt could make her feel so intensely alive. 'Someone must know where Jamie is,' she said a little breathlessly.

'Spies come expensive these days; even the town drifters and vagrants have their price.'

'I'll pay.'

'And who can afford it better?' He retrieved his gun. 'The only quality I envy in your improvident brat is his ability to find your weaknesses. You're a fool about him.'

'I suppose so,' she agreed cheerfully. 'but he's rather the same about me.'

'I'll send a boy for my things though I don't doubt you'll have thrown them from the window before he arrives.' He sighed with mock extravagance. 'All that seems left is for me to await your summons. I'll not keep you waiting. After all, there need be only a few steps between us.'

In fury at his cool confidence she scraped up his clothes and flung them from the window to billow about him as he emerged. He scooped them up, threw them in the phaeton and took up the reins. 'Bolts never kept me out in the old days,' he called, 'and they won't now. This is still a rogue town no matter how it looks on the surface.'

Yes, she thought, remembering his revolver, still the rogue town where no man had moved without a weapon, or any woman who could shoot, and she had been the most expert of all. Irish Paddy Harrigan had taught her to shoot and taught her well, and she had kept up her marksmanship since the time when, a lonely desperate girl, she had left the baby Jamie in Betsy Witherstone's care and escaped to Sydney. On the awful journey down, the revolver at her waist had been her only protection against spite, vengeance, or rape by her fellow travellers or the robbers of the road. Now she never went to bed at night without tucking her revolver under her pillow.

She stopped dead. What was it Kurt had said? *'There need be only a few steps between us.'* She ran upstairs and through the master bedroom – signs of occupation there too – to what had once been Brick's dressing-room and, yes, the blue-painted door stood open. How *dared* he use these stairs from the hotel office to her bedroom, Brick's private stairs into the house. She slammed and bolted the door. She would have extra bolts fitted for this door belonged to the past: how often she had lain waiting for Brick's tread, counting his steps, to be reassured as he locked the door against the demands of the hotel and the outside world. She trembled. She wanted him here, now, for the magic of their life together was in this room, their own private precious world. She would die if he did not follow her, and soon, for no matter how furiously he came she would soothe him as she had always done. She would win him back. In this room he would not, could not, resist her.

So began the drift of clinging, cloying Indian-summer days and lonely nights that seemed to have no real end or beginning and in which she felt sealed off in some claustrophobic hothouse, enduring Abby's complaints at Kurt's tardiness in sending help – at least the locks had been changed. She saw little of Gondola though Abby reported he had established rapport with the hotel stable-hands, working with the horses, shining carriages, running his twisted little run on his twisted little legs with messages and taking on any odd job that would earn him a few coins, wandering back to sleep in the outhouse but as a cat, alert to the faintest sound. Raunie let him be for she knew he would come running at her call. She saw no one else except Isaac, who came with firewood for the tea Abby was always brewing and to crop and pull at the overgrown garden, and the hotel maids who brought the trays and stared, irritating her, for the whole town must know by now that the O'Shea house was occupied and by its mistress. Surely Jamie would hear and come running? But no Jamie, though Abby asked discreet questions about the town. Those she enquired of always turned out to be newcomers, strangers to the town's fables, who had certainly heard of the O'Sheas, but that was all. As for Jamie O'Shea – or Lorne, or whatever he called himself – all anyone seemed clear about was that gangs of young bloods rode in and out of town, as gangs had always done, stayed a while to kick up the usual rumpus around the pubs, then rode on their way. The town closed its doors on such gangs and stayed tight until all was quiet again. Raunie felt curiously isolated and depressed.

Kurt finally sent a girl with a strong accent and an equally strong scent of garlic about her – Dutch or German, Raunie did not know or care. Kurt's note had stated simply that Dulcima was strong enough to hoist furniture about which she had promised not to throw at anyone, as was her habit, and willing to live in provided she could choose her room. They soon discovered why for they were disturbed at odd hours by catcalls and whistles at her window that opened onto the lane, or by the racket of youths hoisting her inside after her time off. Abby promptly dismissed her but Dulcima refused to leave – she did her work, didn't she? Besides, she liked the place. Since she promised not to bring her swains inside they decided to make the best of it; after all, they could always do worse.

There was no message, nothing from Kurt, and Raunie was forced, finally, to send for him. He had no idea where Jamie was nor, it seemed, had anyone else. Impossible, she ridiculed, someone must know his whereabouts. Kurt gave his usual maddening shrug. The boy could be wandering the roads like the young gipsy he was, or town-and-pub hopping back to Sydney, or – had she considered? – even shipped out of the country . . .

'Jamie wouldn't leave Australia any more than he would leave me.' Even so, it lay in her mind tormenting her.

'Everyone's close-mouthed on the fields, you know that. Diggers are cagey, giving out nothing without something in return. It takes time and patience to unlock tongues.'

'Pay them what they ask,' she brazened, recklessly, for her money was dwindling and she would soon have to borrow on her jewels, or even sell a piece here and there. 'If you don't find him, I must. Do you want me to go to the police? Or go looking for him myself?'

'You won't risk the police. And how would you seek him out? Go riding about in the wilderness bailing up diggers? You're a poor rider. You wouldn't cover much ground in a dray. And your carriage isn't built for potholes.'

He was right, of course, and she grew more depressed. Bushfires ringed the town. Even so, unhappy and bored, she consented to drive out with him but the roads and gullies were deserted, heavy with smoke and haunted by black stinging flies and mosquitoes from the mud where water should have been. Dust coated her gloves and lay in the folds of her clothes and she refused to go again. In despair she ordered Abby to pack for Sydney, then changed her mind.

Abby was difficult, for Kitty Wickler was sending messages that Herbert was off helping a mate with his claim but she did not know where. 'He's deserted her,' Raunie scoffed. 'He's always deserting her.' All the same, she gave Abby money she could not afford, anything to mollify the woman and keep her in town for Abigail was all she had – and Sweet Jesus shaking his fists at her from street-corners and planting himself on his box outside the Irish Boy, haranguing her and the tipplers rolling from the bars. She devoured the life of the hotel from behind her curtains, recognising none who came and went about the yards and outhouses. She refused to go near the mine or the store – let people come to her. But according to Abby there was new staff at the O'Shea store, at the hotel, and out at the mine, and nobody came. It was as if she had ceased to exist; the town, incredibly, had forgotten her. Terrified of becoming a recluse she forced herself out with Abby to promenade Pall Mall on the gala Saturday night, past tailors and jewellers and bakeries and 'la modes' amid the click of bowling alleys and music from the concert halls and the German girls waltzing to the German band. But she recognised no one – where was the old Bendigo? She kept away from the O'Shea store for she had worked too hard there on first coming to Bendigo. Rosa's Robes, where she had once spent so lavishly, was more to her taste, but as she fingered ribbons and feathers she did not want, wandering listlessly from stand to stand, a familiar voice dragged her back to the past with horrifying clarity.

'Well now, if it ain't milady!'

Barring her way was the Duchess, corseted within an inch of her life and breath, her ravaged over-painted face beneath stiff gluey curls and a bonnet heavy with plumes, laughing with all the lusty bravado of the old days. Two of her women whispered beside the parasol stand and it was apparent that though her speech remained pure London Thames-side the Duchess plied her trade in more opulent surroundings.

'Mrs O'Shea,' Raunie snapped.

'Signora Costello.' With an airy wave of her heavily ringed

hand. 'The better 'alf is a wine importer, along with other profitable sidelines.'

'Alf Brierley's dead?'

The woman hesitated only a moment. 'If he ain't he blooming well should be.'

'So it's bigamy now, is it?'

The Duchess patted her hair. 'We've both things to hide, milady. If I keep a still tongue see y'do the same.'

'I've nothing to hide.'

'No?' The woman laughed. 'What y'doing 'ere without your man, eh? Up to no good, I'll be bound. You always was a sly one.'

Kurt was right, Raunie reflected as she brushed the Duchess from her path. Despite town councillors and municipal by-laws the veil of respectability lay thinly over the old riotous disorder of the town where, in that first rush of seven years before, she and Brick had bargained and intrigued, grabbing before others could grab, plundering with all the need and greed that she could inspire in him, pushing, goading, brushing aside his 'damn you, Egypt' those times he had dug in his heels and resisted. 'It's kill or be killed,' she had warned as they stocked their stores at gruelling prices – after all, diggers must expect to pay for wheat all the way from South Australia as well as for meat from the Riverina; the millers were getting rich, why not the O'Sheas? One passed it on to those who could afford to pay! They acquired a mine and she fought against paying the men a living wage: 'They're failed diggers. Anything you pay them is better than scratching at poor claims.' They built up the old shanty of the Irish Boy till they had assets enough to leave in Kurt Herlicht's clever manipulative (too much so at times she insisted) hands to return to Sydney to spend their gains – but on her terms. She would return only as his wife. Sydney, the city that had left her to starve, even to die in its gutters or the worst of its taverns, would give her respect or give her nothing. And no isolated pile of a house on the North Shore dependent on drunken ferrymen, built for another woman at that! Brick had been so besotted he could refuse her nothing and had built Birubi, isolated, but, Brick

360

insisted, the vanguard of the grand houses of the Sydney élite, to live the life that suited her and be damned to the conservatives and the sterlings. She had grasped her new life with eager hands and shaped it to her ways and wishes.

Kitty sent frantic messages that her children were ailing and Raunie knew she could not keep Abby in town. But watching the woman rattle off in Isaac's cart she felt a desolation such as she had seldom known. She sent for Kurt again and again and he would come meticulously through the front door. No word of Jamie. Nothing. The days and nights seemed endless as she wandered the house to the ticking of the hall clock, the rooms crammed with bitter-sweet memories: the lavish dinners laced with magnums of champagne and hang the expense . . . The wild after-race gatherings with loaded pistols in a row on the marble mantel while the men paid court to women in luxurious gowns brought from Melbourne modistes in the spanking new coaches of Cobb & Co. She ran her finger around a bullet hole under the south window, souvenir of a four-day debauch by a gang of negroes who'd held a shooting match to finish off the proceeds of their strike; a bullet that had missed her by a fraction yet she had laughed at it . . . More bullet holes from the 'forty-niners', the Californians who'd galloped on stolen horses into the hills after 'rangers', their murderous Bowie knives out in a drunken flash . . . The excitement of the gold escort hugged by blue-clad troops bringing out the whole town to see, children running and shouting as they followed their 'fairy coach' as they called it . . . Sunday fist-fights ending in pitched battles with pick handles, scattering churchgoers . . . Revolvers shooting off in the night from claims, warning thieves that guns were loaded and at the ready . . . Watching from this very window for Brick to ride in from Melbourne, only half alive without him as she was only half alive now. And the time, in a gloriously drunken spree, he had ridden Glenora up the spanking new stairway of the Irish Boy, to test it he shouted, to crash in a welter of timber and dust but rising from the rubble unhurt like a phoenix from its ashes, laughing with her and the world, both of them half mad with success and each other . . .

The savage outlawry of the riff-raff dregs of Eureka . . . And her protests at his journeys into the Riverina: 'Come with me then and follow the cattle down,' he would thunder. 'I must see to my lands and my stock. I'm a bushman.' Always the wanderer, in a way the explorer. But always returning to Bendigo, and her.

Why didn't he come now? She had left hints as to her destination so why wasn't he here? Through the long dead afternoons she lay behind closed shutters enduring the heat, Dulcima closeted with a novelette and peppermints. Sometimes she would coax the girl to cards but Dulcima was more of a cheat than herself and was packed off to bed for insolence. Raunie would draw the curtains against the blackness of the frontier road and lie sleepless. Other nights she would sit by her window staring out at the hotel lights making great streaks across the road, teased by voices throbbing in song, aching to be with vigorous gay people under hard bright lights. But she would not, must not, give Kurt the opportunity to climb those stairs, Brick's stairs, to her bed. From time to time she sent for him insisting he find Jamie no matter the cost. His casual air maddened her. She had little money so gave him rings and brooches and bracelets, thankful Abby was not there to scold for Abigail would never let her part with her gems. Lonely, almost penniless, confused and growing desperate she was ready to promise anything and everything if only Kurt would bring Jamie home.

One morning she surprised Dulcima stuffing pillowcases with her best shawls and scarves, a bundle of jet hairnets stuffed down her front. Raunie dismissed the girl with threats to hand her over to the police if she came near the house again. Now she was truly alone. Even Sweet Jesus seemed to have deserted his box. Isaac no longer wandered the garden and she hadn't set eyes on Gondola for days. She picked at her food. Searching cupboards she found brandy, quite a lot of brandy. Half crazy with loneliness, her longing for Brick, and the spirit, she let the chain off the blue door. She would go down into the hotel and laugh with Kurt, dance with Kurt, flirt with Kurt, let Kurt devour her if he must . . . She paused, appalled at her reflection in the hall mirror, wild-haired, her négligé bedraggled and food-stained. She looked like a mad woman. Hating herself, she bolted the door and poured more brandy, neat. Brandy, it seemed, was her only friend.

Jamie was skilled at dressing hurriedly and in semi-darkness but this morning he was hard pressed for the coach left at six. Early as it was he could hear maids up and down the stairs of the 'hotel', actually a seedy theatrical lodging-house, with hot water for early risers, but a plunge of his head in the basin of ice-cold water to startle him awake must suffice. Even so, he paused in dragging on his shirt to draw aside the mosquito-netting on the girl in the bed. Her blonde hair was touched by the first faint light, hair that had caught his attention as he lounged beside Good Old Harry, bored with the third-rate operetta, bored with Good Old Harry, his friends and their pursuits as he was bored with Melbourne's baked-hard streets lined with respectable iron-lace terraces, shuttered as if terrified of footpads. Good Old Harry had dragged him from balls to theatres and various functions to celebrate something or other, persuading, monopolising, shadowing; watching him, Jamie felt, as persistently as some bodyguard-spy. Indeed he was beginning to wonder if Harry was precisely that! He wanted Bendigo for Easter and if Good Old Harry wouldn't come with him, Good Old Harry could go to Hell. Good Old Harry had agreed, finally, to leave Melbourne but only for Ballarat for he dared not anger his father further. Paul Ventril had threatened to cut him off without a cent and then where would they be? Someone had to find the spending money! He must go home and placate the old man. They had compromised. Ballarat it would be.

Actually, it was the girl's voice that had brought him to the stage door for he had never heard sweeter, with some-thing irresistible about it. She had fixed large clear eyes on him, studying him, he felt with approval, so was surprised at her rebuff.

'I'm taking supper with a gent from Ballarat. Everyone's rich in Ballarat.'

'I'm not rich but flush enough to buy oysters and ices and all the champagne you can drink.' He'd scrape up enough for that for one supper should do it, it always had. Watching from a doorway he had seen her take a cab alone, no gent from Ballarat, or from anywhere else it seemed. Yet it wasn't until his third approach that she had agreed to sup with him and had eaten hungrily though nervously, dropping her fork and spilling her wine, prattling with a tension he found intriguing for he was accustomed to confident women who took the initiative. She would be a great actress one day, she insisted with passion, not just a singer in the chorus. She would study, she would tour Europe no matter what it cost her, she would become famous . . . a dream so far removed from the modest restaurant in Collins Street that was all he could afford but that she seemed to find so grand, that they laughed together over her vision. She had not demurred further. Even so, she puzzled him by not asking for money or even seeming to expect it. She did not cry or protest or beg, just left everything to him, which was as well for she had fumbled so badly he had almost left her bed. But in the end she had surprised him, not least by the fact that she was a virgin. He hadn't altogether enjoyed the feeling of violation it gave for he had known none but harlots which, in a way, he preferred – they taught a man. You always knew where you were with the Cypriots.

Despite a watercart rattling by in the lane she slept on, her cheek resting on her arm flung forward over the pillow as if reaching out for the day – or for him perhaps? The idea pleased him. Lucy Marigold Finney she had admitted; Lucinda Amora was only for the stage, singers were expected to flaunt Italian names. She seemed to want to impart confidences . . . Her brother was a rhymester but a stylish one, writing rigmarole for the shopkeepers, while her father manufactured shell lime, but the very best, after the directions of Signor Angelo Daniello, modeller and plasterer to the King of Naples. Of course, so much fine dust about the house was a great trial, and bad for a singer's throat . . . He had let her keep her small pretensions. Her other arm hung limp over the side of the bed, the little blue ring he had given her (he carried a pocketful of them) glowing in the candle-light. There was still a faint flower scent about her and the room, verbena, rose perhaps, and in sleep her face was that of a child. In a way she awed him and he wasn't used to the feeling, it filled him with emotions he didn't understand and didn't want.

He let the netting drop. He didn't want to be held by her, or by any one girl. Women were for your passing fancy and leisure hours – his needs, he supposed, now that he was older. The light was growing and he could see his way but he hated daylight of late – days could be hell for he was in debt and deeper every day, a far cry from the odd IOU that gave a zest to life. One could lose oneself at night in cards and the playhouses and women but the day returned to confront you, reveal you, and he didn't like what it revealed. His luck had deserted him, his precious luck that, falter as it might, had always returned to set him on his feet again – Raunie's luck he called it. Gipsy luck. But it was no more and he was uneasy, scared if the truth were known though he'd die before he showed his uncertainty. The usurer had turned out to be a Herlicht man. Perhaps he had always known it would be so yet couldn't face it for, after all, how could it be otherwise? Yet he had taken the loan at cruel interest because nothing else offered. He was buying time now, paying a bit here, some there, waiting for his luck to change – as change it must. It always had. It would again.

He set three sovereigns on the bedside table, hesitated and retrieved two; one was inclined to overpay, particularly for a virgin, so he was assured by those for ever seeking one to cure the clap and willing to pay lavishly to lie with her. He didn't believe that old nonsense but it was astounding how many did. Anyway, he took good care of himself! Surprising himself he paused with his hand on the doorknob to look back at the girl. A fumbling hesitant child with an amazing voice . . . She slept on, her arm flung forward over the pillow. Curiously, he wanted to linger and that surprised him further but he flung open the door and, blowing warmth into his hands, set off through the still, cool, early-morning streets to meet Good Old Harry Ventril at the coach-station.

The paddle-wheeler, an old lump doomed to the dying cedar trade, puffed its way south belching black smoke, loping and labouring in the morning swell as if putting in time till the nor'easter rose near midday to nudge it along. Brick had paced the deck alone for some time, leaning over the rail, drawing in as a flavour the semi-tropical intensity of blue and green and gold under the piercing morning light. Now others were venturing on deck to stretch their limbs, picking their way over flour casks and sugar bags to lean on the rails and stare, the young mothers fencing off corners to rest their babes, the young perching on boxes and bales to kick their heels. The sun climbed the late summer sky, blazing against the thickly-timbered cliffs leading to the hills and valleys of the southern coast, the sea foaming in on sand crescents of beaches where aborigines hacked at the carcass of a washed-up whale or fished from the headlands, or rowed out in their bark canoes to follow the coaster and return the waves of children, or just stare.

'Too much of it – land I mean.' A harsh male voice grumbled at Brick's elbow, vision temporarily blurred by smoke from an ornate pipe. 'Nowt but emptiness. Bears down on a man, so to speak.'

'I don't feel it so.'

'You're born to the place, I reckon. I was bred to the Great Dock Road.' He glowered at a native canoe. 'Give it back to the blackfellows, I say. Never tame it.'

'I take it you're not here to stay.'

The man shrugged. 'Can't take to the place. But I'm noan daft, I've seven mouths to feed and another on the way and we've meat three times a day, lad, better than on Merseyside. But when I've made m'pile 'twill be a different kettle of fish; I'll have the brass to sail back and forth.' He grinned. 'Aye, I'd like to lord it over Liverpool.'

'And are you making your pile?'

'Noan so bad, with a snug little chophouse in Sydney. Now it's to the south to open red plush and chondeleers for Melbourne epicureans, toffs with the brass to splurge on specialities like venison and game, and small birds if I can get 'em. Specially larks. Larks are the thing! The wife, see, has a dash of Italian and knows how to cook 'em: trusses 'em up quick as a wink, brushes 'em with egg, rolls 'em in breadcrumbs, lark-spits and roasts 'em ten minutes over a quick fire bastin' all the time with butter – ten minutes by the clock. Succulent!' He smacked his lips. 'You've noan had larks the way the wife cooks 'em. Never.'

'I've never eaten larks and don't intend to.'

He was a little offended, but curious. 'So what's your line?'

'You could call me a man of parts. The land, mostly.'

'Home on the sheep's back, eh? You'll make your pile if the goddamned back-country don't get y'first.'

'You've travelled it?'

'I'm noan daft there either! I stay by the shore.' He shot out a tobacco-stained hand. 'George Bloom trading as Georges Beauvour (he pronounced it Boovoor) restooratoor.' He fumbled in his pocket, presumably for his card. 'Never liked the Froggies, who does, but they do give summat to a place – class, if you get my meaning?'

'Brick O'Shea.'

'O'Shea?' He tapped the card on the rail. 'Heard that somewhere.' His head shot up. 'Why, you're the . . .' He looked more scared than surprised.

'Nigger, you'd call me back "home" if you weren't calling me blackfellow. In this country I'm Black Brick O'Shea to friends in jovial mood, to those not so jovial I'm the darky or "the one with the touch o' the tarbrush". Actually, I'm a quarter-caste. A quadroon.'

Georges Boovoor knocked out his pipe. 'As I said, I've a long tail. Mouths to feed. And a pile o' paperwork to do before we dock.' Slipping the card back in his pocket, he fled.

Brick paced again, impatient for journey's end. He would spend a day or so in Melbourne making token visits to Raunie's favourite hotels but he was sure she was in Bendigo – how she was drawn back to that flat hot country town –

most likely with Jamie. What exactly he would do when he found her he had not considered, except to drag the truth from her; it was enough that she confronted him and did not attempt to evade truth any longer for he was burning bridges and tying ends. And to one end he had diverged to Parramatta to find the scrap of flesh and bone that was Jamie's son sitting in his own excreta surrounded by dog faeces, while his grandmother slapped sheets about in clouds of steam. The baby's black curls were matted, his delicate little face pinched by the morning chill but he sat strong-backed and alert. He had taken the filthy soggy crust from the child's dirty fingers and its screams had risen above his own shouts at the dreadful hag of a grandmother.

'Has he no clothes?' He picked at the baby's sole garment, a ragged shirt.

'Only what covers 'im, sir.' The crone's voice turned to a whine. 'I do the best I can since his ma run orf with her fancy man leaving the brat to eat me out of 'ouse and 'ome.'

'He has no teeth,' he laughed. 'Or has he . . .' He knew little about babies this age but running a finger round the raw gums he had it soundly bitten.

'Willy Wilberforce gets through his crust well enough.'

'Willy *what?*'

'The toff what freed the slaves. I 'eard tell of 'im, see, and says to m'self, Rosy Watts, if y'can raise the child through colic and fever and all the rest of it 'til he's grown he can free his gran from the washtub.' She wiped her dripping nose on a pillow-case with stubbornness more than hope. ' 'Tis a name as good as any other.'

'Willy Wilberforce!' The baby's lips had trembled at his laughter. 'Such a name does not cry,' he added sternly and the child's fears had dissolved into a chuckle. 'Nor does it sit in dung.' He had swept up the child, filth and all, shouting above the slap and slam of wet sheets. 'I'm taking him off your hands. You'll be well paid and his mother recom-pensed, but the pair of you will make your marks on paper before the law or I'll have you charged with neglect and you'll finish up in gaol for there's many here to give evidence as to how I found the child.'

'I'm sure I want the best for 'im, Mr O'Shea, and I'll see his ma makes no fuss neither.'

'Then clean him up. I'll fetch him in the morning.' And he sent Willy Wilberforce Watts-Lorne-O'Shea, one name as good as another, off to Erins Pride by coach in Fay Witherstone's care. The women would fatten him up nicely.

The sun was almost overhead. The air began to shiver and the breeze to whine. Skin tingled with the sting of the nor'easter and salt stung the lips. Clothes billowed and blew. The steamer came alive to shake and turn and shudder like a toy boat in a big pond, shimmering its way down the long foaming coast of the Pacific.

Chapter Eighteen

BENDIGO WAS *en fête*: the hotels were crowding with visitors in for the race-meetings and sports and the Easter Fair, with the highlight of the Monday Procession. For the more sophisticated the Shamrock Concert Hall, the Haymarket, the Lyceum, along with every corner public-house, competed in featuring popular artistes. The town crier was already hoarse. Posters nailed to trees informed the world that a circus was due, not just circus acts but a menagerie, and excited children were hoarding their pennies. Bridge Street's Chinatown was polishing its cymbals and gongs, collecting crackers and assembling its giant dragon. The Irish Boy had squeezed in extra beds, and tables into its gleaming restaurant. The bars were well stocked with imported liquors, particularly French champagne, and the gaming-rooms were poised for record business.

Kurt Herlicht was virtually tied to his office with little time for anything but management, riding out only when necessary to the O'Shea mine and the slaughter-yards and the store. But he worked with an acute sense of the inner door leading up to Raunie's bedroom, Raunie so close and, as always, desirable. Her appearance in Bendigo could easily have proved disastrous for his plans but he had acted promptly in sending Jamie off with Good Old Harry, ostensibly to enjoy the fleshpots of Melbourne but actually to keep the boy free of his mother's influence, at the same time putting him in touch with his own (well-primed) usurer. The hasty device had worked, if not without a hitch here and there, for Good Old Harry had telegraphed that Jamie was itching to get back to Bendigo for Easter but he had managed to coax him to Ballarat. An awkward compromise though a necessary one, for Jamie was about to crack, deep enough in debt to stake the Irish Boy with O'Shea to honour the debt; one of the man's convenient quirks, honouring gambling debts. He, Herlicht, could not stop now; the Irish Boy was almost his again. He had waited plotted and planned these six years to win it back.

There was shouting . . . from the stables, or was it the coach-house? Cursing, he sprang to his feet. That Neapolitan buffoon was causing trouble again, he knew it; the wretch had been trouble since wheedling his way about the Irish Boy with all the traits of the vagrant, the runaway, the brigand. He'd ordered him off but to no avail. He'd beaten him but somehow the creature crept back to burrow into dark corners of the stables or coach-house or grain shed, grooming the horses, coveting them, stealing one or the other to ride about the countryside. He'd beaten him again for lighting fires to cook his Italian messes but it made no difference, back he came, grinning, supplicating, winning over the men who made a pet of him, amusing them with his attempts at English, teaching them to shoot, doubtless with a stolen gun – Raunie's perhaps? The commotion, whatever it was, was growing. Men were shouting at each other . . .

Kurt took a whip from a hook, not an ordinary whip but a cat-o'-nine-tails, an instrument not seen much in recent years, a relic of convict days. He shook the thongs loose. Smoke was coming from the stables – no, the shed. A furious argument was in progress as he ran across the coaching yard. Men were stamping out a fire dangerously close to the dividing wall of the grain shed and the horses' stalls. The cripple was swift and adept on his short legs but Kurt barred his path, grasped him by his collar and flung him to the ground. With a cold fury he beat him methodically and persistently till Gondola lay, a curled-up twisted thing, moaning at the feet of his hated *padrone*.

Raunie started up from a half sleep, her heart pounding. No, the pounding came from a distance – the door-knocker. She struggled from the bed, her head swimming, trying to concentrate on the sound – there it was again. Brick! Swaying slightly from vertigo and not a little panic she clutched at the bed-head, soothed by the sharp coolness of brass, striving to collect her wits. Her husband had come to tell her he hated her and that he loved a freckle-faced Irish girl who was to bear his child – no, the child was no more. Think. *Think!* She had wanted him to come, ached for him, but now she was afraid. He had come to kill her, convinced it was she who had destroyed Alannah's child-to-be – *his* child. He was capable of murder; hadn't he killed the half-breed Dgeralli long ago? And only he knew how many others. Her moist hair clung to her neck and she smoothed it from her face. She must look her best, using all her guile to placate him and win him back. The knocker was persistent. If she did not let him in he would try other entrances – windows left open? She couldn't remember. She couldn't even remember when she'd last seen Dulcima and she shook her head to clear it . . . she had discharged Dulcima, she remembered, and now she was quite alone; even Abigail had deserted her. Her dwarf groom had deserted her; Kurt was right, she should not have brought the fool. She stared down at the glass-panelled door. A shadow made a dim pattern against the glass but man or woman she could not tell. Not tall enough for Brick. Abby – that was it. Abigail had come back! She skimmed the stairs to fling open the door. It was Kurt Herlicht. She had not even considered Kurt.

'The town's still out and about so I'm surprised you left me standing here.' He brushed past her, closing the door behind him. He was resplendent in dress clothes, the crisp black and white elegant against his fair sleek hair and blue eyes. She clutched her untidy peignoir about her, aware of her shining unpainted face. 'You haven't send a demand, much less a message, in days.' He stared at her intently. 'What is it? Are you ill?'

She must look far worse than she imagined, she thought miserably. He tipped up her chin. Useless to flinch or try to avoid his gaze; besides, she was glad of any human being who cared if she were even alive, and with an impulsive movement she rested her cheek against his sleeve. 'It's the

372

house,' she whispered. 'It's so quiet and lonely. Sometimes I think I am going mad.'

'You won't go mad.' He put an arm about her. 'Not now.' But she drew back, looking about her in surprise.

'It's still daylight.'

'Turned five o'clock of a fine day. It's not good to hide yourself away like this, Raunie. Or to drink alone. Come out of this mausoleum or you will be ill – or go mad, you know it.'

'Yes, I know it.' She licked her dry lips in a misery of indecision.

'You haven't even set foot in the hotel yet. People are asking why not.'

'What people?'

'Those who remember you – they seem to be coming to light. Tonight is a gala in honour of an opera company working the Bendigo-Maryborough-Castlemaine circuit and people are coming in from miles around. I have a special table, with visitors up from Melbourne out to enjoy themselves so come and look your best. You're not meant to live in dark places. Come out into the light. I'll be back for you at seven.' She found it wonderful to be coaxed. But he didn't touch her again, and she wanted him to coax her, stimulate her, lead her out like the old forceful Kurt. It was exactly what she needed. She had hidden herself away too long.

It was not easy to dress herself for Abby always knew where everything was. She lacked her most luxurious clothes but did her best. Her hair was the difficult part. Finally she caught it up behind her ears with combs and let its richness fall over her shoulders in coils. Excited, she scrabbled in her jewel box, now sadly almost empty, for her gipsy charms, her old protection against *mallochio* – evil influences – seldom worn these days for Brick was impatient of superstition. She ran her fingers over the figure of a pig surmounting a boar's tooth, so old its origin was lost in time. It clinked against her lucky cowrie shell that Brick had given her long ago. Tonight she would wear her talismans, tonight they would not be *mochardi* – taboo – tonight she would be herself, a gipsy. She strung the charms proudly about her neck to rest in the hollow between her breasts. Let people whisper and wonder if they would: she did not care. Her gauzy shining shawl brought out the colour and sparkle of her eyes and the effect pleased her. She looked very young, she decided happily, swinging about the room, invigorated, her tiredness and boredom seeping away. How could she bear to grow old? To be unwanted and neglected must be the most terrible fate a woman could endure. She was haunted by fear of age, for with the years came loss of beauty and without her beauty she was lost. But tonight she was young. *Young!*

She took Kurt's arm with confidence as he led her into the full blaze of the hotel lights. The music and talk, the fragrance of massed flowers mingling with the more subtle perfume of women struck her as a sunlight flash or a sudden burst of rain, enhancing her sense of colour, sound and scent. It was like old times, better than old times, for the Irish Boy had become a splendid glittering palace matching anything she had seen in Melbourne, with its long lavish bar, and the elaborate theatre at the restaurant end grown out of the plank-boarded stage for the 'free and easys' that had acquired such a reputation during the notorious years when the town had been full of rip-roaring blood-houses. Since then Brick, with Kurt on the bandwagon, had created a legend in this expensive showplace where the landed gentry of squatters, and the wealthy townsfolk, could flaunt their clothes, their wives, their affluence, and their mistresses if they desired and dared. What could Jamie improve here? she wondered with some amusement. But being Jamie he would have ideas, too many ideas perhaps. A dance troupe was entertaining with pseudo-Grecian tableaux *à la* Emma Hamilton, but she felt eyes turn as Kurt led her to the long table sparkling with silver and crystal where frilled shirt fronts, oiled hair and the naked shoulders of women gleamed as brightly as their jewels. The smell of rich food almost sent her reeling and she realised she had not eaten a proper meal in days – or had she? The recent past was something of a blank. Champagne corks popped, a stimulating sound as background to the singers and dancers who came and went. Who were these expensively dressed expansive men whose eyes lingered on her? Kurt pronounced names and whispered identities – a mine-manager, a seed-merchant, a horse-dealer. A jeweller up from Melbourne to open a branch pinched her knee under the table and likened her eyes to emeralds, then spoilt the compliment by an allusion to cat's eyes. Dabbling in gold-buying too, he boasted, and doing nicely thank you. She turned her back to him to fascinate a gaudy gent sidling back and forth to the gaming-rooms. Farther down was a miller grown rich on South Australian wheat imported in the boom years, and opposite a butcher grown rich the same way – the richest burgher in Bendigo, Kurt teased; O'Shea had better look to his laurels! And be nice to the wives, he advised, legal and otherwise for they set the tune. Raunie ignored them as coarse noisy *hausfraus*, their perfumes and clothes harsh and overpowering. The cuisine was elaborate and the champagne expensive and Kurt was lavish with both. The horse-dealer pressed her hand boasting of his race-winnings. He would give a dinner in her honour, she was too splendid a filly to be hidden away. She flirted with them all and watched the eyes of their women grow cold. If a man did leave her side he joined a tight male circle to talk softly and seriously, or burst into peals of laughter at some private joke, or grin at his companions in a conspiratorial manner as if plotting, as doubtless they all were.

'Picked up the widow Purcell's allotment in Mitchell Street. I've a hunch the railway station will be around there.'

'Land takes too long to appreciate. I'm investing in breweries. You can depend on the grog.'

The comings and goings to the gaming-rooms grew brisk, young blades with keen faces and older men with hard ones. Jamie would be in some gaming-house tonight, she brooded, perhaps even in here . . . The idea startled and disturbed; was it possible he was hiding from her? Doubts nagged and for the first time she felt uncertain of her power over her son, even over Brick, and suspicious of these shrewd-eyed people, doubly suspicious of Kurt and tried to draw away from him. The old magic must not be allowed to work, for in Kurt Herlicht there had always been something to make her uneasy even when they had been lovers, particularly when they had been lovers. His eyes followed her when she danced with the mine-owner – or was it the seed-merchant – and in an abrupt change of mood and music he led her out in a waltz. Stimulated by champagne, excited by the colour and lights and the admiration of men, she was warmly conscious of Kurt's hand on her waist and his breath on her cheek. She seemed to float within the circle of his arms in some melodious hazy house of pleasure and for a while forgot even Jamie. But returning to the table she found a large female flanked by a flamboyant Italian with black whiskers and curls and be-ringed fingers. The Duchess! How dared she intrude here threatening by her presence, as she had threatened on the *May Queen*, at the Thames Hulk, coming and going throughout Raunie's life reminding her of a world she had discarded. The tip of the woman's fan brushed the talismans at her throat.

'Something to fall back on when times are bad, eh, milady?'

'Don't call me "milady".'

This time the fan tip brushed her shoulders. 'Mrs O'Shea and m'self are old friends,' she informed the restaurant. Heads turned and a terrible anger infected the warm and glorious haze in which Raunie moved.

'Friends?' she exploded. 'You're no friend of mine, you trussed-up trollop, and you don't sit at my table in my hotel. Get out and take your fancy man with you. *Out.*' She picked up a bowl of flowers and fruit and brought it down hard on the Duchess's head, water oozing over the woman's glued curls and high plumes and fake pearls. Above the pandemonium Raunie screamed at her, at the restaurant, at Bendigo. 'Out of here, you whore. Out. *Out!*' Gripping the woman by her convolutions of hair she dragged at its pins, shaking her with the strength of fury until her fingers were prised loose by the horrified guests and the Duchess's demented screaming and blaspheming faded into distance. Someone pressed a glass of champagne into her hand and she drank it without a word or pause. She didn't give a damn for the Irish Boy or Bendigo or Kurt Herlicht. Certainly not for the Duchess. She had waited years for such a triumph as this.

It was through the same haze that she sensed Kurt – was it
Kurt? – leading her up the steps to her house and through
rooms bathed in pink – no, an amber glow; the amber light of
her sitting-room lamp. He was drawing curtains and the
room became a pink cathedral – no, an amber one, closing in
to become a cave where all was mute and dim with her
bedroom at the end of a long luminous tunnel. Kurt was
holding her – or was it Brick? Yes, it was Brick, running his
hands up her arms to caress her throat. She did not draw
back, she could not for it was Brick, she knew it, he had come
at last and she leant against him, drifting off with him to all
the old wonderful sensations. He was the one she loved and
wanted and all was right and full of promise. There was
music far off and they were laughing together as they often
laughed, easily, lightly, ribaldly – but he was gone as
suddenly as he had come and she was desolate, for Kurt was
with her again and she wanted to kill Kurt Herlicht because
he was not Brick.

'Dance for me,' he whispered. 'The way you used to
dance.'

'That way?' Her voice sounded vague and far off but she
smiled at the misty shape of the man caressing her. She
didn't want to kill him so he must be Brick after all and she
laughed with excitement, giggling in a foolish happy way.
The music was soft and beguiling to match his voice, his
entreating voice, which was odd for Brick never entreated,
Brick O'Shea demanded.

'Dance for me,' he demanded – ah yes, this was Brick, 'the
way you used to dance.'

The music was possessing her; wonderful music, close and
compelling. She could not resist it any more than she could
resist him, and humming some half-remembered song she
moved sensuously and languorously, swaying to the haunting, enchanting music that drifted from somewhere. His
hands were on her and over her and she moved within them
slowly and happily. Her movements quickened with the
music that had a gipsy sound to it, or she fancied it did, and
she fondled her gipsy talismans, kissing the little shell with
soft and gentle murmurs. With an excited laugh she moved

from his arms to dance the way she had danced on the *May Queen* long ago, with the wide white rollers dashing against the ravaged old East Indiaman, a sixteen-year-old widow with an unexpected and unwanted child growing within her, terrified of the raw country to which she was bound and the man who was to become her employer. But she had loved Brick O'Shea from the first and had danced her way to him *via* one of the worst taverns on the Rocks, surviving it as she had survived all such squalid purlieus and men she hadn't loved, or only loved a little like Alister; danced and manoeuvred and shaped a path to grand houses and places, all to gain Brick's notice, to impress him, and finally to possess him for she did possess him and always would. She laughed with him in all the excitement of the old days when they had first lived together here, and their world had been full of promise and she wanted those days again in this beloved house and nothing must hamper her for she could refuse him nothing. She kicked off her shoes and her bare feet felt wonderful. She could not bear clothes on her hot moist body and flung them aside too, and loosened her long black hair and raised her arms above her head – was that a gipsy fiddle? The clapping of her hands made an insistent tantalising rhythm as her arms twisted and her feet moved in long-discarded but always remembered patterns, gipsy patterns, pagan patterns. Her arms rose higher and her movements grew wilder, joyous and abandoned. Her shawl trailed and tangled about her hips and she kicked it aside and danced naked as she had as a small child in London hovels for a coin, until her mother found her and dragged her off. She shivered with delight as Brick's hands moved over her bare shoulders and breasts and throat. He put his lips to her throat in well loved and remembered caresses . . . But there was something different about his touch as he held her breasts cupped, pressing them back and up. Her skin burned against his hands, such smooth hands which was odd for they did not seem like Brick's hands; then she forgot the difference, the oddness, for it no longer mattered. Her legs burned. She could barely stand. Blessedly he was holding her and drawing her off somewhere.

378

'Raunie . . . Ah, Raunie.'

There was something different about his voice too, not like Brick's voice, but it was too late, she could not resist for she was feeling intensely now and obeying his commands even though they were different demands from the pattern she had always shared with Brick. Her starved body was responding and all else was blotted out and she was reaching for him, clawing for him, drawing him in deeply and hungrily there in the quiet dim room that had always meant happiness to her. He spread her legs and lay between them, then came down heavily upon her as he always did for she could bear a great weight – Brick's weight – yet this was not the same weight, not quite. But she must not be interrupted, she dared not, absorbed in her husband, her lover . . . He opened her legs and closed them sharply to encircle his hips. She locked her heels hard in the small of his back and pressed to him with her thighs and his penetration was as sharp and exquisite as it had always been – yet not the same. Not quite. The same Brick, yet not quite. Her little whimpers of pleasure were flawed for it was Kurt within her, she knew it now, and there was bitterness and loss for she did not love Kurt Herlicht, she loved Brick. And there was something else, a voice thundering at her, a hated voice penetrating the warmth of physical completion.

'The wages of sin is death,' the voice thundered. 'The harlots and strumpets and evils of the earth shall be consumed by the flames of Hell.' Sweet Jesus! He was watching her, watching them both and she moaned, then jarred against her lover and all was spoiled. Nothing was the same . . . Sweet Jesus was her enemy . . . Alannah was her enemy . . . Moll Noakes was her enemy . . . The Duchess . . . How many others? She had many enemies. Abby had forsaken her. Jamie had deserted her. Her dwarf had deserted her – a bitter thing that. And Kurt? Kurt was making love to her . . . They lay breathing deeply together until the room was quiet and still around them.

'Sweet Jesus was in the room,' she told him.

He laughed softly at her foolishness. 'Go to sleep.'

'Have you sent him away? Send him away.'

'Be quiet now.' He yawned and turned over, away from her. She stared at the wall a long time until she heard his deep breathing. He even snored a little. She did not love Kurt Herlicht. She did not even like him, not really. But finally, she too slept.

When she woke she was alone. Kurt must have left very early for there was nothing yet of the hotel's morning bustle. He had managed, discreetly – when had Kurt not? – and quietly she assumed, to extricate her from her 'contretemps' with the Duchess; then, without committing the indiscretion of using her inner stairs, had escorted her formally and openly through her front door. She had wanted Brick through it all but he had been with her only because she had willed him there, conjured up by the fumes of champagne and the lights and music and the simple joy of feeling, of making love. She had opened doors she had meant to keep closed. They must not be opened again. She would keep her servants close – but she had no servants, she was alone. Then Abby must return. But if Abby refused to come? Then she, Raunie, must leave Bendigo . . . But where to run? To hide? She dragged herself from her bed to bolt and chain all doors and without bothering to dress sat by her window watching the road, alert for Kurt's knock, for it would come, she knew it. It was midday before she heard the rattle of the chain on the inner door and crept down the steps to hold herself against it as if to give it added strength against him, sensing his fist on the wood, seeming to feel his very breath.

'I know you're there, Raunie. You can't hide from me for ever. Or from the world.' Pressing against the door she closed her eyes and ears against him, keeping him out. 'You need me as much as I need you, you know it. Expect me tonight.'

She made no sound until she heard him go, then let out her breath in a tiny whimper of fear and hate – yes, hate – not only for Kurt Herlicht but for herself.

Gondola hated the manager, the director – *il padrone* – of the Irish Boy with a deadly and growing hatred. He had hated him at Birubi when he moved close to the mistress. He had hated him when he whispered with her or put his hand on her arm, hating him even more when he made the mistress angry. He hated him here in this town that he, Gondola, had come to regard as his own for it was as dry and hot and earthy as his native Campania. It seldom rained and he liked that for *Italiani* sank into misery in rain. He had not really liked Sydney, too close to the ocean; *Italiani* were not fond of the sea either – ah, the terrors of the voyage out! He prayed to the Blessed Virgin, even more importantly and with awe to the miracle-working S. Januarius, that the mistress would stay on in her house for if she stayed in Bendigo he, Gondola, stayed.

He smoothed the mutton fat into his raw and aching back, his flogged back, contorting his contorted self to do it. The wounds of his life were many, they never went away and the most he could do was smooth and soothe. But he had made friends in this town, Isaac for one. Isaac would not let him starve, Isaac was a Christian if a testy one. And he had found various small corners of the grain shed and stables where he could curl up and snooze in the heat of the day, knowing the mistress was in her big house on the other side of the wall but letting him be, knowing he would never desert her even if he wandered off now and then. Places where he could hide his battered pan and make a small fire to brew his coffee and cook his sausages or stew his minestrone and slice his peperoni or salami; everything begged or stolen when necessary from his countrymen in the Whipstick. They were his people, in a way his family, something of the old life when as a street child unwanted and ridiculed he had begged stolen or scrounged his meal of beans, a princely repast in that teeming world where he was known as *il gobbo*, the hunchback. Somehow he had survived the streets of Naples, that world of noise and crowding odours, before his next world of the *basso*, the underground cellar in the back street where he had been taken in by the Boldinis, circus tumblers, for his agility and quickness to learn. Twisted legs and hump or no, he did all they taught him and more for his limbs seemed able to stretch and move any way he wished them to go. He became an expert shot. He acted the comic as skilfully as any from the *commedia dell'arte* to become the pride of the

Boldinis as they wandered the Abruzzo and the Molise, then Lazio, and north into Venetia, sometimes joining travelling circuses as a troupe. He had not liked Venice, too much water and not a horse to be seen; besides, he had lost himself in its *calles* and the Boldinis had been forced to leave without him. That happened sometimes but he always found them again when he needed them. He had lost himself in Sydney too, stealing fruit and running from a constable on his quick short legs. When he had finally escaped the law there were no Boldinis, they had moved south. Miraculously, the mistress O'Shea had taken him in and he would do anything for her for she laughed with him not at him and let him carry her revolver with its carved ivory handle, a frivolous-looking fancy weapon but not a toy, ah no. Above all she let him ride her horses, the best, so he would be her groom, her servant, her slave if she wished it until death and beyond – he said prayers to many saints that it would be so. Naturally there were things about Birubi that he did not like: the son of the house kicked him but being kicked about the world was a part of life, besides, the son was of the mother, gipsy mother and son, and he understood that. He tolerated the master O'Shea, a busy gruff powerful man, a true *condottiere* to be respected but avoided. Yes, he tolerated the men of the O'Shea household, but Herlicht, *il padrone*, was hated with a deadly and lasting fire.

On the whole life was good – except that he was restless. He could not help it for a circus had come to town, not any circus he knew but, *magnifico!*, one with a menagerie. He liked working with beasts, they obeyed him and when he performed with them, in control and gained applause for his skills, he became as tall and straight and handsome as the most powerful in the land. He would never desert the mistress – well, not for long. She knew he would return to her. But what harm could it do to pay the circus a visit for a day? Two days perhaps? Three . . .

Raunie sent a boy to Eaglehawk but he returned to say he couldn't find the Wickler tent. She knew he lied; he hadn't even made the trip, just pocketed the coins. She sent another boy but still no Abby and she felt trapped by her own walls, drifting through the Easter days in a kind of languid squalor. The house became a stifling smothering fortress in which she turned with distaste from food but was forced to take in the trays; otherwise the girls left them for the dogs to fight over or to be smothered in flies. The world maintained a forbidding silence as if it were somewhere far off, only returning now and then in bursts of music and song, the rattle of carriages and pounding of horses. The long hot silences of the holy days of Easter were broken only by church bells. She knew she could not lock Kurt out for long and in desperate moments would open a window to breathe fresh air and let in the world, even if it were only the monotonous chug-chug of the engine bang in the middle of Pall Mall that never stopped except on Sundays. Once she saw movement amid the shrubs and saw Isaac stringing up vines, and the sight steadied her for it meant life was going on as usual. Isaac was as earnest a gardener as he was an Evangelist, though a taciturn one, moving head-down with a rough competence about his fruit and flowers. She saw him glance up now and then at her closed house and decided he might be worth a few questions and went down and out, startled by the bright sunlight, to admire his work, which made him grunt and glower – not an amiable old man at all.

'Thought you'd gone back to Sydney, Ma'am, house shuttered an' all.'

'You know I'm here so don't pretend otherwise. What news of the town?'

'If y' didn't lock y'self away you'd know it's a real Sodom an' Gomorrah with riff-raff crowding in for the racing an' dicing an' few for chapel or church. More strumpets to tempt decent men. An' half-naked dancers an' tumblers an' savage beasts out there at that circus—'

'A circus?' How isolated she had been. It was entirely possible Gondola had run off to join it.

'—with your own pub, the Irish Boy – an' I speak the truth, Ma'am, though y' won't want to hear it – the worst of the lot. Miners will gamble, hard to stop 'em, but your place is run for the nobs, with the working man prey to empty pockets an' his urge to fill 'em scarce tolerated or given the boot.'

'It's a man's own fault if he gambles.'

'But he's no chance at all where tables are rigged an' the police bribed.'

'Mind your tongue, you foolish old man. What would you know? You don't even belong to Bendigo.'

'Foolish maybe but not stupid. I'm not long up from Geelong, true, but I look an' listen but there's none so blind as will not see an' that's y'self, Ma'am, for y' don't really want to know, I reckon. But 'tis your pub an' you've a bad lot running it, all light an' colour out front to hide what goes on in back rooms, led by that foreigner making another pile out o' cock-fighting an' ratting, an' bull-terriers roughened an' savaged up for the bull-fighting out in the scrub for them who'll bet on anything outside the law. A grown man has a chance, Ma'am, but 'tis the reckless young 'uns that don't know what's being done to 'em. They've heard all about Eureka, see, our own little war over at Ballarat, over an' done with now, we know it, but they keep it going, young blades on the rampage with the police doing nought, palms greased or too scared to touch young nobs from the stations, as most of 'em are. They have a leader, a black-haired lad who knows where the police are an' how to dodge 'em.'

'Black-haired? Would his name be Jamie by any chance?'

'Never heard the name, Ma'am, all I heard was that he's a handsome wild sort o' lad, about seventeen.'

Her hands trembled as she picked up a creeper trail and held it out. 'I weary of idle chatter, Isaac.' She could scarcely speak. 'Nail this up then get about your work.'

It was the late start from Melbourne that had put them far behind. They had stood waiting, shivering a little in the chill early morning. The great coach was immaculate in its polished brass and harness and paintwork, the horses chafing to be off, the driver itching to take up the ribbons but the staff too busy and harassed to answer questions – how could anyone misplace a child? Details were vague except that the mother was near-hysterical. Whether her child had wandered off or just hadn't turned up or was ill or injured somewhere nobody knew, and after a time as they paced or stood on one foot then the other nobody cared, just blamed Cobb & Co., weary of this end-of-Easter and wanting home. But over one hundred miles through Keilor, Kyneton, Elphinstone and Castlemaine loomed before them before they could, literally, put their feet up, and no sign yet of moving off.

Brick paced too, but apart to escape garrulous matrons – did Mr O'Shea know Mrs Patchett of View Place? Regrettably, Mr O'Shea did not, he had been absent from Bendigo for some time. Then he must know Alderman Smythe, everyone knew Alderman Smythe. Indeed he did, Madam, he only wished he didn't, sending her off in a great huff. Brick seldom travelled by coach, he had lived his life in the saddle and sadly missed Glenora but speed was important. He regretted his wasted time in Melbourne, in and out of hotels Raunie might favour, but with no sign of her. He did not press for information for he hadn't really expected her to stay in the city; she would be in Bendigo, he was certain of it now – and with Jamie.

They could delay no longer, child or no child, the Company had a reputation for punctuality, besides, there was the mail. The tearful mother's baggage was being taken off when the child was swept along Bourke Street by exhausted grandparents, fuddled old darlings who'd confused arrangements and departure points. The child was undamaged and vigorous and enjoying the silly mix-up and mother and child were hated from then on. The sun was climbing as the post-horn sounded – no five-thirty arrival in Bendigo that night. They'd be lucky if they pulled in to the Shamrock by eight.

Jamie, trailing a reluctant Good Old Harry, rode into Bendigo from the south. Their last 'rest' had been on the outskirts of Castlemaine, at a notorious grog shanty clinging to the town's fringe of tents and mud-brick and slab-and-clay humpies of old Forrest Creekers, its back room a haunt of the best, and worst, poker players. He had done well, winning spending money which, as he'd rather anticipated, he'd been forced to collect at gunpoint. They moved out in a hurry too but it had been worth it for he was now independent enough to ignore Good Old Harry and his sulks and his digs at the Princess Royal and splurge happily at the Irish Boy, thumbing his nose at the town and at Kurt – after all, what was three thousand pounds? Flushed with shanty grog and his jingling pockets he didn't give a damn for Kurt Herlicht. He didn't give a damn for Constable Spencer either – warned out of Ballarat! Old Spencer had never gone that far before, Spencer was O'Shea's crony but this time he'd lost his woolly head and his temper.

'I'll have no such bestiality around Ballarat, Jamie O'Shea, from you or that gang you lord it over.'

'It's Ventril's "gang". And don't call me O'Shea.'

'Out o' this town, the lot o' you. And if your Pa don't like it he can talk it out with me. That's if we ever see him around these parts again.'

'And don't call O'Shea my father.'

'That's between the pair o' you. Out of Ballarat till I give you leave to come back. And the Ventrils won't like what I have to say to them either.'

He hadn't even cared much for the sport for there had been something rather childish in hanging a live goose by its feet, greasing its head and neck then riding full tilt to drag off its head. It was the brisk betting that had got him in. Run out of Ballarat! They wouldn't do it to him in Bendigo. Bendigo was 'home'.

With other riders they were caught up in a crowd of boys and youths, shouting at each other and kicking up the dust and enjoying punch-ups – of course, the scrappy tail-end of the Monday Procession. They could hear its racket ahead as it wound its roundabout way from Market Square through the town streets. How often as an eager boy had he struggled for a place amid the townsfolk, the crowd swollen by those in from the gullies: the Irish from Irishtown far down the

Bendigo Valley, the Cornish from Long Gully, Germans from Kilfenora and Italians from the Whipstick scrub, in to watch the rattling floats of commerce and industry and manufacture with the coats of the brewery horses polished shinier than their mirror-bright harness. He had tramped with the town youths to the beat of the big drum and sung with the German Band . . . He broke into a canter uncaring if Good Old Harry followed or not, dodging roadside vendors with their 'Toffees' and 'Muffins' and 'Pies all hot' and 'Rosy apples six a penny'. Posters proclaimed a circus and his heart gave a childish leap for the joys and excitement of his growing up; he had loved a circus since running off at the age of four to become a conjuror's assistant. Good Old Harry or not, he'd be in that tent tonight!

They were being drawn along in the flow of breakaway floats and vendors and hawkers and family parties making their way to the Fairground at the lower end of Pall Mall close by the Bridge, far enough from the most respectable streets (as they saw themselves) to escape the lights and noise but, to the horrors of Temperance, happily adjacent to the rash of pubs on the Mundy Street corners – the lock-up would be crowded already. They tethered their mounts and wandered the garish clutter of gipsy caravans and over-decorated tents, and carts topped by platforms where sideshow performers gave a tantalising taste of the delights within. Two sweating youths turned the windlass handle of the clanking merry-go-round while another played a concertina. Jamie shot behind a booth to dodge Mrs Malamud, still peddling her goats' milk and still, he swore, sporting a selfsame bonnet of his youth although the worse for its mastication by a long line of goats. Good Old Harry had disappeared and he felt a certain relief for he wanted free of Good Old Harry, at least for the moment. A blind man was going about with this hurdy-gurdy and his devoted wife, picking pockets. There was a Punch and Judy Show. There was a Hindu ice cream man. And the *pièce de résistance* of all fairs, the boxing tent fronted by a spruiker holding aloft the gloved hand of a cauliflower-eared bruiser.

'Who'll have a glove with Bully Butcher? He'll knock your

block off but put it on again real nice, that's his promise and his pleasure. Don't judge him by his powerful mawleys, folks, he's a reg'lar lamb. Who'll have a glove with Bully?'

Kurt had his fingers in surprising pies, no doubt of it! A character was feeding a squealing cat into an odd kind of contraption and drawing a string of sausages from the opposite end to wind the meat about his neck like a muffler. Great hilarity from the crowd. What looked like coloured water turned out to be an elixir to cure all ills, but even more miraculous was a magic paste to cure corns, bunions, dandruff and, it seemed, every other unfortunate disability of life.

'Rub it into your private parts, sir, give new vigour to your life – and your wife. A secret recipe handed down from the days of the Arabian Nights, a true love salve . . . ' – a series of violent knowing winks – 'and we all know how they made love in the days of howdahs and harems.' Muddling geography and social customs for the sake of dramatic alliteration.

An outraged husband knocked him off his platform for such talk before respectable women. A fight ensued as to whether to run the vile-mouthed creature out of town. The crowd left them to a decision and straggled over to Professor Baltasar's Variety Show where the Prof. strutted in a pretence of a South American uniform with an accent to match as he introduced with admiring leers a young *danseuse* a-glitter with spangles. The girl was slim and fair and very young with something about her that reminded Jamie of Lucy Marigold Finney – Lucinda Amora. Damn the girl, he didn't want to be reminded of her, a skinny scrap of a girl, not much good as a lover either for she had cried out, and oddly he heard that cry in his dreams, thrilling in a way yet disturbing; he had never been obliged to hurt a girl before. He had never been required to be careful; whores were paid for what you did to them. Sometimes they didn't even take your money. They liked young boys.

The circus proved a poor thing with a patched tent and those performers in evidence garbed in faded and much-mended costumes. But the children crowded in awe about the cages of a tired lion, chattering monkeys and strange birds. There was a troupe of performing dogs, and a morose seal. A repellent fellow from Calabria coiled snakes about his skinny neck. An Auguste with enormous mouth, red and white striped face and a bulbous nose cavorted in baggy pants pretending to push children off the merry-go-round. Another, with the true white-painted face of the clown, mimed nonsense, tormenting a made-up horse with rear legs so short and twisted the beast ambled lopsided to everyone's delight. Jamie stared at those twisted human legs for there was something familiar about them.

The horse stumbled off the makeshift stage and someone filled in with patter till a tiny figure flashed out in a woman's dress and female mask so grotesque a baby screamed in fright. The midget minced in a hotch-potch of knockabout comedy with a gin bottle. The crowd laughed itself hoarse and the tired little circus was saved. But a familiar voice cursed it and the world in a familiar rhetoric of doom.

'"Do not drink wine nor strong drink, thou, nor thy sons with thee."' A bible banged against wood in emphasis. 'Yahweh will have vengeance upon drunkards and scarlet women and fornicators and adulterers . . .'

Someone knocked Sweet Jesus off his platform as someone always did, and another argument ensued as to whether he should be bundled out of town with the depraved pedlar of potions. The busy fellow with the twisted legs, his ridiculous mask now topped by a flaming red wig, performed as a sort of female Roman gladiator, tangling in the net and tripping over the trident, tumbling on and off stage with a marvellous silent agility, struggling with an invisible opponent till the onlookers were beside themselves. They even forgot Sweet Jesus. A conjuror filled in till the funny fellow returned as a miniature knight in papier-mâché shield and paper armour that nevertheless clanked to a pair of false teeth used like castanets. The knight-of-old tumbled on and off a make-believe horse, fumbled with his lance, tripped over it, threw it in the air and retrieved it with a marvellous and practised skill. Falling and blundering about he struggled with his cardboard visor – more hilarity. He simulated choking within the stubborn helmet; worse, he went through the motions of suffocating with a terrible clank-clank of the awful teeth so real many believed in his imminent death and wide-eyed children began to cry. But he revived, to escape his make-believe horse turning on him to bite and chew and crunch the false teeth, finally tugging so hard at the helmet it fell off in the dust. The performer strode bare-headed to the front of his makeshift stage to bow right and left.

'Gondola!' Jamie shouted.

The midget froze, quivered, then ran. But Jamie was as swift, gaining on him for the crowd hemmed them in considering it all part of the act. Eyes wide, Gondola ran in terror, weaving and dodging, and would have escaped but for a muddy puddle of refuse on the edge of camp. Splashing his way through it he caught, full on, a bucket of waste tossed from a nearby tent that sent him sprawling head first into the mess. Jabbering his mixture of Italian-English he scrambled to his feet picking cabbage leaves out of his ears. The soaked papier-mâché sagged and bits of his paper costume sank into the mud. Jamie grasped the dwarf and held on.

'Talk English,' he roared. 'You know enough to tell me what you're doing in Bendigo besides playing the fool in a circus. Talk or you'll spend the night in the lock-up.' He shook the creature so violently that Gondola's teeth rattled as sharply as had the prop pair now glaring at them from the mud. Behind the dwarf's agitated gibberish Jamie caught one word – 'mistress'.

'My mother?'

What was Raunie doing in Bendigo – yet, why not? She loved the town. Though why had he, Jamie, not been told of her visit? 'You're a filthy mess and not fit to be seen. You'll clean up at the Royal then we'll ride out to the Irish Boy. If my mother's in Bendigo she'll be there or in her house.' Good Old Harry would be hanging about the boxing tent for hours but they each carried a key to his hotel digs. 'Stop screaming or I'll hold your head in the muck again. Pick up your feet, there. Pick up your feet!'

Chapter Nineteen

'YOUR SUPPER, Madam.' It was Emma knocking: Emma was always precise as to her 'madams'. 'Lamb chops, and peas and 'taters fresh from the garden. Fruit tart and cream. If you please, Mrs O'Shea?'

But Emma was swept in before a large woman who bade her place the tray and hurry back to her duties. 'Naa then, Mrs O'Shea, your victuals can wait a wee bit for they're hot and covered.' Hannah McKee folded her formidable arms. 'Y' didna expect me after all these years any more than I expected ye in Bendigo.'

'How dare you force your way in here.'

'I dare for I've things to say aboot the O'Sheas as well as aboot m'self that ye'll thank me for in the end – and it's Mrs McKee when ye speak to me as it was when ye emptied slops in ma first shakedown in this town. No more looking doon your beakie at me, m' gal. Your pub owes me brass which your tailor's dummy in there refuses to pay me. Twenty poonds an' nae a penny less.'

'I haven't twenty pounds to pay you.'

'Ye'll find it, for I helped build up your wee shanty to the place it is with m' cock-a-leekie an' stockpots an' m' potato scones an' baps an' all the rest I've served m' diggers for years past. Now it's fancy Froggy dishes in there nae matter how m' faithfuls beg for home cooking. He's driving 'em oot as he's locked me from m' kitchen so I'll follow m' diggers to other fields. But I need brass to start a lodging-house in Araluen.'

'Mr Herlicht handles such matters.'

'I dinna take orders from that bounder. I take orders from your ain mon.'

'You know he's not here.'

'An' more's the pity for he wouldna rob an old woman to pay for broken plates, already cracked an' used for dogs' dinners an' passing tramps; a fair mon, O'Shea, in the matter of wages no matter what else he may be. That German rogue discharged me, on your orders he swears.'

'Austrian – and I gave no such orders.'

'He's a liar then as well as other things. Never asking where I'll lay m' head an' me with m' gal run off with a coachman and m' guid father dead an' nae a body to care if I starve. Hannah McKee must look oot for herself an' will for I'm nae sorry to leave remembering the Irish Boy when it were a fair hostelry giving all a chance. Now it's spit an' polish and noise an' lights to cover up a wickedness o' gambling outside the law an' the police paid to turn blind eyes. And strumpets in the best rooms crooking their little fingers over m' tea an' pastries—'

'Deal with Mr Herlicht, I tell you.'

'—wi' the worst of 'em the same what travelled wi' us to the fields in '52 hand in glove with that German, her house too close to the Irish Boy for decency an' calling herself Costello when she's nae right to the name. Gi' me m' brass, I said, or I'll tell the mistress what you're really up to. If there's one thing I said, she won't have, it's interference in her son's life. She dotes on the lad.'

'Jamie? What do you know of my son?'

'What everyone else knows though they're too scared to speak up, for Herlicht can be a bad enemy. But I'm nae scared; I'm off when I get m' brass so I'll speak m' piece before I go. When Kurt Herlicht learned you were on your way here he packed your Jamie off to Melbourne care o' that young swell, Harry Ventril, the one they call Good Old Harry, under Herlicht's thumb he is, just where Herlicht will have your own lad before long. He sent them off so you wouldna learn what he's doing to him.'

'What is he doing to him?'

'Herlicht's using your lad to get his hands on the Irish Boy.'

'Everyone know Kurt Herlicht wants the Irish Boy, as

everyone knows it's not Jamie's to give or wager or use as collateral.'

'Which willna stop Herlicht, for the pub will come to your laddie in the end; we heard naught in the old days from his father but "Work it up, boy. Build it up. One day it will be yours."'

'You were always a gossip, Hannah McKee, a dangerous one at that. I won't listen to your rumours and alarms. Get out of my house.'

'Not wi'out m' twenty poonds. I'll have what's mine or stand here till the crack o' doom an' nae a minute less.'

She planted her feet and folded her arms like the rock of colonialism she was and Raunie knew she was beaten. She emptied her reticule on the table: twenty pounds, all she had in the world but for the five tucked under her mattress for emergencies and the woman wasn't getting that. Her jewels were gone except her wedding ring, and one inexpensive but treasured ring Brick had given her long ago, as a sort of joke on his part, but which, poor thing though it was, she loved to display on her right hand where it flopped about in all its vulgarity. Scrabbling among her few remaining trinkets she found it and slipped it on her finger with a gesture of defiance. Down to her last ring and Hannah McKee wasn't getting that either! She found a brooch she had never liked and pushed it across the table. 'That's worth more than twenty pounds. Take it or leave it.'

'Birmingham paste, I reckon.'

'Take it and go. Get out. *Out.*' Like a wild thing she pushed the woman through the door and slammed it on her. She grew wilder. As she was, in *déshabille*, she flew upstairs to her bedroom and down the steps to fling open the office door. The whole noisy brilliance of hotel life hit at her. Kurt sprang to close the hotel door and lock it; she had forgotten how quickly he could move. She noticed his hat and riding crop on his desk – evidently he had just come in. Or was he going out?

'I'm always glad of an eager woman, Raunie, but your timing is deucedly inconvenient. I've just come from the mine. A man injured—' She struck him violently across the mouth. His hand flew to his lips and his fingers came away red, cut by the ornamental ring. He staunched the blood with his handkerchief. 'Whatever your grudge it will have to wait. It's our busy time and no one knows I'm back yet.'

'If I scream I'll bring the whole hotel to the door.'

'I doubt it. You wouldn't be the first woman to get noisy in here. Besides, I choose my staff for discretion.'

'*Your* staff? This hotel is not your anything, Kurt Herlicht. It's mine. Everything is mine.'

He shrugged. 'What is it you want? I have things to do.'

'I want my son.'

'How many times have I told you, I don't know where he is.'

'You lie. You've lied all along.'

'What are you talking about?'

'You shouldn't make enemies of cooks and gardeners. You sent Jamie to Melbourne so we wouldn't meet, so that I wouldn't know that he's in your debt.'

'So that's it! You should have more sense than to listen to a vengeful Scottish hag and a bigoted old digger.'

'What do you want from Jamie?' she shrilled. 'What could you win from him but pin money?' Her voice cracked. He clapped a hand over her mouth and, gripping her tightly, pushed her ahead of him up the steps to her bedroom and slammed and locked the door behind them. He was a powerful man. 'There! Now yell your head off if you want to, no one's likely to hear and even if they do they know better than to intrude here. Do you really think I'm interested in Jamie's loose change? I can get that from any young fool in the Irish Boy's gaming-rooms, or in any town pub. If you must know, and it seems it's time to have it all out, I'm after highter stakes with your son.'

'If you're still hankering after the Irish Boy you can't have it. It's not Jamie's to bet and you know it.'

'I know he's under age but if he's desperate enough – and he's fast approaching that stage – he'll fall back on it, he must, for he has nothing else to bargain with. Did you really believe I'd let O'Shea keep that hotel? I've waited six years to get it back.'

'Brick won it fairly.'

'Maybe. But it was the salt rubbed in the wound that stung, the tossing of a pittance to run a hotel I once owned, and if I can't get at O'Shea direct then I'll get at him through his son. He's vulnerable where Jamie's concerned.'

'You're not getting at Brick through Jamie, you're getting at me. Jamie doesn't belong to Brick, he belongs to me. He's the only thing in the world that is truly mine. Because he wants to be.'

'Your precious son owes me three thousand pounds.'

Stunned, she could only stare. 'Three thousand . . . Impossible. How could it happen? Jamie gambles, of course he gambles, but he's never had more than three hundred pence at a time to play with; he comes to me for a miserable five . . . ten pounds, whatever I can spare. It's a game with him, part of his life with his young friends so they can brag about a few petty debts to make themselves feel reckless, grown-up, something to laugh over together.'

'Three thousand pounds is no petty debt and certainly no laughing matter. Jamie knows he's in deep, not only to me but to others, and if I were willing to wait others are not. Don't you understand that there are those waiting in the wings to hit at O'Shea through Jamie.'

'But the money I gave you? My jewels? What have you done with them?'

'Expenses.'

'What expenses?'

'Stop screaming.'

'You made love to me. That was part of your plan too, wasn't it, to keep me quiet and out of the way. To keep a hold over me—'

'*No.*' He stopped her, sharply. 'It wasn't quite killing two birds with one stone there, Raunie. I've always wanted you. I always shall.' He moved towards her but she backed.

'Don't touch me.'

'Get a hold of yourself. If this money wasn't owed me it would be owed somebody else. What started out as fun for Jamie, betting on his precious luck – his gipsy luck as he calls it – has become an obsession. He's lost his luck and he's scared; he's as superstitious as yourself and plays on in an attempt to get it back. Betting has become a fever with him. You can't stop it. No one can.'

'I'll never let you hurt him.' She was quiet and deadly. 'I'll have his IOUs and I'll have them now.'

'Jamie's IOUs are my trump card in bargaining with O'Shea. They'll be handed over in exchange for the Irish Boy, nothing less, or I'll let the world know of your son's rather nasty little transgressions around Ballarat.'

'Jamie has always played games. What of it?'

'He's been turned out of Ballarat for illegal sporting. It's doubtful if the town will have him back.'

'You're lying. You're always lying.'

'Not this time. And make no mistake, if it served my purpose I'd see he was banned from Bendigo. As for O'Shea, he's always been scrupulous over gaming debts; he'll settle my way, I'm banking on it. A matter of honour with him.'

'Who are you to talk of honour? I won't let you drag Brick into this mess so you'll settle with me. I'll have those IOUs or I'll – I'll—'

'What will you do?' he scoffed. 'You can do nothing so stop talking wildly. Look at yourself, you're half mad, you can't even talk sensibly. You drink too much. Look at yourself, I say.'

He swung her about, forcing her to look in the mirror. She didn't like what she saw. She did look half mad, dishevelled and desperate. Her eyes moved wildly about the room seeking a way out, an answer – and found one. At least a chance. She could threaten him, scare him, for she was an expert shot and he knew it. She wrenched herself from his hold, ran to the bed and groped under her pillow for her revolver, always there. Her fingers closed about it and she pulled back the hammer. At the sound he turned to face her. She raised the weapon.

'The Irish Boy will go to Jamie when and how Brick decides. I won't let you spoil my son's life – or Brick's. Certainly not mine. Give me those IOUs.'

'You're acting like the worst tragedy queen on your own stage. Stop making a fool of yourself and give me that thing.'

It was his off-hand manner that did it. It enraged her. She took a step forward to fire but through her fog of brandy, her love of Jamie, of Brick, her own pride and now humiliation she saw him lunge. Shock stunned her for an instant, just time enough for him to grasp the weapon and try to wrench it from her. She held on, struggling with him. His arms went round her, holding her so tightly and savagely against him she could not move, her arms pinned with the revolver jammed between their bodies. He was trying to prise her fingers from the weapon but she fought him, not only for Jamie and Brick but for herself, for this man had used her, not in the way he had used her son, still he had used her and being used was something she had never been able to bear. She struggled for the weapon. She felt a sudden crippling blow across the back of her hand and her arm jerked with shock and pain and her fingers moved involuntarily, pulling the trigger. The blast shocked them both. She staggered but his grip was like iron. Her vision blurred and all other sensations gave way to piercing clouding pain . . . a weakness . . . a falling away . . .

The revolver dropped to the carpet with a soft little plop and Kurt Herlicht stared at Raunie's still face as she lay limp in the crook of his arm, her eyes staring up unblinking. Blood trickled down the side of her face, now down her neck, seeping over the front of her *négligé*, staining the satin a dull lustreless red. Blood was on his jacket. Blood stained his waistcoat a bright red.

'Raunie,' he whispered, horrified. '*Raunie.*'

He shook her. Nothing. He tried mopping up the blood, dabbing at it but it was useless, she was bleeding her life away. God! He bent and listened to her heart. Nothing. He buried his face in her neck, moaning. He put his lips to hers, willing her to life then, revolted, recoiled; he was kissing a dead woman. He let her drop to the couch. It was clear the bullet had entered the side of her head and lay there somewhere. He could not bear her eyes staring up at him, they seemed to be following his every movement and he brushed them closed. She looked even more beautiful in death than in life. Raunie was dead – *dead*. And he had killed her.

Some reflex action made him pick up the revolver then drop it hastily. No, he had not killed Raunie. She had held the gun, her own revolver, and pulled the trigger as she struggled with him; somehow her hand had twisted back upon itself. It was an accident. But would anyone believe him? This town hated him and would see him hanged. The police were paid to support him but would they in the end? He could not depend on them. Hannah McKee would speak against him. Isaac the gardener. Certainly that wretched Italian buffoon with the absurd name. O'Shea would never believe him. Jamie most certainly would not. He stood staring down at the beautiful dead face and the bleeding body; damn him for a fool for ever touching her again. He paced, wiping his sweating hands then paused – was that the door-knocker? He listened closely. Silence. But of course the sound had come from the hotel; the night was so clear and still that sounds drifted clearly. Get hold of yourself, Herlicht, and think. *Think!* Suicide . . . Why not? A woman brooding behind closed doors with the added mystery of why she had come at all and alone? Trouble with her husband – few would doubt that. Drinking too much? They would believe that too. A moody unhappy woman grown unstable, making herself ill on brandy, so desperate she had killed herself in a fit of depression – would they really believe it? Perhaps. Somehow it was not foolproof, not quite sound, not *final* enough. Besides, he had handled the gun.

Robbery? That was better. It would be entirely believable for it happened all the time: old lags wandering the town, roistering drunken youths on the rampage, preying on women alone. She had resisted the theft of her jewels (the town knew she possessed fine gems with only himself aware of their actual whereabouts), had struggled with the thief and the gun had gone off – his or hers it did not matter – as had actually happened, only the principals were different. Robbery – that was it! A foolproof motive with no one to dispute it.

First, to dispose of the gun, for if he left it lying about it would imply the intruder was a complete fool in forgetting to hide the weapon. He would throw it out in the bush or, easier still, toss it in the water-butt in the yard where it would not be found in a hurry and even if it were would give credence to the robber theory. He moved quickly, pulling out drawers, scattering clothes and knick-knacks and cushions, his mind working on his alibi. No one had seen him return to his office, he was certain of that. His staff knew he had ridden out to the O'Shea mine to settle a dispute so there was every chance they would accept his explanation of being about O'Shea's business all afternoon: he had diverged to inspect the abandoned theatre destined for renovation and had spent time there over the plans. He had ridden on to the allotment offered as site for a new O'Shea store . . . a perfectly feasible explanation of his movements and no one could prove he had been in town at the precise moment of the shooting – no one. All he need do now was ride out of town by back roads then ride in again, giving time for Raunie's body to be found – as it soon must be. Luckily, no one seemed to have heard the shot above the noisy comedy routine in the hotel; in any case the explosion had been muffled. He wrapped the revolver carefully in his handkerchief and stowed it in his pocket. He could not risk the front entrance so he must go by the back way even though there was a moon glow. He peeped from the window. The yard was dimly lighted by a lantern and a couple of bracket flares flickering over the shafts of drays and carts. Otherwise it was deserted for the play was but half over and the stableboys, always a bunch of wags, would have slipped off to catch a glimpse of the entertainment. Almost everyone would be watching the play. He must creep through the back garden to the back gate and, keeping to the wall, work his way round the deserted hotel yard, disposing of the revolver on the way, saddle his horse and away. It had to be so. He had no choice.

He stiffened. A door had opened and closed in the house – the back door. He remembered it was usually left unlocked for the maids to bring the trays. Two sets of footsteps, the heavy steps of men, one set with a curious unevenness . . . Whoever they were they were wandering about downstairs. The steps paused at the bottom of the stairs . . . No time for him to slip into an empty bedroom; besides, bedrooms were likely to be searched. The steps were on the stairs. Luckily, there was a high cupboard just outside the room large enough to conceal a man. The steps were ascending. He moved swiftly. In pulling the cupboard door closed upon himself he glimpsed Jamie O'Shea dragging the Italian, Gondola, behind him. Almost afraid to breathe, Kurt pressed himself against the wall as he heard the two pause at Raunie's bedroom door.

Only stragglers had wandered Bendigo's streets as Jamie, gripping Gondola before him on his horse, rode from Macrae Street to the Irish Boy. From time to time he slapped the dwarf for wriggling or moaning in a way scarcely human. Whether the wailing was peculiar to his race or even his deformity, Jamie didn't know nor did he care, for the hunchback had always repelled him. Even so, he hadn't let Gondola from his sight or grasp as he tipped pails of water over him, then forced him into an assortment of garments purloined from the Princess Royal: a shirt and breeches too big for him tied about his waist with a belt, and boots belonging to the youngest stablehand around. He had gained nothing more from persistent questioning than that servants and mistress had come round by steamer to Melbourne – conveyed in Gondola's usual dramatic mime – then caught the coach to Bendigo, two . . . three . . . more weeks ago, holding up doubtful fingers. The fool didn't seem to know much about time either, and Jamie slapped him again in temper and frustration – why didn't Raunie teach him English? He had always considered the creature half mad but now he was inclined to judge him deliberately obtuse.

The hotel was well-lighted, and its restaurant and concert hall crowded, judging by the great gusts of laughter drifting out, but the O'Shea house boasted only one light and that in Raunie's bedroom, or the room she always used. No outside lamps. Anger had long taken over from surprise for he had mixed feelings about meeting his mother. Had she come chasing him – or Kurt Herlicht? The query nagged for why had Kurt not told him of her visit? He had always admired Herlicht for his success, his bravura, his power, but he had never liked the idea of the man's association with his mother. Further peals of laughter, then a lull and a small sharp sound like a revolver shot . . . It had seemed to come from the house but he was on edge, it could only be a trick of distance, a part of the stage performance. After all, Raunie's presence need have nothing to do with Kurt, or even with himself, it could be that she had left O'Shea at long last. The idea soothed him and, hauling Gondola after him, he picked his way to the front door, cursing the dark and the shrubs and vines – why hadn't she set a gardener to work? Tripping in his voluminous clothes Gondola entangled himself in vines and, cursing, Jamie was forced to pause to set him free with a cuff over the ears for his awkwardness. He knocked. No answer. Peering through the glass he saw the hall dimly lighted from the upstairs glow but the place seemed deserted. Odd that, for even if his mother were at dinner in the hotel where was Abigail? Cursing the stumbling Gondola trying to keep pace, he picked his way round the side of the house, impatiently brushing aside the miniature jungle of shrubs and trees. More tangling in vines, more cursing, more cuffs. The back door was unlocked, so like Raunie, always careless, as were the servants she employed. All was quiet in the house, even so he had the odd feeling that his mother was here, brooding, drinking perhaps – ah yes, Raunie drank too much. He wandered the downstairs rooms – nothing. Perhaps she had fallen asleep up there in her room, yet he knew he was being ridiculous; Raunie asleep at this early hour? But something was wrong about the house . . . there was no sound. Dragging Gondola after him he climbed the stairs to pause in the doorway of his mother's bedroom.

It was a shambles. Exactly as if a thief had blundered about searching for loot. And then he saw his mother. She lay on the couch as if asleep but her body seemed twisted somehow . . . Then he saw her face. It was bleeding and strange and his hands went limp, freeing the resentful unhappy Gondola to sink to the floor and stare about him, bewildered. Jamie blundered forward to pause, shivering, for her face was covered in blood. Blood stained her clothes. He sank on his knees beside her.

'Raunie.' It grew to a wail. '*Raunie*.'

She was dead, he knew it. Shot through the head, he knew that too – so the shot had come from here after all. He stumbled to his feet and with an odd little run fumbled with the doorkey, wrenched open the blue door and hurtled down the steps to the hotel shouting one word over and over: 'Dead! *Dead!*'

Gondola crouched just inside the door staring at his mistress, angry at having been dragged here in such ill-fitting garb for even when he played the fool he did not like to look or feel like one. He was missing his evening performance too! At first he thought his mistress asleep but there was something strange about her for in all the noise she had not moved. Then he saw the blood, and remembered the word the young master had shouted: *dead*. He knew what it meant – *morto*. His mistress was dead and his world fell apart and he was again nothing, less than the deformed child abandoned on the streets of Napoli to steal and struggle and fight for his existence. Since his mistress had taken him in he had not needed to fight. She beat him, yes, but spoiled him too, laughing with him so wonderfully he never had to wonder why they laughed together. Gondola amused her, she said, and she liked to be amused. But she was not laughing now and he must fight again, this time to avenge her. It was *la morte!* Someone had killed his mistress. A sound like a distant buzz of bees came from the hotel and he scrambled to his feet. Footsteps below – no, on the stairs behind him and he swung about in time to see a shadow, a shape, disappear down the house stairs. The shape of a man, Kurt Herlicht, *il padrone*, his mistress's murderer, he knew it! A stampede now on the stairs leading up from the hotel office. They were coming. He, Gondola, could do no more for his mistress here, others would take care of her now. He leaped over the banister to land in the hall below with every bit of his acrobatic skill, upright and firm. He was very strong. People were crowding into the room above but soaring over other voices was the agitated, almost childish, wailing of the young master. He sounded as if he were going mad.

With tremendous speed and agility Gondola ran out of the back door, through the small garden then the kitchen garden and orchard and out of the back gate into the yard, still empty of human life. No sign of *il padrone* but he knew where he was and what he was about – saddling a horse to make his escape. He must not escape. Gondola tightened his belt, kicked off his ill-fitting boots, and on bare feet hardened from childhood on the cobbles of Neapolitan streets padded silently between the carts and drays to find the stable doors closed – of course they were closed, *il padrone* had closed them not wanting to be seen. He peeped through the cracks, breathing in the warm odour of close-packed and restless horseflesh. There seemed only two lanterns burning, one on the back wall of the stables, the other close enough to make out *il padrone* in a stall saddling the big black stallion he, Gondola, regarded as his own, and for this he hated the man even more fiercely. Horses feared fire so he would not harm the beasts. He loved horses, he knew all about them, they were his friends, he had worked with them all his life so they must be stampeded to safety – but a stampede so sharp and sudden it could not be halted or evaded.

The oil flares above his head over the doorway burned fiercely. Climbing on a box he took them down and stood balanced, one in each hand. With swift savage kicks of his powerful feet he broke open the doors and, torches held high, ran swiftly and surely, as only he could run, between the stalls towards the back wall where a window gave on to the lane behind the hotel – his escape. Halfway down he shouted, '*Fuoco! Fuoco!*' waving the torches in wide dramatic arcs in a terrifying display of flame. *Il padrone* stood transfixed, stunned, with his horse half saddled. But the horses came to terrified life as the dwarf ran about lighting everything that would burn – straw, hay, wood splinters, blankets. In the tight confines of the stall the stallion fought to free itself like the mad beast it was become, rearing and kicking out so violently that wood shattered and splintered. The horse crashed down on the man imprisoned with him, hurling him against the wall with a thud that sickened. *Il padrone* made no sound as the horse plunged on him again and again, trampling him under its maddened hoofs before it beat through what remained of the stall to join and lead the kicking rearing terrified horseflesh rushing together to shatter the stable doors in a mêlée of splinters and palings. They thundered as a body across the yard, turning over drays and carts and all else blocking their path. Gondola dashed the lanterns against the splintered doors to make an added blaze. The stables burned fiercely in the warm dry atmosphere with the shattered doors a flame barrier. Gondola knew that once it was ascertained the horses were safe no one would – or could – try to enter. He heard shouts and alarmed voices but did not look back as he climbed out of the window and dropped soundlessly into the narrow lane. He would hide and steal food, then a horse, and ride off somewhere, anywhere, it did not matter. The necessary, the important, the wonderful thing was that the hated *padrone* was dead. He, Gondola, had avenged his mistress.

The coach had been so dogged by mishaps all day that by evening no passenger cared for further explanations or apologies or to bother his or her head over the whys and wherefores, craving only the lights of Bendigo, and home. All were silent, stunned, yet in a way oddly resigned. At Kyneton a young matron, very much *enceinte*, had been taken ill and must be settled at the inn with relatives and a doctor found for Cobb & Co. had a reputation to maintain. Amid the hubbub the mischievous child of the morning had wandered off again looking for bullseyes and of course had lost herself. The passengers began taking out their aggravation on its mother until someone found the brat down a lane stuffing herself with sweetmeats and attempting to do the same to a stray cow. A cockroach had been found floating in the soup of a hastily prepared meal . . . the water was upsetting delicate digestions, as all digestions were by now . . . there was an argument over seating arrangements . . . someone had mislaid a valise . . . and so on, and so on.

Misfortune smiled upon itself. There was, it was agreed, something almost sinister about the day to the point where a clergyman talked earnestly of the Devil and demons, even of witchcraft. The road through the Black Forest seemed as bad as it had ever been. They felt every jolt, or insisted they did, finally hitting a stump that should not have been there, leaving a wheel so badly twisted they must await a wheelwright, who was out hunting, so another hour was endured before he could be found. The joker of the trip, for there was always one, tried to cheer them with the reminder that no one had been injured in the swerving and rocking, and was snubbed for his optimism. The coach became a hated thing to the point of hysteria and it was around ten o'clock when the less than immaculate vehicle entered Bendigo, its weary exasperated passengers rousing only long enough to point out a glow in the sky to the north-east. Cobb & Co. drew up to the Shamrock on this bizarre Easter Monday night to find the place deserted but for a couple of harassed maid-servants. It was the final straw. They had expected a welcome, concerned enquiries, even a show of sympathy, certainly cabs lined up, but Pall Mall was empty of human life. Brick went seeking a mount to find only an elderly porter.

'McDermott! Where is everyone?'

The man peered at him. 'Why, it's Mr O'Shea – it *is* Mr O'Shea, isn't it? My eyes aren't what they were—'

'Stop chattering, man. Is the town sleeping off a drunken orgy?'

'They're all out at the fire, sir, to see if they can help. Some swore it was the Irish Boy—' His eyes widened. 'But that's your hotel, sir.'

'Order a horse saddled. There must be one stableboy left.'

'There's nothing in the stables but a good-for-nothing hack, Mr O'Shea. The gentlemen took everything.'

'Then saddle what you've got. Hurry.'

It was indeed a poor mount and could not be spurred on so they did no more than canter along streets empty but for little knots of people in nightshirts peering over gates at the enflamed sky – it was the Irish Boy right enough. He clambered off where drays were rolling up with their barrels of precious water in a race to claim their five-pound prize. The fire-cart was doing its best from its canvas tank, and a long line of sightseers and locals passed full buckets from the well. But the stables were burning so fiercely no one could get close and they were concentrating on saving the hotel proper. Groups in evening dress stood exclaiming and getting in each other's way or just staring at the garish glow of stables and lean-tos. Distracted neighbours ran about, fearful of their own properties. In the mêlée one voice soared; Sweet Jesus, with his uncanny sense of being at the core of events, bellowing his warnings of Hellfire and the wrath of God as punishment for unspecified sins. Brick dragged him off his perch and thrust a bucket into his hand.

'Stop bellowing and join the line there. Many's the meal you've had at the Irish Boy so get in and help save it.' He caught the arm of a man he recognised, a carter who supplied the hotel with wood and coal. 'Where's my manager?'

The man turned a startled sweating face. 'Why, it's Mr O'Shea.'

'Where's Herlicht? You know Kurt Herlicht, my manager?'

'Ain't sighted him, nor has anyone else. I'm told he rode out to your mine this afternoon and ain't come back yet. But he can't miss the glow of this wherever he might be. No hope of saving the stables as y'can see but the horses are safe, all over town by now. Got everyone out of the hotel, just in case, but it seems right enough. The house is safe too.' Burch, the Irish Boy's head waiter, lumbering by with a bucket, stopped dead.

'It's Mr O'Shea!'

'You're not seeing a ghost, Burch.'

'Have they told you yet—'

'Told me what? I've only this minute arrived after a rotten trip from Melbourne. Let me through, man. If my wife's not in the hotel she'll be in her house. I'm surprised she's not out here in the thick of this.'

'Then you'd better listen, Mr O'Shea, for it's to do with your wife. The police are with her in the house.'

'The police? Good God, man, why?'

'She's been shot, sir.'

'*Shot*? Then let me through.'

'But she's dead, sir. Mrs O'Shea has been shot dead.'

Bendigo gossiped and gloated over rumours along with the known facts of the double tragedy: Mrs O'Shea, who had been staying at her house adjoining the Irish Boy but had seldom been seen about town, had been found by her son, shot through the head. Suicide had been discounted as no weapon had been found in her hand or close by, and robbery became the firm theory; although no windows or door had been forced it was known the back door was left unlocked at that hour. Besides, according to her maid arrived in from Eaglehawk, jewellery was missing. Mrs O'Shea's former maid, Dulcima, would be questioned, no doubt of it, as would Isaac the gardener, and Hannah McKee who had taken the woman's evening meal, all four assuming the status of martyr-culprits in the town's need of a solution. On the same evening, dramatically and rather mysteriously, Kurt Herlicht, the Irish Boy's manager, a man mourned by none but a few loose women, had been burned to death in a fire at the Irish Boy stables. His charred and mangled body found next day displayed terrible injuries apparently inflicted by the horses as they stampeded, and even the man's worst enemy wished him unconscious at the time. How the fire had started was the big mystery but there were those who insisted that Gondola, Mrs O'Shea's groom – now disappeared – was for ever lighting fires about the yard and stables and out-houses, moreover he hated *il padrone* as he called Herlicht, and with good reason for the man beat him often and savagely. Alas for an easy solution, it seemed the dwarf had been with Jamie, Mrs O'Shea's son, all evening. Perhaps, simply, a lantern had been knocked over . . . perhaps . . . perhaps . . . There were no answers and it was doubtful if the inquest would provide any. No weapon had been found though extra police had been called in. Bendigo remained agog.

407

It proved a difficult and tedious inquest of wordy speculation: on the evening of Easter Monday, April 25th, 1859,
Mrs O'Shea had been found shot dead in the bedroom of her
house adjoining the Irish Boy Hotel by her son Jamie
O'Shea – or Lorne, as he preferred to call himself – upon his
riding into town from his lodgings at the Princess Royal
Hotel in Macrae Street with the Italian called Gondola, Mrs
O'Shea's groom, since disappeared, no doubt as a foreigner
and unable to speak English terrified of the event. Suicide
was disposed of for no gun had been found and it could only
be assumed that either Mrs O'Shea had struggled with the
intruder, and the gun, probably her own, had turned back
upon herself, or she had been shot by the unknown thief,
perhaps in panic after robbing her of her jewellery of which it
was known she possessed much. In the absence of evidence
to the contrary the coroner pronounced death by shooting by
an unknown assailant.

As to the death by injury and fire of the Irish Boy's
manager, Kurt Herlicht, fires could start easily and at any
time in warm dry weather in stables and outhouses, and it
was assumed that in the absence of attendants – the
stableboys would be severely dealt with over their absence –
Herlicht had been unsaddling his horse on his return from
an afternoon spent about O'Shea's business. Obviously,
however the fire had begun, it had been frighteningly swift
and had panicked the horses who in their stampede had
inflicted terrible injuries upon the victim rendering him
unconscious for no cries had been heard – again, his cries
could have been drowned by the intermittent but uproarious
laughter from the hotel theatre. All this, unfortunately, was
supposition in the absence of facts. Mr O'Shea had been on
the road by Cobb & Co. at the time. Though no one was
completely satisfied there was no evidence to the contrary
and there could be no other finding but accidental death; in
any case officialdom was relieved to dispose of such unfortunate events. Bad for trade. Even so, the double tragedy
hung in the air for months. And, when other topics of
conversation failed, for years to come.

*

It had seemed natural to Brick to bury his wife in a town in which she had always been happy. Bendigo had turned out *en masse* for the funeral, most from a morbid interest in a woman they knew only by hearsay but a victim of gory tragedy, others because of O'Shea himself – the staff of the Irish Boy, of his store, officials from his mine. Brick had ordered a simple burial but the young cleric was awkward over the words, clearly uneasy, not only because the O'Sheas were a family he knew only through district folklore, and that lurid, but by the presence of a fringe of lavishly dressed but disreputable women flaunting themselves at solid burghers, and the bellowing and shaking of fists by the fanatic they called Sweet Jesus from his box under a nearby tree surrounded by the town's human debris – no doubt of it, the creature belonged in an asylum! Yet there were those who considered the old vagrant's curses rough justice; Sweet Jesus bent on having the last word with his erstwhile enemy.

Young Jamie O'Shea-Lorne, the woman's son by a former husband, stood silent and withdrawn despite his frenzy at his mother's death, bearing the ceremony with a dignity that stopped ribald remarks if not gossip. A young reprobate, a larrikin, remembered by old identities for his wild goings-on when growing up, in trouble most of the way but a handsome stylish larrikin and it was known he had adored his mother. Though father and son had little to say to anyone and less to each other, Brick let Jamie be, for the youth, as much as he himself, was finding it almost impossible to accept that a woman who had been so vividly alive, grasping at life with both hands, was dead. Bendigo would go back to its daily living – the crushers were always there – but he and Jamie must live with the shock of her death. The circumstance of it would become unimportant: what was important was that Raunie had been a large part of his life, abrasive, provocative, a tantalising torment yet an unforgettable one from his first sight of her in his kitchen at Erins Pride; pregnant and wretched about it, hostile to him as her employer and in her eyes exploiter, nursing her burnt fingers, tossing back her beautiful hair at him, proud, wilful, and sly for she had manipulated him along with so many others. But he had lived with those traits as he had lived with the pull of her beautiful body that had brought him back to her again and again, a body he had resisted for so many years to finally enjoy as she had enjoyed his, for he knew that in her own way she had loved him.

The weather held. It was a fine evening as he rode to the Burial Ground. Some day perhaps he would talk to Jamie of his certainty about Gondola's part in Kurt Herlicht's death but now it was let sleeping dogs lie. He had searched town for the dwarf but without success. He had ridden out to the gullies, even to the Whipstick, the strange matted growth that sheltered wood-cutters and charcoal-burners and miners, even small farms on land wrested from the Whipstick mallee, and strange trees, a cross between gum and wattle, hugged by dense scrub, everything so festooned and entangled by vines and creepers that one could not see ahead and the only space was the sky above the thick lacy treetops. Gondola had vanished, yet Brick did not really believe he had left town. The horses from the Irish Boy stables had all been rounded up and no one else had reported a horse stolen, so his hunch was that the dwarf was hiding till interest slackened, awaiting his chance to steal a mount and ride out blindly, somewhere, anywhere. Meanwhile, where would he feel secure awaiting his chance? Beside someone he had loved.

Raunie's grave awaiting its headstone lay in the shelter of trees and shrubs. Nearby was a wooden shed containing grave-diggers' tools, conceivably with a loose paling or two for Gondola to squeeze through and shelter from the night chill. Brick did not have to investigate for he almost tripped over the hunchback curled up by Raunie's grave, asleep. The dwarf started up to crouch back, rubbing his eyes.

'The police will soon pick you up here,' Brick warned. 'There's an empty shepherd's hut out of town on the Echuca road where you can hide till I collect you on my way north. If you're discovered I leave you behind, remember that. There'll be blankets and food enough for some days so lie low. Understood?' Gondola nodded. The master had always been a harsh man but this was *il destino*. He had watched his mistress's burial from a fork high up in a nearby tree and he felt safe beside her grave, except that it grew cold of a night. Besides, he belonged to the master now, to the young master too, he supposed, for the mistress had loved the boy. 'Follow me,' Brick beckoned. 'Not a sound now.' There was no one about but he took a blanket from his saddle-bag and threw it about the hunchback's shoulders, more for concealment than for warmth. He found some bread and cheese. 'Mount behind me. Up with you.'

With one swift movement Gondola sprang to O'Shea's saddle. Wolfing the bread he drew the blanket tight around him. He had food and warmth and, when the master came to collect him, perhaps a horse of his own. He bit deeply into the lump of cheese. He was content. With a horse of his own he would have everything.

Chapter Twenty

THE MORNING was misty and chill as Brick and Jamie rode out of Bendigo with full waterbags, rifles and rations, a spare horse, and Isaac's cart bearing Abigail Luff and her boxes. Brick had offered to send her to Melbourne and round by steamer to Sydney, even to find her a place there, but no, she would stay with her kin for good or ill. He and Luff had always been at war but the woman had been devoted to Raunie so he gave her money enough for some independence knowing full well she would squander it on her tent family. She sat stiffly erect beneath her ancient parasol without a word or a backward glance as Isaac took the turnoff to Eaglehawk and the Wicklers.

The day was warming up as they rode north. A mile out they picked up the wary, chastened and by now hungry Gondola, who revived enough to perform a little dance of triumph at the sight of a mount of his own. Jamie made no comment at the dwarf's reappearance, indeed the boy seemed quite unconcerned, even unaware of what went on about him. They would be three weeks on the road, longer if the tracks were muddy or the horses poor or tiring. Brick did not really mind for it would give him time, perhaps, to come to terms, if flimsy transient ones, with the unhappy youth riding beside him. He had half expected Jamie to run off once the funeral was over but it was as if shock had dulled the boy and Brick let him be. Meanwhile he mopped up Herlicht's life in relation to himself, for he had uncovered grasping, surprising even to him, corners of the man's life: underhand business deals, prostitution, illegal gaming and sporting – even making a few extra shillings shuttling beaten-up pugilists between country fairs and Melbourne shows – loans at exorbitant interest, gold-buying with every cheating device known on the fields, and Brick joined the long line of creditors lining up for the estate. As for his own affairs, his first act was to settle, if reluctantly, Jamie's debts for Raunie's death had altered things. Jamie was his now and it must be a clean slate for the boy as well as for himself. It was the end of an era. Bendigo had served its purpose, Bendigo was in the past and to that end he went from broker to lawyer to agent, all O'Shea property to go under the hammer, even the Irish Boy – particularly the Irish Boy. The legal firm of Willow, Brunt and Haggerty, secure amid new cedar desks and leather chairs, would be kept busy for months, even years to come. He would make a bequest to the town but no fountains or memorial tablets or monstrous effigies: a clinic, a school, a crèche, the civic fathers to choose. No one queried for no one really wanted argument or even answers: the O'Sheas were moving out and on and there was a certain relief in the fact. The O'Sheas had never been respectable – interesting, vigorous, bringing life-blood to the town in the past but respectable, never. Bendigo was building schools and a new Town Hall and planning more fire-brigades and parks and fine residences behind discreet hedges – no more dirty linen in Bendigo's market-place! Bendigo was taking itself seriously in preparing to enjoy its riches.

The road to the little settlement of Echuca on the Murray was flat, straight and dry and they would reach the river by evening. Tomorrow would be another day of flat easy riding to Deniliquin and Taylor's where O'Shea had friends and business contacts. They would turn north-west to Narriah – Narriah station was to go – then north, crossing the Billabong Creek to Hay and Booligal and following the Lachlan to Oorin. Oorin and its out-stations would stay.

It was not until they touched the familiar country of the Lachlan that Jamie roused to bag 'roos for fresh meat and chase emus for the sport of it. Brick noticed him searching for emu eggs which seemed to presage him taking them back to Hennessy, but he left well alone, it was too early to probe. He stood in the doorway of Joey's rough home-to-be, its walls lined with pasted-up newspapers – always something to read, Hackett growled, and when were the young'uns due, he didn't want to lose that job in Gippsland, he could do with some rain for a change. Brick narrowed his eyes towards the desert wilderness of the Darling, his nightmare . . . He had spoken little of that time for he had grown whole again, a slight limp and no worse – he had been lucky. Besides, it was a strange fragmented episode, a blur of a dream-time, leaving him uncertain even now how it had come about, a vagueness as to what had prompted him besides the obvious of roping in wild horses for the stations. Perhaps a need for action, for violent movement in an effort to escape Alannah's haunting eyes – she had not wanted him to leave her. He had set out on a whim, some impulse for he had never risked crazy country before without a plan, to cross the Willandra Billabong towards Hallows station and the Darling country. He had made another error in taking only Yalgu, a fine horseman but a sullen Black, unused to white men and so resentful of them that Brick, like all good bushmen, never let the fellow behind him with a spear. Still, he had thought to ease him out; in any case he meant to pick up other Blacks at Hallows. But he had never reached Hallows station. Time had lost itself as he wandered, drifting, one camp as another, one holding-yard as the last, one vista as the next, a vast endless sea of land that seared the soul, as the back country had appalled the early explorers, kangaroos and emus immobile in the static desolation of heat, only an occasional flock of galahs rising for no apparent reason to shatter the silence of everlasting scrub and sand and rubble and stones and saltbush and red ochre earth and ti-tree and the marvellous mulga that sustained stock in drought, and the shock contrast of swamps and lagoons after a wet, festering and odorous under the merciless sun. Time had become nothing, losing itself as he was lost, hypnotised perhaps as he had never been before by distance and isolation and the terrifying silence of the unchanging terrain.

Even so, the desolation had satisfied some immediate need in him, an urge to people its nothingness and give it substance and being by mastering the mobs of wild horses that appeared in clouds of dust on the skyline like Mongol steeds across the steppes, racing after their leaders in a restless savage search for water and feed, arrogant wary beasts adapted to their environment and cunning in their survival. Fired by their beauty and pride he had chased them, for ever it seemed. He should have anticipated a maddened stallion for it happened sometimes; perhaps the gruelling heat, or thirst, perhaps his own loss of firm control in breaking it in, perhaps his abstraction of mind immersed in mirages of blessed water. Perhaps time and the land itself had dulled his reflexes, he did not know, but the unity of man and beast had dissolved causing the brumby to panic and Brick's foot to catch in the makeshift stirrup and the maddened horse to drag him over the murderous fire of hard-baked ground, battering and crunching his body until mercifully releasing him to lie, unable to move and near death, seeing through dim burning eyes the ominous dust-storm building up and when it hit almost burying him alive. Yalgu had absconded – he should have anticipated that too – perhaps through a superstitious fear of the dead thing Brick had appeared. He had lain in agony, near to death and madness, his leg smashed, no doubt his ribs, and his tongue swollen from thirst. If he tried to stand he knew he would never walk again. Then the miracle of Tubbul stumbling by, a Black probably of the Bakandji tribe wandered from his familiar Darling. Tubbul had half carried, half dragged him to vegetation and a makeshift shelter to lie in fever, only leaving him to hunt close by and fight the wild horses at the waterholes for the foul water, otherwise he would surely have died. Tubbul had brought rotten flesh, brushed off the maggots, and they had eaten it half raw. He brought water fouled by the same horses Brick had hunted, slimy to his lips, but he drank it, his stomach in revolt. Brick chewed saltbush so dry it powdered in his fingers and on his lips but he had survived. He had even tried to set his own leg – or had he? – for memory had dimmed while he drifted through some tormenting nether-land, lost in haunted dreams where Alannah's face came and went, accusing, and he did not know why she accused. Raunie accused . . . Barbara – even Barbara was there . . . all three emerging with some green paradise of foaming seas and cooling shade and lush foliage until the shock of reality when he cursed the Black with swollen tongue and hoarse voice, then cursed the world for his pain and hunger and thirst. Always thirst.

But it was not really a long time, days perhaps, until drunken quarrelsome men had stumbled by. One, a bonesetter, had set the bones of 'heelers'. 'Ain't never found much difference between man and beast,' he had boomed, half tipsy but cheerful. The brutality of being pulled about as, maudlin but joking, they held him down to stare up at their faces swimming over him while he bit on something, a lump of wood, till his mouth bled. Mercifully, he had passed out while the man worked a miracle; he had known what he was about, that one; a renegade surgeon perhaps? But they were scared men on the run and had gone as they had come until one, the bonesetter maybe, had sent others to carry him on a mattress of sacking stuffed with grass strung between the sweating rumps of men and beasts, over swaying miles, Tubbul trotting alongside until turning off silently to find his tribe. The great blue had burned on him, lighting mirages of lakes on far horizons on which trees, rigid, thick-trunked and twisted, hung in the air. Sleepless, he had stared up at the great void of night picked out with stars, with the sense of disembodiment the night sky always evoked in him. But he had lived, he had even grown lucid, and walked again almost straight – he would do well enough. The land had nearly beaten him but not quite. Never quite.

Now, with the sullen Jamie, and Gondola who slept curled up by the remains of the camp fire till prodded awake, resigned to his new master and life, they turned north-east, crossing the Willandra Billabong to follow the Lachlan in its great curve east, a long and difficult journey but shorter than retracing their steps, following the river tracks through the small settlements of Condobolin, Forbes and Cowra then turning south through Murringo to join the Great South Road at the dusty little township of Yass. This was the way Joey and Grace would come to Oorin, over five hundred miles of it, a long haul but with water along the way and, equally important, some human contact. Days and nights took on the ritualised rhythm of bush life on the road through hot dry days of a lingering summer. On the great desert stretches they cooked what they shot or trapped, dipping into their precious supplies to make damper and brew mugs of hot raw tea. They grassed their horses where feed was plentiful and urged them on when it was sparse. They forded creeks and swam rivers, for bridges were rare. They plunged into waterholes to wash the clothes on their backs. They slept exhausted round the remains of their camp fires, moving along indifferent tracks over monotonous scrub, their burning eyes soothed by fertile patches of undulating land where trails led off to some homestead, calling briefly for news and supplies but moving on, time losing itself in sunrises and sunsets, in tiny settlements, in shepherds' huts, and sheep, always sheep. An end-of-summer, burnt-brown land under a haze of heat and dust and the smoke of bushfires always dangerous in dryness, smoke rising or hanging white or grey according to the sun over the distant hills, sometimes burning beside them along the road. In kinder hillier country they found wild ducks and kangaroos and assorted birdlife, with fish a-plenty in the rivers and creeks. They met aboriginal tribesmen, and diggers moving north, lonely men who had little to say. They seldom saw a woman. Searching his pockets one morning Brick spilled out Raunie's gipsy charms, temporarily forgotten, unaware that Jamie was watching him. The youth snatched them up.

'These belonged to my mother. You'll not give them to that Irish virago,' he raged.

'I was keeping them for you. Come now, what would Alannah want with them?'

'You never cared about Raunie. Not really. You didn't love her.'

'Oh yes, but in my own way. If that way was different from others I don't try to explain it, I can't. I only know she was a part of my life, a big part, as I of hers. You must understand that.' Jamie, Brick could see, had come to sorrowing but self-pitying life. He held out 'roo meat cooked to a turn but the boy brought his clasped hands down on it hard, thumping it into the fire. Brick shrugged. 'Go hungry then. We've a

417

way to go before you'll eat prime roast mutton.' He stamped out the fire. 'Tomorrow we turn south to Yass.'

'I don't give a damn how or where we go.'

'Then I decide. That goes for the future too.'

'Raunie hated Erins Pride.'

'She had her reasons.'

'There are rumours about you and that girl.'

'There are always rumours. And "that girl" is Mrs Aldercott. Call her so.'

'You always try to act so bloody civilised,' Jamie raged spitefully. 'You'll never really succeed, you know.' He kicked at the embers. 'Your precious "Mrs Aldercott" wants too much of her own way.'

'So do I so we'll be well matched. You just like easy women.'

'I suppose I do.' Yet, oddly, he remembered only blonde hair spread on a pillow and a striving willingness to please that had nothing to do with being 'easy'. Lucy Marigold Finney, singer and would-be actress. No one had such a name, was that why he remembered her? Or because he was the first with her . . . 'You'll marry your "Mrs Aldercott", I know it.'

'Marriage between us is out of the question and you know that. We take what we can.'

'By running off.'

'If you like. And you'd best run with us for there'll be nothing left in the south unless you want to battle it out with Rob at the Pride; you'll come off second best, you always have. My mill goes up for auction soon and I'll spell in Sydney just long enough to put everything else on the market: the house at Neutral Bay, the stables and school, my store, Birubi, and all other investments. Nothing stays but Erins Pride and Oorin.'

'You expect me to live on Brisbane's mud flats? Or out with the wowser Scots on the Brisbane Plains?'

'That or tackle the Darling Downs. If you want more than a shepherd's hut you'll wield a mattock with the rest of us. There's a life there for you if you pitch in. There's certainly a chance for your son.'

418

'You'll never saddle me with Dora's brat.'

'Dora's brat was crawling about an inn yard blue with the cold, his mother run off with a waiter which won't be a bad match for her so be glad of it. My bet is she'll not be back, but if she should turn up she'll never get Willy Wilberforce.'

'Willy *what?*'

Brick laughed. 'As good a name as any, according to his grandmother. Give thanks for small mercies, it could have been a ponderous "David Livingstone".'

Jamie, fretful and uninterested, turned to stare into the monotonous distance, his eyes half-closed under his cabbage-tree hat. A day or so to the Great South Road then easier riding to the fringe of Goulburn and the track to Erins Pride. They walked their horses in the noon heat with the world shimmering about them, sheep huddled and panting in what shade they could find, the only sound Gondola breaking into a favourite little song of Naples. Even the birds dreamed.

May, the lovely turn of season, had a freshness to morning and night, even a bit of a sting in the winds from the south ruffling the feathers of the heat-weary swans and urging them from the sluggish shallows of the almost dry lagoon. Yet there were days when the dying summer would grow valiant and show unexpected life in breathing hotly over the land. Alannah rode a great deal, or wandered happily about Burrendah reacquainting herself with her Place of the Swan, lingering on the verandah or strolling the gardens to return Huie's triumphant grin as he pointed out some special growth. But her favourite walk was still down past the shearing-shed and workshop to her coppice, where she would sit propped against her favourite tree to read or reread her letters:

'Your father has married the Swallow woman.' She could actually feel her aunt's notepaper quiver with indignation. 'And quite without warning. I never thought to see the day when I would be expected to accept, not simply a sales-woman from Hackney even if it is Hackney proper, but a hussy – I *will* say it – for I shall insist to my dying day that

419

Maria Swallow is no better than she should be. However, I refuse to ruin my health or my disposition crying over spilt milk. Your father has made his bed and at least I had the satisfaction of refusing to attend the ceremony such as it was, almost *secretive* from all accounts, and shall have the further satisfaction of refusing her my house.' *Her* house? Lucknow? 'Your father will always be welcome, I hope I know my duty *there*, but that woman, never! No doubt he has written you of his purchase at auction of O'Shea's Mill? Quite a coup, I understand, the town talks of nothing else. As is his way he did not see fit to confide in me but the talk is that he made an excellent deal, but then he was always the shrewd man of business; indeed, his single-mindedness when he wants something has always daunted me. Your husband will find all in order at Lucknow when he brings you down which for your sake I hope will be soon for how you can bear the back-country I do not know; I confess I have never been *quite* the same since my sojourn inland . . .' Anything beyond the Glebe was back-country to Delia Carney. 'We continue to attract pupils of the *highest* respectability, Eveline Purdue's recommendations are *invaluable* . . .

Alannah turned to her father's letter. Behind its formality it quivered as violently as her aunt's. 'I have married Maria Swallow as I'm sure your aunt has informed you. She did not attend, a pity, for I should have liked one member of my family present since Maria did not consider it fair, when you had just settled in, to make you feel *obliged* to come . . .' She stirred impatiently. Her father had never succeeded in subtlety with her; it was clear he had not wished her at his wedding perhaps because Maria did not. But she did not resent his marriage, or Maria, she simply did not want to become involved in their life together. 'I never thought,' he continued, 'to be brother to a snob and I hope I am not father to one. It is my hope that you will grace Brighton from time to time but I speak with honesty when I say it is now Maria's home to command as she sees fit – as we both see fit – and if your aunt cannot accept that I feel certain you will.' He was hurt and angry and, so, unreasonable. 'No matter how you feel about returning to Ireland, and I am never quite certain of your feelings on that score, I shall never go back. Do you not ponder, Alannah, as I do, exactly how far we have come from the Mourne Mountains? . . .'

No mention of his acquisition of O'Shea's Mill. Then he did not wish her to know and was diverting her with mountains. 'There are no Mourne Mountains here,' Con had complained. 'There are other mountains,' she had replied. Her father had accepted that premise and had worked with the country not against it, sliding into it reasonably, combining its best with what he brought to it and he had brought a great deal. He moved with assurance in his new environment where Con had despised Australia and it had hit back. The country did not care how one felt or what one craved, it demanded and took, never giving an inch, and to survive one must meet it on its own terms. As for herself, she still had not accepted what she could not change. She knelt to dip her hand in the curling edge of the Creek and mop her warm cheeks. The water was very cold. Yes, there were other mountains, and the snows, it was predicted, would be early and heavy this year. She watched the tiny circles radiate out as she strolled to the remains of the old stone bridge where she had lain in Brick's arms, one a part of the other, that warm spring night long ago – which was not long ago, after all. She knelt to run her palm over the grass, fancying she could feel the hollow where she had lain with him. Even now the ground seemed urgent with their needs.

'O'Shea has returned to Erins Pride,' Simon had told her as if saying Huie would grow fine strawberries this year. 'Just walked in the way he does, without warning, with Jamie and that strange Italian groom. One can rightly call O'Shea a sudden man. The county's agog with rumours . . . but of course O'Shea's affairs are no longer my business.' Shuffling papers briskly he sounded aggrieved, even a little spiteful. 'I just hope he stays long enough to see Joey and Grace decently married. And decide what to do about that child with the absurd name.'

'Willy Wilberforce? Somehow name and baby suit each other.'

'The general opinion is that he is Jamie's child. I for one don't doubt it.'

He was uneasy, for anything outside conventional behaviour always disturbed him though he did try not to make issues of such facts – a discreet, well-mannered man, a civilised man as he regarded himself. Now he looked wise, even a little secretive; why, she thought, with indulgent amusement, he could quite easily develop into the local gossip. But her idle speculation was lost in the certainty that soon Brick O'Shea would come for her.

There had been some initial awkwardness on O'Shea's arrival for only garbled accounts of the tragedy at Bendigo had drifted through to Erins Pride. The name Herlicht meant nothing other than that he was O'Shea's Bendigo manager, but the man had died horribly on the same night as Mrs O'Shea, so badly injured by stampeding horses he had been unable to escape the gutting of the Irish Boy stables – arson or pure accident no one seemed to know. But they did wonder and whisper over O'Shea's wife, shot it was said, resisting a thief since her jewels were missing, as was her revolver for it was known she always carried one. There seemed no definite answer to any of it and it was certainly too much for Hetty who warned the kitchen against asking questions. If Mr O'Shea wished to discuss the tragedy he would raise the subject. Meanwhile Erins Pride must go about its business which was the immediate task of feeding up the travellers, even the odd little hunchback, purely a Christian act on Hetty's part but a 'wipe your feet' as he came by the kitchen helped keep him in his place. Hetty Witherstone distrusted foreigners, particularly Italians born in the shadow of some terrible volcano likely to blow up at any minute. Gondola was quite outside Hetty's experience and understanding. Besides, she was too occupied with countering the shock of the master's decision to emigrate to the wilds of this new state of Queensland, again outside her experience and understanding. Mercifully, the Pride would go on – Erins Pride would always go on – even so the entire business was unnerving. Hetty hated change. Everything in its place and God in his Heaven was Hetty Witherstone's need and creed.

But she was in her element in imparting hoarded county gossip and domestic news: Barney Cook had disappeared again for the umpteenth time, gone walkabout or, more likely, in gaol. 'He's no good, Mr O'Shea, never was, never will be.' If only the master would see fit to take him north to where wild tribes would put the fear of heathen gods in him; better still, point the bone. Leaving Mrs Carney to oversee the Bridge Academy, the Aldercotts had settled into Burrendah, the schoolmaster tutoring in Goulburn between running his school on the station, but her own boys were doing no better there than they had at the Pride and the sooner they were off to Oorin the better, with Joey, happily, their idol – which brought her to Joey and Grace. 'They'll be wed before you leave for Sydney, Mr O'Shea, or I'll not answer for the consequences. The girl's like a taut spring, sitting on her packed boxes as it were, waiting. Just waiting.' Grace Charlton had made her bed as Mrs Carney would say, even if it were only sacking stuffed with leaves and grass for a start, but she, Hetty Witherstone, wouldn't have it on her conscience that the girl shared it with Joey without God's blessing. They were all glad Richie had been sent for – he could easily be replaced in Sydney. Now would Mr O'Shea please consider the lad for Oorin? Richie had long fretted to throw in his lot with the back-country and would do well as stockman and drover, and what he didn't know he'd learn along the way. Daisy Elston, already lonely for her George, and her girls were on the high seas home with nary a husband snared between them. Billy Warwick had taken a second wife. And was it true Mrs Noakes had taken a few steps? And would she continue to improve?

'The doctors doubt that. All the same she throws in her lot with me, up over the Range in a sling seat if necessary. Luckily, Nurse Puttering fancies the challenge of a new state. Queensland already trembles.'

And Willy Wilberforce? He was growing a vigorous lump, his cheeks filling out, smiling a lot and eating everything within range of his hands. He was bouncing himself around Belle's kitchen with many a rap on his knuckles to leave things be. The women had made him clothes from scraps of their own and he would be warm in winter, if multi-coloured.

'Leave him with us, sir, at least till he grows a mite. Another child about the place makes no difference. He's too young for such a journey.'

'You're getting soft, Hetty Witherstone. I was dragged about the country eating sparse and bunking where I could and I survived. This one will do better.'

'Then take Fay for she's fearful of being parted from him. She sings to him now, even if her lullabies are ribald ditties picked up from the men. But I'd rather have that than see her strut a music-hall stage showing off her legs. Her mother would turn in her grave.'

'I doubt it,' Brick laughed. 'However, if her father's as willing as the girl she comes with us and no need for you to fuss, Puttering keeps her well in hand. The women and baby will go by steamer to Moreton Bay where I'll meet them; Jamie, Gondola – and Barney when I catch up with him – will trail overland with me for I've places and folk to visit on the way. My Newcastle mill must be set up for auction, it's not complete but well-stocked.'

It was all too much for Hetty. She stood, flushed and a little troubled, watching him stride off, not young any longer but still straight and strong-muscled, scarcely limping at all, a fine figure of a man as she always insisted, with plenty of living left to him – but no wife. Sadder still, no sons to carry on, only Jamie, spoilt and wild and always at war with him; she had never envied O'Shea there. She shook her head, desolate over a man without sons but, supremely satisfied with her own world, ran her palms up her side hair and smoothed down her apron. She even began to sing about her kitchen in her off-key voice when O'Shea found Barney drunk in a grog shanty beside the Wollondilly, sobered him by plunging his head in the stream then locked him up at the Pride till they left for Sydney. Hetty didn't envy O'Shea Barney Cook either.

Happily oblivious to his fate, Willy Wilberforce played in the dirt under the big tree, always a playground for the children of Erins Pride, his toys a few sticks and stones, absorbed in popping a stone into his mouth and, where other babes would choke, moving it deftly and thoughtfully about, spitting it into his palm, gazing at it gleaming with his saliva, then throwing it aside to try another. Brick gouged a stone from his mouth and the child's eyes blazed and he hit out with his small fists. His hair was as black and curly as Jamie's but his skin paler, with the same delicate features but not as graceful in movement, of more solid build. Jamie and the resilient slut of a Dora had produced a child that would grow with the features, the sly intelligence, the stubbornness, perhaps the innate profligacy of its father, and the durable strength of its peasant mother – not a bad combination for this country, Brick decided. He sensed Jamie pause beside him and shift from one foot to the other before waving an airy hand.

'He'll choke himself.'

'I think not.' Brick paused. 'Pick him up.'

'That grub?'

'It's clean dirt. And he won't bite you – well, not too hard. Pick him up.'

Jamie finally obeyed, if reluctantly, to hold the child awkwardly. Willy Wilberforce squirmed his indignation, then when he found escape impossible gripped Jamie's curls and tugged in tearful anger. Jamie swore and they struggled with each other. Seeing them close Brick's last doubt, if he had any, dissolved for the line would go on; deny it all his life which he probably would this was Jamie's son – and Raunie's grandchild. How she would have hated *that!* At least she had not grown old, she had died as beautiful and firm and strong, as physically desirable as she had ever been, an unpredictable fascinating woman with whom his life had been entangled. Squealing and squirming, wanting to return to his play, Willy Wilberforce dragged at his father's hair. Then tiring, he was still, staring at the youth, his childish gaze disconcerting.

'You're going on eighteen,' Brick reminded Jamie.

'An old man.' He laughed and the child in his arms made curious bubbly sounds.

'Time for man's work. Time to take on a child too.'

'I disown this one.'

'Even so he comes with us.'

The baby grew tired of just staring and dashed his fists full-pelt into his father's face. Jamie shook his head clear. 'Do I have to fight you the same way to show who's master here?' he shouted.

A poor enough start, Brick decided. But a start all the same.

Simon was at his desk in Burrendah's recently completed schoolroom. He had an hour before classes and was working on Burrendah's accounts. But he worked with a restlessness that disturbed concentration. It was not only that he missed Sydney and Lucknow, an ever-present loss, but the sting of autumn was affecting him sorely. His eyes smarted under the dry winds and he was always running out of pocket-handkerchiefs. He felt a reluctance even to turn pages and in a determined effort to shake off his ennui drew his ledgers resolutely towards him. But looking up, he paused.

His wife was walking up the verandah steps, slowly, unusual for her for he saw urgency in Alannah's slightest movement, a natural trait and one of the things he loved about her – but then, he loved many things about his wife. She stimulated him by her energy, even in those awful breeks she had adopted but which she no longer wore. 'A childish rebellion, I think,' she would laugh, 'to shock my aunt, to shock the world, to let it know I was alive and meant business. I needed to do it then. Do you think I'm growing up at last?' Her throat was a golden brown – her Aunt Delia would have been horrified – and her hair was sunbleached for she often forgot her hat or deliberately ignored it. She must toughen up, she insisted, laughing at her often sunburnt nose. He bent to his work again and did not look up until he had completed his row of figures, as she knew he would, then he pushed all aside, folded his hands and turned in his chair to where she stood poised in the doorway. The morning sun made a crown behind her head. The sight of her pleased him immensely.

'You've tired yourself already.'

'I can't think why so early in the day. Too much sun perhaps for it's still strong. And I had to go back for my hat. I forget it too often, don't I?'

'I should tie it about your neck each morning.' He gave his spectacles their habitual push and pat and set his pen on the desk instead of its rest and she knew he was not his usual precise self. She was as familiar with his work habits as she was with the faintly worried expression she had learned to live with, even at times to find engaging, and she knew that when he took up the pen again there would be a tiny inkspot. The desk was peppered with such spots as if he were being constantly interrupted without time to place the pen correctly but, far more likely, was too disturbed to do so. The spots had grown more numerous since he had returned to Burrendah. He removed his spectacles and pinched the skin of his nose, red from pressure. 'I need new spectacles,' he explained as he did often, rubbing the skin behind his ears. He would never take time to get the glasses eased. He looked serious and concerned, very young and rather handsome. 'You're busy,' she murmured uneasily.

'Never too busy for you.' He pushed the ledgers aside, stood, and stamped his feet. 'I need more exercise. I should take long walks with you, that would be very pleasant, but there's always so much to be done.' He straightened and met her eyes. 'I feel you have something important to say to me.'

'To ask, rather.' She took a deep breath. 'How can one be certain that what one does, or says, is right at the time? I know that sounds stupid and confusing but I've never been sure that what I do is right, at a precise moment I mean, for me or for others. I don't know it now.'

'Aren't you confusing the right thing with the best thing?'

'Perhaps.'

'Otherwise, it seems one can only follow one's feelings.'

'Feelings are unstable pointers, or it seems so where mine are concerned for now, this minute, my feelings are driving

427

me to tell you something that perhaps should be kept hidden
– I don't *know*, Simon, really I don't. Perhaps all would be
best kept secret yet I don't even know if that is what I mean. I
am confused and hesitant and don't know what to do. All I
am certain of is that I can't live with dishonesty any longer.
My dishonesty, I mean.'

'You dishonest? Nonsense. If you want to confess you've
spent some shocking amount on curtains or some other
household item, it is unnecessary.' He smiled gently. 'After
all, I keep the books.'

'Simon!' It was a small anguished wail. 'It has nothing to
do with curtains or bookcases or even a pianoforte—'

'You fret for the child.'

'I suppose I do without actually realising it. But if I do
I know it's for something insubstantial, something that was
almost there but not quite. It's just that one . . . wonders . . .
what it would have been like. One can't help it.'

'I don't speak of it for that reason.'

'Simon . . . please listen. Don't you notice that I always say
my child? It was *my* child.'

'Of course it was your child.' An urgent fly buzzed against
the window pane. Carefully and methodically he rolled up a
sheet of paper and smacked it dead.

'My child. Not yours.'

It sounded so loud and bald and awful that for a moment
she died. She could only stand in the dreadful stillness and
wait for him to speak, for he must speak, say something,
anything, now that she had brought it into the open. He
must *do* something – kill her if he wanted to. But even though
it was terrible to hear her own words it was not nearly as
terrible as repeating them alone and unshared in her mind as
she had done for so long. And for that reason, selfishly
perhaps, she had drawn him into the heavy burden of her
secret. 'Did you hear me? It was not your child.'

'I heard you. Of course I heard you.'

'Then you still don't understand. You were not the father.
I had to tell you this for there is a turning point in our lives.'

'Don't say any more.' He faced her squarely. 'I forbid you
to say more about it.' There was something so determined in

428

his voice and stance that she found him daunting – Simon daunting? – and obeyed. 'I am stopping this agony for you, for us both, for you are trying to put into words something that I long ago suspected. I've lived with indecision too; the quandary of whether or not to tell you that if I did not exactly *know* I guessed.'

'Guessed? But you must have had reason for your suspicion.' Then she gave a small resigned lift and fall of her shoulders. 'But of course, on our marriage you knew I was not a virgin.'

'No – or rather let me say I did not give the matter thought. It never entered my head to query your . . . intactness, shall we say. Why should I? I knew nothing of a woman's physical components, nothing but the clothed shape of women which, I confess, did stir me at times – oh yes, I gazed on women, wondering as men do. But I was taught that women were devices of the Devil. I lived very much with those constant terrors of the Church, the Devil and Hell, they were my companions in adolescence. Unfortunately, I grew up an over-serious Enthusiast untouched by the warmth of the Movement, the passion of it . . . My knowledge and experience of life came from books and those I was required to read were quite inadequate in teaching me the relationship between man and woman. My ignorance was profound – until I met you. I loved you instantly, Alannah, so all was right and good for me with no need to explore further. Moreover, what toleration I now show for the human condition you have instilled in me. You have always been good for me and if a woman is precious to a man he holds, or tries to hold, that which makes him happy.'

'If you suspected you must have wondered who?'

'I didn't dare. Besides, it didn't seem important nor does it now. I choose not to wonder. What is important is that there is no lasting division between us. I choose to be happy with you and to that end this episode is of the past. I insist it be so and will not discuss it again.' He opened a small cupboard. 'I have something for you.' He took out a small linen bundle, unwrapped it and set its contents on his desk. She gasped.

'My Celtic cross! Where did you find it?'

'It was returned to me. How, does not matter now. All that is important is that you have it back. It is a handsome thing so you must wear it. And now, my dear, I must get back to my work.' His fingers were already running expertly down a column of figures. She was dismissed. She tied her hat strings securely for a little wind had sprung up. 'I shall finish my walk before facing Grace and her packing and unpacking.' She sighed. 'She accumulates. If I don't watch her she'll pack half Burrendah.'

'Joey will off-load.'

She smiled. 'He might at that.' Joey Bowes was more decisive these days – sharper. Whatever else had happened to him in those weeks wandering about Sydney, Joey had learned something of independence and assurance. He might even learn to stand up to Grace for the good of themselves, and Oorin.

'Watch the sky. Change of season you know. We'll have a storm before the day's out, you'll see.' She went off smiling to herself at his air of country certainty. Pen in hand, Simon watched her on her way: so much left unsaid, so much unresolved but it must remain so for words damaged. No more idle words. Certainly he would hold to himself, as he had for so long, the conviction that soon now Brick O'Shea would come to claim Alannah.

Grace Charlton and Joey Bowes were married by the Reverend Boogle under the trees at Burrendah with friends and well-wishers gathered to wish them a safe journey. They left the next morning with an eager Richie and their heavily-packed dray on their journey of five hundred miles, give or take a few, travelling as far as Forbes with a family from Marulan. Brick had made a kind of peace with Joey but both knew things would never be quite the same again and perhaps as well, Brick decided, for he had never wanted or deserved hero-worship from Joey Bowes. In the madness that had driven him then he had blamed the youth openly for Alannah's 'accident' and he knew Joey would never quite forgive him. Perhaps time would smooth things over . . . He

430

had ridden to Burrendah to see them off and in the general settling down afterwards went in search of Alannah. Neither had forced a meeting and they had met only in the company of others but they could no longer skirt issues. Her coppice was cool with an end-of-summer heaviness when he found her picking ferns, her hair loose over her open collar. She looked very young, he thought. Too young. And vulnerable. His heart seemed to stop.

'I leave for Sydney in two days,' he said without preamble.

She straightened, wiping her damp hands on her skirt. 'Don't go, will you, without explaining to Simon how the press works.' She spoke with a curious breathlessness, her words tumbling. 'Imagine, a wool press! He just stands, if not exactly scratching his head over it, wanting to do so. They like him here after all, or perhaps they're just getting used to him for he tries, really he does. He was a little afraid, you see. After all, he belongs to Staffordshire and he can't change that, not really. Just as Aunt Delia belongs to Stonemore—'

'Two days, Alannah.' He moved close to her. 'I'll be in Sydney just long enough to put my properties on the market. They'll be left in good hands.' He paused and she knew he was thinking of her father but these days he never mentioned Owen Moynan. 'There's something you must know,' he went on. 'Raunie caused the child's death. She undermined the steps. She did not actually admit to it, she never would, but I know it was so. The baby became an obsession.'

'She loved you.' She felt nothing for Raunie now, she only knew that the dead woman had been her enemy, destroying her child because Brick had fathered it, in the savage vengeance of a savage woman.

'Possessed me. Perhaps possession is a kind of love . . . But it's all over. Finished.'

'There's something you must know. I told Simon the truth – all but that you were the father. Somehow he guessed the baby was not his but refuses to speak of the matter again. He never will, I know it.'

He made a quick little movement, of impatience she thought. 'I'm heading north with a mixed bag of emigrants, the women and the child by sea, the rest of us overland: an old crippled convict woman who'll complain by signs if she can't use words but I'll get her there if we all die in the doing of it. Her nurse with the battle strategy of a Napoleon that yet could prove useful in subduing hostile natives. A servant girl I've bribed with a piano and singing lessons and a husband but who would come none the less, as nursemaid to a bastard baby I've endowed with my name; I gave it to his father, perhaps the son will like it better. A youth who hates me as his father but will come because he has nowhere else to go; Jamie has always preferred not to starve. A buffoon of a Neapolitan who's likely to finish up hanged for some crime whether he commits it or not, and a renegade Black who's likely to hang with him. Finally, Black Brick O'Shea, to use the more pleasant of my names, nearing fifty, with more than a few of the wounds of life, decently hidden I hope.' His arms went about her. 'And there's a place for you, a special place . . .'

'I won't cry,' she said fiercely. 'Not the way I used to cry. Wasn't it awful, all those tears? At nothing. *Nothing!*'

'It was always at something.' The lost child was between them, a shadowy incomplete memory, a thought where there had been possibility. They would have loved it, boy or girl, together or apart and it would have been a fortunate and beloved child. 'I'm building again, Alannah – a house, a dynasty. The House of O'Shea. To that end I must have sons, but I'll have no other but you to bear them. Ah, girl . . .' He held her tightly and it was more than she could bear and she pressed to him, clinging, seeking his lips, and their brief precious life together crowded in. Memories enchanted. 'I know,' he murmured, 'it would be so easy this way, but it's not enough. Not for me. Not now.' He held her off, willing her eyes. 'You'll walk by my side before the world or not at all.' His words were not gentle now, they were hard and determined. 'Since you cannot come as wife you must come as mistress and I'll have no faint-hearted woman—' But he broke off at the longing and the agony in her eyes and pressed her face hard down against his chest and held it there.

'Don't look like that – don't. I can't bear it either. Don't.'

Jamie galloped Burrendah's home paddock exercising his wild black mare to the mad yelping of dogs. Fay Witherstone, her face paler than usual under her wide-brimmed hat, shifted Willy Wilberforce to her other hip as she waited to resume the journey into Goulburn and the Sydney coach; they had turned off to pay final respects to Burrendah and now Ida and Dan stood with the hands to wave them God-speed. Startled, she backed as Gondola brought up the horses. Brick O'Shea mounted his own.

'Don't let the child see you're afraid,' he warned the girl. 'Give him back to me and climb on your horse; Gondola will rope it to his own. You'll learn to ride well before you tackle Queensland. That wilderness is no gentle canter round a home paddock. Now up with you!'

He thumped Willy Wilberforce before him on the saddle, the baby's plump little legs splayed, a quaint man-child in the pint-sized cabbage-tree hat, shirt, breeches and boots Hetty and the women had made him for the long journey. The child clutched the saddle, wide-eyed at his height from the ground and the restless beast beneath him. The horse shied, Willy Wilberforce screamed and twisted about, but Brick laughed down at the puckered face and somehow the distraction stopped the baby's tears. 'Face the world, Willy Wilberforce,' he boomed, tying him to his own body with a padded band. 'It's not so bad.' He shouted orders to Jamie, to the jester-dwarf, to the scared Fay clinging to her mount, and to Barney bringing up the pack-horses. The baby screamed again somewhere between terror and delight and Alannah hastened to calm him, patting his knee. Brick bent and covered her hand with his own. She glanced down the hill at the man standing in Burrendah's doorway, watching and waiting. She turned back to meet Brick's eyes and the child was quiet, staring from one to the other.

'What can I do?' she whispered.

'You will come,' he told her. 'Not now. Not yet perhaps, but you will come. You know it. I know it. Meanwhile!' He straightened and waved the others to follow.

'Hang on, Willy Wilberforce,' he shouted. 'Hang on. We've work to do.'

Glossary

Aborigine, Aboriginal
Both in common usage but often applied incorrectly. Aborigine is the noun and Aboriginal the adjective. Correctly, the Australian native is the Australian Aborigine.

blood-house
A disreputable public-house.

blower
A show-off. A braggart.

Botany Bay
Early name for the Colony of New South Wales.

brumby
A wild horse. Mobs of brumbies wandered the outback (and in parts still do), the descendants of stock, some fine blood stock, others everyday stock horses, escaped from cattle stations or turned loose to fend for themselves.

bussing
Kissing.

cabbage-tree hat
A wide-brimmed hat woven from the fibres of the cabbage-tree palm.

Mrs Chisholm
Caroline Chisholm, the pioneer philanthropist who began her work among the destitute female immigrants of Sydney in the early 1840s. Born into a farming family of Wootton, near Northampton, England, in 1808, she died at Fulham, London, in 1877 and is buried in Northampton's Billing Road Cemetery, her grave marked 'The Emigrants Friend'. Her portrait is on the Australian five-dollar note.

currency

Term covering whites – particularly young whites – born in Australia, distinguishing them from immigrants:

One of the many names for a convict:

Term used for a wide variety of notes and coins, as distinct from English gold pieces called 'sterling'.

dead men

Empty bottles.

dolly pot

Crushing bowl for extracting gold from the quartz.

Dunbar

In August 1857, the clipper ship *Dunbar*, seeking the entrance to Port Jackson in darkness and in a fierce gale, was washed onto the rocks just south of the Gap. Only one, a seaman, survived out of a complement of one hundred and twenty.

Eureka

On the goldfields of Ballarat, Victoria, on the morning of 3rd December, 1854, after a brief fight, troops dispersed miners barricaded in a stockade, the culmination of diggers' protests over licence fees.

fustians

Trousers of a tough cotton cloth. Also called moleskins.

galah

Cockatoo; hence a boastful fool.

Indian, Nigger, Black

Terms used by early settlers for the Australian Aborigine.

jen

Aboriginal woman – strictly, a wife. Nowadays spelt 'gin'.

Joe Joe

The diggers' cry, warning of goldfield police, nicknamed 'Joes' after Charles Joseph La Trobe (Latrobe), the governor who introduced the hated licence tax in Victoria.

logs

The lockup.

new chum

A newly landed inexperienced immigrant.

old lag

Ex-convict or ticket-of-leave man.

post-'n'-rails

Applied to the tea brewed by workmen erecting post-and-rail wooden fencing, a term afterwards adopted by bushmen travellers.

quartzopolis

The community of quartz mines on Bendigo.

Queensland

Proclaimed a state on 11th May, 1859. Formerly called Moreton Bay.

The Rocks

The crowded squalid district of old Dawes Point, likened to London's St Giles.

scauf

Food

sheep-walk

In Australia, a narrow track over the hills trodden out by sheep. (In U.K., pasture-land for sheep.)

sly-grogger

An unlicensed dealer in liquor, his stock usually of a rough 'rot-gut' brew.

squatter

Originally, the derogatory term for stockholders who wandered the inland seeking fresh grazing for their stock and who 'squatted' on Crown Land where and how they pleased. The term has evolved as one for the long-established, affluent, landowning class of rural Australia.

sterling and pure merinos

The 'upper crust' of the free settlers.

ti-tree or tea-tree

In Australia, a shrub from whose leaves bushmen brewed a substitute for tea.

traps

Mounted police.

Vandemonians

People from Van Diemen's Land (Tasmania). A derogatory term for goldfields' police, some of whom were ex-convicts recruited from Tasmania, and hated for their ruthless hunting out of diggers' licences.

Yealanbidgee River

The Murrumbidgee.